PENGUIN TWENTIETH-CENTURY CLASSICS
THE BLACK GIRL IN SEARCH OF GOD
AND SOME LESSER TALES

Bernard Shaw was born in Dublin in 1856. Although essentially shy, he created the persona of G.B.S., the showman, satirist, controversialist, critic, pundit, wit, intellectual buffoon and dramatist. Commentators brought a new adjective into English: Shavian, a term used to embody all his brilliant qualities.

After his arrival in London in 1876 he became an active Socialist and a brilliant platform speaker. He wrote on many social aspects of the day; on *Common Sense about the War* (1914), *How to Settle the Irish Question* (1917) and *The Intelligent Woman's Guide to Socialism and Capitalism* (1928). He undertook his own education at the British Museum and consequently became keenly interested in cultural subjects. Thus his prolific output included music, art and theatre reviews, which were collected into several volumes, such as *Music in London 1890–1894* (3 vols., 1931); *Pen Portraits and Reviews* (1931); and *Our Theatres in the Nineties* (3 vols., 1931). He also wrote five novels and some shorter fiction, including *The Black Girl in Search of God and Some Lesser Tales* and *Cashel Byron's Profession*, both published in Penguin's Bernard Shaw Library.

He conducted a strong attack on the London theatre and was closely associated with the intellectual revival of British theatre. His many plays fall into several categories: 'Plays Pleasant'; 'Plays Unpleasant'; his comedies; chronicle-plays; 'metabiological Pentateuch' (*Back to Methuselah*, a series of plays); and 'political extravaganzas'. Bernard Shaw died in 1950.

Title-page of The Black Girl *as first published by Constable in 1932*

THE BLACK GIRL IN SEARCH OF GOD

and some lesser tales

BERNARD SHAW

*Wood Engravings
by John Farleigh*

*

DEFINITIVE TEXT
*under the editorial
supervision of*
DAN H. LAURENCE

PENGUIN BOOKS

PENGUIN BOOKS

Published by the Penguin Group
Penguin Books Ltd, 27 Wrights Lane, London w8 5TZ, England
Penguin Putnam Inc., 375 Hudson Street, New York, New York 10014, USA
Penguin Books Australia Ltd, Ringwood, Victoria, Australia
Penguin Books Canada Ltd, 10 Alcorn Avenue, Toronto, Ontario, Canada M4V 3B2
Penguin Books (NZ) Ltd, Private Bag 102902, NSMC, Auckland, New Zealand

Penguin Books Ltd, Registered Offices: Harmondsworth, Middlesex, England

This collection first published by Constable 1934
Published in Penguin Books 1946
Reprinted with illustrations 1966
5 7 9 10 8 6 4

Copyright 1932, 1934 by George Bernard Shaw
Copyright © 1959, 1961 The Public Trustee as
Executor of the Estate of George Bernard Shaw
All rights reserved

Printed and bound in Great Britain by
Clays Ltd, St Ives plc

The Black Girl in Search of God was first published as *The Adventures of the Black Girl in Her Search for God* late in 1932. The remaining items in this volume were first collected in *Short Stories, Scraps and Shavings*, 1932. They were published individually as follows: 'Aerial Football' in *The Neolith*, November 1907; 'The Emperor and the Little Girl', written for a Belgian war charity for children, in the *New York Tribune Magazine*, 22 October 1916; 'The Miraculous Revenge' in *Time*, March 1885; 'The Theatre of the Future' in *The Grand Magazine*, February 1905; 'A Dressing Room Secret' in the *Souvenir of the Shakespeare Ball*, ed. Mrs George Cornwallis-West, 1911, published in aid of the Shakespeare Memorial Fund; 'Still after The Doll's House' in *Time*, February 1890; 'Death of an Old Revolutionary Hero' in *The Clarion*, 24 March 1905; 'The Serenade' in *The Magazine of Music*, November 1885; 'A Sunday on the Surrey Hills' in the *Pall Mall Gazette*, 25 April 1888; 'Cannonfodder' in *The Clarion*, 21 November 1902. 'Beauty's Duty', 'Don Giovanni Explains', and 'A Glimpse of the Domesticity of Franklyn Barnabas' are not recorded as having been published before their appearance in 1932.

Except in the United States of America, this book is sold subject
to the condition that it shall not, by way of trade or otherwise, be lent,
re-sold, hired out, or otherwise circulated without the publisher's
prior consent in any form of binding or cover other than that in
which it is published and without a similar condition including this
condition being imposed on the subsequent purchaser

CONTENTS

Preface to the Black Girl in Search of God	7
The Black Girl in Search of God	27
Aerial Football: the New Game	85
The Emperor and the Little Girl	101
The Miraculous Revenge	117
The Theatre of the Future	147
A Dressing Room Secret	181
Don Giovanni Explains	191
Beauty's Duty	219
Still after The Doll's House	225
A Glimpse of the Domesticity of Franklyn Barnabas	243
Death of an Old Revolutionary Hero	295
The Serenade	309
A Sunday on the Surrey Hills	321
Cannonfodder	329

PREFACE TO THE BLACK GIRL IN SEARCH OF GOD

WAS inspired to write this tale when I was held up in Knysna for five weeks in the African summer and English winter of 1932. My intention was to write a play in the ordinary course of my business as a playwright; but I found myself writing the story of the black girl instead. And now, the story being written, I proceed to speculate on what it means, though I cannot too often repeat that I am as liable as anyone else to err in my interpretation, and that pioneer writers, like other pioneers, often mistake their destination as Columbus did. That is how they sometimes run away in pious horror from the conclusions to which their revelations manifestly lead. I hold, as firmly as St Thomas Aquinas, that all truths, ancient or modern, are divinely inspired; but I know by observation and introspection that the instrument on which the inspiring force plays may be a very faulty one, and may even end, like Bunyan in The Holy War, by making the most ridiculous nonsense of his message.

However, here is my own account of the matter for what it is worth.

It is often said, by the heedless, that we are a conservative species, impervious to new ideas. I have not found it so. I am often appalled at the avidity and credulity with which new ideas are snatched at and adopted without a scrap of sound evidence. People will believe anything that amuses them, gratifies them, or promises them some sort of profit. I console myself, as Stuart Mill did, with the notion that in time the silly ideas will lose their charm and drop out of fashion and out of existence; that the false promises, when broken, will pass through cynical derision into oblivion; and that after this sifting process the sound ideas, being indestructible (for even if suppressed or forgotten they are rediscovered again and again) will survive and be added to the body of ascertained knowledge we call Science. In this way we acquire a well tested stock of ideas to furnish our minds, such furnishings being education proper as distinguished from the pseudo-education of the schools and universities.

Unfortunately there is a snag in this simple scheme. It forgets the prudent old precept, 'Dont throw out your dirty water until you get in your clean' which is the very devil unless completed by 'This also I say unto you, that when you get your fresh water you must throw out the dirty, and be particularly careful not to let the two get mixed.'

Now this is just what we never do. We persist in pouring the clean water into the dirty; and our minds are always muddled in consequence. The educated human of today has a mind which can be compared only to a store in which the very latest and most precious acquisitions are flung on top of a noisome heap of rag-and-bottle refuse and worthless antiquities from the museum lumber room. The store is always bankrupt; and the men in possession include William the Conqueror and Henry the Seventh, Moses and Jesus, St Augustine and Sir Isaac Newton, Calvin and Wesley, Queen Victoria and H. G. Wells; whilst among the distraining creditors are Karl Marx, Einstein, and dozens of people more or less like Stuart Mill and myself. No mind can operate reasonably in such a mess. And as our current schooling and colleging and graduating consists in reproducing this mess in the minds of

PREFACE

every fresh generation of children, we are provoking revolutionary emergencies in which persons muddled by university degrees will have to be politically disfranchised and disqualified as, in effect, certified lunatics, and the direction of affairs given over to the self-educated and the simpletons.

The most conspicuous example of this insane practice of continually taking in new ideas without ever clearing out the ideas they supersede, is the standing of the Bible in those countries in which the extraordinary artistic value of the English translation has given it a magical power over its readers. That power is now waning because, as sixteenth-century English is a dying tongue, new translations are being forced on us by the plain fact that the old one is no longer intelligible to the masses. These new versions have – the good ones by their admirable homeliness and the ordinary ones by their newspapery everydayness – suddenly placed the Bible narratives in a light of familiar realism which obliges their readers to apply common sense tests to them.

But the influence of these modern versions is not yet very wide. It seems to me that those who find the old version unintelligible and boresome do not resort to modern versions: they simply give up reading the Bible. The few who are caught and interested by the new versions, stumble on them by accidents which, being accidents, are necessarily rare. But they still hear Lessons read in church in the old version in a specially reverent tone; children at Sunday School are made to learn its verses by heart, and are rewarded by little cards inscribed with its texts; and bedrooms and nurseries are still decorated with its precepts, warnings, and consolations. The British and Foreign Bible Society has distributed more than three million copies annually for a century past; and though many of these copies may be mere churchgoers' luggage, never opened on weekdays, or gifts in discharge of the duties of godparents; yet they count. There is still on the statute book a law which no statesman dare repeal, which makes it felony for a professed Christian to question the scientific truth and supernatural authority of any word of Holy Scripture, the penalties extending to ruinous outlawry; and the same acceptance of the Bible as an infallible encyclopedia is one of the Articles of the Church of England, though another Article, and that the very first, flatly denies the corporeal and voracious nature of God insisted on in the Pentateuch.

In all these instances the Bible means the translation authorized by King James the First of the best examples in ancient Jewish literature of natural and political history, of poetry, morality, theology, and rhapsody. The translation was extraordinarily well done because to the translators what they were translating was not merely a curious collection of ancient books written by different authors in different stages of culture, but the Word of God divinely revealed through his chosen and expressly inspired scribes. In this conviction they carried out their work with boundless reverence and care and achieved a beautifully artistic result. It did not seem possible to them that they could better the original texts; for who could improve on God's own style? And as they could not conceive that divine revelation could conflict with what they believed to be the truths of their religion, they did not hesitate to translate a negative by a positive where such a conflict seemed to arise, as they could hardly trust their own fallible knowledge of ancient Hebrew when it contradicted the very foundations of their faith, nor could they doubt that God would, as they prayed, take care that his message should not suffer corruption in their hands. In this state of exaltation they made a translation so magnificent that to this day the common human Britisher or citizen of the United States of North America accepts and worships

PREFACE

it as a single book by a single author, the book being the Book of Books and the author being God. Its charm, its promise of salvation, its pathos, and its majesty have been raised to transcendence by Handel, who can still make atheists cry and give materialists the thrill of the sublime with his Messiah. Even the ignorant, to whom religion is crude fetishism and magic, prize it as a paper talisman that will exorcize ghosts, prevent witnesses from lying, and, if carried devoutly in a soldier's pocket, stop bullets.

Now it is clear that this Bible worship, though at its best it may achieve sublimity by keeping its head in the skies, may also make itself both ridiculous and dangerous by having its feet off the ground. It is a matter of daily experience that a book taken as an infallible revelation, whether the author is Moses, Ezekiel, Paul, Swedenborg, Joseph Smith, Mary Baker Eddy, or Karl Marx, may bring such hope, consolation, interest, and happiness into our individual lives that we may well cherish it as a key of Paradise. But if the paradise be a fool's paradise, as it must be when its materials are imaginary, then it must not be made the foundation of a State, and must be classed with anodynes, opiates, and anaesthetics. It is not for nothing that the fanatically religious founders of the new Russia dismissed the religion of the Greek Church as 'dope.' That is precisely what a religion becomes when it is divorced from reality. It is useful to ambitious rulers in corrupt political systems as a sedative to popular turbulence (that is why the tyrant always makes much of the priest); but in the long run civilization must get back to honest reality or perish.

At present one party is keeping the Bible in the clouds in the name of religion, and another is trying to get rid of it altogether in the name of Science. Both names are so recklessly taken in vain that a Bishop of Birmingham once warned his flock that the scientific party is drawing nearer to Christ than the Church congregations. I, who am a sort of unofficial Bishop of Everywhere, have repeatedly warned the scientists that the Quakers are fundamentally far more scientific than the official biologists. In this confusion I venture to suggest that we neither leave the Bible in the clouds nor attempt the impossible task of suppressing it. Why not simply bring it down to the ground, and take it for what it really is?

To maintain good humor I am quite willing to concede to my Protestant friends that the Bible in the clouds was sometimes turned to good account in the struggles to maintain Protestant Freethought (such as it was) against the Churches and Empires. The soldier who had his Bible in one hand and his weapon in the other fought with the strength of ten under Cromwell, William of Orange, and Gustavus Adolphus. The very old-fashioned may still permit themselves a little romance about the Huguenots at La Rochelle, the psalm of the Ironsides at Dunbar, the ships that broke the boom and relieved the siege of Londonderry, and even about Dugald Dalgetty. But the struggle between Guelph and Ghibelline is so completely over that in the 1914–18 war the ministers of the Guelph king did not even know what his name meant, and made him discard it in the face of the Ghibelline Kaiser and the Holy Roman Empire. In the revival of that war the soldier, equipped with a few atomic bombs, fought with the strength of a million; but the idolized Bible was still at the back of the popular newspapers, full of the spirit of the campaigns of Joshua, holding up our sword as the sword of the Lord and Gideon, and hounding us on to the slaughter of those modern Amalekites and Canaanites, the Germans, as idolators and children of the devil. Though the formula (King and Country) was different, the spirit was the same: it was the old imaginary conflict of Jehovah against Baal; only, as the Germans were also fighting for King and Country, and were quite as convinced as we that Jehovah, the Lord strong and mighty, the Lord mighty in battle, the Lord of Hosts (now called big battalions), was their God, and that ours was his enemy, they fought as hard and felt quite as virtuous. But the wounds to civilization were so serious that we do not as yet know whether they are not going to prove mortal, because they are being kept open by the Old Testament spirit and methods and superstitions.

The situation is past trifling. The ancient worshippers of Jehovah, armed with sword and spear, and demoralized by a clever boy with a sling, could not murder and destroy wholesale. But with machine gun and amphibious tank, aeroplane and gas bomb, operating on cities where millions of inhabitants are depending for light and heat, water and food, on centralized mechanical organs like great steel hearts and arteries, that can be smashed in half an hour by a boy in a bomber, we really must take care that the boy is better educated than Noah and Joshua. In plain words, as we cannot get rid of the Bible, it will get rid of us unless we learn to read it 'in the proper spirit,' which I take to be the spirit of intellectual integrity that obliges honest thinkers to read every line which pretends to divine authority with all their wits about them, and to judge it exactly as they judge the Koran, the Upanishads, the Arabian Nights, this morning's leading article in The Times, or last week's cartoon in Punch, knowing that all written words are equally open to inspiration from the eternal fount and equally subject to error from the mortal imperfection of their authors.

Then say, of what use is the Bible nowadays to anyone but the antiquary and the literary connoisseur? Why not boot it into the dustbin? Well, there is a *prima facie* case to be made out for that. Let us first do justice to it.

What about the tables of the law? the ten commandments? They did not suffice even for the wandering desert tribe upon whom they were imposed by Moses, who, like Mahomet later on, could get them respected only by pretending that they were supernaturally revealed to him. They had to be supplemented by the elaborate codes of Leviticus and Deuteronomy, which the most fanatically observant Jew could not now obey without outraging our modern morality and violating our criminal law. They are mere lumber nowadays; for their simpler validities are the necessary commonplaces of human society and need no Bible to reveal them or give them authority. The second commandment, taken to heart by Islam, is broken and ignored throughout Christendom, though its warning against the enchantments of fine art is worthy the deepest consideration, and, had its author known the magic of word-music as he knew that of the graven image, might stand as a warning against our idolatry of the Bible. The whole ten are unsuited and inadequate to modern needs, as they say not a word against those forms of robbery, legalized by the robbers, which have uprooted the moral foundation of our society and will condemn us to slow social decay if we are not wakened up, as Russia has been, by a crashing collapse.

In addition to these negative drawbacks there is the positive one that the religion inculcated in the earlier books is a crudely atrocious ritual of human sacrifice to propitiate a murderous tribal deity who was, for example, induced to spare the human race from destruction in a second deluge by the pleasure given him by the smell of roasting flesh when Noah 'took of every clean beast and of every clean fowl, and offered burnt offerings on the altar.' And though this ritual is in the later books fiercely repudiated, and its god denied in express terms, by the prophet Micah, shewing how it was outgrown as the Jews progressed in culture, yet the tradition of a blood sacrifice whereby the vengeance of a terribly angry god can be bought off by a vicarious and hideously cruel blood sacrifice persists even through the New Testament,

PREFACE

where it attaches itself to the torture and execution of Jesus by the Roman governor of Jerusalem, idolizing that horror in Noah's fashion as a means by which we can all cheat our consciences, evade our moral responsibilities, and turn our shame into self-congratulation by loading all our infamies on to the scourged shoulders of Christ. It would be hard to imagine a more demoralizing and unchristian doctrine: indeed it would not be at all unreasonable for the Intellectual Co-operation Committee of the League of Nations to follow the example of the Roman Catholic Church by objecting to the promiscuous circulation of the Bible (except under conditions amounting to careful spiritual direction) until the supernatural claims made for its authority are finally and unequivocally dropped.

As to Bible science, it has over the nineteenth-century materialistic fashion in biology the advantage of being a science of life and not an attempt to substitute physics and chemistry for it; but it is hopelessly pre-evolutionary; its descriptions of the origin of life and morals are obviously fairy tales; its astronomy is terra-centric; its notions of the starry universe are childish; its history is epical and legendary: in short, people whose education in these departments is derived from the Bible are so absurdly misinformed as to be unfit for public employment, parental responsibility, or the franchise. As an encyclopedia, therefore, the Bible must be classed with the first edition of the Encyclopaedia Britannica as a record of what men once believed, and a measure of how far they have left their obsolete beliefs behind.

Granted all this, the fact remains that a great deal of the Bible is much more alive than this morning's paper and last night's parliamentary debate. Its chronicles are better reading than most of our fashionable histories, and less intentionally mendacious. In revolutionary invective and Utopian aspiration it cuts the ground from under the feet of Ruskin, Carlyle, and Karl Marx; and in epics of great leaders and great rascals it makes Homer seem superficial and Shakespear unbalanced. And its one great love poem is the only one that can satisfy a man who is really in love. Shelley's Epipsychidion is, in comparison, literary gas and gaiters.

In sum, it is an epitome, illustrated with the most stirring examples, of the history of a tribe of mentally vigorous, imaginative, aggressively acquisitive humans who developed into a nation through ruthless conquest, encouraged by the delusion that they were 'the chosen people of God' and, as such, the natural inheritors of all the earth, with a reversion to a blissful eternity hereafter in the kingdom of heaven. And the epitome in no way suppresses the fact that this delusion led at last to their dispersion, denationalization, and bigoted persecution by better disciplined States which, though equally confident of a monopoly of divine favor earned by their own merits, paid the Jews the compliment of adopting their gods and prophets, as, on the whole, more useful to rulers than the available alternatives.

Now the difference between an illiterate savage and a person who has read such an epitome (with due skipping of its genealogical rubbish and the occasional nonsenses produced by attempts to translate from imperfectly understood tongues) is enormous. A community on which such a historical curriculum is imposed in family and school may be more dangerous to its neighbors, and in greater peril of collapse from intolerance and megalomania, than a community that reads either nothing or silly novels, football results, and city articles; but it is beyond all question a more highly educated one. It is therefore not in the least surprising nor unreasonable that when the only generally available alternative to Bible education is no liberal education at all, many who have no illusions about the Bible, and fully comprehend its drawbacks, vote for Bible education *faute de mieux*.

PREFACE

This is why mere criticism of Bible education cuts so little ice. Ancient Hebrew history and literature, half fabulous as it is, is better than no history and no literature; and I neither regret nor resent my own Bible education, especially as my mind soon grew strong enough to take it at its real value. At worst the Bible gives a child a better start in life than the gutter.

This testimonial will please our Bible idolators; but it must not for a moment soothe them into believing that their fetishism can now be defended by the plea that it was better to be Noah or Abraham or Sir Isaac Newton than a London street arab. Street arabs are not very common in these days of compulsory attendance at the public elementary school. The alternative to the book of Genesis at present is not mere ignorant nescience, but H. G. Wells's Outline of History, and the host of imitations and supplements which its huge success has called into existence. Within the last two hundred years a body of history, literature, poetry, science, and art has been inspired and created by precisely the same mysterious impulse that inspired and created the Bible. In all these departments it leaves the Bible just nowhere. It is the Bible-educated human who is now the ignoramus. If you doubt it, try to pass an examination for any practical employment by giving Bible answers to the examiners' questions. You will be fortunate if you are merely plucked and not certified as a lunatic. Throughout the whole range of Science which the Bible was formerly supposed to cover with an infallible authority, it is now hopelessly superseded, with one exception. That exception is the science of theology, which is still completely off the ground – so metaphysical, as the learned say, that our materialist scientists contemptuously deny it the right to call itself science at all.

But there is no surer symptom of a sordid and fundamentally stupid mind, however powerful it may be in many practical activities, than a contempt for metaphysics. A person may be supremely able as a mathematician, engineer, parliamentary tactician, or racing bookmaker; but if that person has contemplated the universe all through life without ever asking 'What the devil does it all mean?' he (or she) is one of those people for whom Calvin accounted by placing them in his category of the predestinately damned.

Hence the Bible, scientifically obsolete in all other respects, remains interesting as a record of how the idea of God, which is the first effort of civilized mankind to account for the existence and origin and purpose of as much of the universe as we are conscious of, develops from a childish idolatry of a thundering, earthquaking, famine striking, pestilence launching, blinding, deafening, killing, destructively omnipotent Bogey Man, maker of night and day and sun and moon, of the four seasons and their miracles of seed and harvest, to a braver idealization of a benevolent sage, a just judge, an affectionate father, evolving finally into the incorporeal word that never becomes flesh, at which point modern science and philosophy takes up the problem with its *Vis Naturae*, its *Élan Vital*, its Life Force, its Evolutionary Appetite, its still more abstract Categorical Imperative, and what not.

Now the study of this history of the development of a hypothesis from savage idolatry to a highly cultivated metaphysic is as interesting, instructive, and reassuring as any study can be to an open mind and an honest intellect. But we spoil it all by that lazy and sluttish practice of not throwing out the dirty water when we get in the clean. The Bible presents us with a succession of gods, each being a striking improvement on the previous one, marking an Ascent of Man to a nobler and deeper conception of Nature, every step involving a purification of the water of life and calling for a thorough emptying and cleansing of the vessel before its replenishment by a fresh and cleaner supply. But we baffle the blessing by just sloshing the water from the new fountain into the contents of the dirty old bucket, and repeat this folly until our minds are in such a filthy mess that we are objects of pity to the superficial but clearheaded atheists who are content without metaphysics and can see nothing in the whole business but its confusions and absurdities. Practical men of business refuse to be bothered with such crazy matters at all.

Take the situation in detail as it develops through the Bible. The God of Noah is not the God of Job. Contemplate first the angry deity who drowned every living thing on earth, except one family of each species, in a fit of raging disgust at their wickedness, and then allowed the head of the one human family to appease him by 'the sweet savour' of a heap of burning flesh! Is he identical with the tolerant, argumentative, academic, urbane philosophical deity who entertained the devil familiarly and made a wager with him that he could not drive Job to despair of divine benevolence? People who cannot see the difference between these two Gods cannot pass the most elementary test of intelligence: they cannot distinguish between similars and dissimilars.

But though Job's God is a great advance on Noah's God, he is a very bad debater, unless indeed we give him credit for deliberately saving himself from defeat by the old expedient: 'No case: abuse the plaintiff's attorney.' Job having raised the problem of the existence of evil and its incompatibility with omnipotent benevolence, it is no valid reply to jeer at him for being unable to create a whale or to play with it as with a bird. And there is a very suspicious touch of Noah's God in the offer to overlook the complicity of Job's friends in his doubts in consideration of a sacrifice of seven bullocks and seven rams. God's attempt at an argument is only a repetition and elaboration of the sneers of Elihu, and is so abruptly tacked on to them that one concludes that it must be a pious forgery to conceal the fact that the original poem left the problem of evil unsolved and Job's criticism unanswered, as indeed it remained until Creative Evolution solved it.

When we come to Micah we find him throwing out the dirty water fearlessly. He will not have Noah's God, nor even Job's God with his seven bullocks and seven rams. He raises the conception of God to the highest point it has ever attained by his fiercely contemptuous denunciation of the blood sacrifices, and his inspired and inspiring demand 'What doth the Lord require of thee but to do justly, and to love mercy, and to walk humbly with thy God?' Before this victory of the human spirit over crude superstition Noah's God and Job's God go down like skittles: there is an end of them. And yet our children are taught, not to exult in this great triumph of spiritual insight over mere animal terror of the Bogey Man, but to believe that Micah's God and Job's God and Noah's God are one and the same, and that every good child must revere the spirit of justice and mercy and humility equally with the appetite for burnt flesh and human sacrifice, such indiscriminate and nonsensical reverence being inculcated as religion.

Later on comes Jesus, who dares a further flight. He suggests that godhead is something which incorporates itself in Man: in himself, for instance. He is immediately stoned by his horrified hearers, who can see nothing in the suggestion but a monstrous attempt on his part to impersonate Jehovah. This misunderstanding, typical of dirty water theology, was made an article of religion eighteen hundred years later by Emanuel Swedenborg. But the unadulterated suggestion of Jesus is an advance on the theology of Micah; for Man walking humbly before an external God is an ineffective creature compared to Man exploring as the instrument and embodiment of God with no other guide than the spark of divinity within him. It is certainly the greatest break in

PREFACE

the Bible between the old and the new testament. Yet the dirty water still spoils it; for we find Paul holding up Christ to the Ephesians as 'an offering and a sacrifice to God for a sweet smelling savour,' thereby dragging Christianity back and down to the level of Noah. None of the apostles rose above that level; and the result was that the great advances made by Micah and Jesus were cancelled; and historical Christianity was built up on the sacrificial altars of Jehovah, with Jesus as the sacrifice. What he and Micah would say if they could return and see their names and credit attached to the idolatries they abhorred can be imagined only by those who understand and sympathize with them.

Jesus could be reproached for having chosen his disciples very unwisely if we could believe that he had any real choice. There are moments when one is tempted to say that there was not one Christian among them, and that Judas was the only one who shewed any gleams of common sense. Because Jesus had mental powers and insight quite beyond their comprehension they worshipped him as a superhuman and indeed supernatural phenomenon, and made his memory the nucleus of their crude belief in magic, their Noahism, their sentimentality, their masochist Puritanism, and their simple morality with its punitive sanctions, decent and honest and amiable enough, some of it, but never for a moment on the intellectual level of Jesus, and at worst pregnant with all the horrors of the later wars of religion, the Jew burnings under Torquemada, and the atrocious renewal of his persecution under Hitler in the present century.

Most unfortunately the death of Jesus helped to vulgarize his reputation and obscure his doctrine. The Romans, though they executed their own political criminals by throwing them from the Tarpeian rock, punished slave revolts by crucifixion. They crucified six thousand of the followers of the revolutionary gladiator,

Spartacus, a century before Jesus was denounced to them by the Jewish high priest as an agitator of the same kidney. He was accordingly tortured and killed in this hideous manner, with the infinitely more hideous result that the cross and the other instruments of his torture were made the symbols of the faith legally established in his name three hundred years later. They are still accepted as such throughout Christendom. The crucifixion thus became to the Churches what the Chamber of Horrors is to a waxwork: the irresistible attraction for children and for the crudest adult worshippers. Christ's clean water of life is befouled by the dirtiest of dirty water from the idolatries of his savage forefathers; and our prelates and proconsuls take Caiaphas and Pontius Pilate for their models in the name of their despised and rejected victim.

The case was further complicated by the pitiable fact that Jesus himself, shaken by the despair which unsettled the reason of Swift and Ruskin and many others at the spectacle of human cruelty, injustice, misery, folly, and apparently hopeless political incapacity, and perhaps also by the worship of his disciples and of the multitude, had allowed Peter to persuade him that he was the Messiah, and that death could not prevail against him nor prevent his returning to judge the world and establish his reign on earth for ever and ever. As this romance came as easily within the mental range of his disciples as his social doctrine had been far over their heads, 'Crosstianity' became established on the authority of Jesus himself. Later on, in a curious record of the visions of a drug addict which was absurdly admitted to the canon under the title of Revelation, a thousand years was ordained as the period that was to elapse before Jesus was to return as he had promised. In 1000 A.D. the last possibility of the promised advent expired; but by that time people were so used to the delay that they readily substituted for the Second Advent a Second Postpone-

PREFACE

ment. Pseudo-Christianity was, and always will be, fact proof.

The whole business is in a muddle which has held out not only because the views of Jesus are above the heads of all but the best minds, but because his appearance was followed by the relapse in civilization which we call the Dark Ages, from which we are only just emerging sufficiently to begin to pick up Christ's most advanced

thought and filter it from the dirty water into which the apostles and their successors poured it.

Six hundred years after Jesus, Mahomet made a colossal stride ahead from mere stock-and-stone idolatry to a very enlightened Unitarianism; but though he died a conqueror, and therefore escaped being made the chief attraction in an Arabian Chamber of Horrors, he found it impossible to control his Arabs without enticing and intimidating them by promises of a delightful life for the faithful and threats of an eternity of disgusting torment for the wicked after their bodily death, and also, after some honest protests, by accepting the supernatural character thrust on him by the childish superstition of his followers; so that he, too, now needs to be rediscovered in his true nature before Islam can come back to earth as a living faith.

And now I think the adventures of the black girl as revealed to me need no longer puzzle anyone. They could hardly have happened to a white girl steeped from her birth in the pseudo-Christianity of the Churches. I take it that the missionary lifted her straight out of her native tribal fetishism into an unbiassed contemplation of the Bible with its series of gods marking stages in the development of the conception of God from the monster Bogey Man the Everlasting Father, the Prince of Peace. She has still to consider the Church of England's sublimation of God to spirit without body, parts, nor passions, with its corollary that in spite of the fourth gospel God is not Love. Love is not enough (Edith Cavell made that discovery about Patriotism) and the Black Girl finds it wiser to take Voltaire's advice by cultivating her garden and bringing up her piccaninnies than to spend her life imagining that she can find a complete explanation of the universe by laying about her with her knobkerry.

Still, the knobkerry has to be used as far as the way is clear. Mere agnosticism is useless to the police. When the question of the existence of Noah's idol is raised on the point, vital to high civilization, whether our children shall continue to be brought up to worship it and compound for their sins by sacrificing to it, or, more cheaply, by sheltering themselves behind another's sacrifice to it, then whoever hesitates to bring down the knobkerry with might and main is ludicrously unfit to have any part in the government of a modern State. The importance of a message to that effect at the present world crisis is probably at the bottom of my curious and sudden inspiration to write this tale instead of cumbering theatrical literature with another stage comedy.

Ayot St Lawrence
1932–46

THE BLACK GIRL
IN SEARCH OF GOD

In the earliest text of this tale Shaw summed up the mystery of existence from Genesis to Einstein's theory of relativity in the equation 'the square root of minus x'. Out of this he created one of literature's most delicious puns, with the Black Girl misconstruing the equation to refer to the sex of the goddess Myna, thus innocently creating a concept of a female divinity – 'the mother of us all'. In 1934 Shaw, after being charged with inaccuracy in his use of the Einstein theory, dutifully altered the equation to read 'the square root of minus one', destroying in the process his cosmic *jeu d'esprit*. In the present edition we have preferred, after calling the matter to the reader's attention, to allow art to take precedence over accuracy by preserving the original pun.

DAN H. LAURENCE

'WHERE is God?' said the black girl to the missionary who had converted her.

'He has said "Seek and ye shall find me"' said the missionary.

The missionary was a small white woman, not yet thirty: an odd little body who had found no satisfaction for her soul with her very respectable and fairly well-to-do family in her native England, and had settled down in the African forest to teach little African children to love Christ and adore the Cross. She was a born apostle of love. At school she had adored one or other of her teachers with an idolatry that was proof against all snubbing, but had never cared much for girls of her own age and standing. At eighteen she began falling in love with earnest clergymen, and actually became engaged to six of them in succession. But when it came to the point she always broke it off; for these love affairs, full at first of ecstatic happiness and hope, somehow became unreal and eluded her in the end. The clergymen thus suddenly and unaccountably disengaged did not always conceal their sense of relief and escape, as if they too had discovered that the dream was only a dream, or a sort of metaphor by which they had striven to express the real thing, but not itself the real thing.

One of the jilted, however, committed suicide; and this tragedy gave her an extraordinary joy. It seemed to take her from a fool's paradise of false happiness into a real region in which intense suffering became transcendent rapture.

But it put an end to her queer marriage engagements. Not that it was the last of them. But a worldly cousin, of whose wit she was a little afraid, and who roundly called her a coquette and a jilt, one day accused her of playing in her later engagements for another suicide, and told her that many a woman had been hanged for less. And though she knew in a way that this was not true, and that the cousin, being a woman of this world, did not understand; yet she knew also that in the worldly way it was true enough, and that she must give up this strange game of seducing men into engagements which she now knew she would never keep. So she jilted the sixth clergyman and went to plant the cross in darkest Africa; and the last stirring in her of what she repudiated as sin was a flash of rage when he married the cousin, through whose wit and worldly wisdom he at last became a bishop in spite of himself.

The black girl, a fine creature, whose satin skin and shining muscles made the white missionary folk seem like ashen ghosts by contrast, was an interesting but unsatisfactory convert; for instead of taking Christianity with sweet docility exactly as it was administered to her, she met it with unexpected interrogative reactions which forced her teacher to improvize doctrinal replies and invent evidence on the spur of the moment to such an extent that at last she could not conceal from herself that the life of Christ, as she narrated it, had accreted so many circumstantial details and such a body of homemade doctrine that the Evangelists would have been amazed and confounded if they had been alive to hear it all put forward on their authority. Indeed the missionary's choice of a specially remote station, which had been at first an act of devotion, very soon became a necessity, as the appearance of a rival missionary would have led to the discovery that though some of the finest plums in the gospel pudding concocted by her had been picked out of the Bible, and the scenery and *dramatis personae* borrowed from it, yet the resultant religion was, in spite of this element of compilation, really a product of the missionary's own direct inspiration. Only as a solitary pioneer missionary could she be her own Church and determine its canon without fear of being excommunicated as a heretic.

But she was perhaps rash when, having taught the black girl to read, she gave her a bible on her birthday. For when the black girl, receiving her teacher's reply very literally, took her knobkerry and strode off into the African forest in search of God, she took the bible with her as her guidebook.

The first thing she met was a mamba snake, one of the few poisonous snakes that will attack mankind if crossed. Now the missionary, who was fond of making pets of animals because they were affectionate and never asked questions, had taught the black girl never to kill anything if she could help it, and never to be afraid of anything. So she grasped her knobkerry a little tighter and said to the mamba 'I wonder who made you, and why he gave you the will to kill me and the venom to do it with.'

The mamba immediately beckoned her by a twist of its head to follow it, and led her to a pile of rocks on which sat enthroned a well-built aristocratic looking white man with handsome regular features, an imposing beard and luxuriant wavy hair, both as white as isinglass, and a ruthlessly severe expression. He had in his hand a staff which seemed a combination of sceptre, big stick, and great assegai; and with this he immediately killed the mamba, who was approaching him humbly and adoringly.

The black girl, having been taught to fear nothing, felt her heart harden against him, partly because she thought strong men ought to be black, and only missionary ladies white, partly because he had killed her friend the snake, and partly because he wore a ridiculous white nightshirt, and thereby rubbed her up on the one point on which her teacher had never been able to convert her, which was the duty of being ashamed of her person and wearing petticoats. There was a certain contempt in her voice as she addressed him.

'I am seeking God' she said. 'Can you direct me?'

'You have found him' he replied. 'Kneel down and worship me this very instant, you presumptuous creature, or dread my wrath. I am the Lord of Hosts: I made the heavens and the earth and all that in them is. I made the poison of the snake and the milk in your mother's breast.

In my hand are death and all the diseases, the thunder and lightning, the storm and the pestilence, and all the other proofs of my greatness and majesty. On your knees, girl; and when you next come before me, bring me your favorite child and slay it here before me as a sacrifice; for I love the smell of newly spilled blood.'

'I have no child' said the black girl. 'I am a virgin.'

'Then fetch your father and let him slay you' said the Lord of Hosts. 'And see that your relatives bring me plenty of rams and goats and sheep to roast before me as offerings to propitiate me, or I shall certainly smite them with the most horrible plagues so that they may know that I am God.'

'I am not a piccaninny, nor even a grown up ninny, to believe such wicked nonsense' said the black girl; 'and in the name of the true God whom I seek I will scotch you as you scotched that poor mamba.' And she bounded up the rocks at him, brandishing her knobkerry.

But when she reached the top there was nothing there. This so bewildered her that she sat down and took out her bible for guidance. But whether the ants had got at it, or, being a very old book, it had perished by natural decay, all the early pages had crumbled to dust which blew away when she opened it.

So she sighed and got up and resumed her search. Presently she disturbed a sort of cobra called a ringhals, which spat at her and was gliding away when she said 'You no dare spit at me. I want to know who made you, and why you are so unlike me. The mamba's God was no use: he wasnt real when I tried him with my knobkerry. Lead me to yours.'

On that, the ringhals came back and beckoned her to follow him, which she did.

He led her to a pleasant glade in which an oldish gentleman with a soft silvery beard and hair, also in a white nightshirt, was sitting at a table covered with a white cloth and strewn with manuscript poems and pens made of angels' quills. He looked kindly enough; but his turned up moustaches and eyebrows expressed a self-satisfied cunning which the black girl thought silly.

'Good little Spitty-spitty' he said to the snake. 'You have brought somebody to argue with me.' And he gave the snake an egg, which it carried away joyfully into the forest.

'Do not be afraid of me' he said to the black girl. 'I am not a cruel god: I am a reasonable one. I do nothing worse than argue. I am a Nailer at arguing. Dont worship me. Reproach me. Find fault with me. Dont spare my feelings. Throw something in my teeth; so that I can argue about it.'

'Did you make the world?' said the black girl.

'Of course I did' he said.

'Why did you make it with so much evil in it?' she said.

'Splendid!' said the god. 'That is just what I wanted you to ask me. You are a clever intelligent girl. I had a servant named Job once to argue with; but he was so modest and stupid that I had to shower the most frightful misfortunes on him before I could provoke him to complain. His wife told him to curse me and die; and I dont wonder at the poor woman; for I gave him a terrible time, though I made it all up to him afterwards. When at last I got him arguing, he thought a lot of himself. But I soon shewed him up. He acknowledged that I had the better of him. I took him down handsomely, I tell you.'

'I do not want to argue' said the black girl. 'I want to know why, if you really made the world, you made it so badly.'

'Badly!' cried the Nailer. 'Ho! You set yourself up to call me to account! Who are you, pray, that you should criticize me? Can you make a better world yourself? Just try: thats all. Try to make one little bit of it. For instance, make a whale. Put a hook in its nose and bring it to me when you have finished. Do you realize, you ridiculous little insect, that I not only made the whale, but made the sea for him to swim in? The whole mighty ocean, down to its bottomless depths and up to the top of the skies. You think that was easy, I suppose. You think you could do it better yourself. I tell you what, young woman: you want the conceit taken out of you. You couldnt make a mouse; and you set yourself up against me, who made a megatherium. You couldnt make a pond; and you dare talk to me, the maker of the seven seas. You will be ugly and old and dead in fifty years, whilst my majesty will endure for ever; and here you are taking me to task as if you were my aunt. You think, dont you, that you are better than God? What have you to say to that argument?'

'It isnt an argument: it's a sneer' said the black girl. 'You dont seem to know what an argument is.'

'What! I who put down Job, as all the world admits, not know what an argument is! I simply laugh at you, child' said the old gentleman, considerably huffed, but too astonished to take the situation in fully.

'I dont mind your laughing at me' said the black girl; 'but you have not told me why you did not make the world all good instead of a mixture of good and bad. It is no answer to ask me whether I could have made it any better myself. If I were God there would be no tsetse flies. My people would not fall down in fits and have dreadful swellings and commit sins. Why did you put a bag of poison in the mamba's mouth when other snakes can live as well without it? Why did you make the monkeys so ugly and the birds so pretty?'

'Why shouldnt I?' said the old gentleman. 'Answer me that.'

'Why should you? unless you have a taste for mischief' said the black girl.

'Asking conundrums is not arguing' he said. 'It is not playing the game.'

'A God who cannot answer my questions is no use to me' said the black girl. 'Besides, if you had really made everything you would know why you made the whale as ugly as he is in the pictures.'

'If I chose to amuse myself by making him look funny, what is that to you?' he said. 'Who are you to dictate to me how I shall make things?'

'I am tired of you' said the black girl. 'You always come back to the same bad manners. I dont believe you ever made anything. Job must have been very stupid not to find you out. There are too many old men pretending to be gods in this forest.'

She sprang at him with her knobkerry uplifted; but he dived nimbly under the table, which she thought must

have sunk into the earth; for when she reached it there was nothing there. And when she resorted to her bible again the wind snatched thirty more pages out of it and scattered them in dust over the trees.

After this adventure the black girl felt distinctly sulky. She had not found God; her bible was half spoilt; and she had lost her temper twice without any satisfaction whatever. She began to ask herself whether she had not overrated white beards and old age and nightshirts as divine credentials. It was lucky that this was her mood when she came upon a remarkably good looking clean shaven white young man in a Greek tunic. She had never seen anything like him before. In particular there

was a lift and twist about the outer corners of his brows that both interested and repelled her.

'Excuse me, baas' she said. 'You have knowing eyes. I am in search of God. Can you direct me?'

'Do not trouble about that' said the young man. 'Take the world as it comes; for beyond it there is nothing. All roads end at the grave, which is the gate of nothingness; and in the shadow of nothingness everything is vanity. Take my advice and seek no further than the end of your nose. You will always know that there is something beyond that; and in that knowledge you will be hopeful and happy.'

'My mind ranges further' said the black girl. 'It is not right to shut one's eyes. I desire a knowledge of God more than happiness or hope. God is my happiness and my hope.'

'How if you find that there is no God?' said the young man.

'I should be a bad woman if I did not know that God exists' said the black girl.

'Who told you that?' said the young man. 'You should not let people tie up your mind with such limitations. Besides, why should you not be a bad woman?'

'That is nonsense' said the black girl. 'Being a bad woman means being something you ought not to be.'

'Then you must find out what you ought to be before you can tell whether you are a good woman or a bad one.'

'That is true' said the black girl. 'But I know I ought to be a good woman even if it is bad to be good.'

'There is no sense in that' said the young man.

'Not your sort of sense but God's sort of sense' she said. 'I want to have that sort of sense; and I feel that when I have got it I shall be able to find God.'

'How can you tell what you shall find?' he said. 'My counsel to you is to do all the work that comes to you as well as you can while you can, and so fill up with use and honor the days that remain to you before the inevitable end, when there will be neither counsel nor work, neither doing nor knowing, nor even being.'

'There will be a future when I am dead' said the black girl. 'If I cannot live it I can know it.'

'Do you know the past?' said the young man. 'If the past, which has really happened, is beyond your knowledge, how can you hope to know the future, which has not yet happened?'

'Yet it will happen; and I know enough of it to tell you that the sun will rise every day' said the black girl.

'That also is vanity' said the young sage. 'The sun is burning and must some day burn itself out.'

'Life is a flame that is always burning itself out; but it catches fire again every time a child is born. Life is greater than death, and hope than despair. I will do the work that comes to me only if I know that it is good work; and to know that, I must know the past and the future, and must know God.'

'You mean that you must *be* God' he said, looking hard at her.

'As much as I can' said the black girl. 'Thank you. We who are young are the wise ones: I have learned from you that to know God is to be God. You have strengthened my soul. Before I leave you, tell me who you are.'

'I am Koheleth, known to many as Ecclesiastes the preacher' he replied. 'God be with you if you can find him! He is not with me. Learn Greek: it is the language of wisdom. Farewell.'

He made a friendly sign and passed on. The black girl went the opposite way, thinking harder than ever; but the train of thought he had started in her became so puzzling and difficult that at last she fell asleep and walked steadily on in her sleep until she smelt a lion, and, waking suddenly, saw him sitting in the middle of her path, sunning himself like a cat before the hearth: a lion of the kind they call maneless because its mane is handsome and orderly and not like a touzled mop.

'In God's name, Dicky' she said, giving his throat as she passed him a caressing little pull with her fingers which felt as if she had pulled at a warm tuft of moss on a mountain.

King Richard beamed graciously, and followed her

with his eyes as if he had an impulse to go for a walk with her; but she left him too decisively for that; and she, remembering that there are many less amiable and even stronger creatures in the forest than he, proceeded more warily until she met a dark man with wavy black hair, and a number six nose. He had nothing on but a pair of sandals. His face was very much wrinkled; but the wrinkles were those of pity and kindliness, though the number six nose had large courageous nostrils, and the corners of his mouth were resolute. She heard him before she saw him; for he was making strange roaring and hooting noises and seemed in great trouble. When he saw her he stopped roaring and tried to look ordinary and unconcerned.

'Say, baas' said the black girl: 'are you the prophet that goes stripped and naked, wailing like the dragons and mourning like the owls?'

'I do a little in that line' he said apologetically. 'Micah is my name: Micah the Morasthite. Can I do anything for you?'

'I seek God' she answered.

'And have you found Him?' said Micah.

'I found an old man who wanted me to roast animals for him because he loved the smell of cooking, and to sacrifice my children on his altar.'

At this Micah uttered such a lamentable roar that King Richard hastily took cover in the forest and sat watching there with his tail slashing.

'He is an impostor and a horror' roared Micah. 'Can you see yourself coming before the high God with burnt calves of a year old? Would He be pleased with thousands of rams or rivers of oil or the sacrifice of your first born, the fruit of your body, instead of the devotion of your soul? God has shewed your soul what is good; and your soul has told you that He speaks the truth. And what does He require of you but to do justice and love mercy and walk humbly with Him?'

'This is a third God' she said; 'and I like him much better than the one who wanted sacrifices and the one who wanted me to argue with him so that he might sneer at my weakness and ignorance. But doing justice and shewing mercy is only a small part of life when one is not a baas or a judge. And what is the use of walking humbly if you dont know where you are walking to?'

'Walk humbly and God will guide you' said the

THE BLACK GIRL IN SEARCH OF GOD

Prophet. 'What is it to you whither He is leading you?'

'He gave me eyes to guide myself' said the black girl. 'He gave me a mind and left me to use it. How can I now turn on him and tell him to see for me and to think for me?'

Micah's only reply was such a fearful roar that King Richard fairly bolted and ran for two miles without stopping. And the black girl did the same in the opposite direction. But she ran only a mile.

'What am I running away from?' she said to herself, pulling herself up. 'I'm not afraid of that dear noisy old man.'

'Your fears and hopes are only fancies' said a voice close to her, proceeding from a very shortsighted elderly man in spectacles who was sitting on a gnarled log. 'In running away you were acting on a conditioned reflex. It is quite simple. Having lived among lions you have from your childhood associated the sound of a roar with deadly danger. Hence your precipitate flight when that superstitious old jackass brayed at you. This remarkable discovery cost me twentyfive years of devoted research, during which I cut out the brains of innumerable dogs, and observed their spittle by making holes in their cheeks for them to salivate through instead of through their tongues. The whole scientific world is prostrate at my feet in admiration of this colossal achievement and gratitude for the light it has shed on the great problems of human conduct.'

'Why didnt you ask me?' said the black girl. 'I could have told you in twentyfive seconds without hurting those poor dogs.'

'Your ignorance and presumption are unspeakable' said the old myop. 'The fact was known of course to every child; but it had never been proved experimentally in the laboratory; and therefore it was not scientifically known at all. It reached me as an unskilled conjecture: I handed it on as science. Have you ever performed an experiment may I ask?'

'Several' said the black girl. 'I will perform one now. Do you know what you are sitting on?'

'I am sitting on a log grey with age, and covered with an uncomfortable rugged bark' said the myop.

'You are mistaken' said the black girl. 'You are sitting on a sleeping crocodile.'

With a yell which Micah himself might have envied, the myop rose and fled frantically to a neighboring tree, up which he climbed catlike with an agility which in so elderly a gentleman was quite superhuman.

'Come down' said the black girl. 'You ought to

know that crocodiles are only to be found near rivers. I was only trying an experiment. Come down.'

'How am I to come down?' said the myop trembling. 'I should break my neck.'

'How did you get up?' said the black girl.

'I dont know' he replied, almost in tears. 'It is enough to make a man believe in miracles. I couldnt have climbed this tree; and yet here I am and shall never be able to get down again.'

'A very interesting experiment, wasnt it?' said the black girl.

'A shamefully cruel one, you wicked girl' he moaned. 'Pray did it occur to you that you might have killed me? Do you suppose you can give a delicate phsyiological organism like mine a violent shock without the most serious and quite possibly fatal reactions on the heart? I shall never be able to sit on a log again as long as I live. I believe my pulse is quite abnormal, though I cannot count it; for if I let go of this branch I shall drop like a stone.'

'If you can cut half a dog's brain out without causing any reactions on its spittle you need not worry' she said calmly. 'I think African magic much more powerful than your divining by dogs. By saying one word to you I made you climb a tree like a cat. You confess it was a miracle.'

'I wish you would say another word and get me safely down again, confound you for a black witch' he grumbled.

'I will' said the black girl. 'There is a tree snake smelling at the back of your neck.'

The myop was on the ground in a jiffy. He landed finally on his back; but he scrambled to his feet at once and said 'You did not take me in: dont think it. I knew perfectly well you were inventing that snake to frighten me.'

'And yet you were as frightened as if it had been a real snake' said the black girl.

'I was not' said the myop indignantly. 'I was not frightened in the least.'

'You nipped down the tree as if you were' said the black girl.

'That is what is so interesting' said the myop, recovering his self-possession now that he felt safe. 'It was a conditioned reflex. I wonder could I make a dog climb a tree.'

'What for?' said the black girl.

'Why, to place this phenomenon on a scientific basis' said he.

'Nonsense!' said the black girl. 'A dog cant climb a tree.'

'Neither can I without the stimulus of an imaginary crocodile' said the professor. 'How am I to make a dog imagine a crocodile?'

'Introduce him to a few real ones to begin with' said the black girl.

'That would cost a great deal' said the myop, wrinkling his brows. 'Dogs are cheap if you buy them from professional dog-stealers, or lay in a stock when the dog tax becomes due; but crocodiles would run into a lot of money. I must think this out carefully.'

'Before you go' said the black girl 'tell me whether you believe in God.'

'God is an unnecessary and discarded hypothesis' said the myop. 'The universe is only a gigantic system of reflexes reproduced by shocks. If I give you a clip on the knee you will wag your ankle.'

'I will also give you a clip with my knobkerry; so dont do it' said the black girl.

'For scientific purposes it is necessary to inhibit such secondary and apparently irrelevant reflexes by tying the subject down' said the professor. 'Yet they also are quite relevant as examples of reflexes produced by association of ideas. I have spent twentyfive years studying their effects.'

'Effects on what?' said the black girl.

'On a dog's saliva' said the myop.

'Are you any the wiser?' she said.

'I am not interested in wisdom' he replied: 'in fact I do not know what it means and have no reason to believe that it exists. My business is to learn something that was not known before. I impart that knowledge to the world, and thereby add to the body of ascertained scientific truth.'

'How much better will the world be when it is all knowledge and no mercy?' said the black girl. 'Havnt you brains enough to invent some decent way of finding out what you want to know?'

'Brains!' cried the myop, as if he could hardly believe his ears. 'You must be an extraordinarily ignorant young woman. Do you not know that men of science are all brains from head to foot?'

'Tell that to the crocodile' said the black girl. 'And tell me this. Have you ever considered the effect of your experiments on other people's minds and characters? Is it worth while losing your own soul and damning everybody else's to find out something about a dog's spittle?'

'You are using words that have no meaning' said the myop. 'Can you demonstrate the existence of the organ you call a soul on the operating table or in the dissecting room? Can you reproduce the operation you call damning in the laboratory?'

'I can turn a live body with a soul into a dead one without it with a whack of my knobkerry' said the black girl 'and you will soon see the difference and smell it. When people damn their souls by doing something wicked, you soon see the difference too.'

'I have seen a man die: I have never seen one damn his soul' said the myop.

'But you have seen him go to the dogs' said the black girl. 'You have gone to the dogs yourself, havnt you?'

'A quip; and an extremely personal one' said the myop haughtily. 'I leave you.'

So he went his way trying to think of some means of

making a dog climb a tree in order to prove scientifically that he himself could climb one; and the black girl went her opposite way until she came to a hill on the top of which stood a huge cross guarded by a Roman soldier with a spear. Now in spite of all the teachings of the missionary, who found in the horrors of the crucifixion the same strange joy she had found in breaking her own heart and those of her lovers, the black girl hated the cross and thought it a great pity that Jesus had not died peacefully and painlessly and naturally, full of years and wisdom, protecting his granddaughters (her imagination always completed the picture with at least twenty promising black granddaughters) against the selfishness and violence of their parents. So she was averting her head from the cross with an expression of disgust when the Roman soldier sprang at her with his spear at the charge and shouted fiercely 'On your knees, blackamoor, before the instrument and symbol of Roman justice, Roman law, Roman order and Roman peace.'

But the black girl side-stepped the spear and swung her knobkerry so heartily on the nape of his neck that he went down sprawling and trying vainly to co-ordinate the movement of his legs sufficiently to rise. 'That is the blackamoor instrument and symbol of all those fine things' said the black girl, shewing him the knobkerry. 'How do you like it?'

'Hell!' groaned the soldier. 'The tenth legion rabbit punched by a black bitch! This is the end of the world.' And he ceased struggling and lay down and cried like a child.

He recovered before she had gone very far; but being a Roman soldier he could not leave his post to gratify his feelings. The last she saw of him before the brow of the hill cut off their view of one another was the shaking of his fist at her; and the last she heard from him need not be repeated here.

Her next adventure was at a well where she stopped to drink, and suddenly saw a man whom she had not noticed before sitting beside it. As she was about to scoop up some water in her hand he produced a cup from nowhere and said

'Take this and drink in remembrance of me.'

'Thank you, baas' she said, and drank. 'Thank you kindly.'

She gave him back the cup; and he made it disappear like a conjurer, at which she laughed and he laughed too. 'That was clever, baas' she said. 'Great magician, you. You perhaps tell black woman something. I am in search of God. Where is he?'

'Within you' said the conjurer. 'Within me too.'

'I think so' said the girl. 'But what is he?'

'Our father' said the conjurer.

The black girl made a wry face and thought for a moment. 'Why not our mother?' she said then.

It was the conjurer's turn to make a wry face; and he made it. 'Our mothers would have us put them before God' he said. 'If I had been guided by my mother I should perhaps have been a rich man instead of an outcast and a wanderer; but I should not have found God.'

'My father beat me from the time I was little until I was big enough to lay him out with my knobkerry' said the black girl; 'and even after that he tried to sell me to a white baas-soldier who had left his wife across the seas. I have have always refused to say "Our father which art in heaven." I always say "Our grandfather." I will not have a God who is my father.'

'That need not prevent us loving one another like brother and sister' said the conjurer smiling; for the grandfather amendment tickled his sense of humor. Besides, he was a goodnatured fellow who smiled whenever he could.

'A woman does not love her brother' said the black girl. 'Her heart turns from her brother to a stranger as my heart turns to you.'

'Well: let us drop the family: it is only a metaphor' said the conjurer. 'We are members of the same body of mankind, and therefore members one of another. Let us leave it at that.'

'I cannot, baas' she said. 'God tells me that he has nothing to do with bodies, and fathers and mothers, and sisters and brothers.'

'It is a way of saying love one another: that is all' said the conjurer. 'Love them that hate you. Bless them that curse you. Never forget that two blacks do not make a white.'

'I do not want everyone to love me' said the black girl. 'I cannot love everybody. I do not want to. God tells me that I must not hit people with my knobkerry merely because I dislike them, and that their dislike of me – if they happen to dislike me – gives them no right to hit me. But God makes me dislike many people. And there are people who must be killed like snakes, because they rob and kill other people.'

'I wish you would not remind me of these people' said the conjurer. 'They make me very unhappy.'

'It makes things very nice to forget about the unpleasant things' said the black girl; 'but it does not make them believable; and it does not make them right. Do you really and truly love me, baas?'

The conjurer shrank, but immediately smiled kindly as he replied 'Do not let us make a personal matter of it.'

'But it has no sense if it is not a personal matter' said the black girl. 'Suppose I tell you I love you, as you tell me I ought! Do you not feel that I am taking a liberty with you?'

'Certainly not' said the conjurer. 'You must not think that. Though you are black and I am white we are equal before God who made us so.'

'I am not thinking about that at all' said the black girl. 'I forgot when I spoke that I am black and that you are only a poor white. Think of me as a white queen and of yourself as a white king. What is the matter? Why did you start?'

'Nothing. Nothing' said the conjurer. 'Or – Well, I am the poorest of poor whites; yet I have thought of myself as a king. But that was when the wickedness of men had driven me crazy.'

'I have seen worse kings' said the black girl; 'so you need not blush. Well, let you be King Solomon and let me be Queen of Sheba, same as in the bible. I come to you and say that I love you. That means I have come to take possession of you. I come with the love of a lioness and eat you up and make you a part of myself. From this time you will have to think, not of what pleases you, but of what pleases me. I will stand between you and yourself, between you and God. Is not that a terrible tyranny? Love is a devouring thing. Can you imagine heaven with love in it?'

'In my heaven there is nothing else. What else is heaven but love?' said the conjurer, boldly but uncomfortably.

'It is glory. It is the home of God and of his thoughts: there is no billing and cooing there, no clinging to one another like a tick to a sheep. The missionary, my teacher, talks of love; but she has run away from all her lovers to do God's work. The whites turn their eyes away from me lest they should love me. There are companies of men and women who have devoted themselves to God's work; but though they call themselves brotherhoods and sisterhoods they do not speak to one another.'

'So much the worse for them' said the conjurer.

'It is silly, of course' said the black girl. 'We have to live with people and must make the best of them. But does it not shew that our souls need solitude as much as our bodies need love? We need the help of one another's bodies and the help of one another's minds; but our souls need to be alone with God; and when people come loving you and wanting your soul as well as your mind and body, you cry 'Keep your distance: I belong to myself, not to you.'' This "love one another" of yours is worse mockery to me who am in search of God than it is to the warrior who must fight against murder and slavery, or the hunter who must slay or see his children starve.'

'Shall I then say "This commandment I give unto you: that you kill one another"?' said the conjurer.

'It is only the other one turned inside out' said the black girl. 'Neither is a rule to live by. I tell you these cure-all commandments of yours are like the pills the cheap jacks sell us: they are useful once in twenty times perhaps, but in the other nineteen they are no use.

Besides, I am not seeking commandments. I am seeking God.'

'Continue your search; and God be with you' said the conjurer. 'To find him, such as you must go past me.' And with that he vanished.

'That is perhaps your best trick' said the black girl; 'though I am sorry to lose you; for to my mind you are a lovable man and mean well.'

A mile further on she met an ancient fisherman carrying an enormous cathedral on his shoulders.

'Take care: it will break your poor old back' she cried, running to help him.

'Not it' he replied cheerfully. 'I am the rock on which this Church is built.'

'But you are not a rock; and it is too heavy for you!' she said, expecting every moment to see him crushed by its weight.

'No fear' he said, grinning pleasantly at her. 'It is made entirely of paper.' And he danced past her, making all the bells in the cathedral tinkle merrily.

Before he was out of sight several others, dressed in different costumes of black and white and all very carefully soaped and brushed, came along carrying smaller and mostly much uglier paper Churches. They all cried to her 'Do not believe the fisherman. Do not listen to those other fellows. Mine is the true Church.' At last she had to turn aside into the forest to avoid them; for they began throwing stones at one another; and as their aim was almost as bad as if they were blind, the stones came flying all over the road. So she concluded that she would not find God to her taste among them.

When they had passed, or rather when the battle had rolled by, she returned to the road, where she found a very old wandering Jew, who said to her 'Has He come?'

'Has who come?' said the black girl.

'He who promised to come' said the Jew. 'He who

said that I must tarry til He comes. I have tarried beyond all reason. If He does not come soon now it will be too late; for men learn nothing except how to kill one another in greater and greater numbers.'

'That wont be stopped by anybody coming' said the black girl.

'But He will come in glory, sitting on the right hand of God' cried the Jew. 'He said so. He will set everything right.'

'If you wait for other people to come and set everything right' said the black girl 'you will wait for ever.' At that the Jew uttered a wail of despair; spat at her; and tottered away.

She was by this time quite out of conceit with old men; so she was glad to shake him off. She marched on until she came to a shady bank by the wayside; and here she found fifty of her own black people, evidently employed as bearers, sitting down to enjoy a meal at a respectful distance from a group of white gentlemen and ladies. As the ladies wore breeches and sunhelmets the black girl knew that they were explorers, like the men. They had just finished eating. Some of them were dozing: others were writing in note books.

'What expedition is this?' said the black girl to the leader of the bearers.

'It is called the Caravan of the Curious' he replied.

'Are they good whites or bad?' she asked.

'They are thoughtless, and waste much time quarreling about trifles' he said. 'And they ask questions for the sake of asking questions.'

'Hi! you there' cried one of the ladies. 'Go about your business: you cannot stop here. You will upset the men.'

'No more than you' said the black girl.

'Stuff, girl' said the lady: 'I am fifty. I am a neuter. Theyre used to me. Get along with you.'

'You need not fear: they are not white men' said the black girl rather contemptuously. 'Why do you call yourselves the Caravan of the Curious? What are you curious about? Are you curious about God?'

There was such a hearty laugh at this that those who were having a nap woke up and had to have the joke repeated to them.

'Many hundred years have passed since there has been any curiosity on that subject in civilized countries' said one of the gentlemen.

'Not since the fifteenth century, I should say' said another. 'Shakespear is already quite Godless.'

'Shakespear was not everybody' said a third. 'The national anthem belongs to the eighteenth century. In it you find us ordering God about to do our political dirty work.'

'Not the same God' said the second gentleman. 'In the middle ages God was conceived as ordering us about and keeping our noses to the grindstone. With the rise of the bourgeoisie and the shaking off by the feudal aristocracy of the duties that used to be the price of their privileges you get a new god, who is ordered about and has his nose kept to the grindstone by the upper classes. "Confound their politics; frustrate their knavish tricks" and so forth.'

'Yes' said the first gentleman; 'and also a third god of the petty bourgeoisie, whose job it is, when they have filled the recording angel's slate with their trade dishonesties for the week, to wipe the slate clean with his blood on Sunday.'

'Both these gods are still going strong' said the third gentleman. 'If you doubt it, try to provide a decent second verse for the national anthem; or to expunge the Atonement from the prayerbook.'

'That makes six gods that I have met or heard of in my search; but none of them is the God I seek' said the black girl.

'Are you in search of God?' said the first gentleman. 'Had you not better be content with Mumbo Jumbo, or whatever you call the god of your tribe? You will not find any of ours an improvement on him.'

'We have a very miscellaneous collection of Mumbo Jumbos' said the third gentleman, 'and not one that we can honestly recommend to you.'

'That may be so' said the black girl. 'But you had better be careful. The missionaries teach us to believe in your gods. It is all the instruction we get. If we find out out that you do not believe in them and are their enemies we may come and kill you. There are millions of us; and we can shoot as well as you.'

'There is something in that' said the second gentleman. 'We have no right to teach these people what we do not believe. They may take it in deadly earnest. Why not tell them the simple truth that the universe has occurred through Natural Selection, and that God is a fable.'

'It would throw them back on the doctrine of the survival of the fittest' said the first gentleman dubiously; 'and it is not clear that we are the fittest to survive in competition with them. That girl is a fine specimen. We have had to give up employing poor whites for the work of our expedition: the natives are stronger, cleaner, and more intelligent.'

'Besides having much better manners' said one of the ladies.

'Precisely' said the first gentleman. 'I should really prefer to teach them to believe in a god who would give us a chance against them if they started a crusade against European atheism.'

'You cannot teach these people the truth about the universe' said a spectacled lady. 'It is, we now know, a mathematical universe. Ask that girl to divide a quantity by the square root of minus x, and she will not have the faintest notion what you mean. Yet division by the square root of minus x is the key to the universe.'

'A skeleton key' said the second gentleman. 'To me the square root of minus x is flat nonsense. Natural Selection –'

'What is the use of all this?' groaned a depressed gentleman. 'The only thing we know for certain is that the sun is losing its heat, and that we shall presently die of cold. What does anything matter in the face of that fact?'

'Cheer up, Mr Croker' said a lively young gentleman. 'As chief physicist to this expedition I am in a position to inform you authoritatively that unless you reject cosmic radiation and tidal retardation you have just as much reason to believe that the sun is getting hotter and hotter and will eventually cremate us all alive.'

'What comfort is there in that?' said Mr Croker. 'We perish anyhow.'

'Not necessarily' said the first gentleman.

'Yes, necessarily' said Mr Croker rudely. 'The elements of temperature within which life can exist are ascertained and unquestionable. You cannot live at the temperature of frozen air and you cannot live at the temperature of a cremation furnace. No matter which of these temperatures the earth reaches we perish.'

'Pooh!' said the first gentleman. 'Our bodies, which are the only part of us to which your temperatures are fatal, will perish in a few years, mostly in well ventilated bedrooms kept at a comfortable temperature. But what of the something that makes the difference between the live body and the dead one? Is there a rag of proof, a ray of probability even, that it is in any way dependent on temperature? It is certainly not flesh nor blood nor bone, though it has the curious property of building bodily organs for itself in those forms. It is incorporeal: if you try to figure it at all you must figure it as an electromagnetic wave, as a rate of vibration, as a vortex in the ether if there be an ether; that is to say as something that, if it exists at all – and who can question its existence? – can exist on the coldest of the dead stars or in the hottest crater of the sun.'

'Besides' said one of the ladies, 'how do you know that the sun is hot?'

'You ask that in Africa!' said Mr Croker scornfully. 'I feel it to be hot: that is how I know.'

'You feel pepper to be hot' said the lady, returning his scorn with interest; 'but you cannot light a match at it.'

'You feel that a note at the right end of the piano keyboard is higher than a note at the left; yet they are both on the same level' said another lady.

'You feel that a macaw's coloring is loud; but it is really as soundless as a sparrow's' said yet another lady.

'You need not condescend to answer such quibbles' said an authoritative gentleman. 'They are on the level of the three card trick. I am a surgeon; and I know, as a matter of observed fact, that the diameter of the vessels which supply blood to the female brain is excessive according to the standard set by the male brain. The resultant surcharge of blood both overstimulates and confuses the imagination, and so produces an iconosis in which the pungency of pepper suggests heat, the scream of a soprano height, and the flamboyancy of a macaw noise.'

'Your literary style is admirable, Doctor' said the first gentleman; 'but it is beside my point, which is that whether the sun's heat is the heat of pepper or the heat of flame, whether the moon's cold is the coldness of ice or the coldness of a snub to a poor relation, they are just as likely to be inhabited as the earth.'

'The coldest parts of the earth are not inhabited' said Mr Croker.

'The hottest are' said the first gentleman. 'And the coldest probably would be if there were not plenty of accommodation on earth for us in more congenial climates. Besides, there are Emperor penguins in the Antarctic. Why should there not be Emperor salamanders in the sun? Our great grandmothers, who believed in a brimstone hell, knew that the soul, as they called the thing that leaves the body when it dies and makes the difference between life and death, could live eternally in flames. In that they were much more scientific than my friend Croker here.'

'A man who believes in hell could believe in anything'

said Mr Croker, 'even in the inheritance of acquired habits.'

'I thought you believed in evolution, Croker' said a gentleman who was naturalist to the expedition.

'I *do* believe in evolution' said Mr Croker warmly. 'Do you take me for a fundamentalist?'

'If you believe in evolution' said the naturalist 'you must believe that all habits are both acquired and inherited. But you all have the Garden of Eden in your blood still. The way you fellows take in new ideas without ever thinking of throwing out the old ones makes you public dangers. You are all fundamentalists with a top dressing of science. That is why you are the stupidest of conservatives and reactionists in politics and the most bigoted of obstructionists in science itself. When it comes to getting a move on you are all of the same opinion: stop it, flog it, hang it, dynamite it, stamp it out.'

'All of the same opinion!' exclaimed the first lady. 'Have they ever agreed on any subject?'

'They are all looking in the same direction at present!' said a lady with a sarcastic expression.

'What direction?' said the first lady.

'That direction' said the sarcastic lady, pointing to the black girl.

'Are you there still?' said the first lady. 'You were told to go. Get along with you.'

The black girl did not reply. She contemplated the lady gravely and let the knobkerry swing slowly between her fingers. Then she looked at the mathematical lady and said 'Where does it grow?'

'Where does what grow?' said the mathematical lady.

'The root you spoke of' said the black girl. 'The square root of Myna's sex.'

'It grows in the mind' said the lady. 'It is a number. Can you count forwards from one?'

'One, two, three, four, five, do you mean?' said the

black girl, helping herself by her fingers.

'Just so' said the lady. 'Now count backwards from one.'

'One, one less, two less, three less, four less.'

They all clapped their hands. 'Splendid!' cried one. 'Newton!' said another. 'Leibniz!' said a third. 'Einstein!' said a fourth. And then altogether, 'Marvellous! marvellous!'

'I keep telling you' said a lady who was the ethnologist of the expedition 'that the next great civilization will be a black civilization. The white man is played out. He knows it, too, and is committing suicide as fast as he can.'

'Why are you surprised at a little thing like that?' said the black girl. 'Why cannot you white people grow up and be serious as we blacks do? I thought glass beads marvellous when I saw them for the first time; but I soon got used to them. You cry marvellous every time one of you says something silly. The most wonderful things you have are your guns. It must be easier to find God than to find out how to make guns. But you do not care for God: you care for nothing but guns. You use your guns to make slaves of us. Then, because you are too lazy to shoot, you put the guns into our hands and teach us to shoot for you. You will soon teach us to make the guns because you are too lazy to make them yourselves. You have found out how to make drinks that make men forget God, and put their consciences to sleep and make murder seem a delight. You sell these drinks to us and teach us how to make them. And all the time you steal the land from us and starve us and make us hate you as we hate the snakes. What will be the end of that? You will kill one another so fast that those who are left will be too few to resist when our warriors fill themselves with your magic drink and kill you with your own guns. And then our warriors will kill one another as you do, unless they are prevented by God. Oh that I knew where I might find Him! Will none of you help me in my search? Do none of you care?'

'Our guns have saved you from the man-eating lion and the trampling elephant, have they not?' said a huffy gentleman, who had hitherto found the conversation too deep for him.

'Only to deliver us into the hands of the man-beating slave-driver and the trampling baas' said the black girl. 'Lion and elephant shared the land with us. When they ate or trampled on our bodies they spared our souls. When they had enough they asked for no more. But nothing will satisfy your greed. You work generations of us to death until you have each of you more than a hundred of us could eat or spend; and yet you go on forcing us to work harder and harder and longer and longer for less and less food and clothing. You do not know what enough means for yourselves, or less than enough for us. You are for ever grumbling because we have no money to buy the goods you trade in; and your only remedy is to give us less money. This must be because you serve false gods. You are heathens and savages. You know neither how to live nor let others live. When I find God I shall have the strength of mind to destroy you and to teach my people not to destroy themselves.'

'Look!' cried the first lady. 'She is upsetting the men. I told you she would. They have been listening to her seditious rot. Look at their eyes. They are dangerous. I shall put a bullet through her if none of you men will.'

And the lady actually drew a revolver, she was so frightened. But before she could get it out of its leather case the black girl sprang at her; laid her out with her favorite knobkerry stroke; and darted away into the forest. And all the black bearers went into extasies of merriment.

'Let us be thankful that she has restored good humor' said the first gentleman. 'Things looked ugly for a moment. Now all is well. Doctor: will you see to poor Miss Fitzjones's cerebellum.'

'The mistake we made' said the naturalist 'was in not offering her some of our food.'

The black girl hid herself long enough to make sure that she was not being pursued. She knew that what she had done was a flogging matter, and that no plea of defence would avail a black defendant against a white plaintiff. She did not worry about the mounted police; for in that district they were very scarce. But she did not want to have to dodge the caravan continuously; and as one direction was as good as another for her purpose, she turned back on her tracks (for the caravan had been going her way) and so found herself towards evening at the well where she had talked with the conjurer. There she found a booth with many images of wood, plaster, or ivory set out for sale; and lying on the ground beside it was a big wooden cross on which the conjurer was lying with his ankles crossed and his arms stretched out. And the man who kept the booth was carving a statue of him in wood with great speed and skill. They were watched by a handsome Arab gentleman in a turban, with a scimitar in his sash, who was sitting on the coping of the well, and combing his beard.

'Why do you do this, my friend?' said the Arab gentleman. 'You know that it is a breach of the second commandment given by God to Moses. By rights I should smite you dead with my scimitar; but I have suffered and sinned all my life through an infirmity of spirit which renders me incapable of slaying any animal, even a man, in cold blood. Why do you do it?'

'What else can I do if I am not to starve?' said the conjurer. 'I am so utterly rejected of men that my only means of livelihood is to sit as a model to this compassionate artist who pays me sixpence an hour for stretching myself on this cross all day. He himself lives by selling images of me in this ridiculous position. People idolize

me as the Dying Malefactor because they are interested in nothing but the police news. When he has laid in a sufficient stock of images, and I have saved a sufficient number of sixpences, I take a holiday and go about giving people good advice and telling them wholesome truths. If they would only listen to me they would be ever so much happier and better. But they refuse to believe me unless I do conjuring tricks for them; and when I do them they only throw me coppers and sometimes tickeys, and say what a wonderful man I am, and that there has been nobody like me ever on earth; but they go on being foolish and wicked and cruel all the same. It makes me feel that God has forsaken me sometimes.'

'What is a tickey?' said the Arab, rearranging his robe in more becoming folds.

'A threepenny bit' said the conjurer. 'It is coined because proud people are ashamed to be seen giving me coppers, and they think sixpence too much.'

'I should not like people to treat me like that' said the Arab. 'I also have a message to deliver. My people, if left to themselves, would fall down and worship all the images in that booth. If there were no images they would worship stones. My message is that there is no majesty and no might save in Allah the glorious, the great, the one and only. Of Him no mortal has ever dared to make an image: if anyone attempted such a crime I should forget that Allah is merciful, and overcome my infirmity to the extremity of slaying him with my own hand. But who could conceive the greatness of Allah in a bodily form? Not even an image of the finest horse could convey a notion of His beauty and greatness. Well, when I tell them this, they ask me, too, to do conjuring tricks; and when I tell them that I am a man like themselves and that not Allah Himself can violate His own laws – if one could conceive Him as doing anything unlawful – they go away and pretend that I am working miracles. But they believe; for if they doubt I have them slain by those who believe. That is what you should do, my friend.'

'But my message is that they should not kill one another' said the conjurer. 'One has to be consistent.'

'That is quite right as far as their private quarrels are concerned' said the Arab. 'But we must kill those who are unfit to live. We must weed the garden as well as water it.'

'Who is to be the judge of our fitness to live?' said the conjurer. 'The highest authorities, the imperial governors and the high priests, find that I am unfit to live. Perhaps they are right.'

'Precisely the same conclusion was reached concerning myself' said the Arab. 'I had to run away and hide until I had convinced a sufficient number of athletic young men that their elders were mistaken about me: that, in fact, the boot was on the other leg. Then I returned with the athletic young men, and weeded the garden.'

'I admire your courage and practical sagacity' said the conjurer; 'but I am not built that way.'

'Do not admire such qualities' said the Arab. 'I am somewhat ashamed of them. Every desert chieftain displays them abundantly. It is on the superiority of my mind, which has made me the vehicle of divine inspiration, that I value myself. Have you ever written a book?'

'No' said the conjurer sadly: 'I wish I could; for then I could make money enough to come off this tiresome cross and send my message in print all over the world. But I am no author. I have composed a handy sort of short prayer with, I hope, all the essentials in it. But God inspires me to speak, not to write.'

'Writing is useful' said the Arab. 'I have been inspired to write many chapters of the word of Allah, praised be His name! But there are fellows in his world with whom Allah cannot be expected to trouble Himself. His word means nothing to them; so when I have to deal with them I am no longer inspired, and have to rely on my own invention and my own wit. For them I write terrible stories of the Day of Judgment, and of the hell in which evildoers will suffer eternally. I contrast these horrors with enchanting pictures of the paradise maintained for those who do the will of Allah. Such a paradise as will tempt them, you understand: a paradise of gardens and perfumes and beautiful women.'

'And how do you know what is the will of Allah?' said the conjurer.

'As they are incapable of understanding it, my will must serve them for it instead' said the Arab. 'They can understand my will, which is indeed truly the will of Allah at second hand, a little soiled by my mortal passions and necessities, no doubt, but the best I can do for them. Without it I could not manage them at all. Without it they would desert me for the first chief who promised them a bigger earthly plunder. But what other chief can write a book and promise them an eternity of bliss after their death with all the authority of a mind which can surround its own inventions with the majesty of authentic inspiration?'

'You have every qualification for success' said the conjurer politely, and a little wistfully.

'I am the eagle and the serpent' said the Arab. 'Yet in my youth I was proud to be the servant of a widow and drive her camels. Now I am the humble servant of Allah and drive men for Him. For in no other do I recognize majesty and might; and with Him I take refuge from Satan and his brood.'

'What is all this majesty and might without a sense of beauty and the skill to embody it in images that time cannot change into corruption?' said the wood carver, who had been working and listening in silence. 'I have no use for your Allah, who forbids the making of images.'

'Know, dog of an unbeliever,' said the Arab, 'that images have a power of making men fall down and worship them, even when they are images of beasts.'

'Or of the sons of carpenters' interjected the conjurer.

'When I drove the camels' continued the Arab, not quite catching the interruption, 'I carried in my pack idols of men seated on thrones with the heads of hawks on their shoulders and scourges in their hands. The Christians who began by worshipping God in the form of a man, now worship Him in the form of a lamb. This is the punishment decreed by Allah for the sin of presuming to imitate the work of His hands. But do not on that account dare to deny Allah His sense of beauty. Even your model here who is sharing your sin will remind you that the lilies of Allah are more lovely than the robes of Solomon in all his glory. Allah makes the skies His pictures and His children His statues, and does not withhold them from our earthly vision. He permits you to make lovely robes and saddles and trappings, and carpets to kneel on before Him, and windows like flower beds of precious stones. Yet you will be meddling in the work He reserves for Himself, and making idols. For ever be such sin forbidden to my people!'

'Pooh!' said the sculptor 'your Allah is a bungler; and he knows it. I have in my booth in a curtained-off corner some Greek gods so beautiful that Allah himself may well burst with envy when he compares them with his own amateur attempts. I tell you Allah made this hand of mine because his own hands are too clumsy, if indeed he have any hands at all. The artist-god is himself an artist, never satisfied with His work, always perfecting it to the limit of His powers, always aware that though He must stop when He reaches that limit, yet there is a further perfection without which the picture has no meaning. Your Allah can make a woman. Can he make the Goddess of Love? No: only an artist can do that. See!' he said, rising to go into his booth. 'Can Allah make *her*?' And he brought from the cur-

tained corner a marble Venus and placed her on the counter.

'Her limbs are cold' said the black girl, who had been listening all this time unnoticed.

'Well said!' cried the Arab. 'A living failure is better than a dead masterpiece; and Allah is justified against this most presumptuous idolater, whom I must have slain with a blow had you not slain him with a word.'

'I still live' said the artist, unabashed. 'That girl's limbs will one day be colder than any marble. Cut my goddess in two: she is still white marble to the core. Cut that girl in two with your scimitar, and see what you will find there.'

'Your talk no longer interests me' said the Arab. 'Maiden: there is yet room in my house for another wife. You are beautiful: your skin is like black satin: you are full of life.'

'How many wives have you?' said the black girl.

'I have long since ceased to count them' replied the Arab; 'but there are enough to shew you that I am an experienced husband and know how to make women as happy as Allah permits.'

'I do not seek happiness: I seek God' said the black girl.

'Have you not found Him yet?' said the conjurer.

'I have found many gods' said the black girl. 'Everyone I meet has one to offer me; and this image maker here has a whole shopful of them. But to me they are all half dead, except the ones that are half animals like this one on the top shelf, playing a mouth organ, who is half a goat and half a man. That is very true to nature; for I myself am half a goat and half a woman, though I should like to be a goddess. But even these gods who are half goats are half men. Why are they never half women?'

'What about this one?' said the image maker, pointing to Venus.

'Why is her lower half hidden in a sack?' said the black girl. 'She is neither a goddess nor a woman: she is ashamed of half her body, and the other half of her is what the white people call a lady. She is ladylike and beautiful; and a white Governor General would be glad to have her at the head of his house; but to my mind she has no conscience; and that makes her inhuman without making her godlike. I have no use for her.'

'The Word shall be made flesh, not marble' said the conjurer. 'You must not complain because these gods have the bodies of men. If they did not put on humanity for you, how could you, who are human, enter into any communion with them? To make a link between Godhood and Manhood, some god must become man.'

'Or some woman become God' said the black girl. 'That would be far better, because the god who condescends to be human degrades himself; but the woman who becomes God exalts herself.'

'Allah be my refuge from all troublesome women' said the Arab. 'This is the most troublesome woman I have ever met. It is one of the mysterious ways of Allah to make women troublesome when he makes them beautiful. The more reason he gives them to be content, the more dissatisfied they are. This one is dissatisfied even with Allah Himself, in whom is all majesty and all might. Well, maiden, since Allah the glorious and great cannot please you, what god or goddess can?'

'There is a goddess of whom I have heard, and of whom I would know more' said the black girl. 'She is named Myna; and I feel there is something about her that none of the other gods can give.'

'There is no such goddess' said the image maker. 'There are no other gods or goddesses except those I make; and I have never made a goddess named Myna.'

'She most surely exists' said the black girl; 'for the white missy spoke of her with reverence, and said that the key to the universe was the root of her womanhood and that it was bodiless like number, which has neither end nor beginning; for you can count one less and less and less and never come to a beginning; and you can count one more and more and more and never come to an end: thus it is through numbers that you find eternity.'

'Eternity in itself and by itself is nothing' said the

Arab. 'What is eternity to me if I cannot find eternal truth?'

'Only the truth of number is eternal' said the black girl. 'Every other truth passes away or becomes error, like the fancies of our childhood; but one and one are two and one and nine ten and always will be. Therefore I feel that there is something godlike about numbers.'

'You cannot eat and drink numbers' said the image maker. 'You cannot marry them.'

'God has provided other things for us to eat and drink; and we can marry one another' said the black girl.

'Well, you cannot draw nor mould them; and that is enough for me' said the image maker.

'We Arabs can; and in this sign we shall conquer the world. See!' said the Arab. And he stooped and drew figures in the sand.

'The missionary says that God is a magic number that is three in one and one in three' said the black girl.

'That is simple' said the Arab; 'for I am the son of my father and the father of my sons and myself to boot: three in one and one in three. Man's nature is manifold; Allah alone is one. He is unity. He is the core of the onion, the bodiless centre without which there could be no body, He is the number of the innumerable stars, the weight of the imponderable air, the —'

'You are a poet, I believe' said the image maker.

The Arab, thus interrupted, colored deeply; sprang to his feet; and drew his scimitar. 'Do you dare accuse me of being a lewd balladmonger?' he said. 'This is an insult to be wiped out in blood.'

'Sorry' said the image maker. 'I meant no offence. Why are you ashamed to make a ballad which outlives a thousand men, and not ashamed to make a corpse, which any fool can make, and which he has to hide in the earth when he has made it lest it stink him to death?'

'That is true' said the Arab, sheathing his weapon, and sitting down again. 'It is one of the mysteries of Allah that when Satan makes impure verses Allah sends a divine tune to cleanse them. Nevertheless I was an honest cameldriver, and never took money for singing, though I confess I was much addicted to it.'

'I too have not been righteous overmuch' said the conjurer. 'I have been called a gluttonous man and a winebibber. I have not fasted. I have broken the sabbath. I have been kind to women who were no better than they should be. I have been unkind to my mother and shunned my family; for a man's true household is that in which God is the father and we are all His children, and not the belittling house and shop in which he must stay within reach of his mother's breast until he is weaned.'

'A man needs many wives and a large household to prevent this cramping of his mind' said the Arab. 'He should distribute his affection. Until he has known many women he cannot know the value of any; for value is a matter of comparison. I did not know what an old angel I had in my first wife until I found what I had in my last.'

'And your wives?' said the black girl. 'Are they also to know many men in order that they may learn your value?'

'I take refuge with Allah against this black daughter of Satan' cried the Arab vehemently. 'Learn to hold your peace, woman, when men are talking and wisdom is their topic. God made Man before he made Woman.'

'Second thoughts are best' said the black girl. 'If it is as you say, God must have created Woman because He found Man insufficient. By what right do you demand fifty wives and condemn each of them to one husband?'

'Had I my life to live over again' said the Arab 'I would be a celibate monk and shut my door upon women and their questions. But consider this. If I have only one wife I deny all other women any share in me, though many women will desire me in proportion to my excellence and their discernment. The enlightened woman who desires the best father for her children will ask for a fiftieth share in me rather than a piece of human refuse all to herself. Why should she suffer this injustice when there is no need for it?'

'But how is she to know your value unless she has known fifty men to compare with you?' said the black girl.

'The child who has fifty fathers has no father' cried the Arab.

'What matter if it have a mother?' said the black girl. 'Besides, what you say is not true. One of the fifty will be its father.'

'Know then' said the Arab 'that there are many shameless women who have known men without number; but they do not bear children, whereas I, who covet and possess every desirable woman my eyes light on, have a large posterity. And from this it plainly appears that injustice to women is one of the mysteries of Allah, against whom it is vain to rebel. Allah is great and glorious; and in him alone is there majesty and might; but his justice is beyond our understanding. My wives, who pamper themselves too much, bring forth their children in torments that wring my heart when I hear their cries; and these torments we men are spared. This is not just; but if you have no better remedy for such injustice than to let women do what men do and men do what women do, will you tell me to lie in and bear children? I can reply only that Allah will not have it so. It is against nature.'

'I know that we cannot go against nature' said the black girl. 'You cannot bear children; but a woman could have several husbands and could still bear children provided she had no more than one husband at a time.'

'Among the other injustices of Allah' said the Arab 'is His ordinance that a woman must have the last word. I am dumb.'

'What happens' said the image maker 'when fifty women assemble round one man, and each must have the last word?'

'The hell in which the one man expiates all his sins and takes refuge with Allah the merciful' said the Arab, with deep feeling.

'I shall not find God where men are talking about women' said the black girl, turning to go.

'Nor where women are talking about men' shouted the image maker after her.

She waved her hand in assent and left them. Nothing particular happened after that until she came to a prim little villa with a very amateurish garden which was being cultivated by a wizened old gentleman whose eyes were so striking that his face seemed all eyes, his nose so remarkable that his face seemed all nose, and his mouth so expressive of a comically malicious relish that his face seemed all mouth until the black girl combined these three incompatibles by deciding that his face was all intelligence.

'Excuse me, baas' she said: 'may I speak to you?'

'What do you want?' said the old gentleman.

'I want to ask my way to God' she said; 'and as you have the most knowing face I have ever seen, I thought I would ask you.'

'Come in' said he. 'I have found, after a good deal of consideration, that the best place to seek God is in a garden. You can dig for Him here.'

'That is not my idea of seeking for God at all' said the black girl, disappointed. 'I will go on, thank you.'

'Has your own idea, as you call it, led you to Him yet?'

'No' said the black girl, stopping: 'I cannot say that it has. But I do not like your idea.'

'Many people who have found God have not liked Him and have spent the rest of their lives running away from Him. Why do you suppose you would like Him?'

'I dont know' said the black girl. 'But the missionary has a line of poetry that says that we needs must love the highest when we see it.'

'That poet was a fool' said the old gentleman. 'We hate it; we crucify it; we poison it with hemlock; we chain it to a stake and burn it alive. All my life I have striven in my little way to do God's work and teach His enemies to laugh at themselves; but if you told me God was coming down the road I should creep into the nearest mousehole and not dare to breathe until He had passed. For if He saw me or smelt me, might He not put His foot on me and squelch me, as I would squelch any venomous little thing that broke my commandments? These fellows who run after God crying "Oh that I knew where I might find Him" must have a tremendous opinion of themselves to think that they could stand before Him. Has the missionary ever told you the story of Jupiter and Semele?'

'No' said the black girl. 'What is that story?'

'Jupiter is one of the names of God' said the old gentleman. 'You know that He has many names, dont you?'

'The last man I met called Him Allah' she said.

'Just so' said the old gentleman. 'Well, Jupiter fell in love with Semele, and was considerate enough to appear and behave just like a man to her. But she thought herself good enough to be loved by a god in all the greatness of his godhood. So she insisted on his coming to her in the full panoply of his divinity.'

'What happened when he did?' asked the black girl.

'Just what she might have known would happen if she had had any sense' said the old gentleman. 'She shrivelled up and cracked like a flea in the fire. So take care. Do not be a fool like Semele. God is at your elbow, and He has been there all the time; but in His divine mercy He has not revealed Himself to you lest too full a knowledge of Him should drive you mad. Make a little garden for yourself: dig and plant and weed and prune; and be content if He jogs your elbow when you are gardening unskilfully, and blesses you when you are gardening well.'

'And shall we never be able to bear His full presence?' said the black girl.

'I trust not' said the old philosopher. 'For we shall

never be able to bear His full presence until we have fulfilled all His purposes and become gods ourselves. But as His purposes are infinite, and we are most briefly finite, we shall never, thank God, be able to catch up with His purposes. So much the better for us. If our work were done we should be of no further use: that would be the end of us; for He would hardly keep us alive for the pleasure of looking at us, ugly and ephemeral insects as we are. Therefore come in and help to cultivate this garden to His glory. The rest you had better leave to Him.'

So she laid down her knobkerry and went in and gardened with him. And from time to time other people came in and helped. At first this made the black girl jealous; but she hated feeling like that, and soon got used to their comings and goings.

One day she found a redhaired Irishman laboring in the back garden where they grew the kitchen stuff.

'Who let you in here?' she said.

'Faith, I let myself in' said the Irishman. 'Why wouldnt I?'

'But the garden belongs to the old gentleman' said the black girl.

'I'm a Socialist' said the Irishman 'and dont admit that gardens belong to annybody. That oul' fella is cracked and past his work and needs somewan to dig his podatoes for him. Theres a lot been found out about podatoes since he learnt to dig them.'

'Then you did not come in to search for God?' said the black girl.

'Divvle a search' said the Irishman. 'Sure God can search for me if He wants me. My own belief is that He's not all that He sets up to be. He's not properly made and finished yet. Theres somethin in us thats dhrivin at Him, and somethin out of us thats dhrivin at Him: thats certain; and the only other thing thats certain is that the somethin makes plenty of mistakes in thryin to get there. We'v got to find out its way for it as best we can, you and I; for theres a hell of a lot of other people thinkin of nothin but their own bellies.' And he spat on his hands and went on digging.

Both the black girl and the old gentleman thought the Irishman rather a coarse fellow (as indeed he was) but as he was useful and would not go away, they did their best to teach him nicer habits and refine his language. But nothing would ever persuade him that God was anything more solid and satisfactory than an eternal but as yet unfulfilled purpose, or that it could ever be fulfilled if the fulfilment were not made reasonably easy and hopeful by Socialism.

Still, when they had taught him manners and cleanliness they got used to him and even to his dreadful jokes. One day the old gentleman said to her 'It is not right that a fine young woman like you should not have a husband and children. I am much too old for you: so you had better marry that Irishman.'

As she had become very devoted to the old gentleman she was fearfully angry at first at his wanting her to marry anyone else, and even spent a whole night planning to drive the Irishman out of the place with her knobkerry. She could not bring herself to admit that the old gentleman had been born sixty years too early for her, and must in the course of nature die and leave her without a companion. But the old gentleman rubbed these flat facts into her so hard that at last she gave in and the two went together into the kitchen garden and told the Irishman that she was going to marry him.

He snatched up his spade with a yell of dismay and made a dash for the garden gate. But the black girl had taken the precaution to lock it; and before he could climb it they overtook him and held him fast.

'Is it me marry a black heathen niggerwoman?' he

cried piteously, forgetting all his lately acquired refinements of speech. 'Lemme go, will yous. I dont want to marry annywan.'

But the black girl held him in a grip of iron (softly padded, however); and the old gentleman pointed out to him that if he ran away he would only fall into the clutches of some strange woman who cared nothing about searching for God, and who would have a pale ashy skin instead of the shining black satin he was accustomed to. At last, after half an hour or so of argument and coaxing, and a glass of the old gentleman's best burgundy to encourage him, he said 'Well, I dont mind if I do.'

So they were married; and the black girl managed the Irishman and the children (who were charmingly coffee-colored) very capably, and even came to be quite fond of them. Between them and the garden and mending her husband's clothes (which she could not persuade him to leave off wearing) she was kept so busy that her search for God was crowded out of her head most of the time; but there were moments, especially when she was drying her favorite piccaninny, who was very docile and quiet, after his bath, in which her mind went back to her search; only now she saw how funny it was that an unsettled girl should start off to pay God a visit, thinking herself the centre of the universe, and taught by the missionary to regard God as somebody who had nothing better to do than to watch everything she did and worry himself about her salvation. She even tickled the piccaninny and asked him 'Suppose I had found God at home what should I have done when He hinted that I was staying too long and that He had other things to attend to?' It was a question which the piccaninny was quite unable to answer: he only chuckled hysterically and tried to grab her wrists. It was only when the piccaninnies grew up and became independent of her, and the Irishman had become an unconscious habit of hers, as if he were a part of herself, that they ceased to take her

THE BLACK GIRL IN SEARCH OF GOD

away from herself and she was left once more with the leisure and loneliness that threw her back on such questions. And by that time her strengthened mind had taken her far beyond the stage at which there is any fun in smashing idols with knobkerries.

AERIAL FOOTBALL: THE NEW GAME

(From The Neolith of November 1907)

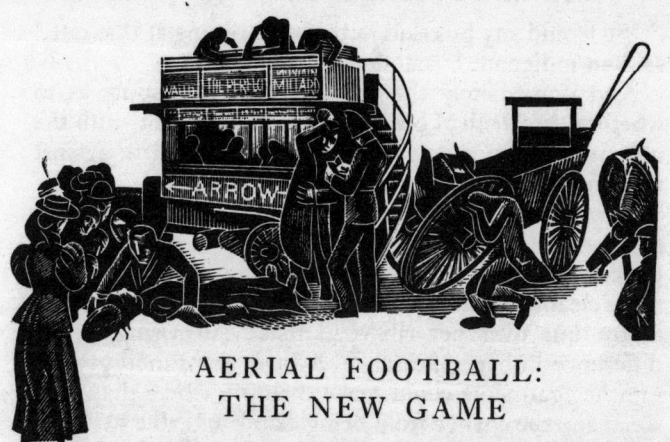

AERIAL FOOTBALL: THE NEW GAME

'Is she dead?' said the motor bus driver, looking very sick, as the medical student from the Free Hospital picked up Mrs Hairns in the Gray's Inn Road.

'She smells frightfully of your petrol,' said the student.

The driver sniffed at her. 'Thats not petrol,' he said. 'It's methylated spirit. She's been drinking. Youll bear me witness that she smells of drink.'

'Dont you know all youve done yet?' said the policeman. 'Youve killed his lordship.'

'What lordship?' said the driver, changing from tallow color to green.

'The back end of the bus swung right into the carriage,' panted the footman. 'I heard his lordship's neck crack.' The footman wept, not because he loved his late employer, but because sudden death affected him that way.

'The Bishop of St Pancras,' said a boy, in explanation.

'Oh, my good Lord!' said the motorman, in great trouble. 'How could I help it?' he added, after wiping his brow, appealing to the crowd, which seemed to have been in solution in the air, so suddenly had it precipitated round the accident. 'The bus skidded.'

'So would any bus skid in this mud, going at that rate,' said an indignant bystander.

And immediately the crowd began to dispute as to whether the bus had been going too fast or not, with the motorman passionately maintaining the negative against the affirmative of the whole Gray's Inn Road.

Mrs Hairns certainly did smell of drink. She had done so more or less for forty years whenever she had twopence to spare. She had never been a nice looking woman nor a cleanly dressed one; and the passage of the crowded motor bus over her ribs had made surprisingly little difference in her appearance. A little more mud ground into her garments could make them no worse than they were; and the change from being drunk and able to shuffle home and being drunk and incapable was not startling.

As to the bishop, there was not a scratch nor a speck of mud on him. He had not been touched. He had been boyishly proud of being a bishop, and had expressed his pride by holding his neck very stiff. Consequently it broke when the carriage was stopped suddenly by the swinging round of the tail of the bus.

Mrs Hairns was taken aback when the bus suddenly swooped round at her. That made no difference, because no presence of mind on her part could have saved her. It did not hurt her at all. A single broken rib touching a lung is painful; but when an overwhelming shock annihilates your nerves, and an overwhelming weight makes bone dust of all your ribs, and wraps them up in a squash with your heart and lungs, sympathy becomes ridiculous. The game is up. The remediable has become irremediable: the temporal, eternal. A really flexible mind accepts the situation and thinks a great deal about it before there is time even to die. The suddenest death is a long business compared with the lightning work of imagining an experience of, say, a thousand years.

Mrs Hairns was squashed clean out of the Gray's Inn Road on to the foot of a hill with a city on the top. It was

AERIAL FOOTBALL: THE NEW GAME

rather like Orvieto, of which city there was a photograph in the drawing room of the Vicar of St Pancras, who employed Mrs Hairns as a charwoman whenever he attempted to reclaim her, and was beaten every time by her acquired taste for methylated spirits, which enabled her to drink furniture polish with avidity, though you could trust her with untold dozens of mere hock. Beyond getting the photograph focussed on her retina occasionally whilst dusting, Mrs Hairns knew nothing about Orvieto. A place so unlike Pentonville Hill suggested dread and discomfort to her. She felt sure it must be almost as bad as heaven, which she associated with teetotalism, cleanliness, self-control, being particular, and all sorts of horrors. Now that she found herself actually on the road to it, she looked up at it with the utmost misgiving until a superior voice behind her made her start and attempt a shambling curtsey. It was the bishop.

'Can I obtain a conveyance anywhere here,' he said, 'to take me up to the gate?'

'I cant say, I'm sure, sir,' said Mrs Hairns: 'I'm a stranger here.'

The bishop passed on the moment she said 'cant say,' taking no further interest in her, and resigned himself to walk up.

There was a horse grazing a little way off. As Mrs Hairns noticed it, a faint ray of heavenly comfort stole into her soul. Though for many years – ever since the passing away of the last rays of her youth at twentyfour or thereabouts – she had been interested in nothing but methylated alcohol, she had been born with an unaccountable fancy, not for horses exactly, but, as she put it, for a horse. It was an unintelligent and innocent fancy; but it had won her hand in marriage for the late Alfred Hairns, normally and by economic necessity a carman, but by natural vocation a poacher. This rude fancier of the equine was too poor to afford a horse. But after all he was too poor to afford a residence in

London, or a double bed, or even a suit of clothes. Yet he always had a London address; he never appeared in the streets naked; and neither he nor Mrs Hairns slept on the floor. Society had convinced him that the lodging, the bed, and the clothes were indispensable, whether he could afford them or not: accordingly, he had them. The conviction that a horse was equally indispensable was idiosyncratic with him; so he always kept a horse, even when he could by no means afford to keep himself, maintaining that a horse made no difference – that it even paid its way. The same view has been taken of 80 h.p. motor cars.

Bonavia Banks was attracted by his idiosyncrasy, which was also her own. She easily persuaded him that a wife was as indispensable as a horse, and equally made no difference. She became Mrs Alfred Hairns, and bore thirteen children, of whom eleven died in infancy owing to the malversation of their parental care by the horse. Finally the horse died; and the heartbroken Hairns was tempted to buy a magnificent thoroughbred for four pounds from the widow of a gentleman who had paid two hundred and thirty for him only three days before. Hairns, whilst leading his bargain home, was savaged by him so that he died of lockjaw the day after the horse was shot. Thus perished miserably Alfred Hairns, the victim of the bond between man and beast which proclaims that all life is one.

The horse raised its muzzle from the grass; looked at Mrs Hairns carelessly; switched its tail; moved on a few steps to an uncropped patch of verdure; and was about to continue its repast when, as if some fibre of memory had suddenly vibrated, it erected its ears; raised its neck; and looked more attentively at her. Finally it came to her, stopping only once on the way absent-mindedly to graze, and said, 'Dont you remember me?'

'Chipper!' exclaimed Mrs Hairns. 'It cant be.'

'It *is*,' said Chipper.

AERIAL FOOTBALL: THE NEW GAME

Chipper conversed after the manner of Balaam's ass. That is, Mrs Hairns knew what he was saying too well to notice that he did not actually utter any sound. But for the matter of that neither did she, though she did not notice that also. Conversation in this Orvietan region was wholly telepathic.

'Have I got to walk up that hill, Chipper?' said Mrs Hairns.

'Yes,' said Chipper, 'unless I carry you.'

'Would you mind?' said Mrs Hairns shyly.

'Not at all,' said Chipper.

'Aint there a vehicle?' said Mrs Hairns. 'I cant ride bare-backed. Not that I can ride anyhow.'

'Then you must walk,' said Chipper. 'Hold on to my mane; and I'll help you up.'

They got up somehow, and were close to the gate before it occurred to Mrs Hairns to ask what place it was, and to ask herself why she was going there.

'It's heaven,' said Chipper.

'Oh Lord!' said Mrs Hairns, stopping dead. 'Why didnt you tell me before? I never done anything to get me into heaven.'

'True,' said Chipper. 'Would you rather go to hell?'

'Dont be so silly, Chipper,' said Mrs Hairns. 'Aint there nothin between hell and heaven? We aint all saints; but then we aint all devils neither. Surely to gracious there must be a place for everyday sort of people that dont set up to be too particular.'

'This is the only place I know,' said Chipper; 'and it's certainly heaven.'

'Belike there might be some kitchens in it,' said Mrs Hairns. 'You wont let on that I used to get a bit overcome once in a way, Chipper, will you?'

Chipper snuffed up a noseful of Mrs Hairns's aura. 'I should keep on the lee side of St Peter,' he said. 'Thats Peter,' he added, jerking his head in the direction of an elderly gentleman with a pair of keys of XII century design.

AERIAL FOOTBALL: THE NEW GAME

The keys were more for ornament than use, apparently; for the gate stood wide open; and a stone placed against it to keep it from blowing-to was covered with moss, and had evidently not been moved for centuries. This surprised Mrs Hairns, because it had been strongly impressed on her in her childhood on earth that the gates of heaven were always shut tight, and that it was no end of a business to get them opened.

A group of angels stood in the carriage way. Their wings, purple and gold, heliotrope and silver, amber and black, and all sorts of fine colors, struck Mrs Hairns as lovely. One of them had a sword with a blade of lambent garnet-colored flame. Another, with one leg naked from the knee down, and a wading boot on the other, had a straight slender trumpet, which seemed long enough to reach to the horizon and yet was as handy as an umbrella. Through the first floor window of one of the turrets of the gate Mrs Hairns saw Matthew, Mark, Luke, and John in bed with their breeches on according to the old rhyme. Seeing that, she knew this was really the gate of heaven. Nothing else would have quite convinced her.

Chipper addressed himself to Peter. 'This woman is drunk,' said Chipper.

'So I see,' said St Peter.

'Ow Chipper!' said Mrs Hairns reproachfully. 'How could you?' They all looked at her; and she began to cry. The angel with the sword of flame drew it across her eyes and dried her tears. The flame did not hurt, and was wonderfully reviving.

'I'm afraid she's hopeless,' said Chipper. 'Her own children will have nothing to do with her.'

'Which planet?' said the angel with the trumpet.

'Tellus,' answered Chipper.

'What am I to tell them?' said Mrs Hairns.

The angels laughed. Peter roared. 'Come!' said the trumpet angel: 'she can make puns. Whats wrong with her?'

'She's a liar and a thief,' said Chipper.

'All the inhabitants of Tellus are liars and thieves,' said the trumpet angel.

'I mean she is what even they call a liar and a thief,' said Chipper.

'Oh!' said the sword angel, looking very grave.

'I'm only making it easy for you,' said Chipper to Mrs Hairns; 'so that they shant expect too much.' Then, to Peter, 'I brought her up because she once got out and walked on a hot Sunday when I was dragging her up a hill with her husband, three of his friends, their wives, eight children, a baby, and three dozen of beer.'

'Fancy your remembering!' said Mrs Hairns. 'Did I really?'

'It was so unlike you, if I may say so,' said Chipper, 'that I have never forgotten it.'

'I dessay it *was* silly of me,' said Mrs Hairns apologetically.

Just then the bishop arrived. He had been energetically climbing the hill by the little foot tracks which cut across the zig-zags of the road, and had consequently been overtaken by Chipper, who knew better.

'Is this the gate of heaven?' said the bishop.

'It is,' said Peter.

'The *front* gate?' said the bishop suspiciously. 'You are sure it is not the tradesman's entrance?'

'It is everybody's entrance,' said Peter.

'An unusual arrangement, and in my opinion an inconvenient one,' said the bishop. He turned from Peter to the angels. 'Gentlemen,' he said. 'I am the Bishop of St Pancras.'

'If you come to that,' said a youth in a dalmatic, putting his head out of one of the turret windows, 'I am St Pancras himself.'

'As your bishop, I am glad to meet you,' said the bishop. 'I take a personal interest in every member of my flock. But for the moment I must ask you to excuse me,

as I have pressing business at court. By your leave, gentlemen' – and he shouldered his way firmly through the group of angels into heaven and trotted sturdily up the street. He turned only once, for a moment, to say, 'Better announce me,' and went his way. The angels stared after him quite dumbfounded. Then the trumpet angel made a post horn of his trumpet, and first root-a-tooted at the sky, and then swept the trumpet downwards like the ray of a searchlight. It reached along the street to the bishop's coat tails; and the next blast swept him like a dry leaf clean round a corner and out of sight.

The angels smiled a beautifully grave smile. Mrs Hairns could not help laughing. 'Aint he a tease!' she said to Chipper, indicating the trumpet angel.

'Hadnt you better follow the bishop in?' said Chipper.

Mrs Hairns looked apprehensively at Peter (she was not afraid of the angels), and asked him might she go in.

'Anybody may go in,' said Peter. 'What do you suppose the gate is for?'

'I didnt understand, sir,' said Mrs Hairns. And she was approaching the threshold timidly when the bishop came back, flushed and indignant.

'I have been through the whole city in a very high wind,' said the bishop; 'and I cannot find it. I question whether this is really heaven at all.'

'Find what?' said Peter.

'The Throne, sir,' said the bishop severely.

'*This* is the throne,' said St Pancras, who was still looking out of the window, with his cheeks on his palms and his palms propped on his elbows.

'*This!*' said the bishop. 'Which?'

'The city,' said St Pancras.

'But – but – where is He?' said the bishop.

'Here, of course,' said the sword angel.

'*Here!* Where?' said the bishop hurriedly, lowering his voice and looking apprehensively round from one to the other until he finished with the trumpet angel, who had sat down to take off his wading boot and shake a stone out of it.

'He is the presence in which we live,' said the sword angel, speaking very harmoniously.

'That is why they are angels,' St Pancras explained.

'What are you looking about for?' said the trumpet angel, standing up with his boot comfortable again. 'Did you expect to see somebody in a shovel hat and apron, with a nose, and a handkerchief to blow it with?'

The bishop reddened. 'Sir,' he said, 'you are profane. You are blasphemous. You are even wanting in good taste. But for the charity my profession imposes on me I should be tempted to question whether you are in the truest sense of the word a gentleman. Good morning.' And he shook the dust of heaven from his feet and walked away.

'Aint he a cure!' said Mrs Hairns. 'But I'm glad theres no throne, nor nobody, nor nothin. Itll be more like King's Cross.' She looked at them rather desolately; for something in the sword angel's voice had made her feel very humble and even ashamed of being drunk. They all looked back at her gravely; and she would have cried again, only she knew it would be of no use after the sword had touched her eyes: her tears were dried for ever. She twisted a corner of her jacket – a deplorable jacket – in her restless fingers; and there was a silence, unbroken until the snoring of Matthew, Mark, Luke, and John became painfully audible, and made her look forlornly up at their common little wooden beds, and at the flyblown illuminated text on the wall above them: 'A broken and a contrite heart, O Lord, thou wilt not despise.'

'I wonder,' she said, 'would one of you gentlemen say a prayer for a poor drunken old charwoman that has buried eleven, and nobody's enemy but her own, before I offer to go in.'

Suddenly she sat down stunned in the middle of the

AERIAL FOOTBALL: THE NEW GAME

way; for every angel threw up his hands and wings with an amazing outcry; the sword flamed all over the sky; the trumpet searched the corners of the horizon and filled the universe with ringing notes; and the stars became visible in broad daylight and sent back an echo which affected Mrs Hairns like an enormous draught of some new and delightful sort of methylated spirit.

'Oh, not such a fuss about me, gentlemen,' she said. 'Theyll think it's a queen or a lady from Tavistock Square or the like.' And she felt shyer than ever about going in. The sword angel smiled, and was going to speak to her when the bishop came back, pegging along more sturdily than ever.

'Gentlemen,' he said: 'I have been thinking over what passed just now; and whilst my reason tells me that I was entirely justified in acting and speaking as I did, still, your point of view may be a tenable one, and your method of expressing it, however unbecoming, effective for its purpose. I also find myself the victim of an uncontrollable impulse to act in a manner which I cannot excuse, though refraint is unfortunately beyond my powers of self-inhibition.'

And with that speech he snatched off his apron; made a ball of it; stuffed it into his shovel hat; and kicked the hat into space. Before it could descend, the sword angel, with a single cut of his wings, sprang into the air whooping with ecstasy, and kicked it a mile higher. St Pancras, who had no wings, but shot up by mere levitation, was on it in a second and was shooting off with it when the trumpet angel collared him and passed it to the amber and black angel. By that time Matthew, Mark, Luke, and John were out of bed and after Peter into the blue vault above, where a football match was already in full swing between the angels and the saints, with Sirius for one goal and the sun for the other. The bishop looked in amazement for a moment at the flying scrum; then, with a yell, sprang into the air and

AERIAL FOOTBALL: THE NEW GAME

actually got up nearly fifty feet, but was falling from that dangerous height when the saint he patronized swooped and caught him up into the game. Twenty seconds later his hat was halfway to the moon; and the exultant shouts

of the angels had dwindled to mere curlew pipings, whilst the celestial players looked smaller than swifts circling over Rome in summer.

Now was Mrs Hairns's opportunity to creep in

through the gate unnoticed. As her foot approached the threshold the houses of the heavenly street shone friendly in the sunshine before her; and the mosaics in the pavement glowed like flower beds of jewels.

'She's dead,' said the student from the Free Hospital. 'I think there was a spark left when I took hold of her to straighten her out; but it was only a spark. She's dead now all right enough – I mean poor woman!'

Hafod y Bryn
31 July 1907

THE EMPEROR
AND THE LITTLE GIRL

*(Written for the Vestiaire Marie-José,
a Belgian war charity for children,
in 1916)*

THE EMPEROR
AND THE LITTLE GIRL

IT was one of those nights when you feel nervous and think you see people in the shadows, or even ghosts, because there was a moon, it kept going in and out of the clouds; and a lot of clouds were scurrying across the sky, some so white that you could see the moon through them, others like brown feathers that just dimmed her, and some big dark ones that you knew would blacken out the moon altogether when they caught her. Some people get frightened on such nights and keep indoors in the light and warmth where they are not alone, and the night is shut out by the curtains, but others find themselves very restless, and want to go out and wander about and watch the moon. They like the dark because they can imagine all sorts of things about the places they cant see, and fancy that wonderful kinds of people will come out of the blacknesses and have adventures with them.

On this particular night, it was not half so dangerous to be out in the dark as it had been that afternoon to be out in the light, because it was in one of the places where the English and the French were fighting the Germans. In the day time everyone had to hide in the trenches. If they shewed their heads for a moment: bang! they were shot. There were curtains hung to prevent you from crossing certain fields, only these curtains were not like window curtains: they were really shells, showers of bombshells bursting and digging great holes in the ground, and blowing people and cattle and trees all to

THE EMPEROR AND THE LITTLE GIRL

bits; so they were called fire curtains. At night there were no fire curtains; and the soldiers who were up all night watching to shoot you could not see you so easily. Still, it was dangerous enough to prevent you imagining ghosts and robbers. Instead, you could not help thinking about the shells and bullets, and about all the dead and wounded men who were still lying where they had been shot. It is not surprising that there was nobody walking about to enjoy the moonlight and to look at the fireworks; for there were fireworks. From time to time the men who were watching to shoot sent up shells that dropped a bright star in the sky, and lit up quite plainly everything and everybody that was in sight on the ground. When this happened, all the men who were stealing about spying on the enemy, or looking for wounded men, or putting up barbed wire fences to protect their trenches, fell flat on their faces and pretended to be dead until the star went out.

Just a little after half-past eleven, in a place where no men were stealing about, and the star shells were all too far off to shew the ground very distinctly, somebody came stalking along in a strange manner; for he was not looking for wounded, nor spying, nor doing any of the things that the soldiers did; he was only wandering about, stopping and then going on again, but never stooping to pick up anything. Sometimes when a star shell came so near that you could see him pretty plainly, he stopped and stood very stiffly upright, and folded his arms. When it was dark again he walked on with a curious striding step, like the step of a very proud man; and yet he had to walk slowly, and watch where he was going, because the ground was all blown into great hollows and pits by bombshells: besides, he might have tripped over a dead soldier. The reason he carried himself so stiffly and haughtily was that he was the German Emperor: if he came at a certain angle between you and the moon or a star shell, you could see the end of his turned up

THE EMPEROR AND THE LITTLE GIRL

moustache, just as you see it in the pictures. But mostly you could not see him at all; for what with the clouds and most of the star shells being so far off, you very seldom saw anything until you were very close up.

It was so dark that though the Emperor walked very carefully, he stumbled into a great pit, called a crater, made by a mine that had been blown up, and very nearly pitched head foremost to the bottom of it. But he saved himself by clutching at something. He thought it was a tuft of grass; but it was a Frenchman's beard; and the Frenchman was dead. Then the moon came out for a moment; and the Emperor saw that quite a number of soldiers, some French and some German, had been blown up in that mine, and were lying about in the crater. It seemed to him that they were all staring at him.

The Emperor had a dreadful shock. Before he could think of what he was doing he said to the dead men the German words, 'Ich habe es nicht gewollt,' which means, in English, 'It is not my doing,' or 'I never intended to,' or, sometimes, 'It wasnt me': just what you say say when you are scolded for doing something wrong. Then he scrambled out of the pit, and walked away from it in another direction. But his inside felt so bad that he had to sit down when he had gone only a little way. At least he could have gone on if he had tried: but an ammunition case which lay in his path was so convenient to sit on, that he thought he would rest until he felt better.

The next thing that happened was very surprising; for a brown thing came out of the darkness; and he would have taken it for a dog if it had not clinked and squeaked as well as made footsteps. When it came nearer he saw it was a little girl; and she was much too young to be up at a quarter to twelve in the middle of the night. The clinking and squeaking was because she was carrying a tin can. And she was crying, not loudly, but just whimpering. When she saw the Emperor, she was not a bit frightened or surprised: she only stopped crying with a great sniff and sob, and said 'I'm sorry; but all my water is gone.'

'What a pity!' said the Emperor, who was accustomed to children. 'Are you very *very* thirsty? I have a flask, you see; but I'm afraid what is in it would be too strong for you to drink.'

'I dont want to drink,' said the little girl, quite surprised. 'Dont you? Arnt you wounded?'

'No,' said the Emperor. 'What are you crying for?'

The little girl almost began to cry again. 'The soldiers were very unkind to me,' she said, going closer up to the Emperor, and leaning against his knee. 'There are four of them in a mine crater over there. There is a Tommy and a Hairy and two Boches.'

'You must not call a German soldier a Boche,' said the Emperor severely. 'That is very very wrong.'

'No,' said the little girl: 'it is quite right, I assure you. An English soldier is a Tommy; and a French soldier is a Hairy; and a German soldier is a Boche. My mother calls them like that. Everybody does. One of the Boches wears spectacles, and is like a college teacher. The other has been lying out for two nights. None of them can move. They are very bad. I gave them water, and at first they thanked me and prayed that God would bless me, except the college teacher. Then a shell came; and though it was quite far off, they drove me away and said that if I didnt go straight home as fast as I could a bear would come out of the wood and eat me, and my father would beat me with a strap. The college teacher told them out loud that they were softies, and that I didnt matter; but he whispered to me to go home quickly. May I stay with you, please? My father would not beat me, I know: but I am afraid of the bear.'

'You may stay with me,' said the Emperor; 'and I will not let the bear touch you. There really isnt any bear.'

'Are you sure?' said the little girl. 'The Tommy said

there was. He said it was a great big bear that boiled little children in his inside after eating them.'

'The English never tell the truth,' said the Emperor.

'He was very kind at first,' said the little girl, beginning to cry again. 'I dont think he would have said it if he didnt believe it, unless the pain of his wound made him fancy things like bears.'

'Dont cry,' said the Emperor. 'He did not mean to be unkind: they were all afraid you would be wounded like themselves, and wanted you to go home so as to be out of danger.'

'Oh, I'm quite used to shells,' said the little girl. 'I go about at night giving water to the wounded, because my father was left lying out for five nights and he suffered dreadfully from thirst.'

'Ich habe es nicht gewollt,' said the Emperor, feeling very sick again.

'Are you a Boche?' said the little girl; for the Emperor had spoken to her before in French. 'You speak French very well; but I thought you were English?'

'I am half English,' said the Emperor.

'Thats funny,' said the little girl. 'You must be very careful; for both sides will try to shoot you.'

The Emperor gave a queer little laugh; and the moon came out and shewed him to the girl more plainly than before. 'You have a very nice cloak, and your uniform is very clean,' she said. 'How can you keep it so clean when you have to lie down in the dirt when a star shell shines?'

'I do not lie down. I stand up. That is how I keep my uniform clean,' said the Emperor.

'But you mustnt stand up,' said the little girl. 'If they see you they will fire at us.'

'Very well, then,' said the Emperor. 'For your sake I will lie down when you are with me; but now you must let me take you home. Where is your house?'

The little girl laughed. 'We havnt a house,' she said.

THE EMPEROR AND THE LITTLE GIRL

'First the Germans shelled our village. Then they took it; and the French shelled it. Then the English came and shelled the Germans out of it. Now all three of them shell it. Our house has been struck seven times, and our cowhouse nineteen times. And just fancy: not even the cow was killed. My papa says it has cost 25,000 francs to knock down our cowhouse. He is very proud of it.'

'Ich habe es nicht gewollt,' said the Emperor, coming all over bad again. When he felt better he said, 'Where do you live now?'

'Anywhere we can,' said the girl. 'Oh, it is quite easy: you soon get used to it. What are you? Are you a stretcher bearer?'

'No, my child,' said the Emperor. 'I am what is called a Kaiser.'

'I did not know there was more than one,' said the little girl.

'There are three,' said the Kaiser.

'Do they all have to turn their moustaches up?' said the little girl.

'No,' said the Kaiser. 'They are allowed to wear beards when their moustaches wont turn up.'

'They should put them in curl papers like I do with my hair at Easter,' said the little girl. 'What does a Kaiser do? Does he fight, or does he pick up the wounded?'

'He doesnt exactly *do* anything,' said the Emperor. 'He thinks.'

'What does he think?' said the little girl, who, like all young things, knew so little about people that when she met them she had to ask them a great many questions, and was sometimes told not to be inquisitive, though her mother usually said, 'Ask no questions, and youll be told no lies.'

'If the Kaiser were to tell, that wouldnt be thinking, would it?' said the Emperor. 'It would be talking.'

'It must be very funny to be a Kaiser,' said the little

THE EMPEROR AND THE LITTLE GIRL

girl. 'But anyhow, what are you doing here so late when you are not wounded?'

'Will you promise not to tell anybody if I tell you?' said the Emperor. 'It's a secret.'

'I promise faithfully,' said the girl. 'Please do tell me. I love secrets.'

'Then,' said the Emperor, 'I had to tell all my soldiers this morning that I was very sorry I could not go into the trenches and fight under fire as they do, and that the reason was, I had to think hard for them all, that if I were killed they would not know what to do and they would all be beaten and killed.'

'That was very naughty of you,' said the little girl; 'for it wasnt true, you know: was it? When my brother was killed another man just stepped into his place and the battle went on just as if nothing had happened. I think they might have stopped just for a minute; but they didnt. If you were killed, wouldnt somebody step into your place?'

'Yes,' said the Emperor. 'My son would.'

'Then why did you tell them such an awful fib?' said the little girl.

'I was made to,' said the Emperor. 'That is what a Kaiser is for, to be made get up and say things that neither he nor anyone else believes. I saw it in the faces of some of the men today that they didnt believe me, and thought I was a coward making excuses. So when the night came I went to bed and pretended to go asleep; but when they were all gone I got up and stole out here by myself to make sure that I was not afraid. That is why I stand up when the star shells shine.'

'Why not do it in the day time?' said the little girl. 'Thats when the real danger is.'

'They wouldnt let me,' said the Emperor.

'Poor Kaiser!' said the little girl. 'I'm so sorry for you. I hope you wont be wounded. If you are, I'll bring you some water.'

THE EMPEROR AND THE LITTLE GIRL

The Emperor felt so fond of her when she said this that he gave her a kiss before he got up and took her by the hand to lead her away to a place of safety. And she felt so fond of him that she never thought of anything else for the moment. This was how it happened that neither of them noticed that a star shell had just lit up right over them, and that the tall figure of the

THE EMPEROR AND THE LITTLE GIRL

Emperor could be seen by its light from ever so far, though the girl, who was a little thing in a dingy brown dress, and whose face was, to tell the truth, not very clean, looked at a little distance like nothing but an ant heap.

The next moment there was a fearful sound: the sound of a shell rushing through the air so fast that it left the bang of the cannon behind it as it came straight towards them. The Emperor turned round quickly to look; and as he did so two more stars broke out, and another shell began racing towards them from a great distance. And this was a very big one: the Emperor could see it tearing through the air like a great mad elephant, making a noise like a train in a tunnel. The first shell burst not very far away with such a splitting crack that it seemed to be right in the Emperor's ear. And all the time the second shell was coming with a terrible rush.

The Emperor threw himself on his face and clutched the earth with his fists trying to bury himself out of danger. Then he remembered the little girl; and it seemed to him so awful that she should be blown to pieces that he forgot about himself and tried to jump up and throw himself on top of her to shield her.

But you can think of things far quicker than you can do them; and shells are nearly as quick as thinking. Before the Emperor had got his fingers out of the clay, and his knees doubled up to rise, there was a most tremendous noise. The Emperor had never heard anything so awful, though he was used to shells at a distance. You couldnt call it a bang, or a roar, or a smash: it was a fearful, tearing, shattering, enormous bang-smash-roar-thunder-clap-earthquake sound like the end of the world. The Emperor really believed for a whole minute that he had been blown inside out; for shells do sometimes blow people inside out when they dont actually hit them. When he got up, he did not know whether he was standing on his head or his heels; indeed he was not standing

THE EMPEROR AND THE LITTLE GIRL

on either; for he fell down again several times. And when at last he managed to keep on his feet by steadying himself against something, he found that the something was a tree that had been quite a long distance away from him when the shell came, so he knew he had been blown all that way by the explosion. And the first thing he said to himself was 'Where is the child?'

'Here,' said a voice in the tree over his head. It was the little girl's voice.

'Gott sei dank!' said the Emperor, greatly relieved, which is the German for 'Thanks be to God!' 'Are you hurt, my child? I thought you were blown to pieces.'

'I *am* blown to pieces,' said the little girl's voice. 'Blown into just two thousand and thirtyseven little tiny weeny pieces. The shell came right into my lap. The biggest bit left is my little toe; it's over there nearly half a mile off; one of my thumb nails is over there half a mile the other way; and there are four eyelashes in the crater where the four men have left their bodies; one for each; and one of my front teeth is sticking in the strap of your helmet. But I dont wonder at that, because it was coming loose. All the rest of me is just burnt up and blown into dust.'

'Ich habe es nicht gewollt,' said the Emperor in a voice that would have made anybody pity him. But the little girl didnt pity him at all: she only said:

'Oh, who cares whether you did or not, *now*? I *did* laugh when I saw you flop down on your face in your lovely uniform. I laughed so much that I didnt feel the shell, though it must have given me such a dig. You look funny still, holding on to that tree and swaying about just like Granpapa when he was drunk.'

The Emperor heard her laughing; but what surprised him very much was, he heard other people laughing too, like men with gruff voices.

'Who else is laughing?' he said. 'Is there anyone with you?'

'Oh, lots and lots,' said the voice of the little girl. 'The four men who were in the crater are up here. The first shell set them free.'

'Du hast es nicht gewollt, Willem, was?' said one of the gruff voices; and then all the voices laughed; for it was funny to hear a common soldier call the Emperor Billy.

'You must not deny me the respect you have taught me to consider my due,' said the Emperor. 'I did not make myself Kaiser. You brought me up to it, and denied me the natural equality and innocent play of an ordinary human being. I command you now to treat me as the idol you made me and not as the simple man that God made me.'

'It's no use talking to them,' said the little girl's voice. 'They have all flown away. They didnt care enough about you to listen to you. There is nobody left but me and the Boche in spectacles.'

A man's voice came down from the tree. 'I go not with them because I desire not to associate with soldiers,' it said. 'They know that you made me a professor for telling lies about your grandfather.'

'Fool,' said the Emperor, rudely: 'did you ever tell them the truth about your own grandfather?'

There was no answer; and after a little silence the girl's voice said, 'He has gone away too. I dont believe his grandfather was any better than yours or mine. I think I must go too. I am very sorry; for I used to like you before I was set free by the shell. But now, somehow, you dont seem to matter.'

'My child,' said the Emperor, full of grief at her wanting to leave him. 'I matter as much as I ever did.'

'Yes,' said the little girl's voice: 'but you dont matter to *me*. You never did, you see, except when I was foolish enough to be afraid that you would kill me. I thought it would hurt instead of setting me free. Now that I *am* set free, and it's ever so much nicer than being hungry and cold and frightened, you dont matter a bit. So goodbye.'

'Wait a moment,' said the Emperor in a begging voice. 'There is no hurry; and I'm very lonely.'

'Why dont you make your soldiers fire the big gun at you as they did at me?' said the little girl's voice. 'Then you will be set free, and we can fly about together as you like. Unless you do, I cant stay with you.'

'I may not,' said the Emperor.

'Why not?' said the little girl's voice.

'Because it is not usual,' said the Emperor; 'and the Emperor who does anything unusual is lost, because he is nothing himself but a Usuality.'

'That is a very long word: I never heard it before,' said the little girl's voice. 'Does it mean a clod that cant get away from the earth, no matter how hard it tries?'

'Yes,' said the Emperor. 'Just that.'

'Then we must wait until the Tommies or the Hairies give you a dig with a great shell,' said the little girl's voice.

THE EMPEROR AND THE LITTLE GIRL

'Dont be downhearted: I think it very likely they will if you stand up in the light. Now I am going to kiss you goodbye because you kissed me very nicely before I was set free. But I'm afraid you wont be able to feel it.'

And she was quite right; for though the Emperor tried his hardest to feel it he felt nothing. And what made it very tantalizing was that he saw something. For he turned up his face to where the voice came from when she said she would kiss him; and then he saw flying down from the tree the most lovely little rosy body of a tiny girl with wings, perfectly clean and not minding a bit that it had nothing on; and it put its arms round his neck and kissed him before it flew away. He saw it quite distinctly; and this was very curious, because there was no light except dim moonlight in which it should have looked grey or white, like an owl, instead of rosy and pretty. He felt a dreadful pang of grief at parting from her; but it was all spoiled by some real men suddenly speaking to him. He had never noticed them coming. They were two of his officers; and they asked him with great respect whether the shell had hurt him. The little angel disappeared at the first word they spoke. He was so angry at their driving it away that he could not trust himself to speak to them for fully a minute; and then all he said was to ask them rudely the way back to prison. Then, seeing that they did not understand what he meant, and were staring at him as if he were mad, he asked again the way back to his quarters, meaning his tent. They pointed it out: and he strode along in front of them until he reached it, all the sentinels challenging him, and saluting him when the officers answered them. Then he said goodnight, very shortly, and was going in to bed when one of them asked him timidly whether they were to make any report of what had happened. And all the Emperor said was 'You are a couple of — fools,' and the — was a most dreadful swear.

Then they stared at one another, and one of them said,

THE EMPEROR AND THE LITTLE GIRL

'The All Highest is as drunk as be —,' and that — also was a wicked swear. It was lucky that the Emperor was thinking about the little girl, and did not overhear what the officer said. But it would not really have mattered; for all soldiers use bad words without meaning anything.

THE MIRACULOUS REVENGE

(From Time, March 1885)

THE MIRACULOUS REVENGE

I ARRIVED in Dublin on the evening of the 5th of August, and drove to the residence of my uncle, the Cardinal Archbishop. He is, like most of my family, deficient in feeling, and consequently cold to me personally. He lives in a dingy house, with a side-long view of the portico of his cathedral from the front windows, and of a monster national school from the back. My uncle maintains no retinue. The people believe that he is waited upon by angels. When I knocked at the door, an old woman, his only servant, opened it, and informed me that her master was then officiating in the cathedral, and that he had directed her to prepare dinner for me in his absence. An unpleasant smell of salt fish made me ask her what the dinner consisted of. She assured me that she had cooked all that could be permitted in His Holiness's house on a Friday. On my asking her further why on a Friday, she replied that Friday was a fast day. I bade her tell His Holiness that I had hoped to have the pleasure of calling on him shortly, and drove to a hotel in Sackville Street, where I engaged apartments and dined.

After dinner I resumed my eternal search – I know not for what: it drives me to and fro like another Cain. I sought in the streets without success. I went to the theatre. The music was execrable, the scenery poor. I had seen the play a month before in London, with the same beautiful artist in the chief part. Two years had passed since, seeing her for the first time, I had hoped that she, perhaps, might be the long-sought mystery. It had proved otherwise. On this night I looked at her and listened to her for the sake of that bygone hope, and applauded her generously when the curtain fell. But I went out lonely still. When I had supped at a restaurant, I returned to my hotel, and tried to read. In vain. The sound of feet in the corridors as the other occupants of the hotel went to bed distracted my attention from my book. Suddenly it occurred to me that I had never quite understood my uncle's character. He, father to a great flock of poor and ignorant Irish; an austere and saintly man, to whom livers of hopeless lives daily appealed for help heavenward; who was reputed never to have sent away a troubled peasant without relieving him of his burden by sharing it; whose knees were worn less by the altar steps than by the tears and embraces of the guilty and wretched: *he* had refused to humor my light extravagances, or to find time to talk with me of books, flowers, and music. Had I not been mad to expect it? Now that I needed sympathy myself, I did him justice. I desired to be with a true-hearted man, and to mingle my tears with his.

I looked at my watch. It was nearly an hour past midnight. In the corridor the lights were out, except one jet at the end. I threw a cloak upon my shoulders, put on a Spanish hat, and left my apartment, listening to the echoes of my measured steps retreating through the deserted passages. A strange sight arrested me on the landing of the grand staircase. Through an open door I saw the moonlight shining through the windows of a saloon in which some entertainment had recently taken place. I looked at my watch again: it was but one o'clock; and yet the guests had departed. I entered the room, my boots ringing loudly on the waxed boards. On a chair lay

THE MIRACULOUS REVENGE

a child's cloak and a broken toy. The entertainment had been a children's party. I stood for a time looking at the shadow of my cloaked figure upon the floor, and at the disordered decorations, ghostly in the white light. Then I saw that there was a grand piano, still open, in the middle of the room. My fingers throbbed, as I sat down before it, and expressed all that I felt in a grand hymn which seemed to thrill the cold stillness of the shadows into a deep hum of approbation, and to people the

THE MIRACULOUS REVENGE

radiance of the moon with angels. Soon there was a stir without too, as if the the rapture were spreading abroad. I took up the chant triumphantly with my voice, and the empty saloon resounded as though to the thunder of an orchestra.

'Hallo, sir!' 'Confound you, sir –' 'Do you suppose that this –' 'What the deuce – ?'

I turned; and silence followed. Six men, partially dressed, and with dishevelled hair, stood regarding me angrily. They all carried candles. One of them had a bootjack, which he held like a truncheon. Another, the foremost, had a pistol. The night porter was behind trembling.

'Sir,' said the man with the revolver, coarsely, 'may I ask whether you are mad, that you disturb people at this hour with such an unearthly noise?'

'Is it possible that you dislike it?' I replied, courteously.

'Dislike it!' said he, stamping with rage. 'Why – damn everything – do you suppose we were enjoying it?'

'Take care: he's mad,' whispered the man with the bootjack.

I began to laugh. Evidently they did think me mad. Unaccustomed to my habits, and ignorant of music as they probably were, the mistake, however absurd, was not unnatural. I rose. They came closer to one another; and the night porter ran away.

'Gentlemen,' I said, 'I am sorry for you. Had you lain still and listened, we should all have been the better and happier. But what you have done, you cannot undo. Kindly inform the night porter that I am gone to visit my uncle, the Cardinal Archbishop. Adieu!'

I strode past them, and left them whispering among themselves. Some minutes later I knocked at the door of the Cardinal's house. Presently a window on the first floor was opened; and the moonbeams fell on a grey head, with a black cap that seemed ashy pale against the unfathomable gloom of the shadow beneath the stone sill.

'Who are you?'

'I am Zeno Legge.'

'What do you want at this hour?'

The question wounded me. 'My dear uncle,' I exclaimed, 'I know you do not intend it, but you make me feel unwelcome. Come down and let me in, I beg.'

'Go to your hotel,' he said sternly. 'I will see you in the morning. Goodnight.' He disappeared and closed the window.

I felt that if I let this rebuff pass, I should not feel kindly towards my uncle in the morning, nor, indeed, at any future time. I therefore plied the knocker with my right hand, and kept the bell ringing with my left until I heard the door-chain rattle within. The Cardinal's expression was grave nearly to moroseness as he confronted me on the threshold.

'Uncle,' I cried, grasping his hand, 'do not reproach me. Your door is never shut against the wretched. I am wretched. Let us sit up all night and talk.'

'You may thank my position and not my charity for your admission, Zeno,' he said. 'For the sake of the neighbors, I had rather you played the fool in my study than upon my doorstep at this hour. Walk upstairs quietly, if you please. My housekeeper is a hard-working woman: the little sleep she allows herself must not be disturbed.'

'You have a noble heart, uncle. I shall creep like a mouse.'

'This is my study,' he said, as we entered an ill-furnished den on the second floor. 'The only refreshment I can offer you, if you desire any, is a bunch of raisins. The doctors have forbidden you to touch stimulants, I believe.'

'By heaven –!' He raised his finger. 'Pardon me: I was wrong to swear. But I had totally forgotten the doctors. At dinner I had a bottle of Graves.'

'Humph! You have no business to be travelling alone.

Your mother promised me that Bushy should come over here with you.'

'Pshaw! Bushy is not a man of feeling. Besides, he is a coward. He refused to come with me because I purchased a revolver.'

'He should have taken the revolver from you, and kept to his post.'

'Why will you persist in treating me like a child, uncle? I am very impressionable, I grant you; but I have gone round the world alone, and do not need to be dry-nursed through a tour in Ireland.'

'What do you intend to do during your stay here?'

I had no plans; and instead of answering I shrugged my shoulders and looked round the apartment. There was a statuet of the Virgin upon my uncle's desk. I looked at its face, as he was wont to look in the midst of his labors. I saw there eternal peace. The air became luminous with an infinite network of the jewelled rings of Paradise descending in roseate clouds upon us.

'Uncle,' I said, bursting into the sweetest tears I had ever shed, 'my wanderings are over. I will enter the Church, if you will help me. Let us read together the third part of Faust; for I understand it at last.'

'Hush, man,' he said, half rising with an expression of alarm. 'Control yourself.'

'Do not let my tears mislead you. I am calm and strong. Quick, let us have Goethe:

> *Das Unbeschreibliche,*
> *Hier ist gethan;*
> *Das Ewig-Weibliche,*
> *Zieht uns hinan.*'

'Come, come. Dry your eyes and be quiet. I have no library here.'

'But I have – in my portmanteau at the hotel,' I said, rising. 'Let me go for it, I will return in fifteen minutes.'

'The devil is in you, I believe. Cannot –'

I interrupted him with a shout of laughter. 'Cardinal,' I said noisily, 'you have become profane; and a profane priest is always the best of good fellows. Let us have some wine; and I will sing you a German beer song.'

'Heaven forgive me if I do you wrong,' he said; 'but I believe God has laid the expiation of some sin on your unhappy head. Will you favor me with your attention for a while? I have something to say to you, and I have also to get some sleep before my hour for rising, which is half-past five.'

'My usual hour for retiring – when I retire at all. But proceed. My fault is not inattention, but over-susceptibility.'

'Well, then, I want you to go to Wicklow. My reasons –'

'No matter what they may be,' said I, rising again. 'It is enough that you desire me to go. I shall start forthwith.'

'Zeno! will you sit down and listen to me?'

I sank upon my chair reluctantly. 'Ardor is a crime in your eyes, even when it is shewn in your service,' I said. 'May I turn down the light?'

'Why?'

'To bring on my sombre mood, in which I am able to listen with tireless patience.'

'I will turn it down myself. Will that do?'

I thanked him, and composed myself to listen in the shadow. My eyes, I felt, glittered. I was like Poe's raven.

'Now for my reasons for sending you to Wicklow. First, for your own sake. If you stay in town, or in any place where excitement can be obtained by any means, you will be in Swift's Hospital in a week. You must live in the country, under the eye of one upon whom I can depend. And you must have something to do to keep you out of mischief, and away from your music and painting and poetry, which, Sir John Richards writes to me, are dangerous for you in your present morbid state. Second, because I can entrust you with a task which, in the hands of a sensible man, might bring discredit on the Church. In short, I want you to investigate a miracle.'

He looked attentively at me. I sat like a statue.

'You understand me?' he said.

'Nevermore,' I replied hoarsely. 'Pardon me,' I added, amused at the trick my imagination had played me, 'I understand you perfectly. Proceed.'

'I hope you do. Well, four miles distant from the town of Wicklow is a village called Four Mile Water. The resident priest is Father Hickey. You have heard of the miracles at Knock?'

I winked.

'I did not ask you what you think of them, but whether you have heard of them. I see you have. I need not tell you that even a miracle may do more harm than good to the Church in this country, unless it can be proved so thoroughly that her powerful and jealous enemies are silenced by the testimony of followers of their heresy. Therefore, when I saw in a Wexford newspaper last week a description of a strange manifestation of the Divine Power which was said to have taken place at Four Mile Water, I was troubled in my mind about it. So I wrote to Father Hickey, bidding him give me an account of the matter if it were true, and, if not, to denounce from the altar the author of the report, and to contradict it in the paper at once. This is his reply. He says – well, the first part is about Church matters: I need not trouble you with it. He goes on to say –'

'One moment. Is that his own handwriting? It does not look like a man's.'

'He suffers from rheumatism in the fingers of his right hand; and his niece, who is an orphan, and lives with him, acts as his amanuensis. Well –'

'Stay. What is her name?'

'Her name? Kate Hickey.'

'How old is she?'

'Tush, man, she is only a little girl. If she were old enough to concern you, I should not send you into her way. Have you any more questions to ask about her?'

'None. I can fancy her in a white veil at the rite of confirmation, a type of faith and innocence. Enough of her. What says the Reverend Hickey of the apparitions?'

'They are not apparitions. I will read you what he says. Ahem! "In reply to your inquiries concerning the late miraculous event in this parish, I have to inform you that I can vouch for its truth, and that I can be confirmed not only by the inhabitants of the place, who are all Catholics, but by every person acquainted with the former situation of the graveyard referred to, including the Protestant Archdeacon of Baltinglas, who spends six weeks annually in the neighborhood. The newspaper account is incomplete and inaccurate. The following are the facts: About four years ago, a man named Wolfe Tone Fitzgerald settled in this village as a farrier. His antecedents did not transpire; and he had no family. He lived by himself; was very careless of his person; and when in his cups, as he often was, regarded the honor neither of God nor man in his conversation. Indeed if it were not speaking ill of the dead, one might say that he was a dirty, drunken, blasphemous blackguard. Worse again, he was, I fear, an atheist; for he never attended Mass, and gave His Holiness worse language even than he gave the Queen. I should have mentioned that he was a bitter rebel, and boasted that his grandfather had been out in '98, and his father with Smith O'Brien. At last he went by the name of Brimstone Billy, and was held up in the village as the type of all wickedness.

'"You are aware that our graveyard, situate on the north side of the water, is famous throughout the country as the burial-place of the nuns of St Ursula, the hermit of Four Mile Water, and many other holy people. No

Protestant has ever ventured to enforce his legal right of interment there, though two have died in the parish within my own recollection. Three weeks ago, this Fitzgerald died in a fit brought on by drink; and a great hullabaloo was raised in the village when it became known that he would be buried in the graveyard. The body had to be watched to prevent its being stolen and buried at the cross-roads. My people were greatly disappointed when they were told I could do nothing to stop the burial, particularly as I of course refused to read any service on the occasion. However, I bade them not interfere; and the interment was effected on the 14th of July, late in the evening, and long after the legal hour. There was no disturbance. Next morning, the graveyard was found moved to the south side of the water, with the one newly-filled grave left behind on the north side; and thus they both remain. The departed saints would not lie with the reprobate. I can testify to it on the oath of a Christian priest; and if this will not satisfy those outside the Church, everyone, as I said before, who remembers where the graveyard was two months ago, can confirm me.

' "I respectfully suggest that a thorough investigation into the truth of this miracle be proposed to a committee of Protestant gentlemen. They shall not be asked to accept a single fact on hearsay from my people. The ordnance maps shew where the graveyard was; and anyone can see for himself where it is. I need not tell your Eminence what a rebuke this would be to those enemies of the holy Church that have sought to put a stain on her by discrediting the late wonderful manifestations at Knock Chapel. If they come to Four Mile Water, they need cross-examine no one. They will be asked to believe nothing but their own senses.

' "Awaiting your Eminence's counsel to guide me further in the matter,

' "I am, etc." '

THE MIRACULOUS REVENGE

'Well, Zeno,' said my uncle: 'what do you think of Father Hickey now?'

'Uncle: do not ask me. Beneath this roof I desire to believe everything. The Reverend Hickey has appealed strongly to my love of legend. Let us admire the poetry of his narrative, and ignore the balance of probability between a Christian priest telling a lie on his oath and a graveyard swimming across a river in the middle of the night and forgetting to return.'

'Tom Hickey is not telling a lie, sir. You may take my word for that. But he may be mistaken.'

'Such a mistake amounts to insanity. It is true that I myself, awaking suddenly in the depth of night, have found myself convinced that the position of my bed had been reversed. But on opening my eyes the illusion ceased. I fear Mr Hickey is mad. Your best course is this. Send down to Four Mile Water a perfectly sane investigator; an acute observer; one whose perceptive faculties, at once healthy and subtle, are absolutely unclouded by religious prejudice. In a word, send me. I will report to you the true state of affairs in a few days; and you can then make arrangements for transferring Hickey from the altar to the asylum.'

'Yes, I had intended to send you. You are wonderfully sharp; and you would make a capital detective if you could only keep your mind to one point. But your chief qualification for this business is that you are too crazy to excite the suspicion of those whom you may have to watch. For the affair may be a trick. If so, I hope and believe that Hickey has no hand in it. Still, it is my duty to take every precaution.'

'Cardinal: may I ask whether traces of insanity have ever appeared in our family?'

'Except in you and in my grandmother, no. She was a Pole: and you resemble her personally. Why do you ask?'

'Because it has often occurred to me that you are,

perhaps, a little cracked. Excuse my candor; but a man who has devoted his life to the pursuit of a red hat; who accuses everyone else beside himself of being mad; and who is disposed to listen seriously to a tale of a peripatetic graveyard, can hardly be quite sane. Depend upon it, uncle, you want rest and change. The blood of your Polish grandmother is in your veins.'

'I hope I may not be committing a sin in sending a ribald on the Church's affairs,' he replied, fervently. 'However, we must use the instruments put into our hands. Is it agreed that you go?'

'Had you not delayed me with this story, which I might as well have learned on the spot, I should have been there already.'

'There is no occasion for impatience, Zeno. I must first send to Hickey to find a place for you. I shall tell him that you are going to recover your health, as, in fact, you are. And, Zeno, in Heaven's name be discreet. Try to act like a man of sense. Do not dispute with Hickey on matters of religion. Since you are my nephew, you had better not disgrace me.'

'I shall become an ardent Catholic, and do you infinite credit, uncle.'

'I wish you would, although you would hardly be an acquisition to the Church. And now I must turn you out. It is nearly three o'clock; and I need some sleep. Do you know your way back to your hotel?'

'I need not stir. I can sleep in this chair. Go to bed, and never mind me.'

'I shall not close my eyes until you are safely out of the house. Come, rouse yourself, and say goodnight.'

*

The following is a copy of my first report to the Cardinal:

THE MIRACULOUS REVENGE

Four Mile Water, County Wicklow
10th August

My Dear Uncle,

This miracle is genuine. I have affected perfect credulity in order to throw the Hickeys and the countryfolk off their guard with me. I have listened to their method of convincing sceptical strangers. I have examined the ordnance maps, and cross-examined the neighboring Protestant gentlefolk. I have spent a day upon the ground on each side of the water, and have visited it at midnight. I have considered the upheaval theories, subsidence theories, volcanic theories, and tidal wave theories which the provincial *savants* have suggested. They are all untenable. There is only one scoffer in the district, an Orangeman; and he admits the removal of the cemetery, but says it was dug up and transplanted in the night by a body of men under the command of Father Tom. This also is out of the question. The interment of Brimstone Billy was the first which had taken place for four years; and his is the only grave which bears a trace of recent digging. It is alone on the north bank; and the inhabitants shun it after nightfall. As each passer-by during the day throws a stone upon it, it will soon be marked by a large cairn. The graveyard, with a ruined stone chapel still standing in its midst, is on the south side. You may send down a committee to investigate the matter as soon as you please. There can be no doubt as to the miracle having actually taken place, as recorded by Hickey. As for me, I have grown so accustomed to it that if the county Wicklow were to waltz off with me to Middlesex, I should be quite impatient of any expressions of surprise from my friends in London.

Is not the above a businesslike statement? Away, then, with this stale miracle. If you would see for yourself a miracle which can never pall, a vision of youth and health to be crowned with garlands for ever, come down and see Kate Hickey, whom you suppose to be a little girl. Illusion, my lord cardinal, illusion! She is seventeen, with a bloom and a brogue that would lay your asceticism in ashes at a flash. To her I am the object of wonder, a strange man bred in wicked cities. She is courted by six feet of farming material, chopped off a spare length of coarse humanity by the Almighty, and flung into Wicklow to plough the fields. His name is Phil Langan; and he hates me. I have to consort with him for the sake of Father Tom, whom I entertain vastly by stories of your wild oats sown at Salamanca. I exhausted all my authentic anecdotes the first day; and now I invent gallant escapades with Spanish donnas, in which you figure as a youth of unstable morals. This delights Father Tom infinitely. I feel that I have done you a service by thus casting on the cold sacerdotal abstraction which formerly represented you in Kate's imagination a ray of vivifying passion.

What a country this is! A Hesperidean garden: such skies! Adieu, uncle.

Zeno Legge.

Behold me, then, at Four Mile Water, in love. I had been in love frequently; but not oftener than once a year had I encountered a woman who affected me as seriously as Kate Hickey. She was so shrewd, and yet so flippant! When I spoke of art she yawned. When I deplored the sordidness of the world she laughed, and called me 'poor fellow!' When I told her what a treasure of beauty and freshness she had she ridiculed me. When I reproached her with her brutality she became angry, and sneered at me for being what she called a fine gentleman. One sunny afternoon we were standing at the gate of her uncle's house, she looking down the dusty road for the detestable Langan, I watching the spotless azure sky, when she said:

'How soon are you going back to London?'

'I am not going back to London, Miss Hickey. I am not yet tired of Four Mile Water.'

'I'm sure Four Mile Water ought to be proud of your approbation.'

'You disapprove of my liking it, then? Or is it that you grudge me the happiness I have found there? I think Irish ladies grudge a man a moment's peace.'

'I wonder you have ever prevailed on yourself to associate with Irish ladies, since they are so far beneath you.'

'Did I say they were beneath me, Miss Hickey? I feel that I have made a deep impression on you.'

'Indeed! Yes, youre quite right. I assure you I cant sleep at night for thinking of you, Mr Legge. It's the best a Christian can do, seein you think so mighty little of yourself.'

'You are triply wrong, Miss Hickey: wrong to be sarcastic with me, wrong to pretend that there is anything unreasonable in my belief that you think of me sometimes, and wrong to discourage the candor with which I always avow that I think constantly of myself.'

'Then you had better not speak to me, since I have no manners.'

'Again! Did I say you had no manners? The warmest expressions of regard from my mouth seem to reach your ears transformed into insults. Were I to repeat the Litany of the Blessed Virgin, you would retort as though I had been reproaching you. This is because you hate me. You never misunderstand Langan, whom you love.'

'I dont know what London manners are, Mr Legge; but in Ireland gentlemen are expected to mind their own business. How dare you say I love Mr Langan?'

'Then you do not love him?'

'It is nothing to you whether I love him or not.'

'Nothing to me that you hate me and love another?'

'I didnt say I hated you. Youre not so very clever yourself at understanding what people say, though you

make such a fuss because they dont understand you.'
Here, as she glanced down the road again, she suddenly looked glad.

'Aha!' I said.

'What do you mean by "Aha!"'

'No matter. I will now shew you what a man's sympathy is. As you perceived just then, Langan – who is too tall for his age, by the bye – is coming to pay you a visit. Well, instead of staying with you, as a jealous woman would, I will withdraw.'

'I dont care whether you go or stay, I'm sure. I wonder what you would give to be as fine a man as Mr Langan.'

'All I possess: I swear it! But solely because you admire tall men more than broad views. Mr Langan may be defined geometrically as length without breadth; altitude without position; a line on the landscape, not a point on it.'

'How very clever you are!'

'You do not understand me, I see. Here comes your lover, stepping over the wall like a camel. And here go I, out through the gate like a Christian. Good afternoon, Mr Langan. I am going because Miss Hickey has something to say to you about me which she would rather not say in my presence. You will excuse me?'

'Oh, I'll excuse you,' said he boorishly. I smiled, and went out. Before I was quite out of hearing, Kate whispered vehemently to him, 'I *hate* that fellow.'

I smiled again; but I had scarcely done so when my spirits fell. I walked hastily away with a coarse threatening sound in my ears like that of the clarionets whose sustained low notes darken the woodland in Der Freischütz. I found myself presently at the graveyard. It was a barren place, enclosed by a mud wall with a gate to admit funerals, and numerous gaps to admit the peasantry, who made short cuts across it as they went to and fro between Four Mile Water and the market town. The graves were mounds overgrown with grass; there was no keeper; nor were there flowers, railings or any of the conventionalities that make an English graveyard repulsive. A great thorn bush, near what was called the grave of the holy sisters, was covered with scraps of cloth and flannel, attached by peasant women who had prayed before it. There were three kneeling there as I entered; for the reputation of the place had been revived of late by the miracle; and a ferry had been established close by, to conduct visitors over the route taken by the graveyard. From where I stood I could see on the opposite bank the heap of stones, perceptibly increased since my last visit, marking the deserted grave of Brimstone Billy. I strained my eyes broodingly at it for some minutes, and then descended the river bank and entered the boat.

'Good evenin t'your honor,' said the ferryman, and set to work to draw the boat hand over hand by a rope stretched across the water.

'Good evening. Is your business beginning to fall off yet?'

'Faith, it never was as good as it mightabeen. The people that comes from the south side can see Billy's grave – Lord have mercy on him! – across the wather; and they think bad of payin a penny to put a stone over him. It's them that lives towrst Dublin that makes the journey. Your honor is the third Ive brought from south to north this blessed day.'

'When do most people come? In the afternoon, I suppose?'

'All hours, sur, except afther dusk. There isnt a sowl in the counthry ud come within sight of that grave wanst the sun goes down.'

'And you! do you stay here all night by yourself?'

'The holy heavens forbid! Is it me stay here all night? No, your honor: I tether the boat at siven o'hlyock, and lave Brimstone Billy – God forgimme! – to take care of it t'll mornin.'

'It will be stolen some night, I'm afraid.'

'Arra, who'd dar come next or near it, let alone stale it? Faith, I'd think twice before lookin at it meself in the dark. God bless your honor, and gran'che long life.'

I had given him sixpence. I went to the reprobate's grave and stood at the foot of it, looking at the sky, gorgeous with the descent of the sun. To my English eyes, accustomed to giant trees, broad lawns, and stately mansions, the landscape was wild and inhospitable. The ferryman was already tugging at the rope on his way back (I had told him I did not intend to return that way), and presently I saw him make the painter fast to the south bank; put on his coat; and trudge homeward. I turned towards the grave at my feet. Those who had interred Brimstone Billy, working hastily at an unlawful hour, and in fear of molestation by the people, had hardly dug a grave. They had scooped out earth enough to hide their burden, and no more. A stray goat had kicked away a corner of the mound and exposed the coffin. It occurred to me, as I took some of the stones from the cairn, and heaped them so as to repair the breach, that had the miracle been the work of a body of men, they would have moved the one grave instead of the many. Even from a supernatural point of view, it seemed strange that the sinner should have banished the elect, when, by their superior numbers, they might so much more easily have banished him.

It was almost dark when I left the spot. After a walk of half a mile, I recrossed the water by a bridge, and returned to the farmhouse in which I lodged. Here, finding that I had had enough of solitude, I only stayed to take a cup of tea. Then I went to Father Hickey's cottage.

Kate was alone when I entered. She looked up quickly as I opened the door, and turned away disappointed when she recognized me.

'Be generous for once,' I said. 'I have walked about aimlessly for hours in order to avoid spoiling the beautiful afternoon for you by my presence. When the sun was up I withdrew my shadow from your path. Now that darkness has fallen, shed some light on mine. May I stay half an hour?'

'You may stay as long as you like, of course. My uncle will soon be home. He is clever enough to talk to you.'

'What! More sarcasms! Come, Miss Hickey, help me to spend a pleasant evening. It will only cost you a smile. I am somewhat cast down. Four Mile Water is a paradise; but without you, it would be a little lonely.'

'It must be very lonely for you. I wonder why you came here.'

'Because I heard that the women here were all Zerlinas, like you, and the men Masettos, like Mr Phil – where are you going to?'

'Let me pass, Mr Legge. I had intended never speaking to you again after the way you went on about Mr Langan today; and I wouldnt either, only my uncle made me promise not to take any notice of you, because you were – no matter; but I wont listen to you any more on the subject.'

'Do not go. I swear never to mention his name again. I beg your pardon for what I said: you shall have no further cause for complaint. Will you forgive me?'

She sat down, evidently disappointed by my submission. I took a chair, and placed myself near her. She tapped the floor impatiently with her foot. I saw that there was not a movement I could make, not a look, not a tone of my voice, which did not irritate her.

'You were remarking,' I said, 'that your uncle desired you to take no notice of me because –'

She closed her lips, and did not answer.

'I fear I have offended you again by my curiosity. But indeed, I had no idea that he had forbidden you to tell me the reason.'

'He did not forbid me. Since you are so determined to find out –'

'No: excuse me. I do not wish to know, I am sorry I asked.'

'Indeed! Perhaps you would be sorrier still to be told. I only made a secret of it out of consideration for you.'

'Then your uncle has spoken ill of me behind my back. If that be so, there is no such thing as a true man in Ireland. I would not have believed it on the word of any woman alive save yourself.'

'I never said my uncle was a backbiter. Just to shew you what he thinks of you, I will tell you, whether you want to know it or not, that he bid me not mind you because you were only a poor mad creature, sent down here by your family to be out of harm's way.'

'Oh, Miss Hickey!'

'There now! you have got it out of me; and I wish I had bit my tongue out first. I sometimes think – that I maytnt sin! – that you have a bad angel in you.'

'I am glad you told me this,' I said gently. 'Do not reproach yourself for having done so, I beg. Your uncle has been misled by what he has heard of my family, who are all more or less insane. Far from being mad, I am actually the only rational man named Legge in the three kingdoms. I will prove this to you, and at the same time keep your indiscretion in countenance, by telling you something I ought not to tell you. It is this. I am not here as an invalid or a chance tourist. I am here to investigate the miracle. The Cardinal, a shrewd if somewhat erratic man, selected mine from all the long heads at his disposal to come down here, and find out the truth of Father Hickey's story. Would he have entrusted such a task to a madman, think you?'

'The truth of – who dared to doubt my uncle's word? And so you are a spy, a dirty informer.'

I started. The adjective she had used, though probably the commonest expression of contempt in Ireland, is revolting to an Englishman.

'Miss Hickey,' I said: 'there is in me, as you have

said, a bad angel. Do not shock my good angel – who is a person of taste – quite away from my heart, lest the other be left undisputed monarch of it. Hark! The chapel bell is ringing the angelus. Can you, with that sound softening the darkness of the village night, cherish a feeling of spite against one who admires you?'

'You come between me and my prayers,' she said hysterically, and began to sob. She had scarcely done so, when I heard voices without. Then Langan and the priest entered.

'Oh, Phil,' she cried, running to him, 'take me away from him: I cant bear –' I turned towards him, and shewed him my dog-tooth in a false smile. He felled me at one stroke, as he might have felled a poplar-tree.

'Murdher!' exclaimed the priest. 'What are you doin, Phil?'

'He's an informer,' sobbed Kate. 'He came down here to spy on you, uncle, and to try and shew that the blessed miracle was a make-up. I knew it long before he told me, by his insulting ways. He wanted to make love to me.'

I rose with difficulty from beneath the table, where I had lain motionless for a moment.

'Sir,' I said, 'I am somewhat dazed by the recent action of Mr Langan, whom I beg, the next time he converts himself into a fulling-mill, to do so at the expense of a man more nearly his equal in strength than I. What your niece has told you is partly true. I am indeed the Cardinal's spy; and I have already reported to him that the miracle is a genuine one. A committee of gentlemen will wait on you tomorrow to verify it, at my suggestion. I have thought that the proof might be regarded by them as more complete if you were taken by surprise. Miss Hickey: that I admire all that is admirable in you is but to say that I have a sense of the beautiful. To say that I love you would be mere profanity. Mr Langan: I have in my pocket a loaded pistol, which I carry from a silly English prejudice against your countrymen. Had I been the Hercules of the ploughtail, and you in my place, I should have been a dead man now. Do not redden: you are safe as far as I am concerned.'

'Let me tell you before you leave my house for good.' said Father Hickey, who seemed to have become unreasonably angry, 'that you should never have crossed my threshold if I had known you were a spy: no, not if your uncle were his Holiness the Pope himself.'

Here a frightful thing happened to me. I felt giddy, and put my hand to my head. Three warm drops trickled over it. Instantly I became murderous. My mouth filled with blood, my eyes were blinded with it; I seemed to drown in it. My hand went involuntarily to the pistol. It is my habit to obey my impulses instantaneously. Fortunately the impulse to kill vanished before a sudden perception of how I might miraculously humble the mad vanity in which these foolish people had turned upon me. The blood receded from my ears; and I again heard and saw distinctly.

'And let *me* tell you,' Langan was saying, 'that if you think yourself handier with cold lead than you are with your fists, I'll exchange shots with you, and welcome, whenever you please. Father Tom's credit is the same to me as my own; and if you say a word against it, you lie.'

'His credit is in my hands,' I said. 'I am the Cardinal's witness. Do you defy me?'

'There is the door,' said the priest, holding it open before me. 'Until you can undo the visible work of God's hand your testimony can do no harm to me.'

'Father Hickey,' I replied, 'before the sun rises again upon Four Mile Water, I will undo the visible work of God's hand, and bring the pointing finger of the scoffer upon your altar.'

I bowed to Kate, and walked out. It was so dark that I could not at first see the garden-gate. Before I found it,

THE MIRACULOUS REVENGE

I heard through the window Father Hickey's voice saying, 'I wouldnt for ten pound that this had happened, Phil. He's as mad as a march hare. The Cardinal told me so.'

I returned to my lodging and took a cold bath to cleanse the blood from my neck and shoulder. The effect of the blow I had received was so severe, that even after the bath and a light meal I felt giddy and languid. There was an alarum-clock on the mantelpiece: I wound it; set the alarum for half-past twelve; muffled it so that it should not disturb the people in the adjoining room; and went to bed, where I slept soundly for an hour and a quarter. Then the alarum roused me, and I sprang up before I was thoroughly awake. Had I hesitated, the desire to relapse into perfect sleep would have overpowered me. Although the muscles of my neck were painfully stiff, and my hands unsteady from my nervous disturbance, produced by the interruption of my first slumber, I dressed myself resolutely, and, after taking a draught of cold water, stole out of the house. It was exceedingly dark; and I had some difficulty in finding the cow-house, whence I borrowed a spade, and a truck with wheels, ordinarily used for moving sacks of potatoes. These I carried in my hands until I was beyond earshot of the house, when I put the spade on the truck, and wheeled it along the road to the cemetery. When I approached the water, knowing that no one would dare to come thereabout at such an hour, I made greater haste, no longer concerning myself about the rattling of the wheels. Looking across to the opposite bank, I could see a phosphorescent glow, marking the lonely grave of Brimstone Billy. This helped me to find the ferry station, where, after wandering a little and stumbling often, I found the boat, and embarked with my implements. Guided by the rope, I crossed the water without difficulty; landed; made fast the boat; dragged the truck up the bank; and sat down to rest on the cairn at the grave. For nearly a quarter of an hour I sat watching the patches of jack-o'-lantern fire, and collecting my strength for the work before me. Then the distant bell of the chapel clock tolled one. I rose; took the spade; and in about ten minutes uncovered the coffin, which smelt horribly. Keeping to windward of it, and using the spade as a lever, I contrived with great labor to place it on the truck. I wheeled it without accident to the landing place, where, by placing the shafts of the truck upon the stern of the boat and lifting the foot by main strength, I succeeded in embarking my load after twenty minutes' toil, during which I got covered with clay and perspiration, and several times all but upset the boat. At the southern bank I had less difficulty in getting truck and coffin ashore, and dragging them up to the graveyard.

It was now past two o'clock, and the dawn had begun; so that I had no further trouble from want of light. I wheeled the coffin to a patch of loamy soil which I had noticed in the afternoon near the grave of the holy sisters. I had warmed to my work; my neck no longer pained me; and I began to dig vigorously, soon making a shallow trench, deep enough to hide the coffin with the addition of a mound. The chill pearl-colored morning had by this time quite dissipated the darkness. I could see, and was myself visible, for miles around. This alarmed me, and made me impatient to finish my task.

Nevertheless, I was forced to rest for a moment before placing the coffin in the trench. I wiped my brow and wrists, and again looked about me. The tomb of the holy women, a massive slab supported on four stone spheres, was grey and wet with dew. Near it was the thornbush covered with rags, the newest of which were growing gaudy in the radiance which was stretching up from the coast on the east. It was time to finish my work. I seized the truck; laid it alongside the grave; and gradually prized the coffin off with the spade until it rolled over into the trench with a hollow sound like a drunken remonstrance from the sleeper within. I shovelled the earth round and over it, working as fast as possible. In less than a quarter of an hour it was buried. Ten minutes more sufficed to make the mound symmetrical, and to clear the traces of my work from the adjacent sward.

Then I flung down the spade; threw up my arms; and vented a sigh of relief and triumph. But I recoiled as I saw that I was standing on a barren common, covered with furze. No product of man's handiwork was near me except my truck and spade and the grave of Brimstone Billy, now as lonely as before. I turned towards the water.

On the opposite bank was the cemetery, with the tomb of the holy women, the thornbush with its rags stirring in the morning breeze, and the broken mud wall. The ruined chapel was there too, not a stone shaken from its crumbling walls, not a sign to shew that it and its precinct were less rooted in their place than the eternal hills around.

I looked down at the grave with a pang of compassion for the unfortunate Wolfe Tone Fitzgerald, with whom the blessed would not rest. I was even astonished, though I had worked expressly to this end. But the birds were astir, and the cocks crowing. My landlord was an early riser. I put the spade on the truck again, and hastened back to the farm, where I replaced them in the cow-house. Then I stole into the house, and took a clean pair of boots, an overcoat, and a silk hat. These, with a change of linen, were sufficient to make my appearance respectable. I went out again, bathed in the Four Mile Water, took a last look at the cemetery, and walked to Wicklow, whence I travelled by the first train to Dublin.

*

Some months later, at Cairo, I received a packet of Irish newspapers and a leading article, cut from The Times, on the subject of the miracle. Father Hickey had suffered the meed of his inhospitable conduct. The committee, arriving at Four Mile Water the day after I left, had found the graveyard exactly where it had formerly stood. Father Hickey, taken by surprise, had attempted to defend himself by a confused statement, which led the committee to declare finally that the miracle was a gross imposture. The Times, commenting on this after adducing a number of examples of priestly craft, remarked, 'We are glad to learn that the Rev. Mr Hickey has been permanently relieved of his duties as the parish priest of Four Mile Water by his ecclesiastical superior.

It is less gratifying to have to record that it has been found possible to obtain two hundred signatures to a memorial embodying the absurd defence offered to the committee, and expressing unabated confidence in the integrity of Mr Hickey.'

THE THEATRE OF THE FUTURE
(From The Grand Magazine, February 1905)

THE THEATRE OF THE FUTURE

I

WHEN Gerald Bridges returned from Buenos Ayres after twentytwo years' absence from England, he enjoyed his first morning in London enormously. London looks its best in the spring; and this was the 15th of April, 1910.

Bridges was a millionaire. He had begun life as a choir boy; become an extremely respectable young gentleman in a bank; had been terrified by an imaginative doctor into believing that his chest was delicate and that he would die unless he took a sea voyage; had left the bank to go in a cargo boat (owned by his uncle) to Valparaiso; had allowed this uncle to get rid of him by packing him off to Buenos Ayres with some perfunctory advice that he should 'take up an agency of some sort'; and had there bought an agent's business as a doctor buys a practice or a dairyman a milkwalk. The agency consisted of a nameplate and an office with the rent in arrear; and the vendor drank the purchase money (Gerald's little all, save fifty dollars for immediate bread and butter) in three days, and then became a hotel tout of the most questionable sort. The transaction was so unworthy of a youth of the smallest sharpness that Gerald's uncle jumped at the opportunity of disowning him; and the poor dupe sat down in his new office and waited on Providence hopelessly, without gumption enough to raise a hand to avert imminent destitution. He did not even attempt to sell the agency to someone else: he thought such a step would be dishonest.

He waited exactly three minutes. Then a Yankee walked in and asked could he get him any picrate of selenium. Bridges, remembering that the nameplate described him as a picrate agent, and having been brought up strictly to say what was expected of him on all occasions, replied that he would do his best, and asked the man to call tomorrow. Within the next hour three Germans called and asked the same thing. And Gerald made the same reply. When they were gone, he looked vacantly into the street with his hands in his pockets, wondering how he could find out about picrate of selenium, and what manner of medicine it might be – whether it would be good for his chest, for example. For he had somehow made up his mind that it must be a medicine, retailed in little white papers, like powders for children. But the street brought no counsel; and Gerald came to the conclusion, being very shy, that he had better be out tomorrow when the men came back.

Then another man came in, not a commercial gent like the others, but a person who reminded him of the pictures of Spanish farmers in the Doré Don Quixote, which he had taken in at sixpence a month in his native land. This man sat down close to Gerald, having perhaps sized him up as an honest and simple young man, and by dint of impressing a long explanation with his chubby brown forefinger upon the agent's knee (Gerald was fortunately not ticklesome in that quarter) conveyed to him that he had on his ranch a sort of stone which contained something or other which could be made into something else which some newspaper said had been discovered by somebody to be useful for something that would make common gaslight brighter than electric light. The Doré farmer said that it cost him a lot to get this otherwise useless stone cleared away from his ranch; and that if Gerald could sell it for enough to make it worth his while to take it away at his own expense, the farmer would shew his gratitude in a substantial manner. To prove his good faith, he produced the newspaper, in which Gerald saw without emotion (for he was far too callow to grasp how near ruin he stood) that the substance in demand was called picrate of selenium.

The question was, How to remove the stone from the farm? Gerald thought for a moment of making a personal effort with a carpet bag; but he could not help seeing that it would be much more convenient to get the farmer to put the stone on board ship for his previous visitors. So he asked the farmer at what price per pound (he subsequently had to pretend that this was a slip of the tongue for per ton) he would undertake such a delivery, adding, by way of allurement, that if the stuff was really valuable, the farmer ought to have a fair profit on the transaction. The farmer, delighted to have found an honest man, named a price, and departed with the usual engagement for tomorrow.

And that is the whole story of Gerald's millions. For the farmer's price was so much lower than the buyer's offers that Gerald made more on that single deal than he could have earned in two years at the bank; and so, having 'made' the difference, as he expressed it, by his own business ability, he began to see himself in a new light. Before the market had developed to the point at which other agents began to compete with him, he had learnt all it was necessary to learn about it, and had even ventured to buy some important sources of supply. In short, he kept his start, and was a millionaire when his business suddenly vanished like a railway wreath of summer steam in consequence of the discovery by a gas foreman that picrate of selenium, though a pet salt with the German chemist who had started the process, was not at all necessary for the brightening operation, which could be effected much more easily by using common chalk and certain refuse of the soap and glass manufacturers. And it is noteworthy that whereas Gerald was convinced that he had 'built up' his business by his own industry and astuteness, he regarded its disappearance in quite a different way, as a natural catastrophe reflecting no discredit whatever on his ability.

Gerald saw his business go as he had seen it come, without emotion. He cared nothing for picrate of selenium, never to the end of his days knew what it was, nor handled a sample, nor dreamt that selenium was a metal, nor heard of picric acid. He did not care even for money any more than for any other necessary convenience of a comfortable life. He had never cared enough for any woman to get married. He had not cared enough for England or any other place to desert Buenos Ayres for a single month since his uncle had shoved him into it. He would have remained an unambitious and rather helpless employee all his life had he not blundered into the exact spot at which the discovery of an enormously lucrative use for picrate of selenium, itself a blunder as it turned out, had sent a torrent of gold into his empty pocket. He was a dreamer, a born amateur. Therefore he had a hobby. He collected Shakespeariana, and read the Elizabethan dramatists in the spirit of Charles Lamb and Mr Swinburne. Not that he ever went to the theatre in Buenos Ayres. Not, either, that he read plays intelligently, or could tell the cheapest platitude from the deepest and surest stroke of character dissection, provided both were in blank verse. He loved rhetorical balderdash: it gave him an impression of greatness that nothing else could. He could not stand modern naturalism and realism, nor even much of the translations of Goethe, to whom he greatly preferred Schiller, though the choice was one of evils to him at best. But he rather liked translated Goethe in the comfortable attenuation of Bailey's Festus. He could read Taylor's Philip van Artevelde by the yard, and was versed in the works of Colman, Cumberland, Tobin, and Mrs Centlivre. Otway he ranked very highly indeed; and he quite seriously believed that Webster's imagination was gigantic and Chapman's elevation sublime. There are lots of people like Gerald. And in Buenos Ayres he could idealize the London theatres, and look forward to spending some of his millions in visiting them. He could go to the stalls instead of to the pit as he used to do when he was at the bank. Were there not Societies in London for the performance of the mighty works of Marlowe and Webster? Mermaid Societies, Elizabethan Stage Societies and what not?

So on this sunshiny fifteenth of April, 1910, though he first went to the Courts of Justice to see for himself that Temple Bar was actually gone, and to survey the County Council improvements in the Strand, the real business of his walk began when he started westward to see the theatres, and to choose one for a visit that evening.

Many of the old theatres were gone. The Olympic was gone; the Globe was gone; the Gaiety was gone; Toole's was gone; the Queen's was gone. There was some strangeness to Gerald even in the fact that the Queen herself was gone; that the Q.C.s were now K.C.s; that the postage stamps had on them the conventional male profile which seems to fit all European monarchs. But for every old theatre he could remember, there were now three new ones, of such immoderate architectural pretension that the Strand Theatre had been shamed into a reconstruction which made it look like an annex of the Courts of Justice, whilst Terry's, though frugally retaining its old entrance, was now surmounted by a second-hand steeple, purchased readymade at the demolition of a city church. The new playhouses could be distinguished from cathedrals and museums only by the iron shelters for the queue on rainy nights, which were usually added by an engineering firm after the completion of the edifice, a practice which had already

THE THEATRE OF THE FUTURE

led two architects to suicide, and one, more energetic and practical, to murder.

It was perhaps in consequence of this tragedy that the very newest theatre, on the site of St Martin's Church, had cloisters. There were shops round the cloisters; and the theatre was upstairs, everything being carried up to the stage by hydraulic lifts. It was at the box office of this establishment that Gerald presented himself after hesitating on the threshold of a dozen others on his way from St Clement Danes (now flourishing as The Acropoleum, a combination of circus and music hall in which the arena was stationary – a remarkable novelty – whilst the auditorium revolved round it and made its occupants seasick).

The hall on the first floor was what Gerald would have called a bazaar. You could buy newspapers, gloves, ties, flowers, shoes, studs, and photographs there; and there were saddle-bag couches, and little tables with ash trays on them, under tubbed trees. The box office was a cabin on the left, recognizably evolved from the cabins of old, but much more costly, and having on its door a large enamelled copper plate, inscribed Mr Scroop Dabernoon, Premier Acting Manager Assoluto; Mr Mozart Denbigh, Principal Acting Manager; Mr Lorimer Mavrocordato, Acting Manager; and Mr Roy de Bois Guilbert, Assistant Acting Manager.

As Gerald made for the window of the box office, the cabin door opened; and a tall blond man of fifty, frock-coated, tall-hatted, gloved, spatted and slipped in the manner customary among men whose income depends on their appearance, swung indignantly into the hall, talking at the top of his voice.

'You know it's no good talking to me like that, Denbigh. A rotten piece, a rotten crowd, and a rotten lot of outsiders in front: thats what it is. You tell Scroop that if he thinks he can get a big salary here for going about bragging that he has me on his free list, and then treat

me like that, he's mistaken. See?'

Mr Mozart Denbigh, a younger man, took it humbly enough, though in point of attire he was even more imposing than his angry patron. Not only had he slips and spats, but spats on his wrists and cuffs on his ankles over his spats, that being just then the latest fashion. And he had two jewelled pins in his necktie, chained to an enamelled ring.

'Scroop is as put out about it as any man can be, I assure you,' he pleaded. 'I give you my word those bent wood chairs on the stage were a bit of local color. The author insisted on it.'

'Local color be blithered! Cant you find an author who's a gentleman?'

'Well, you know the class of man they are,' said Denbigh with a sigh. 'What can we do? I pledge you my word the furniture in our new piece was made for Prince Duvallo-Schulzheim, every stick of it. We stuck two hundred guineas on to his price to get it; and theyre making a new set for him. The smoking-room in the last act was made for an Atlantic liner; and the curtain the woman hides behind cost us more than the whole of the rest of the mounting. We do you as handsome as we can, Mr Glossop. Dont say you wont come to see our new piece. We'll meet you in every possible way.'

'No: hang me if I will!' said Mr Glossop. 'Last time you stuck me down beside a bounder in a flannel walking suit. I never saw such a thing in a decent London theatre. I damn nearly got up and walked out. It shant occur again, I can tell you. I dont expose myself twice to that sort of thing.'

'Morning dress!' exclaimed Denbigh. 'Impossible!' He turned to the window, and called through it: 'Who was next Mr Glossop last night, Lorry?'

'Doesnt even know who he put next me!' said Mr Glossop bitterly. 'And this is what they call management here!'

Mr Lorimer Mavrocordato, from the depths of the cabin, replied: 'Duke of Westminster. Not my fault. Said he was lookin round the theatres for a governess to teach walkin and talkin. Said he'd been up in the gallery and couldnt hear. The seat belonged to the Baroness Mercedes de Dion all right; but she gave it up to the Duke for the introduction. He didnt want to take it; but Mr Dabernoon worked it for her.'

'See how hard youve been on us for putting you next a Duke!' said Denbigh to Glossop. 'I wont pretend that we have more titles on our free list than any other theatre in London, because it's not true, though it's very nearly true, mind you: theres only one theatre ahead of us; and we're only behind *them* by one French Viscount. But I tell you for a positive fact that this is the only house that has had a real English patrician in its stalls for four years, seven months, three weeks, and two nights exactly. Thats the doing of Talbot Durberville, whom you think such a lot of as an acting manager. He said he was determined to have his house dressed; and if any aristocratic outsider didnt like it, he could stay at home.'

'Quite right too,' said Mr Glossop sulkily, a little out of countenance over the Duke.

'Yes; but see what came of it! The aristocracy said they couldnt bear to be mistaken for Talbot's free list, and chucked evening dress altogether – went in for the John Burns style of thing, you know – and small blame to them. I shouldnt care to be mixed up with Talbot's crowd myself. But Talbot stuck to it; and as our high and mighties didnt exactly see the point of letting Tommy Dobbs dictate to them what theyd wear, and insult them in public if they didnt wear it, they simply dropped the theatre. We tried to get them back here by allowing dinner jackets; but the mischief was done. You may think that Dabernoon was going too far in standing the Duke's flannel suit; but I tell you straight I'd have passed him in boating flannels myself. Now if he was a foreign Duke, of course: not likely; but you dont catch Mosey Dickson firing out a real English Duke!'

'I say nothing against that,' said Mr Glossop, evidently shaken.

'I knew you wouldnt,' said Mr Denbigh, pressing his advantage. 'We may send you a couple of stalls, then, for next Friday, maynt we?'

Mr Glossop looked gloomy, and did not reply promptly. He was considering the proposal; and it was far from clear that he was considering it favorably. 'See here,' he said suddenly: 'what about my expenses?'

Mr Denbigh was shocked that there should be any room for discussion on that subject. 'As usual, of course,' he said. 'We couldnt think of letting you be out of pocket by coming to our little show.'

'What does that mean? Only a guinea, I suppose: eh?'

Denbigh flinched. 'A guinea!' he echoed forlornly.

'Yes, a guinea. What do you suppose it costs me to come to a west end theatre? You know the sort of woman you expect me to bring with me. You saw Mrs Jack Jimmet's diamonds the other night? Yes, I should think you did. Well, that style is accustomed to see money flung about when she wants anything. Flowers, ices, coffee, suppers, tips, cabs –'

'Of course we send a motor for you,' said Denbigh hastily. 'You can have it from five in the afternoon right up to any hour you like.'

'Thats another thing I want to talk about,' said the implacable Glossop, more aggrieved than ever. 'If you cant send a gentleman something more up-to-date than an old crock of a 1904 six-cylinder car, there are other theatres that can. Do you remember old Dodd, of the Royal?'

'Good Lord, do I remember him! "Box Office, Mr Dodd": that was his style.'

'Well, Dodd was sacked for sending me a one-horse

brougham from a local jobmaster. It was his first attempt to keep up with the times, and his last. Dont you forget it, Denbigh. I dont like being chaffed by smart women about the age of my motor car.'

'That will be all right, you take it from me: right as rain. Honor! We have three new ones: no petrol: the explosion is done by dynamite: the newest thing. I'll send you one. Youll find flowers in it for the lady. And sweets and cigarets and so on. We'll do all we can. And if you keep the pocket expenses down to twelve-and-six – or say fifteen –'

Mr Glossop put his foot down. 'Now look here, Denbigh,' he said: 'do you suppose I'm a professional deadhead?'

Denbigh lifted his eyes and hands in mute protest against so monstrous a suggestion.

'I know what you chaps think well enough,' Glossop went on, unimpressed by this demonstration. 'You think we make money out of keeping your theatre smart. Oh yes you do: I see through you as easy as through that window. Well, let me tell you something: I'm an older man than you; and I can tell you a lot you dont know, clever as you think yourself. I can remember the time when the stalls of the London theatres – the first rate west end houses, mind you – were often filled with people who got in simply by paying. They came without introductions! they wore pretty well anything they liked; they didnt even have to show their card, but just planked their money down, so that you might be sitting next to the man that swept your chimney, or to your cook's doctor, for all you knew. In those days I used sometimes, when the piece was what they called a success, to be kept hanging about until the curtain was going up before theyd give me my couple of stalls, they were so anxious to sell them if they could. And even then, by George! they made a compliment of giving them to me. The downright caddishness of the theatre was something beyond belief. Actors of good standing would act – aye, and let their wives act – before perfect strangers for the sake of a few shillings. Theyre doing it now in the provinces, I dare say. Men that were knighted by Queen Victoria used to do it. They had no more idea that an actor in his own theatre was as much bound to be particular as to who he let in as a gentleman in his own house than if they were running a tube railway. But that isnt my point. What I say is this – and now I'm going to tell you something you wont believe; but it's true. When I went in those old days at my own expense, paying for my own travelling, and thanking the actor manager for my stalls as if he was doing me a favor, my theatregoing cost me LESS than it does now.'

Mr Denbigh tried to look as if he believed it; but his incredulity was obvious.

'Oh yes it did: dont you make any mistake about it. To begin with, theyd done away with fees at all the best houses: cloak room, programs and all. Here I'm blackmailed at every turn: a shilling for my hat, a shilling for my coat, a shilling apiece for two programs, a shilling for the lady to powder herself at the looking-glass in the cloak room, a shilling each for all *her* wraps, a shilling for a cup of coffee, and half-a-crown for an ice. Lucky if you get out of it all for half-a-sovereign!'

'Weve nothing to do with all that,' said Denbigh. 'It's all let out over our heads to a contractor.'

'What's that to me?' said Glossop. 'Besides, the standard's gone up in all sorts of ways. There was a tall man named Irving used to act Shakespear at the old Lyceum when it was a theatre. That was a first class no-fee house. Well, when it was over, you just walked down to Charing Cross station on the District – smoky hole of a steam railway it was then – and went home to West Kensington, two shillings out of pocket, perhaps, and thought youd had a jolly evening. Everybody could afford to go to the theatre then. But now it always means a supper, with wine and one thing and another, ending up with an engagement for Brighton from Saturday to Monday that runs into a lot more. You know jolly well that your theatres are only touting lobbies to your big hotels, and that every farthing you pretend to give me here comes back to you with a hundred per cent profit in your hotel. I know the game better than you do. It was flourishing in the east end long before it came to the west: fortunes were made in Hoxton out of owning one theatre and ten public houses – not counting bars before and behind the curtain – long enough before it was accidentally discovered at the west end that Savoy suppers paid better than Savoy Opera. Nowadays the theatre is thrown in for nothing and a trifle over to people who can afford the suppers. But how many people *can* afford them? thats what I would ask you. Why has Jim Capel given up the theatre? Same reason he's given up his motor cars: cant afford it. When I come to your rotten shows here, I dont get out of it once in five times with any change for three pounds in my pocket. And yet you have the cool cheek to offer me twelve-and-six for my expenses! And when Dabernoon turns up here tonight to earn his big salary by airing his shirt front and receiving us at the top of the staircase, youll tell him Ive been here begging, I suppose; and you two'll ask one another what we deadheads'll be wanting next. Oh, youre a pair of beauties, you are! But you cant get the better of *me*.'

'I assure you weve nothing to do with the hotel,' urged Denbigh, overcome by Glossop's arrogant copiousness.

'More fools you!' bawled Glossop remorselessly. 'You make money for the hotel out of me all the same; and if youre soft enough to start that game without having a share in the hotel or building one of your own, so much the worse for you! I was looking at your sandwich men outside; and I recognized three of them as chaps who ran west end London theatres without knowing how the game was worked. Of course they had to pay for their audience the same as other houses. They all three did it out of pure theatre-struckness – not even to oblige a lady. This theatre might have been built out of solid gold bricks with the money thats been sunk in it; and it could be dashed with diamonds for half whats been sunk in the others. And the Theatrical Wigmakers and Printers Syndicate has just bought Adelphi Terrace for two millions cash-on-the-counter to build a new hotel, and three more theatres to feed it.'

'Well, I'll make it twentyfive shillings: will that do? Only, I ask you as a special favor not to mention it. If the regular market went up to that, we couldnt stand the racket for the rest of the season; and I want this job to see me through til June. Come! to oblige me! You know you enjoy a play as well as anybody.'

'You dont suppose I come here to enjoy plays, do you? Why, I can see any of your cast-off successes at a suburban theatre for a few shillings. Just turn in when the humor takes me, you know. No dress: no smart women to drag about. Nobody knows you and you know nobody: nothing to do but look at the play.'

'Yes; but rather an outside crowd, eh?'

'Oh, if you come to that, acting is an outside game. Some of these outsiders can make the evening pass a lot quicker than you can here. Lots of them had theatres of their own in the west end away back in the nineteenth century. Youll see their names starred all over Camden Town and Camberwell just as if they were important people. It makes me laugh sometimes. And such rum names too! Kendal and Hare, and Irving and Wyndham, and Terry and Campbell, and Brough and Rehan, and Tree and Bourchier, and Weedon Grossmith and Maude, and Alexander and Waller and deuce knows who!'

'Our boy messenger would have more self-respect than to call himself names like that in the face of the public,' said Denbigh, with genuine indignation. 'Roy de Bois Guilbert, he calls himself: see it there on the plate! He invented it himself too.'

'You know,' said Glossop, musing over the curious fact, 'theyve got a way of handling a play so that it's often quite interesting. And then you havnt the supper on your mind.'

'After all,' said Denbigh, plaintively, 'we give you the supper on first nights.'

'Oh yes: if you call *that* a supper, scrambling for mayonnaise and champagne with a newspaper man's elbow in your ribs on one side, and an actress's whitewash coming off on your sleeve on the other. Why dont you chuck those suppers? They were all very well when the newspapers were independent of you. But when you own the hotel, and the theatre, and the newspaper, and the critic as well, what do you want to stuff him with chicken and champagne for? Upon my soul I'll take a theatre myself one of these days just to shew you how to do it.' Mr Glossop's tone was now moody almost to moroseness: he was tired of talking; and the associations of the theatre made him feel bored and irritable. 'Here!' he said, breaking off abruptly: 'I cant spend the whole day talking to you. Ta, ta, Mosey. Send the motor at 6.15; and dont forget the flowers.'

He turned away with a little shiver; splayed his lower lip askew with a coarse grimace; and flung down the stairs thoroughly out of sorts. Denbigh looked after him with a cunning air of petty triumph, and then sent a stage whisper through the window to his colleague within.

'Lorry.'

'Yes?'

'Got Glossop for twentyfive bob.'

'No!!!'

'I have though.'

'What'll he say when he finds out that Tommy Dobbs has put the west end rate to thirty this week?'

'Dont care what he says. Ive done him, greedy bounder! and thats enough for me. More than Dabernoon could, you bet.'

And Denbigh, childishly self-satisfied, went into the cabin to receive the congratulations of his colleague more intimately.

Gerald Bridges, listening to this conversation under cover of studying the framed playbill of the evening's performance, found his hobby revolting against these two men with an intensity which revealed to him for the first time how deep a hold the theatre had upon him. Besides, he was amazed, being a novice in everything theatrical except his old habit of going to the pit for two shillings or half-a-crown, and seeing things 'from the front.' Even in those now old-fashioned days he might, had he gained any inside knowledge of the box office, have learnt enough to have become perfectly familiar with the view of the theatre taken by Glossop and Denbigh, and to have recognized in the practices they were discussing only a development – and not even a very remote or extravagant development – of a system which had flourished under his very nose.

The theatre had always been fairyland to him: he had never reasoned about it as about prosaic things. The bankruptcy of a shopkeeper whose shop was always crowded with customers would have surprised him; but the failure of a play, or the collapse of a management, when the boards inscribed Stalls Full, Dress Circle Full, etc., were never once lacking at a performance, had passed unnoticed by him. Once, in a book of Irish views, he had seen a photograph of an imposing statue of a famous Shakespearean actor, his own contemporary, who had left an enormous fortune at his death; and he had felt incredulous because he had never seen this actor or heard of him in London. And he had once, in reading a biographical sketch of Mrs Siddons, wondered why it was that great actresses formerly worked in the provinces, and then, when they had perfected their gifts, took first place in London, whereas nowadays, it seemed, they learnt their business (as best they could) in London; became famous; and then went into the provinces to make money. But he had never followed up the subject, because he had nobody to discuss it with, and indeed cared for nothing about the theatre save the art and poetry and fascination of it, instinctively barring the idea that all these wonderful figures of romance had to pay rent and buy food and find lodgings and grow old just like himself.

For nearly ten minutes he continued to stare at the playbill without understanding a word of it. Indeed there was little to understand; for it was as full of names as a page from a directory. A sort of nomemania had possessed the compiler of it; for there was hardly an employee in the theatre whose name was not starred as enthusiastically as the names of the actors. And all the names were obviously and grossly fictitious. The members of the band, from the *chef d'orchestre* to the 'principal timpanist and percussionist,' were there. The head carpenter was there as 'chief of staff' (name: Lesseps Isambard); the property man was *premier magasinier*; there were calcium superintendents, calcium operators, chiefs of installation, principal electrical engineers, first and second resistance and amber experts, a chief 'appellant' (with a secretary), four librarians (wardrobe, musical, dramatic, and general business), a keeper of prints, thirtyseven *habilleuses* in attendance on the ladies of the cast, five chamberlains in attendance on the few male actors, two literary advisers, three producers (one for each act), a long series of *collaborateurs de l'Auteur* with inscrutable functions, a *balayeuse* of the Royal Box, a lyric poet, and fifty other impertinences which no imagination could anticipate nor memory retain.

A series of County Council regulations came with a prosaic shock after all this romance. There was an announcement that in the following week three birthdays would be celebrated: of a member of the Royal family, of Shakespear's mother's second cousin's ploughman (recently discovered by Mr Sidney Lee), and of the *premier Suisse des coulisses*, the mode of celebration being the presentation to every person in the house of a richly illustrated souvenir, with a box of cigars or a feather fan, according to sex. Finally the old list of prices survived like an unstriped muscle or a disused process in a bodily organism; but the stalls were now a guinea, and the balcony stalls fifteen shillings. There were also seventeen pages of advertisements.

It was a fascinating document, cheap at a shilling, its marked price. Bridges at last stopped staring vacantly at it, and read it from end to end with growing indignation – for it must be remembered that he had not, like the dwellers in London, had it broken to him gradually as it grew from season to season, line by line, folly by folly. He had not seen a London playbill for ten years, and had been unsuspicious enough even then of the enormous proportion of fiction to fact in theatrical business. The whole affair struck him as monstrous, as something calling for a great social reform, for the devotion of a lifetime, for the expenditure of a fortune, for public agitation, for speeches, petitions to parliament, sermons, a press crusade, and examples made of – he did not exactly know of whom, but of somebody.

Fortunately for himself, he did not understand the art of agitation. But he had the pet delusion of the modern millionaire. He believed that he had made his own millions. Had not others failed to make them? Had he not had to work hard and to keep his wits about him, to be sober and prudent and steady whilst other men were drinking and lazing and talking through their hats, in the years during which he had been keeping his sack under the spout of gold in spite of all the centripetal forces that were drawing it away and the men who were jostling to push him aside? He had come to believe that he could do anything. To reform the theatre root and branch seemed quite as possible to him as the simple intention of buying a ticket with which he had come up the stairs.

He turned from the playbill; went resolutely to the window of the box office; put down two sovereigns and a florin on the ledge; and said authoritatively, 'I want two stalls for tonight, please.'

There had been some stir and talk in the cabin up to this moment; but now there was a dead silence. If there were men in there – and he knew there were – their hearts had ceased beating: their breath was no longer drawn.

At last a single syllable, ghostly, stupended, awe-withered, floated through the window.

'Wot?!!!!!!'

'Two stalls for tonight, please,' repeated Gerald, sweetly and distinctly. He pushed the money further in, adding, 'Two guineas, I think.'

The next thirty seconds were so absolutely void that Bridges began seriously to fear that he had struck the whole department dead. Then the door opened slowly, and Mozart Denbigh reappeared. He was evidently uncertain how to deal with an unprecedented situation; but, though pale, he shewed no lack of courage. He looked Bridges up and down, down and up, from the wide welted soles of his shooting boots to the top of his Panama hat. He hesitated. He was an expert in the price of dress: he knew that, article for article, the unfashionable stranger's clothes had cost more than his own. He smelt money. If the stranger had not been such an inconceivable greenhorn as to offer to buy theatre tickets, he might almost have been the boss of an American theatre syndicate. Mozart put on an inquiring, approachable expression, and waited. Gerald out-waited him. Mozart all but slunk back into his cabin. But his pluck revolted at such an exhibition of resourcelessness before the eyes of Lorimer Mavrocordato, eyes now straining spellbound, through the window. He braced himself; drew out his own card; fingered it; said at last, 'I havnt the pleasure –'

'I know you havnt,' said Bridges. 'I dont want it. I want two stalls; and I proffer two guineas. Is that intelligible?'

This was an attack; and it stiffened Denbigh's wilting backbone like a dose of strychnine. He was not going to take that sort of thing from any man. 'Look here!' he said: 'do you suppose you can walk into a first rate west end London theatre without an introduction merely because you have two guineas in your pocket?'

'I walked into Westminster Abbey this morning without an introduction. I go into the Royal Academy without an introduction to the man at the turnstile. I go into the British Museum without an introduction. I go everywhere without an introduction except into the private houses of people who have to get an introduction to me before they take the liberty of inviting me. I always go into theatres without introductions; and if any difficulty is made, I complain to the County Council and the Lord Chamberlain.'

'Well, I'll be damned!' exclaimed Denbigh, scandalized out of all propriety.

'I fear so; but I hope not,' said Gerald imperturbably. 'Will you sell me the tickets or will you not?'

'No I shant,' retorted Denbigh. 'Is that English?'

'No,' said Gerald. 'You should have said "I wont." '

'Good enough for you,' said Denbigh: 'you wont find much difference in the meaning. Youll get no tickets here; and I'll see that you dont get a stall in the west end of London until you apologize. Go and tell that to the Lord Chamberlain or to your Radical friends on the

County Council. If you want a theatre to do as you like in, you can build one for yourself.'

'Thank you: I will,' said Gerald, pocketing his money, and walking quietly away.

Before he reached the stairs Denbigh was at his side, hatless, friendly, beaming, irresistible.

'Come into my office and have a cigar, old chap,' he said, clapping Gerald affectionately on the shoulder. 'Excuse my humor, wont you? Of course you will. You just tell me what seats you want, here or anywhere else; and I'll work them for you. I must have a talk with you. You dont mind, do you? You can spare ten minutes – as a personal favor. It's a grand game; and I can put you up to every move in it.'

Gerald, with English middle-class unsociability, felt that he ought to snub Mozart; but it was impossible. Pleased, excited, keen on the new scent, Mozart was another man: he wiped out his own immediate past without an effort; and within ten seconds Gerald was seated with him in an office at the back of the cabin.

Their conversation need not be recorded here at any length. Mr Denbigh began by giving Gerald a not too succinct history of his entire life, from which it appeared that his name was neither Mozart Denbigh, nor Moses Dickson, but Henry Wilkinson, which, he explained, was no good either for a pal or a program. He was a thoroughbred Englishman, but was compelled by the financial and artistic prejudice against his countrymen to pretend to be a Jew. Lorimer Mavrocordato was his brother-in-law, the best fellow that ever stepped, Luke Mears by name, having chosen the other name so that he could use his monogram, which he had designed himself. His brother-in-law, he explained, was his wife's brother; and this led him to the subject of Mrs Wilkinson herself, who was no sooner mentioned than he lost all sense of time, space, and proportion, and talked about her with a simple uxoriousness which ended by touching Bridges.

The idol in pressed trousers and flashing hat, in slips and spats and jampot collar and enamelled boots, became the homely breadwinner of a tiny Finchley villa, and the idolator of a little woman who managed to keep his humanity green through all his Mozartian and Mosaic metempsychoses.

But what finally won over Bridges was the fact that when he succeeded at last in getting a word in edgeways, and, after first convincing Denbigh that he had a hundred thousand pounds to spare to back his fancy, went on to propose to him the opening of a Cash-for-Admission theatre, with certain other innovations, he struck at once a genuine and deeply revolted sense of honor and decency in his new acquaintance.

'No,' he said stoutly: 'I hope you wont take it in bad part, old man: upon my soul I do; but though I'm not straitlaced, Ive always played the game and I always shall play the game.'

And it was only when Gerald asked him to sit down again and explain exactly what the game was – a thing it had never occurred yet to Denbigh to consider – that the conscience which the acting manager had always felt at his back, like a rock, turned to water and let him through into the abyss at the bottom of which the disgrace of cash-for-admission was gilded by a bank account with one hundred thousand pounds to its credit. Even when Gerald had turned all his pleas and arguments inside out, and forced him to confess that toadying and humbugging Glossop was not a man's work, and was good neither for Glossop nor himself; that an imposture was none the less an imposture because everybody except the outsiders (meaning all who were not accomplices) knew it to be an imposture; that in spite of the enormous prices paid under his system for success, for social prestige, for dramatic art, and even for a superficial air of gentility, none of these things were really attained – all of which Denbigh at last admitted as true 'if you choose to look at it in that way' – he still, whilst frankly owning that he could not justify his feelings by argument, pleaded that he should feel a cad and a juggins and a number of other indeterminate ignominious things if he did anything but what Dabernoon did, what Durberville did, what, in short, everybody did who was not that abject thing, an outsider.

But he consented at last: Gerald never knew exactly why. That fancy for the theatre which had made him an acting manager instead of any other sort of functionary in the great west end fashion machine for squeezing money out of rich people must have sprung, after all, from some aborted radicle of genuine artistic passion which made him hanker after a theatre which should be a real theatre, driven by the same passion in real actors, real authors, real audiences, instead of a simulacrum galvanized into a show of life by trickery from the box office. All the same, he was too ignorant to conceive that any work of art could do without such trickery: they all seemed to him elaborate make-believes to enable us to escape from reality; so that the humbug of the box office and the comedy of the stage were not only housemates but children of one father, the Father of Lies. That dramatic art was a discovery of reality under the insane chaos of daily phenomena, an attempt to make mere experience intelligible, was quite beyond him. He would not have known what Bridges was talking about, had Bridges possessed brains enough to lay such a proposition before him.

What finally overcame his false shame was probably the hundred thousand pounds, and an offer by Bridges to try their effect on Dabernoon. It then began to leak out that in spite of the extravagant expenditure of the theatrical adventurers, even their money was in many cases a delusion, like everything else they professed to supply. Denbigh boasted that his last principal but one had started with £250 (raised on a bill of sale on furniture that did not belong to him), and, by persuading an actress and an actor that a certain play he had was the chance of their lives, and persuading the author of that play that its production would place the British Empire and the United States at his feet, he had extracted enough from them to raise his three figures to the verge of four. Denbigh was proud to say that with this trifle to start with, he had created such an air of success within a week that he had been able to 'rope in fresh backers' and exploit the supposed London success in the provinces and in the American and Colonial market with sufficient results to keep the management on foot with radiant glory for a whole season. What was bitter to him now was that when at last the chance of his own life had come in the person of the long dreamed of backer who was no needy and desperate gambler, no rich amateur playwright with his desk full of impossible plays, no would-be Hamlet nor pretty stage-struck lady with an opulent protector, no callow novice with a huge patrimony slipping through his fingers so fast that duping and pillaging him was a meaner occupation than pocket picking, but a solid moneyed man with his wits about him, able to stand a several years racket, this heaven-sent person should turn out to be a crank of the first water, not only going to lose his money as effectually as Dabernoon could lose it for him in the most fashionable manner, but bent on buying nothing with it but ignominy, ridicule, and rank exteriority.

Still, he consented to be Gerald's acting manager. Indeed, having consented, he suddenly became aware that he had never for a moment had the least real intention of refusing.

2

The rest of the story would be tedious at full length. It may be summarised in a few observations, and an extract or two from the theatrical advertisements of the time.

THE THEATRE OF THE FUTURE

The announcement of the Cash-for-Admission Theatre was at first laughed at as an attempt to spoof the west end; but when Durberville and Dabernoon said it was in bad taste, the laughter ceased; indignant disgust at a breach of good form by some rank outsider was clamorous at the D'Orsay (the leading box office club); and the insiders agreed to cut the outsiders dead. But as the outsiders had never sought the acquaintance of the insiders, nor were in the least concerned about them; as, indeed, they outnumbered them by several hundred thousand to one, and included the Royal Family, the Peerage, the House of Commons, the Landed Gentry, the Church, the Army, the Navy, the Civil Service, the Bar, the Faculty, ninetynine hundredths of the Stage and ninehundred and ninetynine thousandths of the City, not to mention the entire commercial and industrial world, the effect of Dabernoon's displeasure was so small that he was puzzled and disheartened, and even said it was enough to make a man believe in Ibsen. Next day he discovered by chance that the new acting manager, Mr Wilkinson, far from being a rank outsider, was no other than Mozart Denbigh; and then he laughed knowingly, and allowed his friends to infer that he had been in the new move all along.

But he still deplored the bad taste of the C.F.A. advertisements. For instance:

'This theatre is not suited for the display of evening dress. Hats must be taken off; but in other respects parliamentary and churchgoing dress is good enough for the C.F.A. Theatre.'

Dabernoon, who never went to church, and hardly knew what parliament was, could not understand this.

'Admission to all parts of the house, half-a-crown. On Wednesdays and Saturdays, one shilling.'

Roy de Bois Guilbert, whose native quarter was the Elephant and Castle, was dismissed from his employment

THE THEATRE OF THE FUTURE

with bodily violence by Dabernoon for prophesying that they would soon chuck the half-crown, as nobody but toffs could afford it.

The next sensation was among the dramatic authors. It was made by the following announcement:

'The manager of the C.F.A. Theatre regrets to have to announce that his attempt to procure a new play introducing a married woman in love with her own husband, and without a past, has been wholly unsuccessful. An appeal to our leading dramatic authors to write such a play has elicited a unanimous refusal to compromise their professional reputation by dealing with an abnormal situation and catering for morbid tastes. The management has, therefore, determined to open the C.F.A. Theatre with a revival of the most successful play in English literature, the one which opened the theatre to Shakespear and inaugurated the Elizabethan stage (not Mr William Poel's but an earlier XVI-XVII Century enterprise known by the same name).

'The First and Second Parts of King Henry VI will be played on successive evenings from the opening of the theatre until further notice. Later on, they will be replaced by the Third Part and the Tragedy of King Richard III. These plays will not be altered or revised for representation in any way, as the C.F.A. Theatre has, unfortunately, not succeeded in obtaining the services of a stage manager whose judgment in these matters can be accepted as unquestionably superior to Shakespear's. Mr Algernon Swinburne, however, whose all but idolatrous veneration for the Bard is well known, has undertaken to rewrite the Joan of Arc scenes from the point of view, not only of what Shakespear undoubtedly ought to have written, but of the *entente cordiale* between this country and France.'

All this was child's play compared to the advertisement on the morning of the third day after the opening of the theatre. It ran thus:

THE THEATRE OF THE FUTURE
TWENTY SEATS FOR A SHILLING

In consequence of the derisive and almost unanimous condemnation of the C.F.A. Theatre by the London Press, it is now the cheapest and most comfortable house in London. Only one seat in every twenty is occupied; so that each member of the audience, in addition to his own fauteuil, has nineteen others on which to dispose his hat, overcoat, playbill, opera-glass, etc. etc. He has also twenty times as many cubic feet of air as are required by the Building Act, a most healthful comfort in the present sultry weather. Persons recognizing friends in any part of the house can reach them and sit beside them (if desired) with perfect ease without undue disturbance. No crush need be apprehended in case of fire. Those who have been compelled to give up playgoing by the crowded and stuffy condition of the free list theatres are surprised and delighted by the atmosphere of the C.F.A. No headaches nor influenza next morning. Persons wishing to sleep through the less exciting scenes of Henry VI can have the divisions removed from the adjacent seats and stretch themselves comfortably. They are requested to keep their mouths carefully closed to avoid snoring.

'I call that cheek,' said Mavrocordato to his brother-in-law. 'The public will never stand it.'

'If the public will stand Dabernoon the public will stand anything,' said Wilkinson, who now outGeralded Gerald in his contempt for the free list.

Four days later appeared the following:

'The Manager of the C.F.A. Theatre has to apologize to the public for the disappointment caused after his recent announcements by the crowded condition of the theatre. Only one seat can now be guaranteed to each person, and the ventilation of the house, though carefully attended to, is far from being what the Manager could desire. If the rush continues, the Manager will be compelled to stem it by producing a fashionable comedy; but he trusts that more moderate counsels may still prevail. He specially appeals to those who have seen King Henry VI five times and upwards to discontinue their visits until the rest of the public has had an opportunity of witnessing it. The every-nighters, who now number some hundreds, have no excuse for their selfishness.

'The Manager greatly regrets that the conclusion of the Second Part of King Henry VI was last night reduced to absurdity by the inartistic behavior of the Lancastrian army, which in the excitement of the moment defeated the Yorkists instead of retreating in confusion. In future the numbers of the contending forces will be so apportioned as to make a recurrence of this regrettable incident impossible. The substitution of singlesticks for swords has heightened the realism of the scene. Subalterns desiring to take part should inscribe their names with the stage-door keeper. Opportunities will be provided in rotation, but applications should be made at once, as the list is already excessive, despite the recent enlargement of the stage. No further applications from Radical Clubs for the Jack Cade scenes can be entertained; nor can those whose members have been guilty of using their fists in the battle of Blackheath be reinstated on any terms.

'In consequence of the Drawing Room at Buckingham Palace on the 15th there will be some vacancies in the Court scenes.

'P.S. – The wounded in Charing Cross Hospital are doing well.'

On the day this appeared, the newspapers had in their contents bills 'Latest Advertisements of the C.F.A.' The boom agitated the whole country.

It was perhaps a month or six weeks after this that the acting manager and his principal met one night in the theatre. They had both come to the same door to have a peep at the house, which was full to the last seat. Bridges was in blue serge. Denbigh, in square-toed boots, pepper-and-salt trousers, white double-breasted waistcoat, frock coat, and mutton-chop whiskers, might have been a churchwarden or auctioneer in a country town.

'Heard the latest?' he inquired. Bridges had not. 'Theyre putting up the Third Part of old Henry at the Hippodrome. But thats nothing. Dabernoon's going to open on the C.F.A. principle with a smart comedy. Two shows a night: the first from six to eight at sixpence a head, the second from half-past nine to half-past eleven at a guinea a head and no free list. It's an idea, eh?'

'Good luck to him!' said Bridges, whose hair now had a touch of grey at the temples. 'Good luck to them all! Ive shewn them the way; but I never knew what work was before. It's madly fascinating; but it's killing.'

'Yes,' said Denbigh. 'Youll never get away from it now. Once at it, always at it.'

'Who's that man in the third row, the fifth from the end? I seem to know his face, somehow.'

'Man named Glossop,' replied Wilkinson. 'That dowdy little scared rabbit of a woman next him is his wife; and the three children are either his own or some of his pals'; he brings lots of children here. He came the first night, and wanted a seat for nothing. When I refused and tried to get his half-crown, he said he'd never paid for a seat at a west end theatre in his life and never would; but I bounced him into letting me toss up which of us should pay for him. He lost; so I got his half-crown after all. He's been here more than twenty times since. Offers me five shillings a night, and provide his own costume and sword, if we'll let him go on and maffick in the battle of Blackheath.' Here Wilkinson looked reflectively in the direction of Glossop, and then surveyed the crowded house with humbled wonder. 'You know,' he said, 'I dont half believe it yet. I think night after night here that it's all a dream – that I shall wake up and find myself in the old lobby working-in the old lot, and smelling that queer mixture of dinner and powder and scent and brilliantine and starch and kid reviver and sable and skunk and trouser-under-a-hot-iron. Here you never smell anything more exciting than umbrellas and buttered toast: a respectable moral kind of smell. Just look at them! Just think of it's being all money! not a scrap of paper in it from floor to ceiling! And look at the stage! Look at the real right down legitimate acting! Think of Durberville's wife doing Queen Margaret and letting you put her in the bill as Mrs Dobbs! Why, that woman said to me last Easter twelvemonth, 'Mosey,' she says: 'I know I cant act; but Ive got a personality,' she says; 'and, after all, it's personality you want on the stage.' I'd like to see her face if you told her now that she couldnt act and was going on her personality. I believe she could have acted all along, only Durberville used to sit on her when she tried it and tell her not to be stagey. It's wonderful.'

'It's simple enough, after all,' said Gerald. 'Why did you never think of it for yourself?'

'It looks simple now that it's been done, like everything else; but, you see, we were trained not to think of it. We werent fools any more than you; but you had the advantage of being an utter outsider. Dont make any mistake about it: it takes a jolly sight more cleverness and knowledge of the world to do Dabernoon's business than to do our business. He has to make bricks without straw: he has to fake it, fake it, fake it, all the time. Here, what have we to do? Nothing but sit and take the money. The public does it all for us, because the public wants us. I dont do five shillings worth of work in the lobby now: a commissionaire, a turnstile, and a policeman can run the front of the house as well as I can. We dont make this a success: it *is* a success. But the New Olympic isnt a success: it's Durberville who bounces the public into fancying it's a success; and jolly well he does it too. He's just sold the American rights of the piece for four thousand pounds.'

'To somebody who was not up to the game, I suppose?'

'No, to a man who played the game off on him two years ago by selling him a rotten piece at a silver-mine price. Thats whats so queer about the business: when you go into it you get to believe in it yourself until you wont touch a piece that hasnt been through the whole fake routine. Thats when you came in so tremendously as an outsider. You dont mind my saying so, do you? And youre not a bit altered. Youre just like a little child about the theatre still, you know, in spite of all the eye-openers youve had here.'

'Well, it's a playhouse; and play is a child's business. I often think of that passage, "Except ye become as little children," and so on – eh?'

'Yes, oh yes – it's perfectly true. Not a doubt of it,' said Wilkinson. 'Good old Shakespear! always touches the spot.'

'Sh-sh-sh-sh-sh!' came from the audience as the curtain went up, and the first lines came rolling and wailing from the stage, the actor making no attempt whatever to degrade them into prose:

Hung be the heavens with black! Yield, day, to night!
Comets, importing change of times and States,
Brandish your crystal tresses in the sky –

A DRESSING ROOM SECRET

*(From the Haymarket Theatre program of
The Dark Lady of the Sonnets
24 November 1910)*

A DRESSING ROOM SECRET

It was trying-on day; and the last touches were being given to the costumes for the Shakespear Ball as the wearers faced the looking-glass at the costumier's.

'It's no use,' said Iago discontentedly. 'I dont look right; and I dont feel right.'

'I assure you, sir,' said the costumier: 'you are a perfect picture.'

'I may look a picture,' said Iago; 'but I dont look the character.'

'What character?' said the costumier.

'The character of Iago, of course. *My* character.'

'Sir,' said the costumier: 'shall I tell you a secret that would ruin me if it became known that I betrayed it?'

'Has it anything to do with this dress?'

'It has everything to do with it, sir.'

'Then fire away.'

'Well, sir, the truth is, that we cannot dress Iago in character, because he is not a character.'

'Not a character! Iago not a character! Are you mad? Are you drunk? Are you hopelessly illiterate? Are you imbecile? Or are you simply blasphemous?'

'I know it seems presumptuous, sir, after so many great critics have written long chapters analyzing the character of Iago: that profound, complex, enigmatic creation of our greatest dramatic poet. But if you notice, sir, nobody has ever had to write long chapters about *my* character.'

A DRESSING ROOM SECRET

'Why on earth should they?'

'Why indeed, sir! No enigma about me. No profundity. If my character was much written about, you would be the first to suspect that I hadnt any.'

'If that bust of Shakespear could speak,' said Iago, severely, 'it would ask to be removed at once to a suitable niche in the façade of the Shakespear Memorial National Theatre, instead of being left here to be insulted.'

'Not a bit of it,' said the bust of Shakespear. 'As a matter of fact, I *can* speak. It is not easy for a bust to speak; but when I hear an honest man rebuked for talking common sense, even the stones would speak. And I am only plaster.'

'This is a silly trick,' gasped Iago, struggling with the effects of the start the Bard had given him. 'You have a phonograph in that bust. You might at least have made it a blank verse phonograph.'

'On my honor, sir,' protested the pale costumier, all disordered, 'not a word has ever passed between me and that bust – I beg your pardon, me and Mr Shakespear – before this hour.'

'The reason you cannot get the dress and the make-up right is very simple,' said the bust. 'I made a mess of Iago because villains are such infernally dull and disagreeable people that I never could go through with them. I can stand five minutes of a villain, like Don John in – in – oh, whats its name? – *you* know – that box office play with the comic constable in it. But if I had to spread a villain out and make his part a big one, I always ended, in spite of myself, by making him rather a pleasant sort of chap. I used to feel very bad about it. It was all right as long as they were doing reasonably pleasant things; but when it came to making them commit all sorts of murders and tell all sorts of lies and do all sorts of mischief, I felt ashamed. I had no right to do it.'

'Surely,' said Iago, 'you dont call Iago a pleasant sort of chap!'

A DRESSING ROOM SECRET

'One of the most popular characters on the stage,' said the bust.

'Me!' said Iago, stupent.

The bust nodded, and immediately fell on the floor on its nose, as the sculptor had not balanced it for nodding.

The costumier rushed forward, and, with many apologies and solicitous expressions of regret, dusted the Bard and replaced him on his pedestal, fortunately unbroken.

'I remember the play you were in,' said the bust, quite unperturbed by its misadventure. 'I let myself go on the verse: thundering good stuff it was: you could hear the souls of the people crying out in the mere sound of the lines. I didnt bother about the sense – just flung about all the splendid words I could find. Oh, it was noble, I tell you: drums and trumpets; and the Propontick and the Hellespont; and a malignant and a turbaned Turk in Aleppo; and eyes that dropt tears as fast as the Arabian trees their medicinal gum: the most impossible, far-fetched nonsense; but such music! Well, I started that play with two frightful villains, one male and one female.'

'Female!' said Iago. 'You forget. There is no female villain in Othello.'

'I tell you theres no villain at all in it,' said the immortal William. 'But I started with a female villain.'

'Who?' said the costumier.

'Desdemona, of course,' replied the Bard. 'I had a tremendous notion of a supersubtle and utterly corrupt Venetian lady who was to drive Othello to despair by betraying him. It's all in the first act. But I weakened on it. She turned amiable on my hands, in spite of me. Besides, I saw that it wasnt necessary – that I could get a far more smashing effect by making her quite innocent. I yielded to that temptation: I never could resist an effect. It was a sin against human nature; and I was well paid out; for the change turned the play into a farce.'

A DRESSING ROOM SECRET

'A farce!' exclaimed Iago and the costumier simultaneously, unable to believe their ears. 'Othello a farce!'

'Nothing else,' said the bust dogmatically. '*You* think a farce is a play in which some funny rough-and-tumble makes the people laugh. Thats only your ignorance. What I call a farce is a play in which the misunderstandings are not natural but mechanical. By making Desdemona a decent poor devil of an honest woman, and Othello a really superior sort of man, I took away all natural reason for his jealousy. To make the situation natural I must either have made her a bad woman as I originally intended, or him a jealous, treacherous, selfish man, like Leontes in The Tale. But I couldnt belittle Othello in that way; so, like a fool, I belittled him the other way by making him the dupe of a farcical trick with a handkerchief that wouldnt have held water off the stage for five minutes. Thats why the play is no use with a thoughtful audience. It's nothing but wanton mischief and murder. I apologize for it; though, by Jingo! I should like to see any of your modern chaps write anything half so good.'

'I always said that Emilia was the real part for the leading lady,' said the costumier.

'But you didnt change your mind about me,' pleaded Iago.

'Yes I did,' said Shakespear. 'I started on you with a quite clear notion of drawing the most detestable sort of man I know: a fellow who goes in for being frank and genial, unpretentious and second rate, content to be a satellite of men with more style, but who is loathsomely coarse, and has that stupid sort of selfishness that makes a man incapable of understanding the mischief his dirty tricks may do, or refraining from them if there is the most wretched trifle to be gained by them. But my contempt and loathing for the creature – what was worse, the intense boredom of him – beat me before I

A DRESSING ROOM SECRET

got into the second act. The really true and natural things he said were so sickeningly coarse that I couldnt go on fouling my play with them. He began to be clever and witty in spite of me. Then it was all up. It was Richard III over again. I made him a humorous dog. I went further: I gave him my own divine contempt for the follies of mankind and for himself, instead of his own proper infernal envy of man's divinity. That sort of thing was always happening to me. Some plays it improved; but it knocked the bottom out of Othello. It doesnt amuse really sensible people to see a woman strangled by mistake. Of course some people would go anywhere to see a woman strangled, mistake or no mistake; but such riff-raff are no use to me, though their money is as good as anyone else's.'

The bust, whose powers of conversation were beginning to alarm the costumier, hard pressed as he was for time, was about to proceed when the door flew open and Lady Macbeth rushed in. As it happened, she was Iago's wife; so the costumier did not think it necessary to remind her that this was the gentlemen's dressing room. Besides, she was a person of exalted social station; and he was so afraid of her that he did not even venture to shut the door lest such an action might seem to imply a rebuke to her for leaving it open.

'I feel quite sure this dress is all wrong,' she said. 'They keep telling me I'm a perfect picture; but I dont feel a bit like Lady Macbeth.'

'Heaven forbid you should, madam!' said the costumier. 'We can change your appearance, but not your nature.'

'Nonsense!' said the lady: 'my nature changes with every new dress I put on. Goodness Gracious, whats that?' she exclaimed, as the bust chuckled approvingly.

'It's the bust,' said Iago. 'He talks like one o'clock. I really believe it's the old man himself.'

'Rubbish!' said the lady. 'A bust cant talk.'

A DRESSING ROOM SECRET

'Yes it can,' said Shakespear. '*I* am talking; and *I* am a bust.'

'But I tell you you cant,' said the lady; 'it's not good sense.'

'Well, stop me if you can,' said Shakespear. 'Nobody ever could in Bess's time.'

'Nothing will ever make me believe it,' said the lady. 'It's mere medieval superstition. But I put it to you, do I look in this dress as if I could commit a murder?'

'Dont worry about it,' said the Bard. 'You are another of my failures. I meant Lady Mac to be something really awful; but she turned into my wife, who never commited a murder in her life – at least not a quick one.'

'Your wife! Ann Hathaway!! Was she like Lady Macbeth?'

'Very', said Shakespear, with conviction. 'If you notice, Lady Macbeth has only one consistent characteristic, which is, that she thinks everything her husband does is wrong and that she can do it better. If I'd ever murdered anybody she'd have bullied me for making a mess of it and gone upstairs to improve on it herself. Whenever we gave a party, she apologized to the company for my behavior. Apart from that, I defy you to find any sort of sense in Lady Macbeth. I couldnt conceive anybody murdering a man like that. All I could do when it came to the point was just to brazen it out that she did it, and then give her a little touch of nature or two – from Ann – to make people believe she was real.'

'I am disillusioned, disenchanted, disgusted,' said the lady. 'You might at least have held your tongue about it until after the Ball.'

'You ought to think the better of me for it,' said the bust. 'I was really a gentle creature. It was so awful to be born about ten times as clever as anyone else – to like people and yet to have to despise their vanities and illusions. People are such fools, even the most likeable

A DRESSING ROOM SECRET

ones, as far as brains go. I wasnt cruel enough to enjoy my superiority.'

'Such conceit!' said the lady, turning up her nose.

'Whats a man to do?' said the Bard. 'Do you suppose I could go round pretending to be an ordinary person?'

'I believe you have no conscience,' said the lady. 'It has often been noticed.'

'Conscience!' cried the bust. 'Why, it spoilt my best character. I started to write a play about Henry V. I wanted to shew him in his dissolute youth; and I planned a very remarkable character, a sort of Hamlet sowing his wild oats, to be always with the Prince, pointing the moral and adorning the tale – excuse the anachronism: Dr Johnson, I believe: the only man that ever wrote anything sensible about me. Poins was the name of this paragon. Well, if youll believe me, I had hardly got well into the play when a wretched super whom I intended for a cowardly footpad just to come on in a couple of scenes to rob some merchant and then be robbed himself by the Prince and Poins – a creature of absolutely no importance – suddenly turned into a magnificent reincarnation of Silenus, a monumental comic part. He killed Poins; he killed the whole plan of the play. I revelled in him; wallowed in him; made a delightful little circle of disreputable people for him to move and shine in. I felt sure that no matter how my other characters might go back on me, he never would. But I reckoned without my conscience. One evening, as I was walking through Eastcheap with a young friend (a young man with his life before him), I passed a fat old man, half drunk, leering at a woman who ought to have been young but wasnt. The next moment my conscience was saying in my ear 'William: is this funny?' I preached at my young friend until he pretended he had an appointment and left me. Then I went home and spoilt the end of the play. I didnt do it well. I couldnt do it right. But I had to make that old man perish miserably; and I had to hang his wretched

A DRESSING ROOM SECRET

parasites or throw them into the gutter and the hospital. One should think before one begins things of this sort. By the way, would you mind shutting the door? I am catching cold.'

'So sorry,' said the lady. 'My fault.' And she ran to the door and shut it before the costumier could anticipate her.

Too late.

'I am going to sneeze,' said the bust; 'and I dont know that I can.'

With an effort it succeeded just a little in retracting its nostrils and screwing up its eyes. A fearful explosion followed. Then the bust lay in fragments on the floor.

It never spoke again.

DON GIOVANNI EXPLAINS

DON GIOVANNI EXPLAINS

THAT you may catch the full flavor of my little story I must tell you to begin with that I am a very pretty woman. If you think there is any impropriety in my saying so, then you can turn over to some of the other stories by people whose notions of womanly modesty are the same as your own. The proof of my prettiness is that men waste a good deal of time and money in making themselves ridiculous about me. And so, though I am only a provincial beauty, I know as much about courtship and flirtations as any woman of my age in the world, and can tell you beforehand, if you are a man of the sort I attract, exactly what you will say to me and how you will say it at our first, second, third, or what interview you please. I have been engaged rather often, and broke it off sometimes because I thought he wanted me to, and sometimes made him break it off by shewing him that I wanted him to. In the former case *I* was sorry: in the latter, *he* was; though, in spite of our feelings, the sense of relief at getting loose was generally equal on both sides.

I suppose you – whoever you are – now quite understand my character, or at least think you do. Well, you are welcome to flatter yourself. But let me tell you that flirtation is the one amusement I never went out of my way to seek, and never took any trouble to learn. I am fond of dress, dancing, and lawn tennis, just as you thought. I am also fond of good music, good books, botany, farming, and teaching children, just as you didnt think. And if I am better known about our place as a beauty and a flirt than as a botanist or a teacher, it is because nobody will admit that I have any other business in the world than to make a good marriage.

DON GIOVANNI EXPLAINS

The men, even the nicest of them, seek my society to gloat over my face and figure and not to exercise their minds. I used to like the sense of power being able to torture them gave me; but at last I saw that as they liked the torture just as children liked to be tickled, wielding my sceptre meant simply working pretty hard for their amusement. If it were not for the foolish boys, who dont gloat, but really worship me, poor fellows! and for a few thoroughgoing prigs who are always ready to botanize and to play the bass in pianoforte duet arrangements of Haydn's symphonies, I should count the hours I spend in male society the weariest of my life.

One evening in October, I heard by telegram from some friends in our provincial capital, twentyfive miles off by rail, that they had a box for the opera, with a place to spare for me. (In case you are a cockney, I may tell you that opera companies make tours through the provinces like other theatrical people, and are often a good deal better appreciated there than in London.) There was only just time to rush upstairs, make myself radiant, snatch a cup of tea, and catch the ten to seven train. I went by myself: if I were not able to go about alone, I should simply have to stay always in the house. My brothers have something else to do than to be my footmen; my father and mother are too old and quiet in their tastes to be dragged about to a girl's amusements or kept up to her late hours; and as to a maid, I have enough to do to take care of myself without having to take care of another grown-up woman as well. Besides, being in the train at our place is like being at home: all the guards on the line know us as well as they know their own families. So you need not hold up your hands at my fastness because I habitually go up to town by rail; drive to the theatre; find my friend's box there; drive back to the station; and – culminating impropriety! – come back at night by the half-past eleven train: all without chaperone or escort.

DON GIOVANNI EXPLAINS

The opera was Don Giovanni; and of course the performance was a wretched sell. Most operatic performances are – to those who know enough about music to read operas for themselves, as other people read Shakespear. The Don was a conceited Frenchman, with a toneless, dark, nasal voice, and such a tremolo that he never held a note steady long enough to let us hear whether it was in tune or not. Leporello was a podgy vulgar Italian buffo, who quacked instead of singing. The tenor, a reedy creature, left out Dall sua pace because he couldnt trust himself to get through it. The parts of Masetto and the Commendatore were doubled: I think by the call-boy. As to the women, Donna Anna was fat and fifty; Elvira was a tearing, gasping, 'dramatic' soprano, whose voice I expected to hear break across every time she went higher than F sharp; and Zerlina, a beginner on her trial trip, who finished Batti, batti and Vedrai carino with cadenzas out of the mad scene in Lucia, was encored for both in consequence. The orchestra was reinforced by local amateurs, the brass parts being played on things from the band of the 10th Hussars. Everybody was delighted; and when I said I wasnt, they said, 'Oh! youre so critical and so hard to please. Dont you think youd enjoy yourself far more if you were not so very particular.' The idea of throwing away music like Mozart's on such idiots!

When the call-boy and the Frenchman sank into a pit of red fire to the blaring of the 10th Hussars and the quacking of the podgy creature under the table, I got up to go, disgusted and disappointed, and wondering why people will pay extra prices to hear operas mutilated and maltreated in a way that nobody would stand with a modern comedy or Box and Cox. It was raining like anything when we got out; and we had to wait nearly ten minutes before a cab could be got for me. The delay worried me because I was afraid of losing the last train; and though I was a little soothed when I caught it with

DON GIOVANNI EXPLAINS

three minutes to spare, I was in no very high spirits when the guard locked me into a first class compartment by myself.

At first, I leant back in the corner and tried to sleep. But the train had gone only a little way out of the station when a fog signal went bang bang; and we stopped. Whilst I was waiting, broad awake and very cross, for us to go on again, a dreary rush of rain against the glass made me turn to the window, where, the night being pitchy dark, I saw nothing but the reflection of the inside of the carriage, including, of course, myself. And I never looked prettier in my life. I was positively beautiful. My first sensation was the pleasurable one of gratified vanity. Then came aggravation that it was all thrown away, as there was nobody in the carriage to look at me. In case you, superior reader, should be so plain that it has never been worth your while to study the subject of good looks, let me mention that even handsome people only look really lovely and interesting now and then. There are disappointing days when you are comparatively not worth looking at, and red-letter days when you are irresistible – when you cant look into your own eyes and face without emotion. But you are not like that every day: no quantity of soap and water, paint, powder, bothering about your hair, or dressing, will bring it. When it comes then life is worth living, except that it may happen, as it did with me just then, that you lose all the kudos through being in some out-of-the-way place, or alone, or with your family, who naturally dont concern themselves about your appearance. However, it made me happy enough to prevent my catching cold, as I generally do when I come home late out of humor.

At last there was a great clanking of coupling chains and clashing of buffers: meaning that a goods train was getting out of the way. We started with a jerk; and I settled myself in my corner with my face turned to the window, and had a good look as we went along. Mind: I did not close my eyes for a moment: I was as wide awake as I am now. I thought about a lot of things, the opera running through my head a good deal; and I remember it occurred to me that if Don Giovanni had met me, I might have understood him better than the other women did, and we two have hit it off together. Whether or no, I felt sure he could not have fooled me so easily as he did them, particularly if he had been like the Frenchman with the tremolo. Still, the real Don Giovanni might have been something very different; for experience has taught me that people who are much admired often get wheedled or persecuted into love affairs with persons whom they would have let alone if they themselves had been let alone.

I had got about thus far in my thoughts when I looked round – I dont know why; for I certainly had not the least idea that there was anybody or anything to see; and there, seated right opposite me, was a gentleman, wrapped in a cloak of some exquisitely fine fabric in an 'art shade' of Indian red, that draped perfectly, and would, I could see, wear a whole lifetime and look as nice as new at the end. He had on a superbly shaped cartwheel hat of beautiful black felt. His boots, which came to his knees, were of soft kid, the color of a ripening sloe: I never saw anything like them except a pair of shoes I once bought in Paris for forty francs, which were more like a baby's skin than leather. And to complete him, he had a sword with a guard of plain gold, but shaped so that it was a treasure and a delight to look at.

Why I should have taken all this in before it occurred to me to wonder how he came there, I cant tell; but it was so. Possibly, of course, he was coming from a fancy ball, and had got in while the train was at a standstill outside the station. But when I ventured to glance casually at his face – for I need hardly say that an experienced young woman does not begin by staring right into a man's eyes when she finds herself alone with him in a railway carriage – away went all notion of anything so silly as a fancy ball in connection with *him*. It was a steadfast, tranquil, refined face, looking over and beyond me into space. It made me feel unutterably small, though I remembered with humble thankfulness that I was looking my most spiritual. Then it struck me what nonsense it was: he was only a man. I had no sooner stirred up my baser nature, as it were, by thinking thus, than sudden horror seized me; and I believe I was on the point of making a frantic plunge at the communicator when a slight frown, as if I had disturbed him, shewed for the first time that he was aware of me.

'Pray be quiet,' he said, in a calm, fine voice, that suited his face exactly; and speaking – I noticed even then – with no more sense of my attractiveness than if I had been a naughty little girl of ten or twelve. 'You are alone. I am only what you call a ghost, and have not the slightest interest in meddling with you.'

'A ghost!' I stammered, trying to keep up my courage and pretend I didnt believe in ghosts.

'You had better convince yourself by passing your fan through my arm,' he said coldly, presenting his elbow to me, and fixing me with his eye.

My tongue clove to the roof of my mouth. It came into my head that if I did not do something to get over that moment of terror, my hair would turn grey; and nothing worse could well happen to me than that. I put my shut fan on his sleeve. It went right through as if his arm did not exist; and I screamed as if the fan were a knife going through my own flesh. He was deeply displeased, and said crushingly,

'Since I incommode you, I had better get into another carriage.' And I have no doubt he would have vanished there and then if I, actually trying to catch at his insubstantial cloak, had not said, almost crying,

DON GIOVANNI EXPLAINS

'Oh no, no: please dont. I *darent* stay here by myself after seeing you.'

He did not exactly smile; but he became a little more human in his manner, looking at me with something between pity and interest. 'I shall stay with you if it will save you any anxiety,' he said. 'But you must really conduct yourself like an educated lady, and not scream at me.'

The microscope has not yet been invented that can make visible any living creature smaller than I felt then. 'I beg your pardon, sir,' I said, abjectly: 'I am not used to it.' Then, to change the subject – for he had not taken the least notice of my apology – I added, 'It seems so strange that you should travel by rail.'

'Why?'

'No doubt it is not stranger, when one comes to think of it, than many things that are taken as a matter of course every day,' I said, trying feebly to shew him that I was really an educated lady. 'But couldnt you fly quicker – more quickly, I mean?'

'Fly!' he repeated gravely. 'Am I a bird?'

'No, sir; but I thought a ghost could – not exactly fly, but project itself – himself – yourself, I mean – through space somehow; and – that is, if you are conditioned by time and space.' No sooner were the words out than I felt frightfully priggish.

But priggishness seemed to suit him. He replied quite amiably, 'I am so conditioned. I can move from place to place – project myself, as you call it. But the train saves me the trouble.'

'Yes; but isnt it slower?'

'Having eternity at my disposal, I am not in a hurry.'

I felt that I was a fool not to have seen this. 'Of course,' I said. 'Excuse my stupidity.'

He frowned again, and shook out his cloak a little. Then he said, severely, 'I am willing to answer your questions, and help you to the fullest extent of my

199

DON GIOVANNI EXPLAINS

opportunities and information. But I must tell you that apologies, excuses, regrets, and needless explanations are tedious to me. Be good enough to remember that nothing that you can do can possibly injure, offend, or disappoint me. If you are stupid or insincere it will be useless for me to converse with you: that is all.'

When I had recovered a little from this snubbing, I ventured to say, 'Must I keep on asking you questions? There is a tradition that that is necessary with gho – with people from – with ladies and gentlemen from the other world.'

'The other world!' he said, surprised. 'What other world?'

I felt myself blushing, but did not dare to apologize.

'It is generally necessary to ask ghosts questions for this reason,' he said. 'They have no desire to converse with you; and even were it otherwise, they are not sufficiently in sympathy with you to be able to guess what would interest you. At the same time, as knowledge is the common right of all, no ghost who is not naturally a thief or a miser would refuse information to an inquirer. But you must not expect us to volunteer random conversation.'

'Why?' I said, growing a little restive under his cold superiority.

'Because I have not the slightest interest in making myself agreeable to you.'

'I am very sorry,' I said; 'but I cant think of anything to ask you. There are lots of things, if I could only recollect them. At least, the ones that come into my head seem so personal and unfeeling.'

'If they seem so to you after due consideration of my disembodiment, you are probably a fool,' he replied quietly and gently, like a doctor telling me something the matter with me.

'No doubt I am,' I said, my temper beginning to rise. 'However, if you dont choose to speak civilly, you can keep your information to yourself.'

'Mention when I offend you; and I shall endeavor to avoid doing so,' he said, not a bit put out. 'You had better ask your questions, bearing in mind that between a ghost of some centuries and a girl of twenty years there can be no question of manners.'

He was so adorably patient in his contempt for me that I caved in. Besides, I was four years older than he thought. 'I should like to know, please,' I said, 'who you are: that is, who you were; and whether it hurts much to die. I hope the subject is not a painful one. If so –'

He did not wait for the rest of my ridiculous apologetics. 'My experience of death was so peculiar,' he said, 'that I am really not an authority on the subject. I was a Spanish nobleman, much more highly evolved than most of my contemporaries, who were revengeful, superstitious, ferocious, gluttonous, intensely prejudiced by the traditions of their caste, brutal and incredibly foolish when affected by love, and intellectually dishonest and cowardly. They considered me eccentric, wanting in earnestness, and destitute of moral sense.'

I gasped, overpowered by his surprising flow of language.

'Though I was the last of the Tenario family, members of which had held official positions at court for many generations, I refused to waste my time as a titled lackey; and as my refusal was, according to the ideas of my time and class, extremely indecent, I was held to have disgraced myself. This troubled me very little. I had money, health, and was my own master in every sense. Reading, travelling, and adventure were my favorite pursuits. In my youth and early manhood, my indifference to conventional opinions, and a humorously cynical touch in conversation, gained me from censorious people the names atheist and libertine; but I was in fact no worse than a studious and rather romantic freethinker. On rare occasions, some woman would strike my young fancy; and I would worship her at a distance for a long time, never venturing to seek her acquaintance. If by accident I was thrown into her company, I was too timid, too credulous, too chivalrously respectful, to presume on what bystanders could plainly perceive to be the strongest encouragement; and in the end some more experienced cavalier would bear off the prize without a word of protest from me. At last a widow lady at whose house I sometimes visited, and of whose sentiments towards me I had not the least suspicion, grew desperate at my stupidity, and one evening threw herself into my arms and confessed her passion for me. The surprise, the flattery, my inexperience, and her pretty distress, overwhelmed me. I was incapable of the brutality of repulsing her; and indeed for nearly a month I enjoyed without scruple the pleasure she gave me, and sought her company whenever I could find nothing better to do. It was my first consummated love affair; and though for nearly two years the lady had no reason to complain of my fidelity, I found the romantic side of our intercourse, which seemed never to pall on her, tedious, unreasonable, and even forced and insincere except at rare moments, when the power of love made her beautiful, body and soul. Unfortunately, I had no sooner lost my illusions, my timidity, and my boyish curiosity about women, than I began to attract them irrestistibly. My amusement at this soon changed to dismay. I became the subject of fierce jealousies: in spite of my utmost tact there was not a married friend of mine with whom I did not find myself sooner or later within an ace of a groundless duel. My servant amused himself by making a list of these conquests of mine, not dreaming that I never took advantage of them, much less that my preference for young and unmarried admirers, on which he rallied me as far as he dared, was due to the fact that their innocence and shyness protected me from advances which many matrons of my acquaintance made without the least scruple as soon as they found that none were to be expected from me. I had repeatedly to extricate myself from disagreeable positions by leaving the neighborhood, a method of escape which my wandering habits made easy to me, but which, also, I fear, brought me into disrepute as a vagabond. In the course of time, my servant's foolish opinion of me began to spread; and I at last became reputed an incorrigible rake, in which character I was only additionally fascinating to the woman I most dreaded. Such a reputation grows, as it travels, like a snowball. Absurd stories about me became part of the gossip of the day. My family disowned me; and I had enough Spanish egotism left to disdain all advances towards reconciliation. Shortly afterwards I came actually under the ban of the law. A severely pious young lady, daughter of the Commandant at Seville, was engaged to a friend of mine. Full of what she had heard against me, she held me in the utmost horror; but this my friend, desiring to spare my feelings, concealed from me. One day, I unluckily conceived the idea of making the acquaintance of his future wife. Accordingly, presuming on a tie of blood between the Commandant's family and my own, I ventured on a visit. It was late in the evening when I was shewn into her presence; and in the twilight she mistook me for my friend and greeted me with an embrace. My remonstrances undeceived her; but instead of apologizing for her mistake, which I did not myself understand until afterwards, she raised an alarm, and, when her father arrived sword in hand, accused me of insulting her. The Commandant, without waiting for an explanation, made a determined attempt to murder me, and would assuredly have succeeded if I had not, in self defence, run him through the body. He has since confessed that he was in the wrong; and we are now very good friends; especially as I have never set up any claim to superiority as a swordsman on the strength of our encounter, but have admitted freely that I made a mere lucky thrust in the dark. However, not to anticipate, he died in less than five minutes after I hit him; and my servant and I had to take to our heels to avoid being killed by his household.

'Now, unluckily for me, his daughter was, even for a female Spanish Catholic, extraordinarily virtuous and vindictive. When the town councillors of Seville erected a fine equestrian statue to her father's memory, she, by a few well-placed presents, secured a majority on the council in support of a motion that one of the panels of the pedestal should bear an inscription to the effect that the Commandant was awaiting the vengeance of Heaven upon his murderer. She also raised such a hue and cry, and so hunted me from place to place, that the officers of justice repeatedly begged me to fly from their jurisdiction lest they should be compelled by her exertions and by public opinion to do their duty and arrest me, in spite of my social position. She also refused to marry my friend until I had expiated my crime, as she called it. Poor Ottavio, whose disposition was mild and reasonable, and who was by no means sorry to be rid of a short-tempered and arbitrary father-in-law, knew as well as possible that she was as much to blame as I. So, whilst in her presence he swore by all the saints never to sheathe his sword until it was red with my heart's blood, he privately kept me well informed of her proceedings, and, though he followed her about like a dog – for he was deeply in love – took care that our paths should not cross.

'At last my absurd reputation, my female admirers, and my Sevillian persecutors became so wearisome that I resolved to shake them all off at a blow by settling down as a respectable married man. In the hope that the women of Old Castile might prove less inconveniently susceptible than those of Andalusia, I went to Burgos, and there made the acquaintance of a young lady who was finishing her education at a convent. When I felt satisfied that she was a well-conducted girl with no special attachment to me or to anyone else, I married her. Tranquillity and leisure for study, not happiness, were my objects. But she no sooner discovered – by instinct, I believe – that I had not married her for love, and that I had no very high opinion of her intellect, than she became insanely jealous. Only those who have been watched by a jealous spouse can imagine how intolerable such espionage is. I endured it without word or sign; and she of course discovered nothing. Then she began to torture herself by making inquiries among friends who had correspondents in Seville; and their reports wrought her jealousy to a point at which it became apparent to me that, as she said, I was killing her. One day she so far broke through a certain restraint which my presence put upon her as to say that if I did not either confess my infidelities or prove to her that I loved her, she should die. Now I had nothing to confess; and, as to my loving her, nothing short of my extreme reluctance to mortify any person could have enabled me to conceal the extent to which by this time she wearied me. Clearly there was nothing to be done but to decamp. I had sent away my servant some time before to please her, because she had suspected him of carrying messages between me and my imaginary mistresses; but he was still in my pay, and quite ready to resume our wanderings, since he had himself been brought to the verge of marriage by some foolish intrigue. On receiving a message from me, he came to our house; continued to make my wife suspect that I had an assignation in the cathedral that afternoon; and, whilst she was watching for me there, packed up my pistols with a change of linen, and joined me before sundown on the road to Seville. From Burgos to Seville is a hundred Spanish leagues as the crow flies; and, as there were no railways in those days, I did not believe that my wife could follow me so far, even if she guessed my destination.

'When I turned my horse's head south, Burgos seemed – as indeed it was – a gloomy, iron-barred den of bigots: Seville, fairyland. We arrived safely; but I soon found that my old luck had deserted me. Some time after our journey, I saw a lady in the street apparently in distress. On going to her assistance, I discovered that she was my wife. When she demanded an explanation of my flight, I was at my wit's end, seeing how brutal and how incomprehensible to her must be the naked truth. In desperation, I referred her to my servant, and slipped away the moment he had engaged her attention. Now no sooner was my back turned than, fearful lest a reconciliation between us might lead to his being compelled to return with me to Burgos, the rascal shewed her his old list of my conquests, including 1003 in Spain alone, and many others in countries which I had never visited. Elvira, who would never believe any true statement concerning me, accepted the obviously impossible thousand and three conquests with eager credulity. The list contained the names of six women who had undoubtedly been violently in love with me, and some fifteen to whom I had paid a compliment or two. The rest was a fabrication, many of the names having been copied from the account books of my servant's father, a wine shop keeper.

'When Leporello had made as much mischief as possible between me and my wife, he got rid of her simply by running away. Meanwhile, I had retreated to a house of mine in the country, where I tried to amuse myself by mixing with the peasantry. Their simplicity at first interested, but soon saddened me. My ill luck, too, pursued me. One day, walking upon the village common, I came upon the Commandant's daughter, still in deep mourning, which became her very ill, with poor Ottavio at her heels. Fortunately she did not recognize me in the open daylight; and I might have got away with a polite speech or two and a private exchange

DON GIOVANNI EXPLAINS

of signals with Ottavio, had not my wife appeared, from the clouds, as it seemed – and began to abuse me quite frantically. Had she exercised a little self-control, she might have betrayed me at the first word to Ottavio's betrothed, Doña Aña. But she was quite out of her senses; and I simply said so, whereupon she rushed away raving, and I after her. Once away from Aña, and knowing that I could do no good to Elvira, I went home as fast as I could. I had invited my peasant acquaintances to a dance that evening, the occasion being a wedding between a couple of my tenants who were having a very pleasant party at the expense of my carpets, my furniture, and my cellar. But for this I should have left the place forthwith. As it was I resolved to leave early next morning. Meanwhile, there was nothing for it but to change my dress and receive my guests as pleasantly as possible. They were noisy and clumsy enough after their first strangeness wore off; but my attention was very soon taken from them by the entrance of three masked strangers, in whom I instantly recognized my wife, Aña, and Ottavio. Of course I, pretending that I did not know them, made them welcome, and kept up the dancing. Ottavio presently managed to send me a note to say that Aña had suddenly recollected my voice and had sought out and talked over her grievances with Elvira. They had become fast friends, and had insisted on coming to my party in masks in order to denounce me to my guests. He had not been able to dissuade them; and all he could suggest was that if I saw my way to making a rush to get clear, he would put himself forward as my opponent and play into my hands as far as he dared with Aña's eye on him.

'I was by this time at the end of my patience. I bade Leporello get my pistols and keep them in his pocket. I then joined the dancers, taking for my partner the peasant bride, whom I had before rather avoided, as the bridegroom was inclined to be jealous, and she had

DON GIOVANNI EXPLAINS

shewn some signs of succumbing to the infernal fascination which I still, in spite of myself, exercised. I tried to dance a minuet with her; but that was a failure. Then we went into another circle and tried to waltz. This was also beyond her rustic skill; but when we joined in a country dance, she acquitted herself so vigorously that I soon had to find her a seat in one of the smaller rooms. I noticed that my two fair maskers watched our retirement in great excitement. Turning then to the girl, and speaking to her for the first time *en grand seigneur*, I bade her do instantly whatever she was told. Then I went to the door; closed it; and waited. Presently Leporello hurried in, and begged me, for Heaven's sake, to take care what I did, as my proceedings were being commented on outside. I told him sternly to give the girl a piece of money as a reward for obeying my orders. When he had done so, I said to her peremptorily: "Scream, scream like the devil." She hesitated; but Leporello, seeing that I was not to be trifled with, pinched her arm; and she screamed like not one but a thousand devils. Next moment the door was broken in by the bridegroom and his friends; and we all struggled out with a great hubbub into the saloon. But for Ottavio, who, assuming the leadership, flourished his sword and lectured me, they might have plucked up courage to attack me. I told him that if the girl was hurt it was Leporello's doing. At this the storm of menace and denunciation rose to such a pitch that for a moment I nearly lost my head. When I recovered I wholly lost my temper; drew on them; and would certainly have done mischief but for the persistence with which Ottavio kept in front of me. Finally Leporello produced the pistols; and we got to the door, when he ran for his life. After a moment's consideration I followed his example, and we both took horses at the nearest posthouse, and reached Seville in safety.

'For some time after that, I lived in peace. One

evening my wife descried me from a window; but, after a soft word or two, I got rid of her by wrapping Leporello in my cloak and palming him off on her as myself. As she was, like most jealous women, far too egotistical to suspect that I avoided her simply because she was disagreeable, she spread a report that I had sent her off with Leporello so that I might court her maid in her absence: a statement for which there was no foundation whatever, but which was very generally believed.

'I now come to the curious incident which led to my death. That very evening, Leporello, having escaped from my wife, rejoined me in the square close by the statue of the Commandant, of which I have spoken in connection with the inscription and the Town Council. In the course of our conversation, I happened to laugh. Immediately, to my astonishment, the Commandant, or rather his statue, complained that I was making an unbecoming disturbance. Leporello, who heard him distinctly, was terrified beyond measure; so that I at last, disgusted by his cowardice, forced him to approach the statue and read the inscription, much as I have often forced a shying horse to go up to the object of his apprehension. But the inscription did not reassure the poor fellow; and when, to give the affair a whimsical aspect, I pretended to insist on his inviting the statue home to supper with us, he tried to persuade me that the stone man had actually bowed his head in assent. My curiosity was now greatly excited. I watched the statue carefully, and deliberately asked whether it would come to supper. It said "Yes" in a strange stone throated voice, but did not thank me, which was the more surprising as the Commandant had been of the old school, punctilious in etiquette. I grew alarmed as to the state of my health; for it seemed to me that I must be going mad, or else, since Leporello had heard the voice also, that I was dreaming. I could think of only two possible explanations. We had both fasted since the

DON GIOVANNI EXPLAINS

middle of the day, and were hungry enough, perhaps, to have illusions and infect one another with them. Or someone might have played a trick on us. I determined to satisfy myself on that point by returning next day and examining the place closely. In the meantime, however, we hurried home and fell to supper with a will. Presently, to my utter dismay, my wife rushed in, and, instead of the usual reproaches, made a rambling appeal to me to change my way of life. I first spoke kindly to her, and then tried to laugh her out of her hysterical anxiety. This only made her indignant; and in the end she ran out, but presently came back screaming and fled in the direction of the kitchen. Leporello, who had gone to see whether anything outside had alarmed her, returned panic stricken. He gasped out something about the statue, as I understood him; and tried to lock the door. Then came a loud stolid knocking. It occurred to me that the house was on fire, and the watchman come to give the alarm; for indeed no one on earth but a watchman could have given such a knock. I opened the door, and found the statue standing on the mat. At this my nerves gave way: I recoiled speechless. It followed me a pace or two into the room. Its walk was a little bandy, from the length of time it had been seated on horseback; and its tread shook the house so that at every step I expected the floor to give way and land it in the basement – and indeed I should not have been sorry to get it out of my sight even at the cost of a heavy bill for repairs. There was no use in asking it to sit down: not a chair in the place could have borne its weight. Without any loss of time, it began talking in a voice that vibrated through and through me. I had invited it to supper, it said; and there it was. I could say no less than that I was delighted; and so, with an apology for having sat down without waiting, I told Leporello to lay the table afresh, rather wondering at the same time what a solid stone thing could eat. It then said it would not trouble us,

DON GIOVANNI EXPLAINS

but would entertain me at supper if I had the courage to come with it. Had I not been frightened, I should have politely declined. As it was, I defiantly declared that I was ready to do anything and go anywhere. Leporello had disappeared; but I could hear his teeth chattering under the table. The thing then asked for my hand, which I gave, still affecting to bear myself like a hero. As its stone hand grasped mine, I was seized with severe headache, with pain in the back, giddiness, and extreme weakness. I perspired profusely, and, losing my power of co-ordinating my movements, saw double, and reeled like a man with locomotor ataxy. I was conscious of fearful sights and sounds. The statue seemed to me to be shouting "Aye, aye" in an absurd manner; and I, equally absurdly, shouted "No, no" with all my might, deliriously fancying that we were in the English house of Parliament, which I had visited once in my travels. Suddenly the statue stepped on a weak plank; and the floor gave way at last. I had sunk about twentyfive feet when my body seemed to plunge away from me into the centre of the universe. I gave a terrible gasp as it went, and then found myself dead, and in hell.'

Here he paused for the first time. My hair had been trying to stand on end for the last five minutes. I would have given anything for courage to scream or throw myself out of the carriage. But I only stammered an inquiry as to what the place he had mentioned was like.

'If I speak of it as a place at all,' he replied, 'I only do so in order to make my narrative comprehensible, just as I express myself to you phenomenally as a gentleman in hat, cloak, and boots, although such things are no part of the category to which I belong. Perhaps you do not follow me.'

'Oh, perfectly,' I said. 'I am fond of reading metaphysics.'

'Then I must leave you to reach the answer to your own question by a series of abstractions, the residue of

DON GIOVANNI EXPLAINS

which you will have an opportunity of verifying by experience. Suffice it to say that I found society there composed chiefly of vulgar, hysterical, brutish, weak, good-for-nothing people, all well intentioned, who kept

up the reputation of the place by making themselves and each other as unhappy as they were capable of being. They wearied and disgusted me; and I disconcerted them beyond measure. The Prince of Darkness is not a gentleman. His knowledge and insight are very

remarkable as far as they go; but they do not go above
the level of his crew. He kept up a certain pretence of
liking my company and conversation; and I was polite
to him, and did what I could to prevent him from feeling
his inferiority. Still I felt that the cordiality of our
relations was a strain on us both. One day a companion
of his came to me, and, professing that he respected me
too much to connive at my being ill spoken of behind
my back, told me that the Prince had publicly said that
my coming to the place was all a mistake, and that he
wished I would go to heaven and be blest. This was very
strong language; and I went at once to the Prince, and
told him what I had heard. He first said, in a coarse
conversational style which always grated on me, that my
informant was a liar; but on my refusing to accept that
explanation he sulkily apologized, and assured me, first,
that he had only wished me to go to heaven because he
honestly thought – though he confessed he could not
sympathize with my taste – that I should be more
comfortable there; and, second, that my coming into his
set really was a mistake, as the Commandant, whom he
described as a silly old Portland-stone son of a gun, had
misled them concerning my character; and so, he said,
they had let me through at the wrong end. I asked him
by what right then did he detain me. He answered that
he did not detain me at all, and demanded whether
anybody or anything did or could prevent me from
going where I pleased. I was surprised, and asked him
further why, if hell was indeed Liberty Hall, all the
devils did not go to heaven. I can only make his reply
intelligible to you by saying that the devils do not go
for exactly the same reason that your English betting
men do not frequent the Monday Popular Concerts,
though they are as free to go to them as you are. But the
Devil was good enough to say that perhaps heaven would
suit me. He warned me that the heavenly people were
unfeeling, uppish, precise, and frightfully dry in their

conversation and amusements. However, I could try them; and if I did not like them, I could come back. He should always be glad to see me, though I was not exactly the sort of person the Commandant had led him to expect. He added that he had been against the statue business from the first, as people were growing out of that sort of tomfoolery; and to go on with it in the world at this time of day was simply to make hell ridiculous. I agreed with him, and bade him adieu. He was relieved at the prospect of my departure; but still he had sufficient hankering after my good opinion to ask me not to be too hard on them down there. They had their faults, he said; but, after all, if I wanted real heart and feeling and sentiment, honest, wholesome robust humor, and harmless love of sport, I should have to come to them for it. I told him frankly that I did not intend to come back, and that he was far too clever not to know that I was right. He seemed flattered; and we parted on friendly terms. His vulgarity jarred every fibre in me; but he was quite honest in it, and his popularity was not wholly undeserved.

'Since then, I have travelled more than is usual with persons in my condition. Among us, the temptation to settle down once the congenial circle is found, is almost irresistible. A few, however, still find that a circle perfectly congenial to them has yet to be established. Some of these – myself for example – retain sufficient interest in the earth to visit it occasionally. We are regarded as rather eccentric on that account: in fact, ghosts are the lunatics of what you just now called the other world. With me it is a mere hobby and one that I do not often indulge. I have now answered your question as to who I was, and whether it hurt me to die. Are you satisfied?'

'It is very kind of you, I'm sure, to take so much trouble,' I said, suddenly realizing that he had told me all this from a sense of duty, because I asked for it. 'I should like to know what became of Doña Aña and the others.'

'She nursed Ottavio through a slight illness with such merciless assiduity that he died of it, a circumstance he did not afterwards regret. She put on fresh mourning, and made a feature of her bereavements until she was past forty, when she married a Scotch presbyterian and left Spain. Elvira, finding it impossible to get into society after her connection with me, went back to her convent for a while. Later on she tried hard to get married again; but somehow she did not succeed: I do not know why; for she was a pretty woman. Eventually she had to support herself by giving lessons in singing. The peasant girl, whose name I forget, became famous in a small way for her skill as a laundress.'

'Her name was Zerlina, was it not?'

'Very likely it was; but pray how do you know that?'

'By tradition. Don Giovanni di Tenario is quite well remembered still. There is a very great play, and a very great opera, all about you.'

'You surprise me. I should like to witness a performance of these works. May I ask do they give a fair representation of my character?'

'They represent that women used to fall in love with you.'

'Doubtless; but are they particular in pointing out that I never fell in love with them – that I earnestly endeavored to recall them to a sense of their duty, and inflexibly resisted their advances? Is that made quite clear?'

'No, sir, I am afraid not. Rather the opposite, I think.'

'Strange! how slander clings to a man's reputation. And so I, of all men, am known and execrated as a libertine.'

'Oh, not execrated, I assure you. You are very popular. People would be greatly disappointed if they knew the truth.'

'It may be so. The wives of my friends, when I refused to elope with them, and even threatened to tell their husbands if they did not cease to persecute me, used to call me a fish and a vegetable. Perhaps you sympathize with them.'

'No,' I said. Then – I dont know what possessed me; but of course it was not the same with him as with ordinary men – I put out my hand, and said, 'You were right: they were not true women. If they had known what was due to themselves, they would never have made advances to a man; but I – I – I love –' I stopped, paralysed by the spreading light in his astonished eyes.

'Even to my ghost!' he exclaimed. 'Do you not know, señorita, that young English ladies are not usually supposed to make uninvited declarations to strange gentlemen in railway carriages at night?'

'I know all about it; and I dont care. Of course I should not say it if you were not a ghost. I cant help it. If you were real, I would walk twenty miles to get a glimpse of you; and I would *make* you love me in spite of your coldness.'

'Exactly what they used to say to me! Word for word, except that they said it in Spanish! Stay: you are going to put your arms timidly about my neck; ask me whether I do not love you a very little; and have a quiet little cry on my chest. It is useless: my neck and chest are part of the dust of Seville. Should you ever do it to one of your contemporaries, remember that your weight, concentrated on the nape of a tall man's neck, will fatigue him more than he will admit.'

'Thank you: I had no such intention. One question more before the train stops. Were you as sure of your fascination when you were alive as you are now?'

'Conceited, they used to call it. Not naturally: I was born a shy man. But repeated assurances confirmed me in a favorable opinion of my attractions, which, I beg you to recollect, only embittered my existence.'

The train stopped; and he rose and walked through the wood and glass of the door. I had to wait for the guard to unlock it. I let down the window, and made a bid for a last word and look from him.

'Adieu, Don Giovanni!' I said.

'Lively young English lady, adieu. We shall meet again, within eternity.'

I wonder whether we shall, some day. I hope so.

1 August 1887

BEAUTY'S DUTY

BEAUTY'S DUTY

In a solicitor's private office. A client is stamping up and down. Both are youngish men.

CLIENT. No, Arthur: a separation. I'll put up with it no longer.

SOLICITOR. Listen to me, Horace.

CLIENT. I wont listen to you. I wont listen to anybody. My wife and I have come to the parting of the ways.

SOLICITOR. But, my dear Horace, you have nothing against her.

CLIENT. Nothing against her. Nothing ag –

SOLICITOR. I tell you, nothing. You dont complain of her temper: you dont complain of her housekeeping: you dont complain of anything except that she makes you jealous.

CLIENT. I'm not jealous. But if I could stoop to such a feeling, I should have cause for it.

SOLICITOR. Look here, Horace. If you have cause for a separation on that ground, you have cause for a divorce.

CLIENT. I am perfectly willing to be divorced – I mean to divorce her. But you keep telling me I cant.

SOLICITOR. Neither can you. You dont allege misconduct: but allege talk. Talk isnt good enough.

CLIENT. You mean it isnt bad enough. That shews how little you know about it.

SOLICITOR [*out of patience*] O well then, have it your own way. What do you complain of?

CLIENT. Whats that to you?

SOLICITOR. To me! Why, man, Ive got to tackle your wife here in this room this very morning, and explain to her that you are determined to separate from her. Do you suppose I am going to do that without giving her a reason?

CLIENT. I dont mind telling you this. No other man would have stood –

SOLICITOR. Thats no good. What did you stand? You neednt have any delicacy about telling me. Thats what I'm for. You pay a solicitor for the privilege of telling him all your most private affairs. Just forget that we're old friends, and remember only that I'm your solicitor. Besides, you will tell me nothing that I havnt been told fifty times by husbands sitting in that chair. Dont suppose youre the only man in the world that doesnt get on with his wife.

CLIENT. I bet you what you like youve never heard of a case like mine before.

SOLICITOR. I shall be able to judge of that when you tell me what your case is.

CLIENT. Well, look here. Did you ever hear of a woman coming to her husband and saying that Nature had gifted her with such an extraordinary talent for making people fall in love with her that she considered it a sin not to exercise it.

SOLICITOR. But she has you to make fall in love with her.

CLIENT. Yes: but she's done that; and she says it's so nice, and has improved me so much that she wants to do it again and improve somebody else. She says it's like a genius for bringing up children. The women who have that, she says, keep schools. They are so good at it that they have to be unfaithful to their own children and run after other people's, she says. And in just the same way, she maintains, a woman with a genius for improving men by love ought to improve them by the dozen. What do you think of that?

SOLICITOR [*rather taken with the idea*] Theres something in that, you know.

CLIENT. What!

SOLICITOR. I mean of course, logically. It's improper; but it makes good sense. I wonder whats the proper answer to it?

CLIENT. Thats what she says.

SOLICITOR. Oh. And what do you say to her?

CLIENT. I tell her that the proper answer to it is that she ought to be ashamed of herself.

SOLICITOR. Does that do any good?

CLIENT. No.

SOLICITOR. Has she ceased to care for you?

CLIENT. No. She says she will practise on me to keep her hand in; but that she is getting tired of me and must have some new interest in life. Now what do you say to your paragon?

SOLICITOR. My paragon! Have I said a word in her defence?

CLIENT. Have you said a word in mine?

SOLICITOR. But dont you see what the consequences will be if you separate? You will lose all control over her; and then there will be a divorce.

CLIENT. I havnt any control over her at present.

The Junior Clerk enters.

JUNIOR CLERK. A lady to see you, sir. [*With emotion*] She is a very beautiful lady. Oh, sir, if she is in any trouble, will you help her. If she is accused, do not believe a word against her. I'll stake my life on her innocence.

SOLICITOR [*almost speechless*] Well – ! Really, Mr Guppy! [*Recovering himself a little*] What name?

JUNIOR CLERK. I forgot to ascertain her name, sir.

SOLICITOR. Perhaps you will be so kind as to repair that omission.

JUNIOR CLERK. I hardly dare ask her, sir. It will seem a profanation. But I think - I hope - she will forgive me. [*He goes out*].

CLIENT. It's my wife. She's been trying it on that young lunatic.

STILL AFTER THE DOLL'S HOUSE

*A sequel to Walter Besant's sequel
to Henrik Ibsen's play
(From Time, February 1890)*

THE AUTHOR'S APOLOGY

I hope I need not apologize for assuming that the readers of this story are familiar with Ibsen's epoch-making play A Doll's House, which struck London in the year 1889 and gave Victorian domestic morality its death-blow.

Unfortunately I cannot claim an equal renown for the sequel written by the late Sir Walter Besant in the sincere belief that he was vindicating that morality triumphantly against a most misguided Norwegian heretic. Nor may I reproduce it here, as the copyright does not belong to me. And I am sorry to say I do not remember a word of it, and can only infer its incidents from the allusions in my own sequel to it.

I am therefore as much in the dark as my readers: a poor excuse, but the best I have to offer.

G. B. S.

1931

STILL AFTER
THE DOLL'S HOUSE

NORA did not drive on to the station. Her instinct forbade her to run away from her daughter's death and Christine's tongue. She told the driver at once to turn back to the house she had just left; and then she delivered herself up to deepening, spreading, glowing, burning indignation, that rose in her as she began to realize how possible it was for such people as the Krogstads to bring down their own detestable atmosphere of dread and darkness about a lonely and sensitive girl, until she was driven to kill herself to escape from it. Nora knew that they could not help it – that her resentment could only make them worse and make her worse. By this time, indeed, she had lost all relish for resentment and for the Dutch courage which it gives: she no longer needed to remind herself homiletically that it was bitter and poisonous: it *tasted* so, and she loathed it. Yet she was a woman with an ardent temper; and there were times when the shock of some heartbreaking injustice roused that temper and

STILL AFTER THE DOLL'S HOUSE

made her ireful in spite of her earned wisdom. When she alighted from the carriage, there was a gentleman turning away reluctantly from her door. He would hardly have been recognized at the bank in his heavy shapeless cape and broad-brimmed hat; but she knew him: he always came to her in disguise.

'Krogstad!' she said angrily. Then, with a touching effort to speak kindly, 'What are you doing here?'

'They have just told me you were gone,' he said anxiously. 'They said you had left the town.' He checked himself, and added, suspiciously, 'Perhaps you told them to say that to prevent my troubling you again.'

'Even if I had,' she said, 'you ought to believe in yourself too much to suspect such a thing. I intended to go; but I changed my mind on my way to the train, and turned back. Something happened. Go upstairs: I must explain to Fru Krogh that I shall keep on my rooms.'

Krogstad obeyed the moment the door was opened. He was uneasy under the eyes of the cabman, the servant, and Fru Krogh, who came out, all wonder and inquiry. A maid went up with him to light the gas; and he stood with his back to her, pretending to examine the bookshelf whilst she drew the curtains and remade the expiring fire in the stove. When she was gone he put off the cape, and became the respectable banker again, as far as his coat was concerned. But his manner was furtive and submissive: he prowled about the room, and smoothed his clean-shaven lip with the back of his thumb, as if there was a moustache there to settle.

When Nora came in, he brightened, and helped her officiously to get her long travelling coat off. She was a little impatient of his assistance; and he, feeling this, shrank just an eighth of an inch into himself.

'Krogstad,' she said: 'if you dont want to get hurt and humiliated, you had better go away. I am out of temper with you and yours this evening.' Poor Krogstad dejectedly stretched out his hand towards his hat. 'Still, if you dont mind suffering for my sake, I wish you would stay. I must talk to somebody.'

Krogstad beamed. 'You are really glad to see me!' he said. 'I am always so afraid of inflicting myself on you. You may say what you like to me: you know that. I only wish you would allow me the same liberty.'

'Well, I am not very hard on you, Krogstad. I only forbid one subject – your wife; and you know very well that it does you no good to abuse her. I allowed you to do it until I got quite tired of defending her, not very sincerely, perhaps, because you know I dont like her. Sit down.' She threw herself into a rocking chair near the stove with more of her old buoyancy than most women retain on the brink of fifty; and he took a chair and sat leaning forward and looking at her with his elbows on his knees and his laced fingers down between his straightly trousered calves.

'I never abused her to anybody except you,' he said. 'I know what I owe her. She has made me respectable and kept me respectable. Oh yes,' he urged, catching a satirical twinkle in her glance at his rueful air, 'I know that you dont think much of respectability; but it is a great deal to a man who began life with a false step, as you know I did. Respectability might be a come-down for a genius like you; but if I were not respectable I should be something worse, like Helmer, instead of something better. And I owe that to her. Besides, look at the boys. As I was saying only this morning' – here Krogstad, again meeting her eye, flinched perceptibly – 'I have four sons. The eldest is a professor at the university, in great esteem; the second a lawyer, in good practice; the third an officer of engineers, honorably considered; the fourth stays in the bank, to follow my footste –' ...

He faltered and broke down; for she was shaking her head at him in pitiful reproach.

'The eldest, Nils,' she said quietly, when the silence

was exhausted, 'is a professor of philosophy; and in philosophy he is, by his private convictions, what used to be called a Hegelian of the extreme left – I dont know what the newest name for that is. Hegelians of the extreme left regard orthodox Bible worship just as orthodox Bible worshippers regard African fetishism. If your eldest son dared to avow his opinions or to countenance those who dare avow them, he would lose his chair, his income, his position, and the 'great esteem' you boast of. He is greatly esteemed because he is a hypocrite, setting an example of hypocrisy to our young university students. Your second, the lawyer, is said to be in good practice because, instead of helping poverty to fight injustice in the courts, he is doing the dirty work of rich families, flattering them, voting for them, sharing the social plunder with them. Your officer of engineers is honorably considered because he is careful to flourish the Gospel of Peace in his left hand whilst he twirls the crank of a machine gun with his right. And Nils the Second, if he follows in his father's footsteps, will follow them clandestinely to the door of the woman at whom he publicly holds up his hands in pious horror.'

'I always try to say as little about you as I can,' protested Krogstad weakly. 'I stood up for you the other day at the Board meeting, when they got talking about you over young Robert's goings on.'

'Yes, my dear Nils: you said that I had been one of the best of wives and mothers in the days when I was respectable; and that you never could understand how I came to behave as I did. And when Heyerdahl asked you point-blank whether you would allow young Nils to come to one of my Thursday evenings, you shook your head in the most edifying way and said, Of course not.'

Krogstad made a trembling bite at his pale lip. 'What could I have done? What good would it have been to you if I had injured myself and injured the boy by saying anything but what I was expected to say? Besides, if they

STILL AFTER THE DOLL'S HOUSE

knew that I came here, they would not understand: they would think –'

'Very naturally, too, since you are ashamed of your visits. But if you intend never to do anything that mean people are likely to misunderstand, you will have to level down your life to their meanness. By the bye, do you really believe that they dont know?'

Krogstad sat up straight. 'What do you mean?' he exclaimed. 'Know! I should be ruined if they knew. I hope you never –'

Again he checked himself and looked at her with rising suspicion. 'How did *you* find out what I said to Heyerdahl?'

'Oh, I have friends everywhere – sneaks, I admit, but still friends. And you have envious enemies everywhere.'

Krogstad's brows knitted with a sense of injury. 'And you encourage them, and let them talk about me,' he said.

'Have you not yet found out that there is no exemption from trial by talk? I like to hear about you: the friendly ear is an antidote to the envious mouth. Now tell me the truth about that Board of Directors, Nils. You know that Herr Solicitor Heyerdahl has made his money during the promotion boom of the last six years by sharing spoils with certain brokers in a way that would lead to his being struck off the rolls if anybody were interested in proving the collusion. Do you ever allude to that in speaking to him?'

'Good Lord, no, of course not.'

'Then there is Arnoldson, whose second boy is a hopeless drunkard. You dont visit the sins of the children on the parent by ever pretending to know anything about that, do you?'

'Not when Arnoldson is present, poor fellow. It's not his fault. You would like Arnoldson, Nora, if you knew him. He is not bad hearted, I assure you.'

Nora did not turn aside to discuss Arnoldson's

amiability. 'And Sverdrup?' she continued. 'His father was a barber; and his brutality to his servants and his insolence to his poor relations are notorious. Johansen's wife beats him. Falk's wife ought to beat him, according to his own notions of justice, because he keeps a second house which nobody ever mentions to her. Have you ever remonstrated with Sverdrup, or condoled with Johansen? Do you intend to cut Falk for his immoral conduct?'

'Certainly not,' said Krogstad. 'I have nothing to do with their private affairs. The world could not get on if people set up that sort of censorship over one another. We have to fight shy of Johansen, because one cannot very well ask him without his wife; and one never knows what she will do or say next.'

'Does Christine ever lecture them as she used to lecture me?'

'Catch her at it!' said Krogstad, his frown returning. 'They would soon shew her the door.'

Nora looked at him for a moment with an almost roguish light in her wise old eyes. He leant forward again, and stared glumly at her feet, which Christine was wont to condemn as unbecomingly large.

'Nils,' she said at last: 'youre a great fool.'

'Why?' said Nils, raising his voice – much as an irresolute worm might turn.

'Not to see that your acquaintance with me, and your visits here, are just as well known in the Board room as Heyerdahl's illicit brokerage, Arnoldson's son's drunkenness, Sverdrup's sham family pretensions and the rest of it. They never mention me to you; just as you never mention their cupboard skeletons to them. You think you see through them and that they dont see through you. Each of you thinks the same; and so you all get on very smoothly together. But do you know, Nils, that whenever you get an attack of your lumbago, I always learn the news by people asking me how you are.'

'And you!' exclaimed Krogstad, thunderstruck. 'Do you pretend to know?'

'I generally do not know. I have to say that you have not called on me for a fortnight or a month, or whatever the time may be.'

Krogstad stood up, and buttoned his coat slowly. 'Nora,' he said: 'this is treachery: I cant pass it over. If you knew what a relief these visits have been to me; and how they have helped me to keep up appearances between times, you would, I think, have been more considerate. Goodbye.'

'That is just what I suspected, Nils,' she said, unmoved. 'Nothing makes sin easier than an occasional auricular confession to relieve the conscience and clear the slate for a fresh score. I have noticed for some time that you always come to me when you have done something specially mean. You forgot that your confessor was not sworn to secrecy. I have an inkling of what you have on your mind this time. Oh, not what you said to Heyerdahl: nonsense, Krogstad: you ought to know better than that. I mean about my daughter Emmy. Come: sit down and make a clean breast of it. How did it all happen?'

Krogstad did not sit down. He stood up stiffly, only condescending to an exculpatory sweep apart of his hands and shrug of his shoulders. 'I simply explained to her that her engagement to marry Nils was out of the question. Since you insist on my telling you the truth, Robert has committed forgery.' There was a pause: then he reddened suddenly and snapped at her with the words 'as you did.'

'As I did! Then I do not blame him. Whom did he forge to save?'

'Not to save anyone. He forged to get money for himself, I suppose.'

'Ah Nils, Nils, Nils!' she said, with – as yet – nothing but pure kindness for him. 'And yet you say "as I did." '

'I beg your pardon,' said Krogstad sulkily. 'I should have said "as I myself did." But you have upset me: I wish you hadnt talked about my visits here. Of course you had a right to: I know that.'

'And did you do over again to Emmy what you did to me twenty years ago? Did you take that forged bill in your hand, and tell her that you would fight for your respectability as for life itself, and that she must choose between saving your respectability and bringing disgrace and ruin on one she loved?' Krogstad tried to protest; but there was in his eye a confession that lit up a flame in hers. 'If you did,' she said vehemently, 'all Christine's pains to reform you are lost. Once a scoundrel, always a scoundrel!'

His cheeks reddened like those of a young man. 'I could not let Nils disgrace himself,' he said, with anguish in his voice. 'On my soul I was not thinking of myself so much as of him and the other boys. You dont know what a position like mine is. And I did not threaten her – did not take that tone at all. I appealed to her. It was her own act: she consented freely – quite freely.'

'I hope you did not omit to pat her on the head for being a good and brave girl, and to assure her that she would be rewarded in Heaven.'

'You are repeating my words,' he cried. 'She has been with you: it was she who turned you back on your journey.'

'What!' said Nora, astonished. 'Have you not heard?'

'Heard what?'

'She has drowned herself.'

Krogstad turned white; and a greenish ray travelled slowly down his jaw. Then, with a sickly effort, he got to a chair; collapsed into it; and laid his head and arms on the table. Nora could only look compassionately at him and wait. Presently he raised his face, but only for a moment, to ask whether she had any brandy in the house. She had none; but she went downstairs and borrowed a glass from Fru Krogh. When she came back with it, he was sitting up, staring hard at the table. He would not look at the brandy; and she did not press it on him.

'I never thought – I never dreamt that such a thing was likely or even possible,' he said at last, in shaken tones. She was about to answer; but he checked her with an appeal for mercy. 'Dont say anything: what good can it do now?' But she had no sooner acquiesced silently than he became uneasy to hear what she had to say, and added, 'What could I have done except what I did?'

'If you really thought the worse of Emmy for being my daughter, Nils,' she replied as gently as she could, 'then you could have done nothing else. Christine could have said all that you said and been perfectly true to herself in saying it. You, knowing better, were false to your better knowledge. You have clung to your respectability; but your heart has not been narrow enough to make you content with it. You have hankered after our wider life; but your heart has not been large enough to make you join us. Now see what it has ended in. Emmy could have been saved had she learnt two lessons: an easy one which you could have taught her, and a harder one which perhaps I could have helped her to teach herself. You know that Emmy was brought up to believe that she herself could be nothing if not respectable according to Christine's standards; and that this respectability would depend on the respectability of her father, her brothers, her husband and her mother. When her father became a drunkard, and her brother a forger, there was nothing left to her but herself and the mother. But she was too young and too weak to feel herself of any account; and her mother, you all told her, was a vile and wicked woman. If, in that crisis of humiliation and despair, I had offered her my hard lesson that she was herself worth living for as an independent human being, she would not have understood me. But if Respectability itself, incarnate in the person of the Mayor of the town and the great banker, had just then stepped in to tell her that he was her mother's friend – that her mother had many friends, and was no more vile and wicked than his own wife; do you think she would then have turned away from that great relief and reassurance to the fate you described to me so cruelly twenty years ago – to go down, *under the ice, perhaps. Down in the cold black water. And next spring to come up again, ugly, hairless, unrecognizable.* You see I remember.'

'But,' cried the wretched Krogstad, cowering under her words as if they were blows, 'I would have spoken out if I had only known. How could I tell that such a trumpery affair as it seemed was a great crisis – a matter of life or death – the instant for a great effort? She made no fuss about it.'

'Perhaps she was tranquillized by the prospect of that reward in Heaven that you promised her – you who have so carefully feathered your own earthly nest,' said Nora, for a moment falling into irony. 'But I am afraid, poor girl,' she added seriously, 'that the contrast between the Christian charity of your professions and the wrathfulness of your actions proved too much for her credulity. Her suicide is a proof – one that even Christine cannot challenge – of your destruction of her belief in a hereafter. You see, Nils, this habit of regarding your little respectable set as the only people in the world, and other people as low people, and other people's affairs as trumpery affairs, blinds you to the great opportunities of life, which always arise in the wider world which includes these low people. If Emmy had been Heyerdahl's daughter, you would never have pushed her out of your way like a bill with a bad name on it.'

'Go on,' said Krogstad, doggedly: 'say what you like. I am a miserable hound: a failure. I have always been a failure. I wish I had never met my damned wife.'

'Oh come!' said Nora sharply: 'your wife is much

better than you. She has acted up to her convictions. If you had acted up to yours instead of playing down to hers, you would not now be snivelling there about being a failure. Christine's mind is narrow and her ideal is mean; but such as it is, she has realized it. Your ideal is nobler; but you have never realized it – never even known what it is – only felt it as a vague rebellion against the golden calf you have set up in its place. That is why she is a success, and you a failure; though I will say, to console you, that your failure is more akin to salvation than her success.'

'It is my failure that has made her success,' said Krogstad, bitterly. 'What would she be without me? A governess, not worth twopence.'

'That is the worst of marriage, Krogstad: it always either sacrifices one of the couple to the other or ruins both. Torvald was a success as long as I remained a failure. But it is not always the woman who is sacrificed. Twenty years ago, when I walked out of the doll's house, I saw only my own side of the question.'

'You are not going to admit that you were wrong, are you?' said Krogstad hastily, with a curious air of disappointment.

'No,' replied Nora placidly; 'but I did not see that the man must walk out of the doll's house as well as the woman. That evening, after the ball and the tarantella, I had only had my eyes open for five minutes; and naturally I noticed nothing but the overpowering fact that I was only Torvald's plaything. Now I have had my eyes open for twenty years, during which I have peeped into a great many doll's houses; and I have found that the dolls are not all female. Take your home, for instance! You know that if you had any pluck, Krogstad, you would walk out, and be no longer her puppet, but the captain of your own soul, as some English poet says. She does to you what Torvald did to me: she forces you to do what she thinks is right and becoming for a bank director and a mayor, just as Torvald forced me to do what he thought was right and becoming for the lady wife of a respectable bank manager. I felt that I could find something higher for myself; and I came out and found it.'

'And I,' said Krogstad, 'do not feel that I could find anything higher, though I know that something higher exists. By myself I should fall to something lower: drink, perhaps, like Helmer, or slouch into a slovenly Bohemianism that is lazier than my present life without being any better otherwise. No: there is no use denying it: Christine has kept me up to a better mark than I could have attained without her.'

'Yes, my dear Nils; but youve killed Emmy, which you probably would not have done had you been a slovenly slouching Bohemian.'

'Thats true,' said Krogstad, wincing, yet facing the reminder grimly. 'I shall stop Christine's mouth with that when she next has a fit of sermonizing.'

'What an egotist you are, Nils!' said Nora, not ill-naturedly. 'Now that you have got over the first shock of that poor girl's death, you care no more about it than you will about the next tradesman in difficulties whose application for a loan you will refuse.'

'You are her mother,' he retorted; 'and you dont seem deeply affected.'

'Her life was almost as sad to me as her death, Nils! But the pain of parting from her wore itself out years ago, when she was only the doll's plaything. It would take Christine's sense of the duty of hypocrisy to enable me to pretend to miss what I have done without for twenty years. And my heart has not been empty all that time. I suppose you do not believe Christine's theory that a woman's affections are naturally graduated in strict proportion to blood relationship, and that ever since I left Torvald my heart has been an aching void, and my life barren of the love of children and of the pleasant interest in the promise of those who are too young to stir our envy or cross our ambition. Since I freed myself, I have had enough and to spare of affection from children of all ages, including you, Nils. I rest your soul from Christine, do I not? By the bye, are you watching the hour?'

Krogstad hastily looked at his watch, and made at once for his cape and hat. When he had put them on, he hesitated, and said irresolutely, 'It will not seem my fault to the town, will it?'

'What if it does, Nils? Four-fifths of the townspeople are laborers who never speak to you or yours, and whose opinion you despise. Your own set are in a conspiracy to hold you up as a model of virtue: on reciprocal terms, of course. Now I am outside that conspiracy; and therefore I am held up as a model of vice. Christine's favorite preacher has written a tract in which he declares that my friends visit me for the purpose of indulging in obscene conversation, and that Torvald's drunkenness is my fault; because, I suppose, poor Torvald took to playing with the bottle when I took his doll away from him. His Reverence's head has been turned by the injustice of human affairs, because, owing to the state of the copyright law, he cannot get paid twice over for his tracts, once here and once in America. He and Christine between them will shield you. It was from her that I heard of Emmy's fate; and she said, in her melodramatic way, "Wretched woman: the ruin wrought by your own hand is now complete," and so on. You are quite safe, Nils: the word has already gone round that I am to be made the scapegoat; and tomorrow you will be shaking your head over my depravity more gravely than any of the rest, as becomes the Mayor of the town.'

'I will not, Nora,' he said indignantly. 'How can you think so meanly of me?'

'Well, if I am wrong, you can prove me so – tomorrow. But if I am not wrong –'

STILL AFTER THE DOLL'S HOUSE

'You shall see,' he interrupted, blusteringly.

'If I am not wrong,' she resumed, quietly, 'come back to confession when your conscience troubles you; and you shall be forgiven. Or will you be afraid to come

now, since you have discovered that everybody except Christine knows of your visits?'

'Goodnight,' he said shortly.

'Goodnight,' she said. 'My poor old Krogstad!'

He flung out of the room like a boy in a pet; and she sat down at her writing table, to finish her day's work. But in a moment she heard his step at the threshold again, and, turning in her chair, saw his angry face thrust in at the door, saying,

'Easy for *you* to tell me that if I had any pluck I would

do what you did, and desert my wife and family. A woman can do such things and be made a heroine of, if she is only pretty enough. But the very set that makes a heroine of you would join my set in hounding me out of the place as a blackguard if I did such a thing; though, if Christine left me, they would all say it was my fault – that I must have ill-treated her. It is we who are the slaves of marriage and not you.'

'I verily believe it, Nils,' she said, looking up at him with the kindliest interest. 'Mastery is the worst slavery of all.'

'Ugh!' growled Krogstad: 'there is no use in arguing with a woman.' And he vanished.

Then the house door was heard to bang.

A GLIMPSE OF
THE DOMESTICITY OF
FRANKLYN BARNABAS

A GLIMPSE OF THE DOMESTICITY OF FRANKLYN BARNABAS

IF you have read Back to Methuselah you will remember Franklyn Barnabas, the ex-clergyman who, with his gruff brother Conrad, the biologist, had come to the conclusion that the duration of human life must be extended to three hundred years, not in the least as all the stupid people thought because people would profit by a longer experience, but because it was not worth their while to make any serious attempt to better the world or their own condition when they had only thirty or forty years of full maturity to enjoy before they doddered away into decay and death. The brothers Barnabas were in fact the first discoverers of the strangely obvious truth that it is our expectation of life, and not our experience of it, that determines our conduct and character. Consequently the very vulgar proposition that you cannot change human nature, and therefore cannot make the revolutionary political and economic changes which are now known to be necessary to save our civilization from perishing like all previous recorded ones, is valid only on the assumption that you cannot change the duration of human life. If you can change that, then you can change political conduct through the whole range which lies between the plague-stricken city's policy of 'Let us eat and drink; for tomorrow we die' and the long-sighted and profound policies of the earthly paradises of More, Morris, Wells, and all the other Utopians.

DOMESTICITY OF FRANKLYN BARNABAS

It was with this thesis of the Barnabases that I was concerned when I wrote Back to Methuselah; and though I got interested enough in Franklyn personally to go a little way into his domestic history, I had to discard my researches as both irrelevant and certain to sidetrack my main theme and confuse my biological drama with a domestic comedy.

Also I had amused myself by bringing Franklyn Barnabas into contact with a notable social philosopher of our day for the mere fun of caricaturing him. But this proved a hopeless enterprise; for, like all really great humorists, he had himself exploited his own possibilities so thoroughly in that direction that I could produce nothing but a manifestly inferior copy of a gorgeous original. Still, even a bad caricature may have some value when the original has dissolved into its elements for remanufacture by the Life Force. As we cannot now have a photograph of Shakespear, much less a portrait by a master, we cling to the inhuman caricature by Droeshout as at least a corrective to the commonplace little bust of a commonplace little gent in the shrine in Stratford church; and so I think it possible that my thumbnail sketch, inadequate and libellous as it is, may give a hint or two to some future great biographer as to what the original of Immenso Champernoon was like in the first half of his career, when, in defiance of the very order of nature, he began without a figure as a convivial immensity with vine leaves in his hair, deriding his own aspect, and in middle life slimmed into a Catholic saint, thereby justifying my reminder to those who took him too lightly of old, that Thomas Aquinas began as a comically fat man and ended as The Divine Doctor.

Until the other day I believed that my studies of the Barnabas home out Hampstead way, with my Champernoon caricature, had perished in the waste-paper basket which has swallowed many discarded pages of my works. But they have just turned up in the course of a hunt for

DOMESTICITY OF FRANKLYN BARNABAS

matter wherewith to complete a collected edition of my works; and, being much at a loss for padding for this particular volume of scraps of fiction, I looked through them and thought they might prove not only readable, but perhaps useful to married ladies with interesting husbands who attract husband stealers. Such ladies, if they are at all bearable, have all the trumps in their hands, and need never be beaten if they understand the game and play it with the requisite audacity and contempt for the danger.

Here, then, are a few scraps of the scenes which took place in the suburban villa in which the brothers Barnabas made their famous attempt to persuade our political leaders in the first years after the war to discard their obsolete party programs and raise the slogan of Back to Methuselah.

Conrad Barnabas the biologist is in the library waiting for his brother Franklyn. Franklyn comes in presently looking worried and irritated. The conversation proceeds as follows.

CONRAD. Anything wrong?

FRANKLYN. As usual.

CONRAD. Clara broken out again?

FRANKLYN. She left the house on Saturday saying that she would live with me no longer. My worthy brother-in-law wants to see me about her.

CONRAD. What! Immenso Champernoon! Dont say he's coming here.

FRANKLYN. He is.

CONRAD. Oh, Lord!

FRANKLYN. Perhaps if you start a discussion with him he may forget to talk about Clara. I really cannot stand any more of it. I have been a very good husband to her for twenty years, as husbands go; and now I sometimes regret that we did not separate at our first quarrel.

CONRAD. Well, Clara has been a fairly good wife to you, as wives go. She keeps the house very well.

FRANKLYN. A well-kept house is an excellent thing as far as it goes. But it is not an indispensable condition of life to me. Constitutionally I am an untidy irregular man. We all are, we Barnabases. You are.

CONRAD. But I knew better than to marry. You knew what you were doing, you know.

FRANKLYN. I dont think anyone knows quite what he is doing when he marries.

CONRAD. Widowers do. And they marry.

FRANKLYN. It suits them, perhaps. Besides, a married man forms married habits and becomes dependent on marriage, just as a sailor becomes dependent on the sea. But there are limits. I know a sailor who was torpedoed nine times, and yet went to sea again. But the tenth time finished him: he took a job in the docks. Well, Clara has torpedoed me nine times. If she is going to do it again she may find it once too often.

CONRAD. I cannot make out what you have to quarrel about. Whats wrong with her, or you?

FRANKLYN. If you want to know whats wrong with me, you must ask her. What is wrong with her is that she is a bluestocking.

CONRAD. Oh, come! Thats rather out of date, isnt it? I dont believe the women students at Cambridge know the meaning of the word. You dont object at this time of day to a woman cultivating her mind and being educated?

FRANKLYN. Not at all. Nobody ever does: among our set of people at any rate. A bluestocking is not an educated woman or a woman with a cultivated mind.

CONRAD. What else?

FRANKLYN. A bluestocking is a woman who has a mania for intellectual subjects without having a ray of intellect.

CONRAD. Oho! Thats not a bluestocking: it's a

university professor. When a man is mentally incapable of abstract thought he takes to metaphysics; and they make him a professor. When he is incapable of conceiving quantity in the abstract he takes to mathematics; and they make him a professor. When he is incapable of distinguishing between a clockwork mouse and a real one he takes to biology; and they make him a professor. And so on. The fact is, these chaps are clockwork mice themselves. By tutoring them and coaching them and stuffing them with textbooks you wind them up, and they go. You feel safe with them because you always know how far they will go and how they will go. But Clara is not like that. She hasnt been wound up. She is not a fool.

FRANKLYN. Isnt she?

CONRAD. Well, not that sort of fool. These people have no minds at all: Clara has a very restless mind, not to say a fidgety one. What has she been worrying about now?

FRANKLYN. Indian religions. Theosophy. Yoga. Reincarnation. Karma. Anything from the East.

CONRAD. Damn the East! Are we never to look at home for our religion?

FRANKLYN. Amen. She calls Creative Evolution Western Materialism, cockney blasphemy, and all the rest of it. Says she wont live in the house with it.

CONRAD. But a woman doesnt leave her home for a thing like that. Whats the row, really?

FRANKLYN. Oh, what is the row always, in married life? It's not Creative Evolution, it's because I discuss Creative Evolution with Mrs Etteen and refuse to discuss it with Clara. How can I discuss it with a woman who tells me I dont understand it, and that the truth about it is all in the Vedantas or the Upanishads or the last number of the Theosophical Journal or some other nigger scripture?

CONRAD. Mrs Etteen? Who is she?

FRANKLYN. Oh – er – a lady.

CONRAD. Thank God I'm not married, and can discuss Creative Evolution with anyone I like.

FRANKLYN. And now I shall have to sit here and keep my temper while Immenso gasses about domestic virtue.

CONRAD. Why need to keep your temper? I tell you frankly, I intend to lose mine.

FRANKLYN. It wont make the smallest difference to Immenso.

THE PARLOR MAID [*announcing*] Mr Champernoon. [*She withdraws*].

Immenso Champernoon is a man of colossal mould, with the head of a cherub on the body of a Falstaff, which he carries with ease and not without grace. At forty or thereabouts his hair is still brown and curly. He is friendly, a little shy, and jokes frequently enough to be almost either still enjoying the last or already anticipating the next. He is careless of his dress and person, in marked contrast to Franklyn, who, though untidy as to his papers, looks comparatively valeted and manicured.

FRANKLYN. Conrad's here, Imm. You dont mind, do you?

CONRAD [*striving not to let Immenso's large and genial aspect disarm him*] I can go.

IMMENSO. Not at all. Delighted to see you, doctor. [*He sits down on the sofa, which groans beneath the burden*].

FRANKLYN. Well, what is the latest? Has Clara made up her mind to a separation, or has she discovered a new religion, or have you a treaty of good behavior in your pocket which I am to sign?

IMMENSO. I really forget what she said.

CONRAD. You forget!

IMMENSO. The way I look at it is this. A man is not a balloon.

CONRAD. Some men are damned like one.

IMMENSO [*grinning genially*] Like all men of science you are the dupe of appearances. For instance, *I* am superficially like a balloon. I fancy that was in your mind when you introduced the subject of balloons.

CONRAD. It is just possible. But it was you who introduced the subject.

IMMENSO. Let me suggest an experiment. Procure a balloon; and place it on the lawn. Place me at the same time on the roof. Detach us both simultaneously from the lawn and from the roof. The balloon will immediately shoot up into the heavens and be lost. *I* will, on the contrary, descend to earth with destructive force, and probably make a considerable dent in it. In other words, you will not know where to find the balloon; and you will know where to find me. That is the essential difference.

FRANKLYN. Yes, yes; but what has it to do with Clara?

IMMENSO. This. The earth is my home. If my home were in the skies I could not be a married man. You conceive me at the altar trying to get married, with the bride, the bridesmaids, the best man, the pew opener, and the parson all holding me down. But they would have to let go sooner or later. And then up I would shoot. My head would strike the stars. My coat would be whitened in the milky way. And my wife would be that most pitiful of all widows, a grass widow. The natural occupation of the grass widow is to make hay whilst the sun shines. But my widow could not, because my bulk would obscure the sun. I should be a perpetual eclipse –

FRANKLYN. My dear Imm: I shall be delighted to hear your views on balloons, on grass, and on eclipses when we have nothing else to talk about. I have no doubt they will be extremely entertaining. But just at present I want to know what Clara intends to do, or intends me to do.

IMMENSO. But dont you see that that is just what I am coming to?

CONRAD. I'm damned if *I* do.

DOMESTICITY OF FRANKLYN BARNABAS

IMMENSO. If you ask me –

CONRAD. I dont. It would be much shorter to ask a policeman.

IMMENSO. You could not ask a better man. A policeman would tell you at once that the whole police system, like all other eternally stable systems, depends, not on the wandering policeman but on the fixed point policeman. Not on the rolling stone policeman, a human avalanche who gathers no moss, but on the monumental policeman whom you always know where to find.

FRANKLYN. Again I ask you, Imm, what message have you brought to me from Clara?

IMMENSO. Again I tell you, Frank, I bring to you the message of gravitation which saves me from the fate of the balloon, and of the fixed point policeman on whom Conrad depends for his knowledge of the way to Putney. That is important, because if you cant find the way to Putney you cant find the way to paradise.

FRANKLYN. Yes. You were about to say that Clara told you to tell me – ?

IMMENSO. As a matter of detail she told me not to tell you. But what she said was that you could never live alone, because, as she put it, you are no anchorite.

FRANKLYN. Did you defend me from the monstrously false accusation which that implies?

IMMENSO. I pointed out that she was your anchor, and that if a man's anchor belied its own nature and swam away from him, it could hardly blame him for drifting.

FRANKLYN. And what did she say to that?

IMMENSO. She said there was no use talking to me. She said I was making puns of her distress.

FRANKLYN. And was that all?

IMMENSO. No. You may have noticed that when a woman says there is no use talking to a man, he can very seldom get a word in edgeways for the following half hour.

CONRAD. If she shut you up, she is a woman in a thousand.

IMMENSO. That is an almost perfect example of a modern scientific definition. It has the air of exactitude which arithmetic alone can give. Yet as, from the moment the population exceeds nine hundred and ninetynine, every woman is a woman in a thousand, it means absolutely nothing whatever.

FRANKLYN. We make you a present of modern science, Imm: nobody here worships it any more than you do – [*Conrad is about to protest*] – no, Con: you sit quiet and say nothing. I shall sit quiet and say nothing. When Imm is tired of playing with his own mind, he will perhaps have a human impulse, and relieve my anxiety to learn what Clara intends to do.

IMMENSO [*coloring at the implied reproach*] I am not inconsiderate, I hope. Certainly not intentionally so. But what Clara intends to do is her affair. What you intend to do is your affair. My only comment is that probably neither of you will do it. On the other hand I am deeply concerned, as a Christian, and may I say as a friend – if a brother-in-law may presume so far – with what you both ought to do.

FRANKLYN. And what is that?

IMMENSO. Anchor yourself to the hearthstone. Make that your fixed point. There must be fixed points in life or we shall become a community of balloons. Even for balloons there must be fixed gas works, a necessity quaintly met by the House of Commons. There must be irrevocable contracts. What is the first question we ask a man? His name. What is the second? His address. A man without a name is nobody. A man without an address is a vagabond. A man with two addresses is a libertine. A man with two solicitors and two bankers is a rogue. What is a marriage? Two persons with one name, one address. Not a changeable name, but one rooted in history, buried in parish registers to undergo a glorious resurrection in every generation; not a changeable address, but one hearthstone rooted in the solid earth of the motherland as a rock of ages, one certainty among all the uncertainties, one star among all the planets and meteors, one unshakable and unchangeable thing that is and was and ever shall be. You must have a root; and this matter of the root is also the root of the matter.

FRANKLYN. Marriage is not one of the certainties. Are there any certainties? Everything passes away; everything gets broken; we get tired of everything. Including marriages.

IMMENSO. No. Nothing can pass unless it passes something. A bus passes Piccadilly Circus; but Piccadilly Circus remains. I get tired of Clara; but I remain. So does Clara, by the way. And though everything gets broken you cannot break the thinnest glass goblet without striking it against a fixed object. You cannot break it by striking it against a butterfly. Has Con here ever considered, as a curious point in entomology, that you cannot break a butterfly at all? Foolish people say you can break it on a wheel; but it has never been done. Whistler survived his stodgiest enemies.

CONRAD. We have now got from the hearthstone to the butterfly as the emblem of constancy.

IMMENSO. You are a bachelor, Con: it has been your dreadful fate to sip every flower and change every hour until Polly your passion requited. Has she ever done so? No: she eludes you in every form except that of the Polyglot bible, in which you find the words SUPER HANC PETRAM: Upon this rock will I build my Church. What is that rock? The hearthstone. Come back to the hearthstone, Frank.

FRANKLYN. Like a bad penny.

IMMENSO. Not at all. A bad penny is nailed to the counter. Now it is the chief glory and peculiar quality of the hearthstone that you cannot nail anything to it. Also that though you can stand by it you cannot fall by it without getting your head under the grate. You can stand by it; sit by it: you can even, when Clara is indiscreetly curious, lie by it; but you cannot be nailed to it nor fall by it nor inconvenience yourself in any way by it.

FRANKLYN. What are we to do with this fellow, Con?

CONRAD. It's a pathological case. Theres a disease called echolalia. It sets stupid people gabbling rhymes: that is, words that echo each other. Imm here, being a clever chap, gabbles ideas that echo. He's by way of being a pundit, and is really only a punster.

IMMENSO. Be it so. You may say the same of Plato, of Shakespear. At all events, I keep to the point, which is the home.

FRANKLYN. Clara is the point.

IMMENSO. She is the point inasmuch as you have a tendency to stray from her. But the definition of a point is position without magnitude. Now Clara has both position and magnitude; and you will find that the more you attempt to destroy her position, the more oppressive her magnitude will become.

FRANKLYN. Imm: I know your trick of never arguing, but simply talking every idea out of my head except your own ideas. But it's no use your preaching the virtues of an imaginary world of irrevocable contracts to me. We are struggling out of a tyranny of sacred traditions, immutable laws, and irrevocable contracts into a freedom in which we may prove all things and hold fast to that which is good. If I find married life with Clara intolerable, I shall chuck it and chuck her; and thats all about it.

IMMENSO. Many men begin by chucking the woman they love. The saying that 'each man slays the thing he loves' would be more true if it ran that 'each man chucks the thing he loves'; but he usually chucks it under the chin. In any other sense you will find it difficult to chuck Clara.

CONRAD. Tell me this. Suppose Frank and Clara, instead of having at the outside twentyfive years more to live, had two hundred and fifty! Suppose that having brought up one family to the point at which that family naturally breaks up and the young people depart and make new families of their own, they were left to sit and stare at one another for two centuries, or to begin over again with another family, would you still admit no time limit to their contract? Does it occur to you that under such circumstances it might become unreasonable, or be considered indecent, or even declared illegal, for marriages to last for three centuries?

IMMENSO [*reflectively*] I see. You mean that when a tie has endured for, say, fifty years, it becomes so intimate, so sacred, that it establishes, in effect, a relation far closer than the relation of consanguinity, and should be placed on the list of degrees within which marriage is forbidden; that the two may become one flesh so completely that even as brother and sister they would be more remote from one another, and that consequently marriage between them would become unthinkable through its very perfection. That is an idea which commands my respect. When they made you a man of science, Con, they killed a poet, more's the pity!

CONRAD. I never meant any such infernal nonsense. I meant that only fools stick in the same groove for ever, and that the law of change is a biological law.

IMMENSO. Well, if you come to that, I must remind you – though without prejudice to my eternal and unchangeable derision, loathing, contempt, and utter disbelief in biology and all other ologies whatever except perhaps the doxology – that it is a biological law that Frank and Clara shall have only one life and can bring up only one family, and that they must make the best of it.

CONRAD. I deny that it is a biological law. It is

nothing but a bad habit. We can live as long as we like. Do you know what people really die of?

IMMENSO. Of reasonableness. They do not want to live forever.

CONRAD. Of laziness, and want of conviction, and failure to make their lives worth living. That is why. That is sound scientific biology for you. I believe that we are on the brink of a generation that will live longer. Or else we are on the brink of destruction.

IMMENSO. The slain poet has his revenge. He rises from the dead as a scientific madman.

CONRAD. Gasbag!

IMMENSO. Oh, that this too too solid flesh would melt, thaw, and resolve itself into a gas! Call me a Jack Pudding, Con. That will not smell of the laboratory; but it will hit me in the stomach.

FRANKLYN. I am sorry to again make a digression. What does Clara want me to do? She sends me word that it is her firm intention never to cross my threshold again, and that I must see you about it. I have seen you; and I am as wise as I was before. There is no use asking you whether she gave you any message for me, as you will immediately proceed to deliver the message of the universe. Did she give you a letter?

IMMENSO [*producing a key*] She gave me this. She thinks it is her latchkey; but as a matter of fact I tried to open the door with it, and found it would not work; so I had to ring for admission in the usual course. But she undoubtedly believed that it was the key of this house when she gave it me. It is symbolically the key of your house. Actually, now that I look at it, I believe it is the key of mine. She has been staying with us for a few days. So if you will allow me I will keep it [*he replaces it in his pocket*].

FRANKLYN. Then she is in earnest about never crossing the threshold?

Mrs Franklyn Barnabas (Clara) flounces in through the

window. She is a very active lady of fifty or thereabouts, rather under than over, and is richly but hastily and untidily dressed.

CLARA. I must apologize for entering unannounced by this way instead of through the front door as a stranger should. But Frank can hardly expect me to make a parade of our unhappy differences before the servants.

FRANKLYN. I never suggested for a moment that you should.

CLARA. And Imm took the wrong key: you know how incorrigibly careless he is. Give it back to me.

IMMENSO. Two wrongs will not make a right. I had better keep it.

CLARA. I see Con has come here to talk about me. I wish you would mind your own business, Con.

CONRAD. Damn your silly business! I came here to talk about something serious.

CLARA [*smiling*] Dont be naughty, Con. But it serves me right for spoiling you. And the first thing I see when I come into the place is Savvy playing tennis with that young rector. I call it hypocrisy. She does not believe in the Thirty-nine Articles. What right has she to lead that young man on? One would think that she had seen enough of the tragedy of a marriage between two people of different religious beliefs in this house.

FRANKLYN. I quite agree.

CLARA [*flushing*] Do you indeed? Then I think thats a very nasty thing of you to say. You are always worse when you have been talking to Con behind my back. And Imm has been making mischief, I suppose, as usual.

IMMENSO [*bounding from his chair*] *I* make mischief!!!

CONRAD [*rising angrily*] How can Frank help talking about you to me when you make his life a hell?

FRANKLYN [*who has also risen*] You take offence at

your own words. I am long past caring whether you find my remarks nasty or not.

CLARA. Have you all had tea?

This simple question deflates the three men hopelessly.

CONRAD. Tcha! [*he sits down angrily*].

FRANKLYN [*sitting down limply*] Have you had tea, Imm? I forgot to ask you.

IMMENSO [*sitting down ponderously*] I am banting. I have given up afternoon tea.

CLARA [*snatching her hat off carelessly and throwing it aside*] Who has been here while I have been away? [*She sits*]. What have you been doing? How much was the garden account on Saturday? I saw grapes at six and sixpence a pound not a patch on ours. Did you go through cook's books?

FRANKLYN. I know nothing whatever about it. Campbell will tell you about the garden. I told him not to bother me. I gave cook a cheque for what she asked, and sent her book to my solicitor to check.

CLARA. To your solicitor!

FRANKLYN. You have complained so much about the trouble of housekeeping that I have made up my mind to try another plan.

CLARA [*rising*] Well, did you ever! I shall talk to cook about letting you be so ridiculous: what right had she to ask you for a cheque? it is my house and my business. [*Making for the garden door*] Where is Campbell? [*She goes out*].

FRANKLYN [*slowly*] Why do the servants stay?

CONRAD. Why do you stay?

IMMENSO [*rising*] That raises the question, why do *I* stay? My work, it would appear, is done.

CONRAD. Running away, eh?

IMMENSO. Most moral victories have that appearance.

FRANKLYN. Well, off with you. You have the brother's privilege. You can run away from Clara.

Clara returns, in a much better humor.

CLARA. Imm: are you staying to dinner?

IMMENSO. It has not been suggested.

FRANKLYN. I took it as a matter of course, Imm, if you care to.

CLARA. Youd better. [*Immenso resumes his seat*]. Frank: only fancy! cook's become a Theosophist.

FRANKLYN. Indeed? Did she get that in before you complained about the cheque she got from me?

CLARA [*coaxing*] But dear Frank, what was she to do? She needed the money to keep the house going. You must not blame her.

FRANKLYN. I do not blame her.

CLARA. Well, then, what are you talking about? Come, darling: dont be cross. Dont worry about the house. Cook was very glad to see me back; and no wonder: she must have had a dreadful time of it. Dont make me feel that I am more welcome in the kitchen than I am here. Arnt you going to kiss me?

FRANKLYN. Yes, yes. [*He kisses her*] There, dear, there. You are perfectly welcome.

CLARA. Con looks very cheap. Shall I get you some ammoniated quinine, Con? You look just as you did when you were sickening for the influenza last year twelvemonths.

CONRAD. I am quite well.

CLARA. You always say that. It is really very hard that I cant go away for a week without everybody getting ill.

CONRAD. I tell you I am not ill.

CLARA. Well, if youre not, I must say you are not very cordial in your manner. You know how glad I always am to see you here. I think you might shew that you are glad to see me.

CONRAD. Do you want me to kiss you?

CLARA. You may if you like. Nobody can say that I bear malice. [*She advances her cheek in his direction*].

CONRAD [*desperate*] Oh, very well. [*He gets up and kisses her*].

CLARA. Thats better. Now you have quite a color. [*He is, in fact, blushing slightly*].

Savvy, Franklyn's daughter, looks in. She is rather pleasant as a modern bright young thing; but she jars on her father by her dowdiness and rowdiness. She fears neither God nor man.

SAVVY. Mamma: Campbell's here.

CLARA. What does he want?

SAVVY. Nothing. You said you wanted him. About the grapes.

CLARA [*springing up*] Oh yes, of course. They were six and sixpence at Covent Garden. You dont mind my running away for a moment, do you: I promise to come back in a jiffy. [*She hurries out*].

SAVVY. Has she given in? Or have you?

CONRAD. Stalemate, Savvy.

SAVVY. Does that mean that she is coming back?

FRANKLYN. Yes, dear. Yes.

SAVVY. I'm rather glad, you know. The house was getting into a bit of a mess. [*She goes out*].

IMMENSO. I think you have summed up the situation correctly in one word, Con.

CONRAD. Have I? What word?

IMMENSO. Stalemate. That is exactly what is wrong with Frank.

FRANKLYN. What do you mean?

IMMENSO. My meaning is obvious. You are Clara's mate; and in the course of a too monotonous domestic routine you have become stale.

FRANKLYN. And Clara? Do you find her any fresher?

IMMENSO. Clara, with an instinct that amounts to genius, has recognized the situation. Finding herself stale, she takes herself off and then comes back and woos you afresh. What we have just witnessed here is a renewal of the honeymoon.

CONRAD. Tcha!

IMMENSO. Clara went away a stale mate, and

returned a bride. Why dont you do the same, Frank? Why do you stick here in a groove, like a tram car? An Englishman's house is his castle; and when I am a frequent visitor it may be called the Elephant and Castle. But what is the Elephant and Castle? It is not a place at which tram cars stay: it is a point of continual departure and continual return. It is an ark which sends out doves every minute, and to which the doves return when the waters have abated. I shall write a book describing the adventures of a husband who leaves his wife every month only to return and woo her afresh, thus making himself a perpetual bridegroom, his wife a perpetual bride, and his life a perpetual honeymoon. Thus we reconcile the law of change and the irrevocable contract. Thus John Bull in his daily round of work, John Doin' as you may call him, becomes also Don Juan –

FRANKLYN. For heaven's sake, Imm, if you must make puns, make good ones, I —

Clara returns, looking serious.

CLARA. Frank: whats to be done? Campbell is thinking of turning Roman Catholic. He wants my advice about it.

FRANKLYN. What about the grapes?

CLARA. Do you think the grapes more important than the man's soul? I shall certainly not encourage him. And dont you encourage him either, Imm. You are always defending the Church of Rome; and I live in daily fear of your joining it just for an intellectual lark.

IMMENSO. I suggest to you, Clara, that Campbell's case is not a simple case of the grapes, but of the fox and the grapes. Now *the* fox par excellence was George Fox the quaker. A Roman Catholic fox is therefore an absurdity. Campbell should turn quaker.

CLARA. I never know whether you are serious or not, Imm; and neither does anyone else; but Campbell would not join the Society of Friends: he is too cantankerous. I am greatly concerned about Campbell. He has the Keltic imagination: he is the most dreadful liar. And he has a Scottish philosophic subtlety that is almost Eastern. I advised him to read some Indian poetry. I will lend him the poems of Stupendranath Begorr.

IMMENSO. Stupendranath told me a curious thing about his uncle. He lost all his property by gambling in stocks, and had to live by getting married at the rate of two hundred a year.

CLARA. No man has a right to get married on two hundred a year. His wife must be a slave.

IMMENSO. I dont mean two hundred pounds a year: I mean two hundred marriages a year. Under our tolerant rule polygamy is unlimited in India. This gentleman conferred his high caste on the daughters of Indian snobs by marrying them. They made him handsome presents on each occasion; and these presents furnished him with a large income.

CLARA. But how could he support thousands of wives?

IMMENSO. He did not take them away with him. He left them on their parents' hands.

CLARA. And you approve of this! You advocate it! You support it!

IMMENSO. Not for a moment. I simply mention it.

CLARA. Then why do you mention it? It ought not to be mentioned. You would not mention it if you had not some sympathy with it.

CONRAD. If it is good enough for the British Empire it is good enough for you. You support the British Empire, dont you?

CLARA. Of course I support the British Empire. I am a Briton, I am proud to say. I believe we have a sacred mission to spread British ideas, British feelings, and British institutions over the whole world, because they are the best, the wholesomest, the cleanest, the freest. I would not have anyone in my house who questioned that for a moment. But if your silly story were true, it would mean that Stupendranath's vicious uncle, a black man, a gambler, and a bigamist, was imposing his abominable habits and customs on the British Government. I will write to the Secretary of State for India and have this man prosecuted.

FRANKLYN. My dear: you have been entertaining in our house for fully a quarter of a century scores of people who spend their lives in trying to improve British institutions of one kind or another into something more reasonable. If they had been conventional patriots you would have called them dull and refused to invite them. What is the use of saying that you would not have such people in your house.

CLARA. Tell me this. Have I ever once – once during that quarter of a century, as you pompously call it to cover up the weakness of your argument – have I ever once invited or entertained Stupendranath's uncle or any of his shameless wives?

FRANKLYN. I did not say you had.

CLARA. Then what are you talking about?

FRANKLYN. I dont know. Ask Imm: he started this unfortunate subject.

IMMENSO. I cant help feeling that the future of British ideas depends on totally unreasonable people like Clara.

CLARA. Unreasonable! Pray why –

IMMENSO [*forcibly*] No, Clara: you may put down a husband because his domestic peace and comfort for the next week depends on his submission. But you cannot put down a brother. I can trample on you with impunity, because I can walk out afterwards to a comfortable home as long as I am careful to allow my own wife to trample on me. I say you are an utterly unreasonable woman: and I do not care a dump whether you like it or not. As it happens I am now defending you; and –

DOMESTICITY OF FRANKLYN BARNABAS

CLARA. You are a great fat fool, Imm; and I am perfectly capable of defending myself.

IMMENSO. The Roman conqueror had a slave to whisper to him 'Remember that thou art mortal.' The frankness of the British family relation provides me with a sister to remind me that I am a great fat fool. Why is England still England? Because there are so many people like Clara in it. She believes in her ideas, in her culture, in her morals, and backs them against the universe.

CONRAD. Does that give her any right to shove them down other people's throats with a bayonet?

IMMENSO. Yes: I should say it does. If the German shoves his ideas down our throats with music, and the French with wit, and the Italians with rhetorical paintings and romance, why should not we, being more handy with the bayonet than with any of these things, not carry on our propaganda with cold steel? By doing so we stake our lives and all our possessions on our ideas. Is not that more heroic than merely staking them on the success of an opera, an epigram, or a picture? What are we in India for, if not to lock up Stupendranath's uncle as a bigamist? When we put down the burning of widows and sent the car of Juggernaut to the jobmaster's scrap heap, we did India the only sort of service that could justify our interference with her. When we consented to tolerate Stupendranath's uncle we were hauling down the flag, and surrendering to the oriental. I grant you we have no right to govern India, because the Indians can govern themselves at least as well as we govern ourselves, which is not saying much. But we have a sacred right to persecute India. We have no right in the East except the right of the Crusader. The Catholic Englishman imposing British justice, British religion, and British institutions on the Hindoo is God's apostle. A Liberal Englishman undertaking to regulate oriental polygamy and idolatry is an officious

DOMESTICITY OF FRANKLYN BARNABAS

meddler, an apostate, and, as Clara puts it, a fat fool.

CLARA. Nonsense! Why shouldnt the poor people have their own religions and their own institutions? I am sure they are just as respectable as ours. The Salvation Army killed Aunt Martha by playing under her window when she had worn her nerves to rags with neuralgia and morphia. And you justify such a thing!

FRANKLYN. Serve you right, Imm, for trying to take her part. You had better accept Clara as a true Briton and leave it at that. Why persist in expressing her views when you know very well that she hasnt got any?

CLARA. Dont be rude, Frank. It just comes to this, that when you men say things, they are views; but when I say a thing, you just say anything that comes handy for the sake of contradicting and shewing off your superior male intellects. What I say is that the Salvation Army is noisy. You say that it is as quiet as a church mouse; and you call that a view. It may be a view; but it's a lie; and you ought to be ashamed of pretending to believe it. I say that our institutions are a disgrace, right down from the silly humbugs in parliament to the borough council dustmen who never come when they are wanted and have to be cleaned up after for half a day when they do come. I say we are the most stupid, prejudiced, illiterate, drinking, betting, immoral, lazy, idle, unpunctual, good-for-nothing people on the face of the earth, as you would know if you had to keep the house and deal with them instead of sitting here airing your views. And I say that the Indians, and the Chinese, and the Japanese, and the Burmese are people with souls, and have the most wonderful ancient books of wisdom, and make far better brasswork and pottery than Tottenham Court Road can. These may not be views; but they are facts. Imm there thinks he is ever so much wiser than Confucius or Lao-Tse; but when I read Lao-Tse and then try to read Imm's stuff afterwards it bores me to tears.

IMMENSO. Lao-Tse, being only a sage, cannot draw tears. For that, you need sage and onions.

CLARA. What a silly joke! You great baby.

Savvy looks in again.

SAVVY. Mrs Etteen's motor has just stopped at the gate. Look out. [*She vanishes*].

CLARA. I believe that woman has been here every day since I left.

FRANKLYN [*indignantly*] I have not seen Mrs Etteen for six weeks past. As you object to my seeing her; and I do not care two straws whether I see her or not, you can tell her that I am out, or busy, or anything you please: I will hide myself somewhere until she goes. [*He makes for the door*].

CLARA. No, Frank, you must stay. What – [*He goes out*]. Now that is a beastly thing of Frank to do. He will tell her next time he sees her that I drove him away.

CONRAD. Well, so you did.

CLARA. I did nothing of the sort. I asked him to stay. He makes himself ridiculous over her; and then people say that *I* make him ridiculous – that I am a jealous wife and all sorts of things. You shall just see how jealous I am.

The parlor maid enters, followed by a slender lady, beautifully dressed, with an expression of delicate patience that almost suggests suffering. Her eyes, violet in color, have a softness and depth that make her romantically attractive. Age inscrutable, but certainly under fifty and possibly under forty.

THE PARLOR MAID. Mrs Etteen. [*She withdraws*].

MRS ETTEEN [*approaching Clara and speaking with a deprecating shyness that gives a curious penetration to the audacity of what she says*] I am so disappointed to find you here.

CLARA. Pray why?

MRS ETTEEN. That silly Mrs Topham told me that

you had deserted your husband; and as I have adored him for years, I just rushed to offer myself as an unworthy substitute.

CLARA. Well, I'm sure! Theres nothing like being candid, is there? Have you had tea?

MRS ETTEEN. Yes, thank you. Is this your famous brother, Mr Immenso Champernoon?

Immenso, who has been sitting as if mesmerized, too shy to look at anyone, starts convulsively to his feet and presents himself for inspection with his hands hanging limply at his sides and his eyes directed to the carpet.

CLARA. Yes: thats Immenso. He's no use to you: he's happily married. Imm: this is Mrs Etteen.

IMMENSO [*murmuring thunderously*] Ahooroo. Eh plea. [*He is understood to have said 'How do you do? Very pleased.' They shake hands*].

CLARA. Doctor Conrad Barnabas, Franklyn's brother. Unmarried. Fair game; so he wont interest you.

MRS ETTEEN. You are very naughty, Clara. How do you do, Doctor? I have read your book [*shaking hands*].

CONRAD. How do you do?

CLARA. I can be quite as candid as you, Rosie darling. Sure youve had tea?

MRS ETTEEN. Quite. [*She sits down next Immenso and turns her eyes full on him*]. Mr Champernoon: you are the wisest man in England when you are not talking glorious nonsense. Can you explain something to me?

IMMENSO [*trying to recover his assurance in the dangerous warmth of the violet eyes*] Explanation is not a difficult art. I should say that any fool can explain anything. Whether he can leave you any the wiser is another matter.

MRS ETTEEN. Would you believe that I have been married three times?

IMMENSO. Does that need an explanation? Have you not such a thing in your house as a mirror?

MRS ETTEEN. Oh! Gallant! You make me blush.

CLARA. You be careful, Imm. You are only mortal, like that Roman conqueror you were talking about.

MRS ETTEEN. I should be very proud to make a conquest of you, Mr Champernoon; and, as it happens, what I am going to ask you is why I cannot.

IMMENSO [*rising rather heavily and moving to a distant seat*] Will you think me very boorish if I beg you to begin our acquaintance at the beginning and not at the end?

CLARA. Nothing doing, Rosie.

MRS ETTEEN. I know. But isnt it queer? I am not an ugly woman. I am not a very unamiable woman. I dont think I am an exceptionally stupid woman. I do think I am rather a fascinating woman: at least I always secure the attention of men. I have even infatuated more than one. And the upshot of it all is that I have had three husbands, and have been unable to keep one of them, though I have taken the greatest trouble to charm and please them. And here is Clara, who never cares what she does or says, who buys her clothes anywhere and flings them on anyhow, who bullies us and quarrels with us and rides roughshod over all our poor little susceptibilities, and yet keeps her wonderful husband without an effort, though we all want to take him from her.

CLARA. Whats the matter with my clothes? I dont get them anywhere: I get them from Valentino's, where you get yours; and I pay what I am asked. What more can I do? You dont expect me to spend my life bothering about my appearance, do you? I am not a professional husband stealer.

MRS ETTEEN. You dont need to steal husbands, dear. Youve got the best one in the market for nothing. But we poor pretty things dress and dress, and paint and paint, and dye and dye, and charm and charm, and all in vain. They wont stay with us even if we catch them once in a while. That is what I want you to explain to me, Mr Champernoon. It is so unjust.

IMMENSO [*tackling the subject ponderously and seriously*] I take it that a married life, to be permanent, must be part of nature's daily food. Now nature's daily food is not excessively agreeable. A man cannot live on Bath buns.

MRS ETTEEN. An elephant can.

IMMENSO. A very palpable hit, Mrs Etteen. I had, in fact, compared myself to an elephant just before you came in. And curiously enough, I live very largely on buns. But they are plain currant buns. An attempt to live on Bath buns would result in a surfeit of sweetness. If I call Clara a currant bun –

CLARA. I shall call you a sausage roll; so there!

IMMENSO. My sister, who has no illusions about me, will call me a sausage roll. But you, Mrs Etteen, will draw the moral that by laying yourself out to be exquisitely sweet, you may be making it impossible for a plain man to endure your charm for longer than a very brief honeymoon.

MRS ETTEEN. But why does the same thing not apply to very charming men? Franklyn Barnabas is the most charming man I know; but Clara does not get tired of him. What is your answer to that?

IMMENSO. My answer is that perhaps she does get tired of him.

CLARA. Now hold your tongue, Imm. That was not why I went away.

MRS ETTEEN. Oh! You did go away then?

CLARA. Now that Imm has been inconsiderate enough to let it out, you had better be told that Frank and I separated because he and his brother here have set up a new religion which I simply decline to entertain, and which I hope I have heard the last of.

MRS ETTEEN [*sadly*] The separation did not last very long, did it?

CLARA. Nearly a week. Do you call that nothing?

MRS ETTEEN. You see, he came back.

CLARA. He came back! What do you mean? *I* came back. You dont suppose he left me.

MRS ETTEEN. I hoped it. But why dont you get tired of him if what your brother says is true? Surely Franklyn is a Bath bun, if ever there was one.

IMMENSO. I should describe him rather as a Bath Oliver. A Bath Oliver has no sweetness; but it has a certain Cromwellian cleanness and plainness. Hence, no doubt, the name Oliver.

MRS ETTEEN. That is rather funny. But it leaves me lonely, and Clara triumphant. Doctor Conrad: has science nothing to say?

CONRAD. Yes. Science tells you that the trouble is that Frank is not an amoeba.

MRS ETTEEN. What is an amoeba?

CONRAD. Our common ancestor. An early form of life which you will find in the nearest ditch.

MRS ETTEEN. And where does Franklyn come in?

CONRAD. The amoeba can split himself into two amoebas, and the two can split themselves into four and so on. Well, Frank cannot split himself up into a dozen Franks so that there shall be a Frank for every woman who wants him. Theres only one of him; and Clara's got it. Hadnt you better make up your mind to that?

MRS ETTEEN. But Franklyn can split himself up. There is a place in America called Salt Lake City, where the Mormons live. All the best men there were amoebas. They divided themselves among a dozen or twenty women. Why should not Franklyn divide himself between Clara and me? Why should she have this treasure of a man all to herself?

CLARA. Youd better ask him. If he decides to give you a share you can have the lot.

MRS ETTEEN. Greedy!

CLARA. All or nothing for me, thank you.

MRS ETTEEN. You see what a wonderful man he is. She never gets tired of him.

CLARA. Yes I do. I get tired of him, and of the house, and of the children, and of Conrad, and of Imm; and so would you if you took on my job. But they belong here and I belong here; and you dont, darling; and thats what makes all the difference.

IMMENSO. I think that settles it, Mrs Etteen.

MRS ETTEEN. *I* dont. I have an absolute inner conviction that I belong to Franklyn and that Franklyn belongs to me. We must have been married to one another in a former existence. I feel that Clara is only accepting a fact, as all sensible women do. I began by accepting facts myself. But I now believe that the progress of the world depends on the people who refuse to accept facts and insist on the satisfaction of their instincts.

CLARA. It depends a good deal on the sort of instincts you have, doesnt it?

MRS ETTEEN. Oh, if you satisfy the lower instincts and starve the higher, experience pulls you up very short indeed. Besides, Clara, you dont mean that my admiration for Franklyn is a low instinct. You cannot blame me for sharing your own taste.

CLARA. Admire as much as you please. Women make me ill the way they slobber over Frank; and he never looks really contemptible except when he is encouraging them and purring and making sheep's eyes at them. But I suppose he is there to be admired, like my diamond cross. Mothers have the trouble of keeping children clean and fed and wellbehaved for old maids and old bachelors to pet and admire; and I suppose wives must be content to keep husbands presentable for unattached females to flirt with. But there are limits.

MRS ETTEEN. If you will let me feed him and do all

the troublesome part I will let you come and admire him as often as you like.

CLARA. Rosie: you have the devil's own cheek.

MRS ETTEEN. I! I am the greatest coward alive.

CLARA. But take care. You think that the risk you run is only to be thrown out of the house as you deserve. But that isnt the risk you run at all. You can stay to dinner if you like: Imm is dining with us, and Conrad, and the rector. You can just trot over the house and look for Franklyn if you want to: he is somewhere about, waiting til you have gone. But some day, if you dont take care, you will be taken at your word. For two pins I would just throw over all this marriage business and leave you in possession. It is no sinecure for me, nor for any woman.

MRS ETTEEN [*rising, and not trying to conceal that she is wounded*] If he is waiting for me to go, I had better go. [*She goes to the door. It opens in her face; and Franklyn enters*].

FRANKLYN [*with a courteous air of delighted surprise*] What! You here, Mrs Etteen! How do you do?

MRS ETTEEN. Didnt you know? [*She turns and looks at Clara*].

CLARA. I had to tell her you were waiting for her to go, Frank. If Rosie wont be a lady and tell lies enough to make herself agreeable, she must not complain if the truth hits her harder than she bargains for. People with soft corns shouldnt stand on other people's toes.

Mrs Etteen, greatly distressed, snatches out her handkerchief.

CLARA. Sit down, Rosie; and dont be a fool: you can stay to dinner.

MRS ETTEEN [*struggling inarticulately with her tears*] I am so sorry – [*she cannot go on*].

CLARA. Frank: take her round the garden and talk to her. It is you that have upset her.

MRS ETTEEN. Oh no.

FRANKLYN. Come.

MRS ETTEEN [*taking his arm*] I am so ashamed – so sorry – [*She goes out into the garden on Franklyn's arm*].

CONRAD. You got the best of that, Clara.

CLARA. I should think so, indeed. I always get the best of it. She used to frighten me and fluster me. Thats the worst of the way women are brought up: we are trained never to tell the truth or to face the truth: all we know is how to play cat's cradle with one another; and of course the consequence is that the moment we are faced by anyone who just throws the truth in our faces, we get rattled and make fools of ourselves. Rosie played that game on me and nearly drove me mad. I dont know what I should have done if Frank hadnt taken me in hand and shewed me the trick of it. Then I played it on her. I can play her head off at it. When she tries to terrify me by putting a few of her cards on the table: I put the whole pack on the table, both hers and mine; and as I have the ace of trumps I win every time. She came here as a thief to steal Frank from me. Now she comes as a beggar: and I throw her a scrap of him occasionally. She is having her scrap now, in the garden, poor wretch!

CONRAD. Yes: that is what women are: dogs fighting one another for the best bones. And what are we men? The bones you fight for. You dont catch me getting married.

CLARA. Oh indeed! You are glad enough to come here and be taken care of and pet the children without any expense or responsibility, all the same. You cuckoo! [*She flings the epithet in his face and sweeps scornfully out of the room*].

CONRAD [*rising*] Damn her impudence! I will never enter this house again.

IMMENSO. That will not solve the problem. The bachelor solution is no solution. The bachelor is either a hermit or a cuckoo. Go and get married, Con. Better be a husband than a domestic parasite.

CONRAD. I shall go out of this house, anyhow. Good evening.

IMMENSO. I doubt if she will let you. However, you can try. Good evening.

CONRAD. I will jolly soon see whether she can stop me [*he leaves the room*].

Immenso takes a paper and begins to read; putting his feet up, and making himself quite comfortable on the sofa.

CLARA'S VOICE. Where are you going, Con?

CONRAD'S VOICE. I am going out of this house, never to darken your doors again: thats where I'm going.

CLARA'S VOICE. You are going to do nothing of the sort, because I have locked up all your things in your room.

THE TWO VOICES SIMULTANEOUSLY

I tell you I am going. Give me the key of my room instantly. Do you suppose I am going to stay in a house where I am told to my face that I am a sponge, a parasite, a-a-a-a cuckoo? I'm damned if I'll stand it. You can keep your house and your children and your unfortunate devil of a husband. I tell you I wont. What pleasure is it to you to have me if you grudge every morsel I eat and drink and are jealous every time I talk to Savvy? Youre as jealous as –	Now dont be ridiculous, Con: you know very well you brought it on yourself by saying that Rosie and I were two dogs fighting for a bone. If you go, what am I to say to Frank and Savvy? Am I to tell them the nasty things you said about them? And there is roast chicken being done expressly for you; and I have not the least intention of allowing you to waste it. So be good, and remember that we dine at half-past seven, and that half-past seven means half-past seven and not eight as it usually –

DOMESTICITY OF FRANKLYN BARNABAS

The voices fade out of hearing. Immenso, who at the first sound of them has looked up from his paper to listen, smiles broadly; crosses his shins; and settles himself to read until the rector comes to dinner.

We may as well skip the dinner, as the presence of the rector puts a stop to domestic bickering without adding to the brilliancy of the general conversation. Readers of Back to Methuselah will remember the Reverend William Haslam as a very young man who had been shoved into a Church living, as he expressed it, by his father, who was a friend of the patron and a schoolfellow of the bishop. Being at this stage of his career a complete unbeliever, with only two passions, one for lawn tennis and the other for Savvy Barnabas, and being afflicted with perfect clearness of mind as to his unworthiness as a parson (being a hollow fraud, he calls it) he is not very interesting even in ordinary Hampstead society. In the presence of intellects like those of Champernoon and the Barnabases he is a mere cipher in a continuous collar. Nobody, himself least of all, has the faintest suspicion that he alone of all that gifted company is destined to survive three hundred years and be three times an archbishop.

For the present, then, it makes no difference to the dinner party when he slips away from it at the earliest possible moment with Savvy, and takes refuge in the library, where we may now have a look at them as they sit on the sofa, each with an arm round the other's ribs.

HASLAM. Look here, darling: hadnt you better tell your father that we're going to be married?

SAVVY. He wont care.

HASLAM. But he ought to know, you know.

SAVVY. Well, you can tell him if you like. I am not going to intrude my affairs on him when he doesnt even pretend to take any interest in them. I dont mind telling Nunky.

DOMESTICITY OF FRANKLYN BARNABAS

HASLAM. When is it to be? He may as well know the worst at once.

SAVVY. As soon as you like. Now that both Nunky and Papa have gone raving mad on this stunt of theirs about living for ever, life here is becoming unbearable. They expect a dress to last ten years because they expect me to last three hundred. Promise me that when we are married, I shall never hear the words Creative Evolution again.

HASLAM. I promise. I cant keep Adam and Eve out of the lessons in church; but I can keep Creative Evolution out of them. Oh, by the way! I am afraid you will have to come to church. Do you mind very much?

SAVVY. Not a bit. I had to do it in college, you know. Thatll be all right, Bill.

HASLAM. I always rip through pretty fast; and I never preach more than seven minutes: old Lady Mumford makes such an awful row if I do.

SAVVY. Does that matter?

HASLAM. I should think it does. Her big subscription just barely makes the two ends meet in the church accounts. Consequently in our parish Lady Mumford is to all intents and purposes the Church of England.

Franklyn and Conrad come in.

HASLAM [*to Franklyn*] By the way, sir, I think you ought to know. Would you mind if Savvy and I were to get married?

CONRAD. Hallo!

HASLAM. Yes: I know it sounds rather sudden. But theres no immediate hurry. Any time will do.

SAVVY. No it wont.

HASLAM. I dont mean our marriage, darling.

FRANKLYN. You mean only my consent, is that it?

HASLAM. Well, I suppose that is what it comes to. Ha! ha! Priceless!

FRANKLYN. Well, Savvy: you know your own business best.

CONRAD. There is no gainsaying the urge of Creative Evolution.

SAVVY [*desperately*] Oh, Nunky, do drop it for a moment. [*To Haslam*] Lets get married tomorrow. You can perform the ceremony yourself, cant you?

HASLAM. I think I shall ask the blooming bishop. It would be awful cheek; but I think he'd like it.

Clara, Mrs Etteen, and Immenso come in.

CLARA. Franklyn: go and play billiards. You will not digest your dinner if you sit there talking to Conrad.

FRANKLYN. Oh, goodness gracious, may I not have indigestion and intelligent conversation if I prefer it to running round a billiard table after my health?

CLARA. You will be very disagreeable if you get indigestion. And Con wants to smoke. Off with you.

FRANKLYN. Oh, very well. [*He goes out sulkily*].

CONRAD. Anything for a quiet life. [*He goes out, taking his pipe out of his pocket as he goes*].

CLARA. Savvy: take Rosie and Imm to the drawing room; and let us have some music. Imm hasnt heard Rosie play; and the sooner he gets it over, the better.

MRS ETTEEN [*moving towards the door*] Do you really want any music, Mr Champernoon?

IMMENSO [*going with her*] In moods of battle and victory I want the bagpipes, Mrs Etteen. My wife imitates them on the black keys of the piano. I do the drum, with a dinner gong. [*They go out*].

SAVVY. Come along, Bill.

Haslam rises with alacrity.

CLARA. No: Bill will stay and talk to me. You clear out.

Savvy, surprised, looks at Haslam, whose countenance has fallen; then goes out slowly.

CLARA. Sit down.

Haslam sits down.

CLARA [*sitting down also*] Am I, too, privileged to call you Bill, Mr Haslam?

HASLAM. Certainly, if you like.

CLARA. You mustnt suppose because Mr Barnabas is blind, I am. What are your intentions, young man?

HASLAM [*his eyes twinkling*] I have just declared them to Mr Barnabas.

CLARA. What!

HASLAM [*enjoying his retort immensely*] Priceless!

CLARA. I see nothing priceless about it. I think it was great impudence of you to speak to Mr Barnabas before Savvy had said a word to me. What did Franklyn say?

HASLAM. You came in before he had time to say anything. But it seemed to go down all right.

CLARA. A nice father! Didnt he ask you a single question?

HASLAM. You didnt give him a chance.

CLARA. What means have you?

HASLAM. The stipend is £180; and the rectory lets for £300 a year furnished.

CLARA. Genteel poverty. And nothing to look forward to. They wont make you an archbishop.

HASLAM. I should think not. Ha! ha! Priceless!

CLARA. Very well. All I have to say is that if she is fool enough to marry you *I* cant stop her. So dont hope to get out of it that way. You have let yourself in for it; and now you must make the best of it.

HASLAM. It is rather awful. That is, of course, when it isnt delightful.

CLARA. What about your own people?

HASLAM. Oh, they expect me to make an ass of myself. I am the fool of the family. They look to my brother to marry money.

CLARA. Well, you seem to have a fairly sensible family: thats one comfort. I wish I could say as much for us. You know, dont you, that Con is as mad as a hatter, and that Franklyn is going soft in the same way? They think theyre going to live for three hundred years. I dont know what is to become of us. I have to keep up appearances; but – [*she almost breaks down*].

HASLAM [*much concerned*] Oh, dont take it that way, Mrs Barnabas. I had no idea you were worrying about it. I am really awfully sorry.

CLARA. Did you suppose I was a fool? Or did you think I believed all that stuff about creative evolution, or whatever they call it?

HASLAM. It's only a fad. I assure you men get the wildest fads without going a bit dotty. Jolly good thing for them, too. If they dont take to a fad they take to drink or to gambling on the stock exchange, or to the classics or something horribly tiresome.

CLARA [*a little consoled*] You really think that, Bill?

HASLAM. Quite sure of it. My brother's mad on golf. My mother's mad on gardening. Theyre not intellectual, you know. Mr Barnabas and the doctor have to go mad on something intellectual. This three hundred years stunt is a priceless refuge for them.

CLARA. Well, you comfort me. I need it badly, God knows. Thank you. For myself, I had far rather have a comforting son-in-law than one with lots of money. Savvy'd spend it all anyhow, if you had a million. The way she runs through boots! And theyre fortyfive shillings a pair now.

HASLAM. It's awfully good of you to take to me like this, Mrs Barnabas.

CLARA. There are not so many people in the world that one can take to. [*Looking at him critically*] After all, you may come to be an archbishop yet. Old Archbishop Chettle, who was my father's tutor at Durham, was just as ridiculous as you are.

HASLAM. People dont mind it so much when they come to know me.

CLARA. I am a little ridiculous myself, you know. I cannot suffer fools gladly. You dont seem to mind. Can you put up with me as a mother-in-law? I wont come too often.

HASLAM. You will suit me down to the ground. Fancy

your turning out so pricelessly jolly as this!

CLARA [*pleased*] Very well. Now run off to the drawing room, and ask Rosie to play.

HASLAM. I'd a jolly sight rather hear Savvy play.

CLARA. Savvy doesnt want to play. Rosie is dying for an excuse to play Saint Nepomuk's Eve because it always fetches Franklyn from the billiard room to listen to her. Imm will never think of asking her to play: he will only talk her head off. Be kind to her, and ask her for something by Hugo Wolf.

HASLAM. Rather a lark it would be, wouldnt it, if Uncle Imm were to cut Mr Barnabas out with Mrs Etteen?

CLARA. Imm has no ear for music. She cant do it with the piano anyhow.

A hollow chord of G flat and D flat is heard droning from the drawing room piano. Then The Campbells are Coming is played on the black keys.

A drum obbligato begins on the dinner gong, played at first with childish enjoyment, and proceeding, in a rapid crescendo, to ecstasy.

HASLAM. She is doing it with the piano! Priceless!

CLARA [*indignantly*] Well!

SAVVY [*rushing in*] Mother: do come and stop Uncle Imm. If he starts dancing he will shake the house down. Oh, listen to them. [*She puts her fingers in her ears*].

CLARA [*rushing out*] Stop, stop! Imm. Rosie! Stop that horrible noise.

SAVVY [*shutting the door with a slam*] Did you ever hear anything like it? Uncle Imm is the greatest baby.

The noise suddenly stops with the sound of the dinner gong being torn from Imm's grasp and flung down on the carpet, presumably by Clara. The piano takes the hint and stops also.

SAVVY. What did mother want with you?

HASLAM. To ask me my intentions. Priceless!

SAVVY. Did she make a row?

HASLAM. Not a bit. She was awfully nice about it. She's a stunning good sort.

SAVVY. Bill!!

HASLAM. She is, really. I had no idea. We shall get on first rate.

SAVVY. Then I cry off. She has got round you.

HASLAM. Why? Arnt you glad?

SAVVY. Glad! When I am marrying you to get rid of her! Bill: the match is off. If she has got round you I might just as well stay at home. How does she get round people? Why am I the only person she doesnt think it worth her while to get round?

HASLAM. She didnt get round me: she went straight at me; and over I went. What could I do? I was prepared to hold my end up if she started fighting. But she fell on my neck. It wasnt my fault.

SAVVY. It's too disgusting. All men are the same; theyre no good when it comes to tackling a woman who can see nobody's point of view except her own.

HASLAM. She seems to like me in a sort of way.

SAVVY. She always wanted a son. All women do who like men: the women who want girls only want live dolls. I was a disappointment because I was a girl. And now she comes and grabs you from me, as she grabs everything.

HASLAM. I feel just the same about my father, you know. How mother ever stuck it out with him I cant imagine.

SAVVY. You neednt boast about your mother: look at my father! See how he has stuck it out.

HASLAM. Parents are a ghastly fraud, if you ask me. But theyre necessary, I suppose.

SAVVY. Bill: youre very aggravating. I want to quarrel; and you wont. You have no sand in you.

HASLAM. Whats the good of quarrelling? If I felt like that I should jolly well punch your head and have done with it.

SAVVY [*throwing her arms violently round him and punctuating her epithets with savage kisses*] Pig. Fool. Idiot. Sillybilly.

HASLAM. Darling.

The dinner gong is heard bumping against something outside. They spring apart. Immenso enters in the character of a Highland chieftain carrying the gong like a target, and a hockey stick like a claymore. He has heightened the illusion by draping his shoulder with a travelling rug. He marches about, humming The Campbells. Mrs Etteen follows, half annoyed, half amused, and sits down on the sofa.

SAVVY [*still excited, to Immenso*] Sillybilly, sillybilly, sillybilly! Fat boy of Peckham! [*She snatches a ruler from the writing table. Immenso disposes himself immediately for combat. She makes a feint which he utterly fails to parry, and stabs him with the ruler. He falls ponderously and cautiously*]. Slain! slain! Mrs Etteen will receive your last breath. Come, Bill. [*She runs out*].

HASLAM. Priceless! [*He runs out after her*].

IMMENSO [*rising with difficulty*] 'Unwounded from the dreadful close; but breathless all, Fitzjames arose.'

MRS ETTEEN. Mr Champernoon: would you mind growing up for a moment, and condescending to treat me as an adult person?

IMMENSO. If you insist on our keeping up that dreary affectation I am bound to obey you. [*He throws down the hockey stick, the rug, and finally the gong*]. Farewell, ye real things. How good it is to hear your solid thump on the floor! The human boy sleeps with you there. The literary gasbag floats gently to your feet, madam. [*He sits down on the chair furthest away from her*].

MRS ETTEEN. But you have not floated to my feet. You have floated to the opposite end of the room.

IMMENSO. I need space if I am to treat you as a public meeting. I understand that you prefer that to Fitzjames.

MRS ETTEEN. There is a mystic region between the public meeting and the playground in which you have not been seen yet. It is the region in which men and women meet when they are alone together.

IMMENSO [*troubled and grave*] I had better say at once frankly, Mrs Etteen, that in that region I must put up a notice inscribed Nothing Doing. I am married; and I take marriage honorably and seriously. I am not putting this forward as a criticism of your attitude towards it. I only suggest that our attitudes are incompatible. Therefore will you allow me to continue to regard you as a public meeting?

MRS ETTEEN. By all means, if you can.

A pause. Mrs Etteen bears the silence calmly. Immenso is embarrassed by it.

IMMENSO [*at last*] The difficulty is that there is nothing before the meeting.

MRS ETTEEN. Just so. Come, Mr Champernoon! cant you get over this ridiculous shyness, and behave as Nature intended men and women to behave when they are alone together? Come and quarrel with me, or make love to me, or do something human. Search your soul for something to say to me that will not leave me cold and desolate.

IMMENSO. After searching my soul most carefully, absolutely the only remark that occurs to me is that we have been having wonderfully fine weather for the last fortnight. That is the commonplace but tragic truth.

MRS ETTEEN. That is the only thing you can find words for. But there is something between us that you cannot find words for: even you, who are so great a master of words.

IMMENSO. What, for example?

MRS ETTEEN. Say, a sense of deadly peril.

IMMENSO [*slowly*] Mrs Etteen: there are certain things I cannot say to a lady. One of them is that I feel perfectly safe with her.

MRS ETTEEN. So much the better! Can you really talk to me exactly as you would talk to the baker?

IMMENSO. I cannot say that. The baker is an organic part of society. Without the baker I should perish or live on snails. I am not convinced that beautiful ladies – shall I call them love ladies? – are an organic part of society. Without them I should not perish. I should flourish.

MRS ETTEEN. Without love ladies there would be no love children. Have you noticed that love children, like love ladies, are very beautiful?

IMMENSO. The statistics of illegitimate children –

MRS ETTEEN [*quickly*] I did not say illegitimate children, Mr Champernoon: I said love children. There are more love children born in wedlock than out of it: at least I hope so. But there are very few born at all, either in or out of wedlock.

IMMENSO. I have known some very beautiful persons of the sort you mean. I may be prejudiced against them because I, alas! am not an entrancingly beautiful person; but some of them were infernal rascals.

MRS ETTEEN. Spendthrifts and libertines and so forth, eh?

IMMENSO. I am myself a bit of a spendthrift as far as my means allow. No: I should call them thieves, if people who order goods they cannot pay for are thieves. I should call them rascals, because people who borrow money heartlessly from poorer people than themselves on the security of false promises to pay are in my opinion rascals. And libertines, certainly, of both sexes.

MRS ETTEEN. And yet charming people, all the same. Centres of exquisite happiness. Living fountains of love.

IMMENSO. That is why I hate them. They bring these precious things into contempt. They are living blasphemies.

MRS ETTEEN. And so you have to put up with plain

dowdy people, and have children as ugly as yourself. What sort of world is it where the ugly practical people, the people who can deal with money and material things, and be thoroughly mean about them, succeed, and the beautiful people who live in noble dreams and continually strive to realize them are ruined and despised? Do you suppose they like borrowing from poor people, who are the only ones simple enough to lend, or that they enjoy being dunned by tradesmen? Is it their fault that when they offer love, they are told that unless they steal it they must pay for it with all their worldly goods, with their liberty, with nearly the whole of their lives? Is that right? You are a clever man: you are a professional moralist. Is there nothing wrong in it? Give me an honest answer. Dont preach at me: but tell me as man to woman. Do you not feel sometimes that it is all wrong?

IMMENSO. As a professional moralist I can make out a case against it. I can make out a case for it just as easily. Cases do not impress me. They never impress people who have the knack of making them. It's no use giving tracts to a missionary.

MRS ETTEEN. Yes: I was wrong to argue about it. The moment one argues one goes wrong at once. It is deeper than argument. You may say what you like; but can you feel that the beautiful people are all wrong and that the ugly people are all right? Would you think them beautiful and ugly if you really believed that?

IMMENSO. I have noticed that there are subjective and objective people; and –

MRS ETTEEN. Beautiful subjective people and ugly objective people?

IMMENSO [*uneasy under her greater conviction*] Beauty is a matter of taste, after all. One man's meat is another man's poison. Lots of people do not think my wife beautiful. They are nitwits; but they have a right to their opinion.

MRS ETTEEN [*with dignity*] Mr Champernoon: is it possible that you think I am discussing the question of sex with you?

IMMENSO [*taken aback*] Well – er – Well, good heavens! what else are we discussing?

MRS ETTEEN. *I* am discussing beauty, which is not a matter of taste at all, but a matter of fact as to which no difference of opinion is possible among cultivated people. Can you produce a single person of any culture who thinks the Venus of Milo or the Hermes of Praxiteles ugly? Can you produce a single person who thinks –

IMMENSO. Who thinks me beautiful? Not one.

MRS ETTEEN. I have seen worse, Mr Champernoon. [*He bows*]. You are very like Balzac, of whom Rodin made one of the greatest statues in the world. But dont you see that this sex attraction, though it is so useful for keeping the world peopled, has nothing to do with beauty: that it blinds us to ugliness instead of opening our eyes to beauty. It is what enables us to endure a world full of ugly sights and sounds and people. You can do without the Venus of Milo because the young lady at the refreshment bar can make you forget her. I dont want to talk about such attractions: they are only the bait in the trap of marriage: they vanish when they have served their turn. But have you never known really beautiful people, beautiful as girls, beautiful as matrons, beautiful as grandmothers, or men to match them? Do you not want a world of such beautiful people, instead of what the gentleman in Mr Granville-Barker's play calls 'this farmyard world of sex'? Will you dare to tell me that the world was no worse when the lords of creation were monkeys than it is now that they are men, ugly as most of them are? Do you really want us all to become like ants and bees because ants and bees are industrious and goody goody?

IMMENSO. As I am myself a species of human bumble bee, I cannot give you an unprejudiced opinion.

MRS ETTEEN. No: you shall not ride off on a quip, Mr Champernoon. Stand to your guns. You thought I was going to entice you into a flirtation: you see now that I am trying to convert you to a religion of beauty.

IMMENSO. I am not sure that I do not think you all the more dangerous. You might pervert me intellectually; but on the other ground I am invincible. I cannot flirt. I am not what is called a lady's man, Mrs Etteen.

MRS ETTEEN. You cannot flirt! Mr Champernoon: you are the most incorrigible flirt in England, and the very worst sort of flirt too. You flirt with religions, with traditions, with politics, with everything that is most sacred and important. You flirt with the Church, with the Middle Ages, with the marriage question, with the Jewish question, even with the hideous cult of gluttony and drunkenness. Every one of your discussions of these questions is like a flirtation with a worthless woman: you pay her the most ingenious and delightful compliments, driving all your legitimate loves mad with distress and jealousy: but you are not a bit in earnest: behind all your sincere admiration of her priceless pearls and her pretty paint you loathe the creature's flesh and blood. You are all flirts, you intellectuals. If you flirted with housemaids and dairymaids, or with chorus girls, I could forgive you; but to flirt with ghastly old hags because they were the mistresses of kings and of all the oppressors of the earth is despicable and silly.

IMMENSO [*reddening*] I deny that innuendo. I was in a Liberal set, a Protestant set, an atheist set, a Puritan set. I had everything to lose by defending the Church and the Middle Ages, by denouncing Puritanism, by affirming the existence of God.

MRS ETTEEN. Then you had not even the excuse of wanting money or a knighthood. You flirted with these old, wicked, outworn things from pure devilment, because you were a born coquette.

DOMESTICITY OF FRANKLYN BARNABAS

IMMENSO. I do not admit that these institutions are wicked or outworn. I admit that they are old, which proves at least that they were not jerry built.

MRS ETTEEN. Cruelty is old. Slavery is old. Greed, ambition, plague, pestilence, and famine are old. They are not jerry built either. Are they any the better for that? I am not so clever as you, Mr Champernoon; but I can see that if we did not indulge you by stepping softly about the room because we want to admire your wonderful houses of cards, they would come down at the first resolute footfall. As often as not it is your own foot that comes down when some abominable oppression stings you into earnestness; and –

IMMENSO. And who can expect any house to stand that earth-shaking shock?

MRS ETTEEN. A jibe at your size has got you out of many a controversial difficulty.

IMMENSO. I protest I have exploited it only in the interests of good humor. I laugh at it with the wrong side of my mouth. [*He sits down beside her*]. But I still defend the past. My roots are in the past: so are yours.

MRS ETTEEN. My roots are in the past: my hopes are in the future.

IMMENSO. The past is as much a part of eternity as the future. Beware of ingratitude to the past. What is gratitude? The cynic says, a sense of favors to come. Many people would say that we cannot be grateful to the past because we have nothing to expect from it. But if we had no memory of favors from the past we could have no faith in favors from the future. Why do I uphold the Church: I, who know as much of the crimes of the Churches as you do? Not for what the Church did for men, but for what men did for the Church. It brought us no gifts; but it drew forth gifts from us. And that is just as it should be. I love the Church because Michelangelo painted its churches. You complain of it because the churches did not paint Michelangelo. Well, suppose they had painted him! Suppose they had tarred and feathered him! Would you not place the painting of Michelangelo, with the burning of John Huss or Giordano Bruno or Joan of Arc, among the crimes of the Churches?

MRS ETTEEN. That is a very pretty little juggle with words, and very funny. But when you are talking of Michelangelo you are talking of a man so great that he was literally a demigod. When you talk of the Church, you are talking of a pack of common men calling themselves clergymen and priests, and trying to persuade us that they are demigods by wearing ugly black clothes. Michelangelo did not paint for them: he painted for me, and for people like you and me. We are the spectators for whom he painted: we are the Church which drew out his gifts. It was for us that Bach and Beethoven composed, that Phidias and Rodin made statues, that the poets sang and the philosophers became seers. It is you who are faithless and disloyal in giving the allegiance we owe to them to corrupt gangs of little lawyers and politicians and priests and adventurers organized as States and Churches and dressed up like actors to seem the thing they are not. They pretend to see events with glass eyes, and to hear the music of the spheres with ass's ears. [*She pauses. Immenso is staring before him like a nun in a trance*]. Are you listening? [*He does not answer*]. I know. You are thinking how you can work all this into an article.

IMMENSO [*waking up suddenly*] Damn it, I am. [*He salutes*]. *Touché!*

MRS ETTEEN. *Plait-il?*

IMMENSO. That is what a fencer says to his adversary when he acknowledges a hit. Yes: you got in that time. But why should I not make it into an article? It is my trade.

MRS ETTEEN. Couldnt you make it into an action of some sort. Couldnt you kill somebody, for instance, as all the people who are in earnest do?

IMMENSO. I am prepared to kill. You may think it boasting; but, like Hamlet, I do not hold my life at a pin's fee when my fate cries out. As I am not going to kill anybody—shall I say as we are not going to kill anybody? —I suppose our fate does not cry out.

MRS ETTEEN. Oh yes: I am as great a coward, as futile a creature as you: dont think I dont know it. Shall I tell you why that is?

IMMENSO. You evidently will, whether I say yes or no.

MRS ETTEEN. It is because we have not really finished with the sensualities, the crudities, the vulgarities and superstitions that are holding us back. We have not had time to exhaust them, to survive them, to be forced to provide for a spiritual future on earth when they are all dead in us, just as we are forced to provide for bread in our present old age. We do not live long enough –

IMMENSO [*starting*] What! Are you on this Back-to-Methuselah tack too? Has all this been the craze of my brothers-in-law at second hand?

MRS ETTEEN. Oh, very manly man that you are, it does not occur to you that Franklyn Barnabas may have had this from me. Did he ever speak of it before he met me?

IMMENSO. Now that you mention it, no. But it began with Conrad; and you certainly did not work in his laboratory.

MRS ETTEEN. Conrad never saw the scope of his idea any more than Weismann, from whom he got it. He saw how it affected science: he knew that he had to die when he was just beginning to discover what science really is, and had just found out that the experience of people who die at seventy is only a string of the mistakes of immaturity. He had the skeleton of the great faith; but it was Franklyn who put the flesh on it. And it was I, the woman, who made that flesh for him out of my own. That is my relation to Franklyn. That is what Clara would call the intrigue between us.

IMMENSO [*gravely*] She should call it the tragedy of the man who does not trust his wife. He should tell Clara.

MRS ETTEEN. He tells her everything she can understand. If he tries to tell her more it is thrown back in his face like a blow. She is jealous of me; and with good reason.

IMMENSO. But why should he not explain to her the nature of his interest in you, or rather of your common interest in the great faith, as you call it? It is perfectly innocent.

MRS ETTEEN. Will you go home and tell your wife that you find me a very interesting person, and that though you began by keeping at the other end of the room, you have been sitting almost in my lap for the last five minutes?

IMMENSO [*springs up with an inarticulate exclamation. Then, with Johnsonian courtesy*] I beg your pardon, Mrs Etteen. [*He is about to sit down again further from her, but corrects himself, and sits scrupulously as close to her as before*].

MRS ETTEEN. Have I won your interest fairly or have I not? Have I played a single low trick, or practised a single woman's wile?

IMMENSO. You are not a single woman, Mrs –

MRS ETTEEN. Tut! tut! tut! no puns, no jokes, no evasion. Was it fair play or foul play?

IMMENSO. You have landed a very large fish, Mrs Etteen. But you fished fairly. I wish to announce in all honor that I adore you [*he kisses her hand*]. I say it in all honor; and I mean it. And yet I know I shall not tell my wife. Will that be honorable?

MRS ETTEEN. You make too much fuss about it. Do you suppose that there is not among our literary geniuses some writer whose best books she sometimes devours with just a tiny little more relish than your second best? But she does not tell you so. Is that dishonorable, or is it simply kindness – loving-kindness, as the Bible says.

IMMENSO. I hope so.

MRS ETTEEN. Every good wife should commit a few infidelities to keep her husband in countenance. The extent to which married people strain their relations by pretending that there is only one man or woman in the world for them is so tragic that we have to laugh at it to save ourselves from crying. But we shant be so foolish when we all live three hundred years.

How this conversation ended I cannot tell; for I never followed up the adventure of Immenso Champernoon with Mrs Etteen, and dont believe it came to anything.

DEATH OF AN OLD REVOLUTIONARY HERO

(From The Clarion of 24 March 1905)

DEATH OF AN OLD
REVOLUTIONARY
HERO

So old Joe Budgett of Balwick – Stalwart Joe – is dead at last. The Socialist movement has seldom mourned a more typical thoroughgoer than dear old Joe. We all knew him; for he quarrelled with every one of us at one time or another; and yet is there one who is not sorry to lose him? Those who witnessed that simple funeral at Balwick last Thursday morning, when the remains of a poor workman in a cheap pine coffin were borne through the pelting sleet to their last resting-place on the shoulders of Robert Blatchford and H. M. Hyndman, Sidney Webb and Harold Cox, Jaurès (who had come from Paris expressly to pay this last sad duty to the veteran of the International) and myself, Mr Gerald Balfour and Lord Lansdowne, must have asked themselves what manner of man this was to receive a tribute from persons of such diverse views, and so far removed from him in social position.

Joseph Budgett was a heavily built man; and even at 90 – his age when he died – he was no light weight. My heart was heavy as I helped to shoulder the coffin; but I confess that poor Joe seemed heavier still by the time we reached the grave; for we were not trained to the work; and there was a good deal of sugaring among the bearers: Harold, for instance, did nothing but shelter from the sleet under the pall after the first ten yards; Jaurès and Hyndman argued in French instead of attending to their work; Blatchford, after the manner of highly sympathetic literary geniuses with a strong susceptibility to incongruous humor, was so convulsed with suppressed laughter that his quiverings rattled Joe's bones over the stones without contributing anything to their support; and if it had not been for Webb and myself (Fabians doing the practical work as usual), Joe Budgett would never have got to his grave; for Gerald Balfour and Lord Lansdowne were too far forward to get their shoulders properly under the coffin.

Lord Lansdowne was evidently taken aback to find that there was to be no religious service (Joe having been an uncompromising atheist); but he spoke very feelingly at the graveside. 'It was part of the tragedy of this man's career,' he said, 'that in all the seventy years of active political life during which he agitated ceaselessly on behalf of his own class, he never found either in the Liberal party or in the irregular groups which pretended to represent Labor and Socialism, that incorruptible spirit, that stainless purity of principle, that absolute integrity, aloof from all compromising alliances, which his honest character demanded as the sole and sufficient claim to his support. He regarded the Conservative party as an open enemy; but he rightly preferred an open enemy to a false or half-hearted friend; and so, if we never gained his theoretic approval, we at least always had what we valued far more: his practical support.'

It was at this point that the accident of which so much has been made befell Blatchford. The account of it in the evening papers was much exaggerated. It is true that the editor of The Clarion broke down and covered his face with his handkerchief. It is also true that in an attempt to hurry away from the graveside with his eyes full of tears he tripped over the sexton's spade; but he did not fall into the grave, nor was an impression of the nameplate found on his person afterwards. The capitalist press naturally strives to belittle and make ridiculous

DEATH OF AN OLD REVOLUTIONARY HERO

the obsequies of a political opponent; but I cannot help thinking that it might have shewn better taste than to choose a funeral for a display of its cockney facetiousness.

The rest of the speaking has been so fully reported in all the Labor papers that I need not give any account of it here, except that Webb's advice to the Progressive Municipalities to make Free Funerals a plank in the program of Municipal Socialism was quite practical and sincere, and was not, as The Deptford Times asserted, a thinly veiled threat of wholesale political assassination.

A good deal of misunderstanding has been caused by the report that the reason I did not speak was that Mrs Budgett said it would be a mockery for a man who had done his best to kill her husband to make a speech over his grave, and that Joe would turn in his coffin at the sound of my voice. Now it is quite true that Mrs Budgett actually did say this, and that I took no part in the speaking in deference to her wishes. But the three Labor papers who have rebuked Mrs Budgett for making her husband's funeral the occasion of an attack on the Fabian Society are quite wrong in their interpretation of her remarks. She was not thinking of the Fabian Society at all. The truth is, I once did actually try to kill Joe; and as it happened a good many years ago, and he forgave me handsomely – though Mrs Budgett could never forget it – I may as well do penance now by describing the affair exactly as it happened.

I was quite a young Socialist then; and when I heard one day in spring that old Budgett was passing away whilst the earth was germinating all around, a lump came into my throat: the only one I have ever had. I got used to the news later on, because Joe began dying when he was 75, and never got out of his bed from that time forth except to address a meeting or attend a Socialist Congress. But, as I have just said, I was a young hand then; and an intense desire to see the old revolutionary

DEATH OF AN OLD REVOLUTIONARY HERO

hero before he returned to dust took hold of me. The end of it was that I found myself a couple of days later at his cottage at Balwick, asking Mrs Budgett whether he was strong enough to see me. She said he was not, as his heart was in such a state that the least excitement or any sudden noise might be fatal. But when she saw how disappointed I was, she added that he was so mortal dull that a little company would perhaps do him good; and so, if I would promise not to talk to him, and be careful not to make any noise, she would let me up for a while. I promised eagerly; and we went up together, she warning me not to trip over the high sills or dash my head against the low lintels of the sturdy old oak-framed cottage, and I doing the one at every door in my anxiety to avoid doing the other.

This is perhaps the best place for me to say that Mrs Budgett struck me even then as being extraordinarily devoted to Joe. In fact, I dont think she ventured to regard him as anything so familiar as a husband. She had known both toil and sorrow; for she had had to keep Joe and bring up a family of five by her own exertions. As a boy, Joe had been apprenticed to a bigginwainer, and had served his time and learnt the trade; but when a little thumbed and blackened volume containing Shelley's Queen Mab and Men of England, and Tom Paine's Age of Reason, came in his way, and he heard a speech from Orator Hunt, the famous Man in the White Hat, he threw up his bigginwaining and devoted his life to the cause of the people, entrusting all his business affairs to his faithful wife, who never let him know want. In course of time he almost forgot his trade; for I remember on one occasion, when William Morris, in his abrupt way, said to him 'And what the devil is a bigginwainer?' Joe was quite at a loss, and could describe it only as a branch of the coopering. The consequence was that Mrs Budgett had to work pretty hard as a laundress; but she did not mind hard work: what

weighed on her was the curious fatality that the five
children all turned against Joe. They became strong
chapelgoers and moneymakers, and made their quarrel
with Joe an excuse for doing very little for her, because,
they said, they did not want their earnings wasted in
encouraging him. So there had been sorrow and strife
enough even in that little household.

Joe was sitting up in bed when we entered; and I was
struck at once by the lion-like mane of white hair, the
firmly closed mouth with its muscles developed by half
a century of public speaking, the serene brow, clear
ruddy complexion, and keen bold eyes of the veteran.
He gave my hand a strong hearty grip, and said, in tones
that were still resonant (for he had not then acquired
the senile whistling utterance that pierced the ears and
hearts of the International Socialist Congress at Amsterdam), 'Do I at last see before me that old and tried
friend of the working classes, George Bernard Shaw?
How are you, George?'

Although I was not then old, and had no other feeling
for the working class than an intense desire to abolish
them and replace them by sensible people, Joe's cordial
manner encouraged and set me at ease. He invited me
to sit down; and before my trousers had pressed the
chair he was deep in a flood of reminiscences.

'I served my apprenticeship to the revolution,' he said,
'in the struggle against the Reform Bill of 1832.'

'*Against* it!' I cried.

'Aye, against it,' he said. 'Old as I am, my blood still
boils when I think of the way in which a capitalist tailor
named Place – one of the half-hearted Radical vermin –
worked that infamous conspiracy to enfranchise the
middle classes and deny the vote to the working men. I
spoke against it on every platform in England. The Duke
of Wellington himself said to me that he disapproved of
revolutionists in general, but that he wished there were
a few more in the country of my kidney. Then came

DEATH OF AN OLD REVOLUTIONARY HERO

Chartism with its five points to fool the people and keep them from going to the real root of the matter by abolishing kings, priests, and private property. I shewed up its leaders, and had the satisfaction of seeing them all go to prison and come out without a single follower left to them. Then there was Bright and Cobden trailing the red herring of Free Trade across the trail of the emancipation of the working classes. I exposed them and their silly lies about cheap bread; and if I'd been listened to, no Englishman need ever have wanted bread again. Next came those black blots on our statute books, the Factory Acts, which recognized and regulated and legalized the accursed exploitation of the wives and children of the poor in the factory hells. Why, when I took the field against them, the very employers themselves said I was right and bid me God-speed in that campaign. Then came a worse swindle than the Reform Bill of 1832 – the '67 Bill, that gave just a handful of votes to a few workmen to bolster up the lie that Parliament represents the people instead of the vampires that live by plundering them. Didnt I get this scar over my eye from a stone that hit me while I was speaking against that Bill? But it became law for all that; and it emboldened the capitalists so much that they brought in the Education Act to drive all our children into their prisons of schools, and drill them into submission, and teach them to be more efficient slaves to make profits for their bloodsuckers. I spoke against it until I lost my voice for a whole month; and the people were with me too, heart and soul. It ended, as all double-facedness ends, in the Compromise. But thank God – not that I believe in God, but I use the word in a manner of speaking – I never compromised; and I never will. I left the International because it would not support me against the school Bastilles. And it was high time I did; for the International was a rotten compromise itself – half mere Trade-Unionism, and the other half a little private game of a rare old dodger named Marx – not Harry Marks, you know, but Karl – a compromise between a German and a Jew, *he* was: neither one thing nor the other. Then came the Commune of Paris, that did nothing but get the people of Paris slaughtered like mad dogs, because, as I pointed out at the time, it was too local, and stood for a city instead of for all the world. That put an end to everything for ten years; and then Socialism came up again with all the old mistakes and compromises: the half-hearted Chartist palliatives, the stooping to use the votes that the capitalists had bribed the people with, the pushing middle class men and autocratic swells at the head of it. I soon saw through Hyndman, and went with Morris into the Socialist League. But Morris was just as bad: all he wanted was our pennies to publish his poems – John Bull's Earthly Paradise and such tosh as that – in The Commonweal. I turned the League against him at last and took The Commonweal from him; and then he shewed his true nature by leaving us without means to pay the rent or publish the paper. Nothing came of it but another Reform Bill in 1885. I said "Does it abolish the registration laws and establish Universal Suffrage?" "No," they said. "Then have nothing to do with it," I said; and I spoke against it and agitated against it as I never agitated before. But the spirit of the workers was broken: they submitted to it like sheep. I took to my bed then, and never came out of it until the Dock Strike of 1889.'

'That roused you, did it?' I said, ambiguously, for I was now alive to the danger of jumping to any conclusions as to which side Joe might have taken.

'Could I lie here and see the people led away by a renegade like John Burns?' he exclaimed. 'Oh what a degradation that was! what a spectacle of crawling slavery! to see freeborn men begging for sixpence an hour instead of insisting in a voice of thunder on the

DEATH OF AN OLD REVOLUTIONARY HERO

full product of their labor! That was what Burns's pretended Socialism came to when he was put to the test. Sixpence an hour! But I expected no more. I saw through him from the first, just as I saw through Francis Place, and Fergus O'Connor, and Bronterre O'Brien, and the hypocritical Christian Socialists, and George Odger and Charles Bradlaugh and Hyndman and Morris and Champion and the German wirepullers, Bebel and Liebknecht. Self-seeking humbugs, talkers and compromisers all of them. None of them thorough, none of them genuine right through. The Dock Strike was nothing but a conspiracy between Cardinal Manning and John Burns to get Manning made Pope and to get Burns into the County Council. From that day I resolved that Burns should be driven from the cause of the people if my tongue and pen could do it. I'm organizing the Socialist opposition to him at Battersea – the genuine real Socialist opposition – and we'll have him out at the next election, when the Albert Palace is replaced by flats full of Conservative voters.'

'You are working for the Conservatives, then?'

'Young man: I have opposed the Tories all my life; but theres one thing I hate more than a Tory and thats a traitor.'

'Are all the Labor and Socialist leaders traitors?'

'Traitors! What puts such a thought into your mind? There are hundreds of true men who *ought* to be leaders, and will be when the people come to their senses. But the men that put themselves forward as leaders – that organize strikes and tout for votes and win elections – are all traitors and self-seekers, every man of them. It's the so-called unsuccessful men – the martyrs of the movement – the men that stand up for the people against everybody – mark that, against *everybody:* those are the real men, the salt of the people's cause, the glory of the revolution.'

He paused to take a sip of Liebig from a cup his wife

had brought him when we came in. He did it just as a speaker who is getting hoarse takes a sip of water on the platform. As his historical reminiscences had by this time come pretty well up to date, I thought he was done; but he suddenly switched off from history to moral exhortation.

'Look at me!' he said, 'going on for eighty, and as sound as a bell, except for this complaint in my heart, brought on by its bleeding for the people, and by overwork on the platform. Thats because I am a teetotaler, young man. And why am I a teetotaler? Because the cause of the people has been drink to me and stimulant to me and courage and warmth to me. Have I ever taken money for my principles? Never. The exploiting classes have offered over and over again to finance me. But I have never accepted a penny.'

'Except from your wife,' I remarked, thoughtlessly.

For a moment he was completely taken aback. Then he said, with indescribable majesty, 'Never. It is a foul lie; and whoever told it to you lies in his black throat. Prove to me that my wife has ever accepted a farthing from any oppressor of the people – that she has ever possessed a coin that was not earned by her own honest toil – and I will never look on her face again.'

'Thats not precisely what I mean,' I said, rather lamely; for I perceived that he had missed my point; and I rather doubted whether an explanation would mend matters. But he went on impetuously, being constitutionally a bad listener.

'My wife is a crown of rubies to me,' he said, with feeling. 'But I have always kept her out of the rough and tumble of political strife. It has broken me up; but at least I have shielded *her* from it.' Here he wiped away a tear. 'And when I think,' he went on, 'that there are men who are at this present moment plotting to give the vote to middle class women and deny it to my wife, I feel that I could rise from my bed like a young man and fight

DEATH OF AN OLD REVOLUTIONARY HERO

with my last breath against it as I did against the abomination of 1832.'

'All or nothing is your principle.' I said.

'Thats it,' he responded in a ringing voice, aglow with enthusiasm. 'All or nothing.'

'Well,' I said, 'as it is quite certain that you wont get All, you are practically the propagandist of Nothing: a Nihilist, in fact.'

'I am not ashamed of the word Nihilist,' he said. 'The Nihilists are my brothers.'

'To change the subject,' I said: 'is it really true that your heart is so bad that a sudden noise would kill you?'

'It is,' he said proudly. 'You could snuff me out like a candle by knocking that cup of Liebig's Extract over on to the floor.'

I looked round. A grandfather's clock ticked peacefully in the silence; for Joe, having reminded himself of the Liebig, was now drinking it; and even he could not talk and drink at the same time.

'Mr Budgett,' I said, rising, 'I am not a Nihilist; and it is perfectly clear to me that nothing will ever be done as long as you are about. So here goes!' and I pulled the grandfather's clock right over.

It fell with an appalling crash, striking as it fell until its weights thundered on the boards. Terrified at my own deed, I looked fearfully at the dying man. But Joe did not die. Instead, he sprang out of bed and said, 'What the — — are you doing?'

I thought it best, on the whole, to drop from the window and make for the railway station. Next day I sent him £2 – all I could spare – to pay for repairing the clock. But he sent it back to me with a letter of some thirty pages to say that he could do without a clock, but not without his self-respect.

That was why Mrs Budgett objected to my speaking at the funeral.

I confess, now that advancing years have mellowed

my character, that I was wrong in trying to kill Joe. One must live and let live. He bore no malice whatever for the incident, and used to refer to it with the utmost good humor, always ending up with the assurance that he did not take me seriously, and knew that my real object was simply to give him a hearty laugh.

His end was undoubtedly hastened by his efforts to turn the Labor movement against the new Bill for the Enfranchisement of Women; and he was proud to number a Countess among his converts. He almost lost his temper with me because I said that I should support any Bill that would make a start by giving a parliamentary vote or seat to even one woman, though the property qualification were a million sterling. 'All or nothing!' he said, with a fervor worthy of Ibsen's Brand.

The governing classes keep the mass of people enslaved by taking advantage of their sloth, their stupidity, their ignorance, their poverty, their narrowness, their superstition, and their vices. They could not enslave Joe by such means. He was energetic and clever; he was as well read as most cabinet ministers; he was sufficiently fed, clothed and housed (by his wife); he was a universalist in his breadth of view; he was an atheist; and he had practically no vices. And yet the governing classes tied Joe up with the principles of absolute morality tighter than they could tie a hooligan with a set of handcuffs.

After all, the principles of absolute morality were made for this very purpose; so Joe was hardly to be blamed.

THE SERENADE

(From The Magazine of Music, November 1885)

THE SERENADE

I CELEBRATED my fortieth birthday by one of the amateur theatrical performances for which my house at Beckenham is famous. The piece, written, as usual, by myself, was a fairy play in three acts; and the plot turned upon the possession of a magic horn by the hero, a young Persian prince. My works are so well known that it is unnecessary to describe the action minutely. I need only remind the reader that an important feature in the second act is the interruption of a festival by the sound of the horn, blown by the Prince in the heart of a loadstone mountain in which he has been entombed by a malignant fairy. I had engaged a cornist from the band of my regiment to blow the horn; and it was arranged that he should place himself, not upon the stage, but downstairs in the hall, so that the required effect of extreme distance should be produced.

The entertainment began pleasantly. Some natural disappointment was felt when it became known that I was not to act; but my guests excused me with perfect good humor when I pleaded my double duty as host and stage manager. The best seat in the auditorium was occupied by the beautiful Linda Fitznightingale. The next chair, which I had intended for myself, had been taken (rather coolly) by Porcharlester of the 12th, a young man of amiable disposition, and of some musical talent, which enables him to make the most of a somewhat effeminate baritone voice which he is weak enough to put forward as a tenor.

As Linda's taste for music approached fanaticism, Porcharlester's single accomplishment gave him, in her eyes, an advantage over men of more solid parts and mature age. I resolved to interrupt their conversation as soon as I was at leisure. It was some time before this occurred; for I make it a rule to see for myself that everything needed at the performances in my house is at hand in its proper place. At last Miss Waterloo, who enacted the heroine, complained that my anxiety made her nervous, and begged me to go to the front and rest myself. I complied willingly and hastened to the side of Linda. As I approached, Porcharlester rose, saying, 'I am going to take a peep behind: that is, if non-performers may be admitted.'

'Oh, certainly,' I said, glad to be rid of him. 'But pray do not meddle with anything. The slightest hitch –'

'All right,' he said, interrupting me. 'I know how fidgety you are. I will keep my hands in my pockets all the time.'

'You should not allow him to be disrespectful to you, Colonel Green,' said Linda, when he was gone. 'And I feel sure he will do no end of mischief behind the scenes.'

'Boys will be boys,' I replied. 'Porcharlester's manner is just the same to General Johnston, who is quite an old man. How are your musical studies progressing?'

'I am full of Schubert just now. Oh, Colonel Green, *do* you know Schubert's serenade?'

'Ah! a charming thing. It is something like this, I

think. Diddledi-dum, deediddledi-dum, deedum, deediddledyday.'

'Yes, it is a little like that. Does Mr Porcharlester sing it?'

'He tries to sing it. But he only appears to advantage when he sings trivial music. In nothing that demands serious sentiment, depth of feeling, matured sympathy, as it were –'

'Yes, yes. I know you think Mr Porcharlester flippant. Do you like the serenade?'

'Hm! well, the fact is – Do *you* like it?'

'I love it. I dream of it. I have lived on it for the last three days.'

'I must confess that it has always struck me as being a singularly beautiful piece of music. I hope to have the pleasure of hearing justice done to it by your voice when our little play is over.'

'*I* sing it! Oh, I dare not. Ah! here is Mr Porcharlester. I will make him promise to sing it for us.'

'Green,' said Porcharlester with ill-bred jocosity: 'I dont wish to disturb you groundlessly; but the fellow who is to play the magic horn hasnt turned up.'

'Good heavens!' I exclaimed. 'I ordered him for half-past seven sharp. If he fails, the play will be spoilt.'

I excused myself briefly to Linda, and hurried to the hall. The horn was there, on the table. Porcharlester had resorted to an infamous trick to get rid of me. I was about to return and demand an explanation, when it occurred to me that, after all, the bandsman might have left his instrument there at the morning rehearsal and had perhaps not come. But a servant whom I called told me that the man had arrived with military punctuality at half-past seven, and had, according to my orders, been shewn into the supper room joining the hall, and left there with a glass of wine and a sandwich. Porcharlester, then, had deceived me. As the servant returned to his duties, leaving me alone and angry in the hall, my attention was curiously arrested by the gleaming brass curves of the instrument on the table. Amid the inanimate objects around me the horn seemed silent and motionless in a way apart, as though, pregnant with dreadful sound, it were consciously biding its time for utterance. I stole to the table, and cautiously touched one of the valves with my forefinger. After a moment I ventured to press it down. It clicked. At a sound in the supper room I started back guiltily. Then the prompter's bell tinkled. It was the signal for the cornist to prepare for his cue. I awaited the appearance of the bandsman with some shame, hoping that he would not discover that I had been childishly meddling with his instrument. But he did not come. My anxiety increased; I hurried into the supper room. There, at the head of the table, sat the soldier, fast asleep. Before him were five decanters empty. I seized his shoulder and shook him violently. He grunted; made a drunken blow at me; and relapsed into insensibility.

Swearing, in my anger, to have him shot for this mutiny, I rushed back to the hall. The bell rang again. This second bell was for the horn to sound. The stage was waiting. In that extremity I saw but one way to save the piece from failure. I snatched up the intrument; put the smaller end into my mouth; and puffed vigorously through it. Waste of breath! not a sound responded. I became faint with my exertions; and the polished brass slipped through my clammy hands. The bell again urgently broke the ruinous silence. Then I grasped the horn like a vice; inflated my lungs; jammed the mouthpiece against my lips and set my teeth until it nearly cut me; and spat fiercely into it. The result was a titanic blast. My ears received a deafening shock; the lamp glasses whirred; the hats of my visitors rained from their pegs; and I pressed my bursting temples between my palms as the soldier reeled out, pale as though the last trumpet had roused him, and confronted the throng of amazed guests who appeared on the stairs.

*

For the next three months I studied the art of horn-blowing under the direction of an adept. He worried me by his lower middle class manners and his wearisome trick of repeating that the 'orn, as he called it, resembled the human voice more than any other instrument; but he was competent and conscientious; and I was persevering, in spite of some remonstrances from the neighbors. At last I ventured to ask him whether he considered me sufficiently advanced to play a solo in private for a friend.

'Well, Colonel,' he said, 'I tell you the truth, you havnt a born lip for it: at least, not yet. Then, you see, you blow so tremenjous. If youll believe me, sir, it dont need all the muscle you put into it: it spoils the tone. What was you thinking of playing for your friend?'

'Something that you must teach me. Schubert's serenade.'

He stared at me, and shook his head. 'It aint written for the hinstrument, sir,' he said. 'Youll never play it.'

'The first time I play it through without a mistake, I will give you five guineas, besides our regular terms.'

This overcame his doubts. I found the execution of the serenade, even after diligent practice, uncertain and very difficult. But I succeeded at last.

'If I was you, Colonel,' said my instructor, as he pocketed the five guineas, 'I'd keep that tune to myself, and play summat simpler for my friends. You can play it well enough here after half an hour's exercise; but when I'm not at your elbow youll find it wont come so steady.'

I made light of this hint, the prudence of which I now fully recognize. But at that time I was bent on a long cherished project of serenading Linda. Her house, near the northern end of Park Lane, was favorably situated for the purpose; and I had already bribed a servant to admit me to the small pleasure ground that lay between the house and the roadway. Late in June, I learned that she intended to repose for an evening from the fatigues of society. This was my opportunity. At nine o'clock I placed my horn in a travelling bag, and drove to the Marble Arch, where I alighted and walked to my destination. I was arrested by the voice of Porcharlester calling, 'Hallo, Colonel!' As I did not wish to be questioned, I thought it best to forestall him by asking whither he was bound.

'I am going to see Linda,' he replied. 'She contrived to let me know last night that she would be alone all this evening. I dont mind telling you these things, Colonel: you are a man of honor, and you know how good she is. I adore her. If I could only be certain that it is myself, and not merely my voice that she likes, I should be the happiest man in England.'

'I am quite sure that it cannot be your voice,' I said.

'Thank you,' he exclaimed, grasping my hand: 'it's very kind of you to say so; but I hardly dare flatter myself that you are right. It almost chokes me to look at her. Do you know I have never had the pluck to sing that serenade of Schubert's since she told me it was a favorite of hers?'

'Why? Does she not like your singing of it?'

'I tell you I have never ventured to sing it before her, though she is always at me for it. I am half jealous of that confounded tune. But I would do anything to please her; and I am going to surprise her with it tomorrow at Mrs Locksly Hall's. I have been taking lessons and working like a dog to be able to sing it in really first-rate style. If you meet her, mind you dont breathe a word of this. It is to be a surprise.'

'I have no doubt you will startle her,' I said, exulting at the thought that he would be a day too late. I knew that it would take a finer voice than his to bear comparison with the melancholy sweetness, the sombre menace, the self-contained power with which the instrument I carried would respond to a skilful performer. We parted; and I saw him enter the house of Linda. A few minutes later, I was in the garden, looking up at them from my place in the shadow as they sat near the open window. Their conversation did not reach me: I thought he would never go. The night was a little cold: and the ground was damp. Ten o'clock struck – a quarter past – half past – I almost resolved to go home. Had not the tedium been relieved by some pieces which she played on the pianoforte, I could not have held out. At last they rose; and I was now able to distinguish their words.

'Yes,' she said, 'it is time for you to go.' How heartily I agreed with her! 'But you might have sung the serenade for me. I have played three times for you.'

'I have a frightful cold,' he said. 'I really cannot. Goodnight.'

'What nonsense! You have not the least symptom of a cold. No matter: I will never ask you again. Goodnight, Mr Porcharlester.'

'Do not be savage with me,' he said. 'You shall hear me sing it sooner than you think, perhaps.'

'Ah! you say that very significantly. Sooner than I think! If you are preparing a surprise for me, I will forgive you. I shall see you at Mrs Locksly Hall's tomorrow, I hope.'

He assented, and hurried away, fearful, I suppose, lest he should betray his plan. When he was gone, she came to the window, and looked out at the stars. Gazing at her, I forgot my impatience: my teeth ceased to chatter. I took the horn from my travelling bag. She sighed; closed the window; and drew down a white blind. The sight of her hand alone as she did so would have inspired me to excel all my previous efforts. She seated herself so that I could see the shadow of her figure in profile. My hour was come. Park Lane was nearly still: the traffic in Oxford Street was too distant to be distracting.

I began. At the first note I saw her start and listen. When the completed phrase revealed to her what air I was playing, she laid down her book. The mouthpiece of my instrument was like ice; and my lips were stiff and chilly, so that in spite of my utmost care I was interrupted more than once by those uncouth guggling sounds which the best cornists cannot always avoid. Nevertheless, considering that I was cold and very nervous, I succeeded fairly well. Gaining confidence as I went on, I partly atoned for the imperfection of the beginning by playing the concluding bars with commanding sonority, and even achieving a tolerable shake on the penultimate note.

An encouraging cheer from the street as I finished shewed me that a crowd was collected there, and that immediate flight was out of the question. I replaced the horn in my bag, and made ready to go when the mob should disperse. Meanwhile I gazed at the shadow on the blind. She was writing now. Could she, I think, be writing to me? She rose; and the shadow overspread the window so that I could no longer distinguish her movements. I heard a bell ring. A minute later the door of the house opened. I retreated behind an aloe tub; but on recognizing the servant whom I had bribed, I whistled softly to him. He came towards me with a letter in his hand. My heart beat strongly as I saw it.

'All right, sir,' he said. 'Miss Linda told me to give you this; but you are not to open it, if you please, until you get home.'

'Then she knew who I was,' I said eagerly.

'I suppose so, sir. When I heard her bell, I took care to answer it myself. Then she says to me, "Youll find a gentleman somewhere in the pleasure ground. Give him this note; and beg him to go home at once. He is not to read it here." '

'Is there any crowd outside?'

'All gone, sir. Thank you, sir. Goodnight, sir.'

I ran all the way to Hamilton Place, where I got into a hansom. Ten minutes afterwards I was in my study, opening the letter with unsteady hands. It was not enclosed in an envelope, but folded in three, with a corner turned down. I opened it and read,

"714, Park Lane, Friday.
"Dear Mr Porcharlester" –

– I stopped. Had she then given him credit for my performance? A more immediately important question was whether I had any right to read a letter not addressed to me. Curiosity and love prevailed over this scruple. The letter continued thus:

"I am sorry that you have seen nothing in my fancy for Schubert's serenade except matter for ridicule. Perhaps it was an exaggerated fancy; but I would not have expressed it to you had I not believed you capable of understanding it. If it be any satisfaction to you to know that you have cured me of it thoroughly, pray believe that I shall never again hear the serenade without a strange mixture of mirth and pain. I did not know that a human throat could compass such sounds; and I little thought, when you promised that I should hear your voice sooner than I expected, that you contemplated such a performance. I have only one word more: Adieu. I shall not have the pleasure of meeting you at Mrs Locksly Hall's tomorrow, as my engagements will not permit me to go there. For the same reason I fear I must deny myself the pleasure of receiving you again this season. I am, dear Mr Porcharlester, yours truly,

Linda Fitznightingale."

I felt that to forward this letter to Porcharlester would only pain him uselessly. I felt also that my instructor was right, and that I have not the lip for the French horn.

THE SERENADE

I have accordingly given it up.

Linda is now my wife. I sometimes ask her why she persists in cutting Porcharlester, who has pledged me his word as an officer and a gentleman that he is unconscious of having given her the slightest ground for offence. She always refuses to tell me.

A SUNDAY
ON THE SURREY HILLS

*(From The Pall Mall Gazette,
25 April 1888)*

A SUNDAY ON THE SURREY HILLS

As I am not a born cockney I have no illusions on the subject of the country. The uneven, ankle-twisting roads; the dusty hedges; the ditch with its dead dogs, rank weeds, and swarms of poisonous flies; the groups of children torturing something; the dull, toil-broken, prematurely old agricultural laborer; the savage tramp; the manure heaps with their horrible odor; the chain of mile-stones from inn to inn, from cemetery to cemetery: all these I pass heavily by until a distant telegraph pole or signal-post tells me that the blessed rescuing train is at hand. From the village street into the railway station is a leap across five centuries from the brutalizing torpor of Nature's tyranny over Man into the order and alertness of Man's organized dominion over Nature.

And yet last week I allowed myself to be persuaded by my friend Henry Salt and his wife to 'come down and stay until Monday' among the Surrey hills. Salt, a man of exceptional intelligence on most subjects, is country mad, and keeps a house at a hole called Tilford, down Farnham way, to which he retires at intervals, subsisting on the fungi of the neighborhood, and writing articles advocating that line of diet and justifying the weather and the season to 'pent-up' London. He entertained no doubt that a day at Tilford would convert me from rurophobia to rurolatry; and as he is a sensible companion for a walk and a talk – if only he would, like a sensible man, confine himself to the Thames Embankment – I at last consented to the experiment, and even agreed to be marched to the summit of a scenic imposture called Hindhead, and there shewn the downs of the South Coast, the Portsmouth Road (the Knightsbridge end of which I prefer), and, above all, the place where three men were hanged for murdering someone who had induced them to take a country walk with him.

London was clean, fresh, and dry as I made my way to Waterloo after rising at the unnatural hour of seven on Sunday morning. Opening a book, I took care not to look out of the window between the stations until, after traversing a huge cemetery and a huge camp, we reached Farnham. As usual in the country, it was raining heavily. I asked my way to Tilford, and was told to go straight on for four miles or so. As I had brought nothing that could hurt Salt's feelings by betraying my mistrust of his rustic paradise, I was without an umbrella; and the paradise, of course, took the fullest advantage of the omission. I do not know what the downs of the South Coast may be; but I can vouch for both ups and downs as far as the Surrey roads are concerned. Between Farnham and Tilford there are nearly half a dozen hills and not one viaduct. Over these I trudged uphill on my toes and pounded downhill on my heels, making at each step an oozy quagmire full of liquid gamboge. As the landscape grew less human, the rain came down faster, reducing my book to a pulp and transferring the red of the cover to my saturated grey jacket. Some waterproof variety of bird, screaming with laughter at me from a plantation, made me understand better than before why birds are habitually shot. The road presently passed a pine wood, with a gorgeous carpet of wet moss, and a notice that trespassers will be prosecuted. Truly it is worth while travelling thirty miles to be turned back

A SUNDAY ON THE SURREY HILLS

by the curmudgeonism of a country gentleman. My sleeves by this time struck cold to my wrists. Hanging my arms disconsolately so as to minimize the unpleasant repercussion, I looked down at my clinging knees, and instantly discharged a pint of rain water and black dye over them from my hat brim. At this I laughed, much as criminals broken on the wheel used to laugh at the second stroke. A mile or two more of treadmill and gamboge churning, and I came to the outposts of a village, with a river hurrying over a bed of weeds of wonderful colors, spanned by a bridge constructed on the principle of the Gothic arch, so as to extort from horses the maximum of effort both when drawing carts up one side, and preventing the carts from overrunning them when slithering precipitously down the other.

This was Tilford, uninhabited as far as I could see except by one man, whose surly looks asked me, more plainly than words could, what the devil I wanted there. Then up another hill between meeting house and church, and out upon an exposed stretch of road where the rain and wind had an unobstructed final pelt at me. Salt is mistaken in supposing that he lives at Tilford: as a matter of fact he lives considerably beyond it; and I was on the point of turning whilst I had yet strength enough to get back to London, when he hailed me from his door with a delighted shout of, 'Here he is!' and beamed at me as if my condition left nothing to be desired, and Tilford had done itself the highest credit. In no time my clothes were filling the kitchen with steam; and I, invested in some garments belonging to Salt's brother-in-law, a promising poet whose figure is somewhat dissimilar to mine, was distending myself with my host's latest discoveries in local fungology.

My clothes dried fast. Quite early in the afternoon I put them on again, and found them some two inches shorter and tighter, but warm and desiccated. Nevertheless I had a fit of sneezing; and Mrs Salt produced a

A SUNDAY ON THE SURREY HILLS

bottle of spirits of camphor. Unfamiliar with the violent nature of this remedy, I incautiously took a spoonful of it. It all but killed me; but I had the satisfaction, when I came to, of feeling tolerably sure that the influenza bacillus had not survived it. Then, the rain having ceased, we went out for a walk, and followed the road between the hills, which were like streaks of wet peat beneath the cloudy sky. Eventually we got out upon the uplands, where the mud was replaced by soft quicksand and heather already swept dry by the stark wind from the North Sea. Frensham Pond, like a waterworks denuded of machinery, lay to leeward of us, with a shudder passing over it from head to foot at every squall. I sympathized with it, and looked furtively at Salt, to see whether the ineffable dreariness of the scene had not dashed him. But he was used to it; and, when we got home, began to plan an excursion to Hindhead for the morrow. The mere suggestion brought on a fresh fit of sneezing. I positively declined further camphor; and Mrs Salt, by no means at the end of her resources, administered black currant jam and boiling water, which I rather liked.

Next morning I got up at eight to see the sun and hear the birds. I found, however, that I was up before them; and I neither saw nor heard them until I got back to the metropolis. Salt was jubilant because the wind was north-east, which made rain impossible. So after breakfast we started across the hills to Hindhead, through a mist that made the cows look like mammoths and the ridges like Alpine chains. When we were well out of reach of shelter the rain began. Salt declared that it would be nothing; that it could never hold out against the north-east wind. Nevertheless it did. When, after staggering and slipping up and down places which Salt described as lanes, but which were, in fact, rapidly filling beds of mountain mud torrents, we at last got upon Hindhead (which was exactly like all the other

A SUNDAY ON THE SURREY HILLS

mounds), we could hardly see one another, much less the south coast, through the mist. I saw the place where the men were hanged; and I cannot deny that I felt a certain vindictive satisfaction in the idea of somebody having been served out there.

When we started homeward Salt was in the highest spirits. The discovery of a wet day in a north-east wind elated him as the discovery of a comet elates an astronomer. As to Mrs Salt, the conclusion she drew from it all was that I must come down another day. The rain gave her no more concern than if she had been a duck; and I could not help wondering whether her walking costume was not in reality a skilfully contrived bathing dress. She seemed perfectly happy, though the very sheep were bawling plaintively at the sky, and a cow to which I gave a friendly slap in passing was so saturated that the water squirted up my sleeve to the very armpit. Her chief themes whilst we were on the hill was the gentleness of her dog Nigger, whose movements in the direction of the sheep Salt was meanwhile carefully frustrating. Before we got home, my clothes contained three times as much water as they had gathered the day before. When I again resumed them they seemed to have been borrowed in an emergency from a very young brother.

I need not describe my walk back to Farnham after dinner. It rained all the way; but at least I was getting nearer to London. I have had change of air and a holiday; and I have no doubt I shall be able to throw off their effect in a fortnight or so. Should my experience serve to warn any tempted Londoner against too high an estimate of the vernal delights of the Surrey hills, it will perhaps not have been wasted.

CANNONFODDER

(From The Clarion of 21 November 1902)

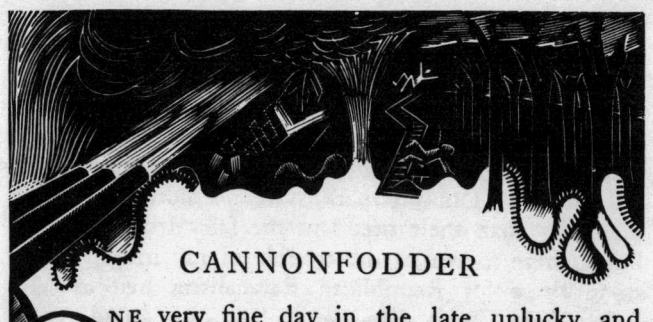

CANNONFODDER

ONE very fine day in the late unlucky and infamous nineteenth century, I found myself on the Lake of Como, with my body basking in the Italian sun and the Italian color, and my mind uneasily busy on the human drawbacks to all that loveliness.

There it was, at its best, the Italian beauty which makes men of all nations homesick for it, whether Italy be their home or not. Worth millions, this beauty, yet displaying itself for nothing to the just and the unjust, the rich and the poor. So undervaluing itself, in fact, that Italian labor, waiting on the pier at Cadenabbia to catch our hawser as we graze the piles, will not look at it, not being quite so cheap itself, though very nearly: to be precise, a penny an hour, one London dock laborer being thus worth six Italians on the stricken field of industry.

On the pier, ready to embark, is a pretty lady in one of those fairy frocks which women never seem to produce until they go abroad, when the gravest tourist may, on any evening, see his respectable wife appear at *table d'hôte* with a dazzling air of having come straight from Vienna, and left her character behind. But as this young lady carries her frock like one born to such luxuries, we surmise that she is American, and speculate as to whether she is coming aboard.

She is; but, not to deceive you, she has nothing whatever to do with my story. I remember nothing of her, except that the gangway through which the fairy frock brushed was held by labor at a penny an hour, and that the friends who sent off the lady in a cloud of kissings and wavings, and messages and invitations, were, chiefly, Mr and Mrs Henry Labouchere and party. The Laboucheres, I may remark, have no more to do with this story than their friend in the fairy frock. But Mr Labouchere increased the trouble of my mind; for he stood there for Republican Radicalism, just as Mrs Labouchere, born Henrietta Hodson, stood, very gracefully, for Dramatic Art, the penny-an-hour basis being none the better for either.

Presently Cadenabbia fades in our wake, Mr Labouchere becoming indistinguishable five minutes before Mrs Labouchere, who still waves her hand so artistically that the young lady in the fairy frock seems quite awkward in comparison.

I am standing on the brink of a sort of hurricane deck, looking down upon the impecunious or frugal mob on the main-deck. Among them are the men who travel third-class because there is no fourth. *I* travel first because there is no double first. Beside me, watching the lake for artistic effects (as I guess; but perhaps he guesses the same about me) is Cosmo Monkhouse, who is soon after to have his obituary notices as a Civil Servant by necessity, and by choice a loving student of the arts, and even a bit of a poet. I like Monkhouse very well: he is, for the matter of that, a more agreeable person than I look. Rather elderly is Cosmo: sufficiently so, at any rate, for his way of life to have stamped its mark on him. I wander into mental arithmetic, and finally come out with a rough calculation that he works six hours a day, and gets ten shillings an hour or thereabouts, allowing for Sundays and holidays. He is, therefore, worth 120 Italian laborers. He represents high-class criticism, my own game at that time. I study his face as he looks straight ahead at the horizon, where the cloud effects are. I find in his flesh an appearance I have noticed in all the elderly men of my acquaintance who have been in love with Art all their lives; who, proud and happy to write about what great artists have done, make the masterpieces of Art the touchstone to try all life by; and who have even achieved some little piece of art work themselves (usually a little poem or tale) which they would never have produced if they had never known the work of their favorite masters. It is a curious sunken look, as if the outermost inch of the man had lost its vitality and would have mummified completely if the evaporation from the submerged reality were not keeping it a little sodden. But as I mark this aspect in Monkhouse, I see also that he is smoking a cigar. All the other dilettanti of my acquaintance smoke too; and the problem that now rises to bother me is whether it is the habit of smoking, or the habit of substituting Art for Life as the diet of the mind, that causes men to die at the surface in this odd fashion. I begin to muse on my own beginnings, and on my early determination not to let myself become a literary man, but to make the pen my instrument, and not my idol. I speedily become very arrogant over this, and am positively thanking Providence for the saving grace that has prevented me from becoming one of the Art-voluptuaries of the literary clubs, when a strange outburst of song comes up from below, uproarious, rowdy, and yet with a note in it as of joy frozen at its source.

I look over the rail. There, just below me, stand three young men, just too big to be called lads, each with a document like an Income Tax return in his hatband, and each with his arm affectionately round his neighbor's neck, singing with all his might. They are a little drunk, but not so drunk as Englishmen would be in like circumstances on English liquor. They are determined to be in the highest spirits; and ribbons in the hat of one of them proclaim a joyful occasion. I try to catch the words of their song, and just manage to make out the general sense of it, which, after the manner of songs, is not sense at all, but nonsense. They sing the joys of a soldier's life, its adventures, its immoralities, its light loves, its drinkings and roysterings, and its indifference to all consequences. Suddenly the poor devil in the middle, who has led the song, and shouted the loudest, stops, and begins to cry. The man on his right breaks down too, from sympathy; but he on the left, the quietest, rallies them; and they sing more defiantly than ever.

A stave or two, and the song goes to pieces again for ever. Its last moanings are dispelled by a fresh start made by the man on the right, who begins a most melting air about parting from home and mother, and so forth. This they rather enjoy: indeed, they finish it quite successfully. With soothed nerves, they talk a little, drink a little, then begin to joke a little and swagger a little; finally bursting into a most martial and devil-may-care song of the conquests that await them when the sword and the bowl and the admiration of women shall be their only occupations. They get through two verses without crying; and then the man in the middle falls on the neck of his comrade, and howls openly and pitifully.

Then I understand the papers in their hatbands. They are conscripts, newly drawn, and on their way to their service. They get off at the next pier. And I remember no more of that evening on Lake Como than if my own embarkation and landing had never taken place.

●

My memory comes to the surface again years later, on a threatening evening at Malta, where I am being rushed by an Orient liner between the lines of the British

Mediterranean squadron. Ahead is darkness and a dirty sea. I do not want to get there; but the Captain does, being a better sailor than I, and on business besides. The fleet drops behind; and the harbor lights are shut off as we turn to the right (starboard, we landsmen call it). As the open sea catches us, we reel almost off our sea-legs, and shake in our pipeclayed shoes, which we wear as piously on the ship as we wear blackened shoes on the land. The pipeclay gives somebody a lot of trouble, and is bad for his lungs; but he would not respect us as gentlemen if we did not insist on it. After all, I am able to appear at the half-deserted dinner that evening; and though the fiddles are on the tables, and the two ladies to windward are twice bowled at me as at a wicket, I eat, drink, and am merry with less misgiving than I had expected. But the weather retains its dirty look; and I am not sorry when we reach Gibraltar, where two persons come on board. The first puts up printed notices that any person daring to take photographs of the rock or harbor will incur the doom of Dreyfus. The other unrolls a pedlar's bag, and publicly offers for sale a large assortment of photographs and models of the said rock and harbor.

I go ashore, and join a party of British pilgrims to visit the fortifications. We are shewn a few obsolete guns, and a few squads of soldiers (we call them Tommies) at drill; and we go away firmly persuaded that we have really seen the business part of the fortress. In that persuasion we liberally tip the military impostor who has pretended to shew us round; and we tell one another, roguishly, that the place is pretty safe for a while yet, eh? One man says that Gibraltar is all rot; that it could be shelled from Ceuta by modern guns; and that nothing but popular sentiment prevents us from dropping it like a hot potato. So indignant do the other Britons become at this, that I have to divert their wrath by suggesting that it is an excellent thing for the Spaniards to have their coast fortified at England's expense, and that we might do worse than offer Portsmouth to the Germans on the same terms. This is received as paradoxical madness; and the talk which ensues shews that we are unusually excited on the subject of England's military greatness.

There is a reason for this. At Malta the news reached us – or, rather, we reached the news – that the Boers have invaded Natal, and that England is at war.

In the afternoon the weather looks dirtier than ever. The sun hides behind slaty clouds; and the sea is restless and irritable, caring nothing for England and her troopships. I wander round the coast. On my return, I come round a corner, and find myself before a big barrack. On the long flagged platform before the barrack sit those who have been spoken of all the morning as 'our Tommies.' Every man has his sea kit with him; and every man is contemplating the comfortless sea and the leaden sky with an expression which the illustrated papers will not reproduce, and could not if they tried. Many of them are, I suspect, young men who had had their first scare of seasickness on their way to Gibraltar, and have not got over it yet. I doubt if any of them think much of the Mausers waiting beyond the waves. They impress me unspeakably; for I have never seen a whole regiment of men intensely unhappy. They do not speak: they do not move. If one of my fellow-sightseers of that morning were to come and talk to them about how irresistible they are when it comes to the bayonet, I doubt whether they would even get up and kill him. They brood and wait. I wait, too, spellbound; but my boat is on the shore, and my bark is on the sea; so I soon have to leave them.

A lady says something about the matter-of-fact quietness of Englishmen in the presence of a call to duty. She means, as I take it, that Englishmen do not behave as the conscripts did on the Lake of Como.

CANNONFODDER

In due time we wallow through the Bay with fearful rollings, and trudge through the Channel head down, overcoat buttoned, and umbrella up. Then the episode sinks again into the sea of oblivion.

*

Recollection rises again on the Ripley Road, where I am lighting a bicycle lamp an hour after sunset. I am bound for Haslemere. I am also tired; and it occurs to me that if I ride hard, I may just catch the Portsmouth train at Guildford, and go to Haslemere in it. The next thing I remember is being told at Guildford that I am in the wrong half of the train. I make a precipitous dash, race along the platform like the wild ass of the desert, jump at a moving footboard, and am pushed and pulled and hustled into pandemonium.

Out of nine men in a third-class compartment, eight are roaring 'God bless you, Tommy Atkins,' at the top of their voices. One of them is distinctly sober; but he is cynically egging on the others by pretending to be as wild as they. The one who is not singing is an innocent-looking young sailor. Room is gradually made for me; and the man who makes it puts his arm affectionately round my neck the moment I sit down. They hail me by the honorable title of Governor, and convey to me that they are all going to the front, except the sailor, who is going to rejoin his ship at Portsmouth. I perceive at once that the sober man is going to do nothing of the sort though he allows it to be assumed that he is. A racecourse possibly; certainly not a battlefield.

We now sing 'Soldiers of the Queen' with tremendous enthusiasm. I sing *fortissimo* to keep out the noise of the others; and this clears me of all suspicion of offensive gentility. My new comrade next propounds the question 'What will Buller do to Kruger?' The question goes round the company; and each strives to exceed his fellow-catechumen in the obscenity of the answer. By the time four have exercised their wit, the possibilities of foul language are exhausted. To my great relief – for I feared they would presently put the question to me – the man whose arm is round my neck releases me, and breaks frantically into 'God bless you, Tommy Atkins,' again. When it flags, the soberest of the reservists (they are all reservists) starts an obscene song on his own account. It is a solo, and my neighbor, not knowing the chorus, is silenced. Now this friendly man who had made room for me, and embraced me, has made himself drunk, and has been roaring songs, and clinging to the subject of Buller and Kruger for two reasons: to wit (1) he wants to forget about his wife, from whom he has parted at Waterloo Station without a notion of how she is going to live until his return (should he ever return); and (2) he wants to prevent himself from crying. The stupid, ribald nonsense the other man is bawling cannot hold his attention for a moment. '*I* dunno what she's to do,' he says to me, even his drunkenness failing him completely. 'I had a bit of drink at the station, you know. I left her there. I dunno whats to become of her.' And he cries feelingly, and cannot for the life of him start the roaring again, though he makes an effort or two.

Then the sailor, perhaps to distract attention from this unsoldierly weakness, pulls out a copy of The Westminster Gazette, on which he has spent a penny, thinking that it is right, on a great political occasion, to buy something that he vaguely understands to be a great political paper. Over The Westminster a debate begins as to the Government. They have all heard that Chamberlain is 'a good man'; and the young sailor has heard reassuring accounts of Lord Rosebery, who will see to it that things are done right. They have never heard of any other statesman, except Lord Salisbury; and we were falling back on Buller again when one of the reservists suddenly conceives that the sailor is claiming to ride to Portsmouth at Service fare, which works out cheaper than the reservists' fare. This piece of favoritism is taken in bad part; and were not the sailor obviously the most powerful man in the carriage, as well as the youngest and decentest, we should quarrel with him over it. As it is, all that happens is an absurd discussion, which shews that, eager as we are to wreak political justice on President Kruger in the most unmentionable ways, we are as ignorant of the nature of a railway ticket as of the relations between the Government and Lord Rosebery. My neighbor has by this time cried himself asleep. He is lulled into deeper slumber by the happy thought of two reservists, who strike up 'Auld Lang Syne.' But they get it so horribly mixed up with 'Home, sweet home' that the sleeper wakes with a yell of 'God bless you, Tommy Atkins'; and all three tunes are raging in an infernal counterpoint when the train stops at Haslemere, and I get out with judicious suddenness; for by that time they are all persuaded that I too am going to the front; and my disappearance probably seems to them a strange combination of a cowardly and unpatriotic desertion with an audacious and successful dash for liberty.

They were very like the Italian conscripts after all, only a good deal drunker, and, being unrestrained by the presence of signorinas in fairy frocks, much more blackguardly. English and Italians alike were being helplessly shovelled into the ranks as *Kanonenfutter*: cannonfodder, as the German generals candidly put it. I am no more sentimental over their homesickness than over their seasickness: both affections soon pass, and leave no bones broken. Nor am I under any illusions as to the possibility of carrying on the arts of war, any more than the arts of peace, by men who understand what they are doing. Had I been in good time for my train, and made my journey in a first-class carriage with Lord

CANNONFODDER

Lansdowne, Mr Brodrick, Lord Methuen, Sir Redvers Buller, and Lord Roberts, the conversation would have come to the same point: namely, the point of the bayonet. So dont suppose that this tale has any moral. I simply tell what I have seen, and what I have heard.

PRINCIPAL WORKS OF BERNARD SHAW

(Dates are of first book publication)

Cashel Byron's Profession, 1886

An Unsocial Socialist, 1887

Fabian Essays in Socialism (edited), 1889

The Quintessence of Ibsenism, 1891

Widowers' Houses, 1893

Plays Pleasant and Unpleasant, 1898
(Widowers' Houses, The Philanderer, Mrs Warren's Profession, Arms and the Man, Candida, The Man of Destiny, You Never Can Tell)

The Perfect Wagnerite, 1898

Fabianism and the Empire (edited), 1900

Love Among the Artists, 1900

Three Plays for Puritans, 1901
(The Devils' Disciple, Caesar and Cleopatra, Captain Brassbound's Conversion)

The Admirable Bashville, 1901

Man and Superman, 1903

The Common Sense of Municipal Trading, 1904

The Irrational Knot, 1905

Dramatic Opinions and Essays, 1906

John Bull's Other Island: Major Barbara: How He Lied to Her Husband, 1907

The Sanity of Art, 1908

The Doctor's Dilemma: Getting Married: The Shewing-up of Blanco Posnet, 1911

Common Sense About the War, 1914

Misalliance: The Dark Lady of the Sonnets: Fanny's First Play, 1914

Androcles and the Lion: Overruled: Pygmalion, 1916

Heartbreak House: Great Catherine: Playlets of the War (O'Flaherty V.C.: The Inca of Perusalem: Augustus Does His Bit: Annajanska, the Bolshevik Empress), 1919

Back to Methuselah, 1921

Saint Joan, 1924

Translations and Tomfooleries, 1926

The Intelligent Woman's Guide to Socialism and Capitalism, 1928

Immaturity, 1930

The Apple Cart, 1930

What I Really Wrote About the War, 1930

Doctors' Delusions: Crude Criminology: Sham Education, 1931

Music in London, 1931

Our Theatres in the Nineties, 1931

Pen Portraits and Reviews, 1931

Fabian Essays in Socialism, 1932

The Adventures of the Black Girl in Her Search for God, 1932

Short Stories, Scraps & Shavings, 1932

The Future of Political Science in America, 1933

Too True to be Good: Village Wooing: On the Rocks, 1934

The Simpleton of the Unexpected Isles: The Six of Calais: The Millionairess, 1936

London Music in 1888-89, 1937

Geneva, 1939

In Good King Charles's Golden Days, 1939

Everybody's Political What's What?, 1944

Sixteen Self Sketches, 1949

Buoyant Billions, 1949

Farfetched Fables, 1951

PENGUIN CLASSICS
www.penguinclassics.com

- *Details about every Penguin Classic*

- *Advanced information about forthcoming titles*

- *Hundreds of author biographies*

- *FREE resources including critical essays on the books and their historical background, reader's and teacher's guides.*

- *Links to other web resources for the Classics*

- *Discussion area*

- *Online review copy ordering for academics*

- *Competitions with prizes, and challenging Classics trivia quizzes*

PENGUIN CLASSICS ONLINE

READ MORE IN PENGUIN

In every corner of the world, on every subject under the sun, Penguin represents quality and variety – the very best in publishing today.

For complete information about books available from Penguin – including Puffins, Penguin Classics and Arkana – and how to order them, write to us at the appropriate address below. Please note that for copyright reasons the selection of books varies from country to country.

In the United Kingdom: Please write to *Dept. EP, Penguin Books Ltd, Bath Road, Harmondsworth, West Drayton, Middlesex UB7 ODA*

In the United States: Please write to *Consumer Sales, Penguin Putnam Inc., P.O. Box 12289 Dept. B, Newark, New Jersey 07101-5289*. VISA and MasterCard holders call 1-800-788-6262 to order Penguin titles

In Canada: Please write to *Penguin Books Canada Ltd, 10 Alcorn Avenue, Suite 300, Toronto, Ontario M4V 3B2*

In Australia: Please write to *Penguin Books Australia Ltd, P.O. Box 257, Ringwood, Victoria 3134*

In New Zealand: Please write to *Penguin Books (NZ) Ltd, Private Bag 102902, North Shore Mail Centre, Auckland 10*

In India: Please write to *Penguin Books India Pvt Ltd, 11 Community Centre, Panchsheel Park, New Delhi 110017*

In the Netherlands: Please write to *Penguin Books Netherlands bv, Postbus 3507, NL-1001 AH Amsterdam*

In Germany: Please write to *Penguin Books Deutschland GmbH, Metzlerstrasse 26, 60594 Frankfurt am Main*

In Spain: Please write to *Penguin Books S. A., Bravo Murillo 19, 1° B, 28015 Madrid*

In Italy: Please write to *Penguin Italia s.r.l., Via Benedetto Croce 2, 20094 Corsico, Milano*

In France: Please write to *Penguin France, Le Carré Wilson, 62 rue Benjamin Baillaud, 31500 Toulouse*

In Japan: Please write to *Penguin Books Japan Ltd, Kaneko Building, 2-3-25 Koraku, Bunkyo-Ku, Tokyo 112*

In South Africa: Please write to *Penguin Books South Africa (Pty) Ltd, Private Bag X14, Parkview, 2122 Johannesburg*

READ MORE IN PENGUIN

Penguin Twentieth-Century Classics offer a selection of the finest works of literature published this century. Spanning the globe from Argentina to America, from France to India, the masters of prose and poetry are represented by Penguin.

If you would like a catalogue of the Twentieth-Century Classics library, please write to:

Penguin Press Marketing, 27 Wrights Lane, London W8 5TZ

(Available while stocks last)

READ MORE IN PENGUIN

THE BERNARD SHAW LIBRARY

'The most influential writer of his age... His plays can scarcely prove other than lastingly delightful since they are the product of vigorous intelligence joined to inexhaustible comic invention' J. I. M. Stewart in the *Oxford History of English Literature*

Androcles and the Lion
The Apple Cart
Back to Methuselah
The Doctor's Dilemma
Heartbreak House
John Bull's Other Island
Last Plays
Major Barbara
Major Critical Essays
Man and Superman
Misalliance and the Fascinating Foundling
Plays Extravagant
(The Millionairess, Too True to be Good, The Simpleton of the Unexpected Isles)
Plays Pleasant
(Arms and the Man, Candida, The Man of Destiny, You Never Can Tell)
Plays Political
(The Apple Cart, On the Rocks, Geneva)
Plays Unpleasant
(Widowers' Houses, The Philanderer, Mrs Warren's Profession)
Pygmalion
Saint Joan
Selected Short Plays
(including The Admirable Bashville and Great Catherine)
Three Plays for Puritans
(The Devil's Disciple, Caesar and Cleopatra, Captain Brassbound's Conversion)